If Love Were All

❧

Judith Henry Wall

simon & schuster

SIMON & SCHUSTER
Rockefeller Center
1230 Avenue of the Americas
New York, NY 10020

Simon and Schuster and colophon are registered trademarks
of Simon & Schuster Inc.

Designed by Jeanette Olender
Manufactured in the United States of America

1   3   5   7   9   10   8   6   4   2

Library of Congress Cataloging-in-Publication Data
Wall, Judith Henry.
If love were all / Judith Henry Wall.
p.   cm.
I. Title.
PS3573.A42556I35   1998
813'.54—dc21   98-15786 CIP
ISBN 0-684-83765-X

acknowledgments

I am grateful to my editor Chuck Adams and
my agent Philippa Brophy for making this
book happen.

I appreciate the interest and input of my son and
his wife, Doug and JoAnna Wall.

And special thanks go to my dear friend
Beverly Peterson. We stand at the opposite ends
of most spectrums, yet our friendship has
endured for more than thirty years.

If Love Were All

chapter one

Charlotte's three children stared at her in stunned silence. She held her breath. *Please let them understand.*

From the living room, the tick of the mantel clock grew louder. The coffeepot perked in the kitchen. Mark was the first to speak. "You're not serious, are you?"

"I don't understand," Vicky said, tears already welling. "Why would you do that?"

Suzanne was looking around the dining room with its faded wallpaper depicting scenes from Colonial Williamsburg, at the empty chair at the head of the table. "It's our home," she whispered with such reverence it made her mother wince.

Charlotte had tried to prepare them. Over the past months she'd inserted something into almost every conversation about how lonely she felt in the big old house, how run-down it had become, how a smaller house would be homier now that she was living alone.

But they had brushed aside her concerns. Suzanne suggested a cat to replace Tiger. Vicky thought Grandma should move in with her. Mark said she hadn't given herself enough time to adjust.

Charlotte decided to wait until her children were all together to tell them she was selling the house and hoped to move before Christmas. Her first opportunity hadn't come until mid-November when they were all in Newberg for the high school homecoming game. Most of the graduates who'd gone off to college came back for the event. And this year, the school's all-state football players from years past were being honored at halftime.

Charlotte's mother went with her to the Friday night game with the Oakland Knights. The whole town turned out for the games, and a sizable percentage of its citizens traveled to the out-of-town games. In small Nebraska towns, no directions were needed to the stadium. You just headed for the lights. They were visible from miles away.

The two women joined the cheer when Mark's name was called, watched as he made his way to the center of the field—tall, broad-shouldered, blond Mark Haberman, now in his second year of law school. A home-town boy who made them proud. Everyone sitting around Charlotte and Hannah turned to offer smiles tinged with sadness. *His father should have been here.*

After the homecoming game, the young graduates would put in an appearance at the homecoming dance, strut around a bit, then head out on their own. There'd been a bonfire. Charlotte could tell by the smell of smoke on their coats.

Yesterday, Suzanne had worked at the drugstore all day and spent the evening with her boyfriend Brady, as she did every Saturday. Vicky slept in, and Mark got up early to study. The two of them spent the rest of the day with friends, watching the Nebraska-Colorado football game on television, then driving over to West Point for pizza—a frequent outing for the residents of Newberg since the town's only eating establishments were Lou's Cafe, the drugstore soda fountain, and the Dairy Dream.

But they had dutifully gone to church with their mother this morning, and it went without saying they would have Sunday dinner before heading back to Lincoln.

Charlotte was too nervous to do more than pick at her food. An annoying tick developed in her right eyelid, and she kept trying to rub it away. It took all her concentration to keep up with the conversation, to ask occasional motherly questions about their weekend. Who had they seen? How was everyone doing?

For dessert, she'd made a fresh apple pie. When they'd finished and were poised to push their chairs back and be on their way, Charlotte took a deep breath—and told them. In an outpouring of words. She'd been thinking about it for a long time. The house made her sad. She needed a change. She could invest the money, not have to rely just on her teaching salary, have a better retirement. She would rent a smaller house for the time being—someplace more economical to heat and easier to care for.

But nothing she said took away the shock and bewilderment written on her children's faces. *Sell their home? Their father had died here.*

Charlotte swallowed back the lump rising in her throat. She loved her children more than anything. Always had. Always would. Her children were more of a religion for her than what she practiced on Sunday morning at the First Lutheran Church on Hoover Street. Did that mean she was obligated to stay on in their childhood home forever?

Maybe it was too soon. Maybe she should wait until Mark had graduated from law school and the girls were out of college. Until they were all married and had homes of their own.

But that meant *years*. And Charlotte felt a sense of urgency. It pressed against her breastbone in the night. It took her breath away at odd moments during the day. Her life was being sucked away.

She needed to move—now, before they celebrated the first Christmas without Stan. If possible, she wanted a new house by then, new traditions, not doing everything exactly the same as they always had in memory of their dad.

If she was going to change anything about her life, she needed to do it while she was still young enough for it to make some sense, before she woke up one morning and realized that she had crossed over some invisible line and was therefore too old for change.

A pretty little house was for rent right across the street from the high school. A pale yellow house with white shutters. Every day she looked to see if the FOR RENT sign was still in the yard. There weren't that many decent rental houses in Newberg. And she didn't want to buy another house. Not yet. Renting left the door open to possibilities.

The realtor said it was a good time to sell. She already had contacted several prospects—growing families who needed a larger house. But Charlotte hadn't let her put a FOR SALE sign out front. She had to tell the children first.

Of course, even if Charlotte sold her house, she'd still live in the same town, still teach school, still be Stan Haberman's widow. But when she'd met with the realtor and actually said out loud that she wanted to sell the house, she'd felt as though she were going to float right off the chair. Of course, she would cry when she walked through the house for the last time—just thinking about it made tears come to her eyes. And driving by the house for the rest of her life would fill her with nostalgia. But if she could move to another house, maybe she could do other things. Like lose fifteen pounds. Go places and do things. Tell Pastor Jenson that this was her last year to teach Sunday school.

She watched while Mark carefully folded his napkin and placed it beside his plate. "It's too soon for you to be making such an important decision," he said, his voice dropping lower in his chest— like Stan's had done when he was being firm.

"It's been eight months," Charlotte reminded him. Which wasn't such a long time. Their grief was still fresh. But it went without saying that her children would get on with their lives because they were young. Their widowed mother had to swim upstream. "I've known for a long time I wouldn't continue to live here—since before your father died. This is a house for a family, not one person."

"But sometimes we're all here," Vicky insisted. "And I always thought I'd bring my children here someday. Don't you want that, Mom—all your children and grandchildren gathered around this table?"

"I'll keep the table," Charlotte said, wishing she hadn't. She'd sounded inane, like her mother. They weren't talking about furniture. They were talking about expectations. Theirs for her. Hers for herself.

"But it wouldn't be the same," Vicky said, crying now, wiping tears away with her napkin. Beautiful raven-haired Vicky with the startling green eyes. Stan thought she would be an actress or a fashion model. But she was majoring in journalism, preparing to follow in her father's footsteps.

"I'm sorry," Charlotte said, her voice less sure. "But I can't stay here waiting for the two or three times a year my family might visit. Can't you understand that just a little? It's lonesome here with your father gone and you children away at school."

"I come home every weekend," Suzanne reminded her.

Charlotte reached over and patted Suzanne's hand. Her youngest child rode the bus from Lincoln every Friday evening to see Brady, who'd gone with her to college last year but decided he didn't need a college degree to work for his father at the John Deere dealership that would someday be his.

"Is this what Dad would have wanted?" Mark asked.

"I have no idea," Charlotte snapped, feeling her insides curl with irritation at his attempt to invoke the will of his dead father.

The girls helped clear the table while Mark put their things in his car. Then they all bundled up and drove out to the cemetery. Charlotte watched while her children reverently touched their father's headstone.

"I love you, Daddy," Vicky whispered.

Charlotte looked four rows over at the grave of her own father, dead more than twenty years now. Her mother usually stopped by on the way home from church with fresh flowers in summer, a spray of holly in winter. But she was in Norfolk, visiting Charlotte's younger sister.

The Newberg cemetery seemed large for a town of only twelve hundred people. But then, even people who moved away were brought back to be planted among their roots for eternity. The cemetery covered a hillside, offering a fine view of the town, with its church spires and the grain elevator rising above the treetops. At the edge of town, the trees stopped abruptly, giving way to fields of corn, milo, and soybeans. A pretty town. Clean and respectable. No crime to speak of. God-fearing citizens—Christians all. Anyone who wasn't wouldn't dare say so.

Charlotte waited until the children had started back to the car before she took her turn touching the granite marker. Stan probably had assumed she'd stay on in the house for the rest of her life. They hadn't talked much about what would happen after he was gone, except to speculate about what the children would do with their lives. And plan his funeral. He wanted "Peace in the Valley" and a wooden casket.

The funeral home didn't have a wooden casket. It would have to be special-ordered. Vicky didn't want her daddy in a casket that would rot. Stan was buried in bronze. No ashes to ashes and dust to dust. His body was entombed for the ages.

On the way back to the house, they stopped by the nursing home to visit Stan's mother, Nellie, who surely wouldn't live much longer. Charlotte and Dr. Linderman were called to the nursing home every week or so, when Nellie's eyes rolled back in her head and her face went slack. "Little strokes," Dr. Linderman called the episodes.

Nellie didn't know the girls and thought Mark was Stan. "What time is it, Son?" she kept asking, as though she had something pressing she needed to do. Vicky fed her the piece of apple pie they'd brought, with Nellie holding her mouth open for the next bite like a baby bird. As they walked down the long hall toward the door, they could hear her calling out, "Does anyone know what time it is?" Mark muttered "Jesus" under his breath.

The Haberman house sat on an acre of land at the corner of Washington Street and Schoolhouse Road. Originally the house had presided over a farm. A toolshed was all that survived of the outbuildings. Like its neighbors, the house was plain and white and sat high on a foundation with only a broad front porch to soften its sternness. Even the churches in Newberg were plain and stern. But then Nebraska was a stern state, inhabited by descendants of sturdy Northern European immigrants who were accustomed to bitter winters, hard work, and few amenities.

It was past four when Mark pulled into the driveway, and they all got out of the car for good-bye hugs. Vicky raced into the house for the botany textbook she'd almost forgotten, Suzanne to call Brady and tell him good-bye.

"I'll call you in a day or two," Mark told his mother. "We need to talk."

"If it's about the house, I'd rather not."

"Legally the house is yours, Mom, but it belongs to all of us— it's our family home. All our memories are centered around this house. I always thought you'd live here the rest of your life, and then one of us would live here when you're gone."

"There aren't any prestigious law firms in Newberg," Charlotte reminded him.

"I might want to retire here someday. Or maintain my residence in Newberg in case I decide to enter politics. If Suzanne marries Brady, she'll always live here. And Vicky talks about buying the *Record* someday, like Dad always wished he could do."

What about me, Charlotte wanted to protest. But the words seemed out of character—not words that would be spoken by the vigilant mother who had raised Mark and his sisters, not by the woman who had selflessly cared for their dying father.

Charlotte glanced up at the corner window. Stan used to watch from there, sitting up in the rented hospital bed where he spent most of his time toward the end, after he could no longer get up and down the stairs even with her help.

"It still seems as though he should be up there, watching for us," Mark said, slipping an arm around her waist.

"Yes," Charlotte agreed, leaning her head against his shoulder.

"You still love him, don't you?"

"Of course I do. I always will. He was the finest man I've ever known."

Mark slipped his other arm around her and embraced her, putting his cheek against her hair. "I love you, Mom."

Charlotte clung to him for a minute, wondering if it was wrong to enjoy a man's strong arms around her if the man was her own son.

❧ Charlotte's footsteps echoed in the now silent house while she put away the china and silver and took the leaf out of the table and carried it down to the basement. She wondered if the table would fit in the dining room at the yellow house.

Restless, she roamed through the big, drafty house that she'd never quite been able to make cozy. The furniture was too far apart in the large rooms, pictures too widely spaced on the walls, area rugs islands afloat on a sea of varnished wood. She'd always wanted to carpet, but they never had the money to spare, and Stan insisted that the hardwood floors gave the house a stately look.

The realtor had suggested that she spruce the place up a bit— paint the entry hall, replace the worn linoleum in the kitchen. But probably whoever bought this house would do so because they recognized its potential. She imagined a young couple who would do the things she'd once dreamed about—remodeling the outdated kitchen, replacing the wooden-framed windows, turning the basement into a rec room, paving the driveway.

Money had always been a problem. Still was. The kids were going to school on scholarships and student loans. They earned their own spending money. But Charlotte helped out. Vicky had wanted to join a sorority more than anything. Mark needed a car to get back and forth to his job at the Criminal Defense Clinic in Omaha. Their textbooks were horrendously expensive. Stan had had only a small life insurance policy. By the time they wanted to increase his coverage, he was uninsurable. But even if she could afford to remodel the house from top to bottom, she wouldn't want to. Not now. The time for that had passed.

She sat at the kitchen table, half-watching an old Bette Davis movie while she graded a set of papers and checked over her lesson plans for tomorrow. Then she carried a glass of wine upstairs to sip while she read in bed.

She retrieved her bathrobe and nightgown from the master bedroom. Only when the children were home did she sleep in the room where Stan had conducted the final year of his life and continued to write a weekly editorial for the *Newberg Record*. The last one had been published two days after his death. "I have been blessed," it began. Such a good, brave man.

The hospital bed was gone from the corner of the large room, the tray of medicines that sat on the bureau had been put away, the desk and computer sent back to the newspaper office. The room no longer smelled of soiled linens and Lysol. But when she tried to sleep there, she found herself listening for Stan.

They'd tried to make love only once after the hospital bed had been delivered. He faded almost immediately. Charlotte tried to help him, but finally he pushed her away. That was one of the few times he cried. At first he wouldn't let her hold him, then he reached for her and buried his face against her breasts. They wept together. And once again he'd made her promise: No more hospital stays. No tubes or life support. No money spent buying another week or month. He would die at home.

Tiger, the family cat, had taken to sleeping with Stan in the hospital bed. Tiger had been with them since the girls were toddlers. For years, he'd patiently endured the indignity of being dressed in doll clothes and pushed around in a doll carriage. Last month Charlotte had had him put to sleep and told the children he had died. He'd stopped asking to go outside and ignored the litter box she'd placed by the basement stairs. The house smelled of cat urine.

She'd held Tiger in her arms, whispering words of endearment until he stopped breathing. Just as she had done with Stan.

After Stan's funeral, Charlotte had taken to sleeping in the guest room, which still gave her an odd little thrill—as though she were in a hotel room. She felt like an adult sleeping there. Which was silly. Who had she been before if not an adult, with a dying husband and three children to care for?

❧ The cancer had begun in Stan's lymph system, and they dared hope for a cure. If you had to have cancer, it was the best kind—everyone told them so, even the oncologist in Omaha. But three years after the first round of treatment, the disease was back. Then he had another remission. And even a third. But at such a cost. He never regained his strength. His lungs filled with fluid. Nausea was a constant problem. Then the cancer metastasized to his liver, and they had to be satisfied with shrinking the tumor—not a remission but a reprieve.

And his status became that of a dying man. People would ask about him in hushed tones, telling her not to give up hope when they knew it was only a matter of time. Even the children stopped talking about "when Daddy gets better." He would never see Vicky and Suzanne graduate from college or Mark from law school. He would never attend their weddings or hold their babies.

For the longest time, he'd kept his office at the *Record*, putting in half days when he could. Then he wrote editorials at the desk in his room or propped up in bed and managed the paper by telephone.

Stan's illness became the focus of family life. When, one by one, the children went off to college, they would call frequently and come home often. When he became bedridden, they carried their meals upstairs. Watched television on the bedroom set. Played gin rummy or bridge when Stan was up to it. Such devoted children. Beautiful children. They didn't get drunk or drive too fast. They worked hard in school, anxious to make their father proud. Every touchdown Mark scored, every basket he made was for his dad. When Vicky was named homecoming queen, she went over to the sidelines where Stan was watching and kissed him rather than the team captain. Suzanne dedicated her valedictory address to her father.

Charlotte had called them home from Lincoln to keep the death watch with her. And they helped plan his funeral, each writing a heart-wrenching tribute to the father they had so loved and revered. There was standing room only in the sanctuary. Women clutched wads of damp tissue in their hands. Men took out pocket handkerchiefs to wipe their eyes. Stan Haberman had been respected by all.

For ten years, Stan had apologized to Charlotte for the turn their life had taken. Too bad she hadn't married someone else and gotten out of Newberg. Seen some of the places she'd only read about in all those books. Had a healthy husband.

And she would tell him she'd never wanted any man but him. It wasn't exactly the truth, but that didn't matter. The exact truth had no relevance. She had married Stan. They'd made a home and family together. Ironically, any stray yearnings she might have fostered vanished in the wake of his illness. She belonged at his side and would be there until the end.

Her children were disappointed when Charlotte didn't purchase a double cemetery plot and install a grave marker with her name already engraved next to their father's, a space left only for the date of her death. "I'm only forty-seven," she protested. "I'm not ready for a tombstone."

But how could she blame them? A grave marker for Harry and Hannah Vogel stood over her own father's grave, with only the date of her mother's death missing. Nothing about the life Charlotte had lived would indicate she had any expectations for widowhood other than teaching school for fifteen or twenty more years, doting on whatever grandchildren came her way, doing good works in the community, going to the cemetery with flowers in hand to mark the passing months and years until she joined her beloved husband in death. And maybe that was exactly how she would live out her years. But she wanted to decide, not just let it happen.

chapter two

I thought I heard someone up here," Suzanne said, peeking over the top of the attic stairwell.

"It's just me and the mice," Charlotte said from where she was sitting on a three-legged stool, surrounded by cardboard boxes.

"Brrr, it's cold up here," Suzanne said, wrapping her quilted bathrobe more closely around her body.

Charlotte watched as her youngest child wound her way through the maze of cast-off furniture and assorted boxes. Suzanne's brown hair was still mussed from sleep, and her right cheek bore crease marks from her pillow. Though not arrestingly beautiful like her raven-haired sister, Suzanne had an appealing sweetness about her. Charlotte could still see in her the big-eyed little girl who always seemed to need more cuddling than her brother and sister.

Suzanne stood behind her mother, putting her hands on Charlotte's shoulders. Charlotte leaned against her, enjoying a moment of physical contact. "Time to get ready for work?" she asked.

"Not yet. What are you looking for?"

"I'm not looking for anything. I'm throwing away twenty-eight years worth of clutter—like this complete collection of canceled checks from 1979," Charlotte said, holding up the shoe box in her lap. "People should probably move every seven years just so they throw away stuff like this on a regular basis."

Suzanne wandered over to a white-painted chest of drawers that still held baby things. Crocheted blankets. Knitted sweaters. The christening gown all three Haberman babies had worn. "What will you do with all this baby stuff?" Suzanne asked, opening first one drawer, then another.

"I'm not sure," Charlotte admitted.

Another chest contained Easter and birthday dresses she'd made for the girls over the years. When they were little, she'd made all their clothes. After she started teaching school, she sewed only for special occasions. The last dress she'd made was Suzanne's formal for the senior prom—navy chiffon with a sequinned bodice. She'd looked like a young Debbie Reynolds.

She had kept too much, thinking one day she'd be glad to have the baby clothes, favorite toys, boxes filled with childish drawings, handmade Mother's Day cards, school papers, newspaper clippings, report cards, letters, certificates. And all those albums of pictures of children growing up and Stan getting sicker. Charlotte herself seldom appeared in the photographs. She was the photographer, the keeper of the record. There were seven albums in all. So much stuff hoarded over the years. She didn't have a clue what to do with it all. Except for a few carefully chosen mementos, she no longer wanted to be responsible for the sentimental clutter of the past.

Suzanne selected a well-worn teddy bear from a large box overflowing with stuffed animals and dolls and leaned against a maple hutch filled with dusty books. The hutch formerly had resided in the dining room but had been replaced by Nellie's lovely china cabinet with glass doors. The only really nice furniture they had were the pieces they'd moved over from Des Moines, after they brought Nellie to live in the Newberg nursing home.

"Or maybe every seven years people could do a major purge and just keep on living in the same house," Suzanne said, hugging the bear to her chest.

"Yes, but no one ever seems to do that."

"Mark called."

"Oh?"

"Yeah. He and Vicky are driving over tomorrow afternoon so we can talk things over. Mark says we put you on the defensive last Sunday. We should start all over again and make a list of pros and cons—talk about things rationally."

"Which means getting me to see things his way, I suppose."

Suzanne shrugged. "I think he's right, Mom. Maybe we can come up with another solution, like helping you fix up the house. It really does need painting."

"And a new furnace, hot-water tank, kitchen. The floors need refinishing, and the roof isn't in such great shape either. But none of that's why I want to move."

"Vicky thinks you want to get married again."

Charlotte laughed. "Which of the town's eligible bachelors does she think I have my eye on? Mr. Olson down at the junkyard? Or one of Nellie's compatriots at the nursing home?"

"I hear the new math teacher at the high school is a widower. And there are other widowers in other towns." She paused. "You wouldn't do that, would you? Get married again?"

"I haven't the faintest idea. Right now, I'd say no. But I don't see what this house has to do with my matrimonial state."

"Wouldn't you feel strange if some man came to see you here—where you lived with Daddy?"

"I don't know, Suzanne. Perhaps. But I will still be the same person no matter where I live. I'm always going to be the woman who was married to your father for twenty-seven years. Moving out of this house won't rewrite my history."

"But it could distance you from it."

"Time does that, honey. Just like you don't come up here and play dolls any more with your sister. And we don't cry now every time we talk about your father." Charlotte stuffed the shoe box of checks in a garbage bag and picked up another. "1983" was written across the top with a Magic Marker. She put it in the garbage bag unopened.

"Don't you want to see what you spent money on that year?" Suzanne asked, tossing the bear back in its box and pulling an old high school yearbook from the hutch. Charlotte recognized it as one of her own. From her senior year. Another lifetime ago.

"I've been doing that. Most of the checks were for groceries, shoes, and orthodontia. The Internal Revenue Service says I only have to keep checks for seven years, so everything else goes. I *am* going to move, Suzanne."

Charlotte picked up the shoe box for 1978—the year her own father died. And her mother still lived in the same house on Iowa Street. She probably had fifty years' worth of canceled checks in her attic.

"I can't bear the thought of strangers living here," Suzanne said, absently leafing through the yearbook pages.

"The family who lived here before your dad and I bought the place probably said the same thing. And the family before that. Ultimately, a house is just a house. The people who live there make it a home."

"Then why can't you just keep on making this house a home?" Suzanne asked. She closed the yearbook and put it back on the shelf, then stooped to pick up a photograph that had slipped from between the pages.

"Because it's time for a change," Charlotte said in a tone that conveyed finality. She took the lid from a cardboard file box and stared down at old tax returns, each year in its own folder. "There should be a law against attics. They just encourage people to be pack rats."

Charlotte looked around the attic at all the boxes yet to be opened, all the possessions yet to be handled, their history remembered, their fate decided. Suddenly she felt overwhelmed.

"Who's the guy?" Suzanne asked, handing the photograph to her mother.

Charlotte looked at the snapshot of herself and a boy, arm-in-arm, both wearing bathing suits, laughing, the municipal swimming pool in the background. "My, oh my. That was a long time ago."

"Well, who is he?" Suzanne demanded.

"Just a boy I once knew. From Pender. He worked in Newberg that summer."

"Where is he now?"

"I don't know. I haven't heard or thought about him in years." Charlotte hesitated, trying to decide what to do with the photograph, then tossed it in the garbage bag and stood up, stretching her cramped muscles. "Let's go have some breakfast."

For years, the tale about how Daddy saved Mommy from drowning had been an often-requested bedtime story. Just when Charlotte thought the children had outgrown it, one of them would resurrect it, begging to hear the story again.

Mark liked his dad's version, which started with fifteen-year-old Stan, who earned his spending money trapping mink and beaver along Logan Creek. If Stan hadn't been headed there, he wouldn't have been cutting across the park at just the right moment to hear the girl's screams and to rescue her from certain death. Stan knew about winter safety from his Boy Scout training and was able to pull the girl from the icy water. He carried the freezing, terrified young girl home to her parents, who'd thought she was safe in her bed and wouldn't have started to look for her until much later. By then her body would have been floating under the ice of the skating pond.

Vicky and Suzanne preferred their mother's version. It was a once-upon-a-time tale about a little girl who loved ice skating more than anything in the world and had taught herself to spin round and round like a top. For her ninth birthday, she got a pair of magical skates that would allow her to spin even faster, so fast she would be nothing but a blur to the amazed people who lined the shore of the skating pond to watch her. That night she dreamed about spinning in those skates, and very early the next morning before anyone else was awake, she slipped out of the house and tramped through the snow to the pond even though she was never, ever supposed to go skating without her mother or father along. But she just had to try out her new skates, and she would be careful, keeping to the edge of the pond where the ice was thick and safe.

She spun and spun around the edge of the deserted pond, faster than ever before. Around and around. She amazed herself at how fast she was spinning. But while she was spinning, she drifted toward the center of the pond. With a crunching sound, the ice began to crack. The girl dropped to her hands and knees and ever so carefully began crawling toward the edge of the pond. She wasn't afraid. It wasn't a big pond. She only had a few feet between herself and solid ice.

But suddenly she was sinking into the icy water with nothing to grab hold of. The weight of the skates was pulling her down into the frigid pond. She thought of her mother and father, and her little sister. How sad they would be if she died. She didn't want to drown. Never to grow up. Never fall in love. Never have children. She began to scream.

A brave and handsome boy heard her screams and came running across the park. Flat on his belly, he inched his way out on the ice until he was close enough to grab the girl's hand. Slowly, he pulled her out of the water and across the ice to safety. He wrapped her in his coat and carried her to her house, skates and all.

And Mark, Vicky, and Suzanne never would have been born if the boy hadn't saved the little girl from drowning, because she grew up to be their mommy, and the brave, handsome boy grew up to be their daddy.

Charlotte had allowed them to believe that, from that day forward, the boy and girl in the story knew in their hearts that they were destined for one another. And even though the boy moved away to another town, the girl knew that he would come back to her someday, and she waited patiently for his return.

The truth of the story was, as Stan unceremoniously dumped

Charlotte on the front porch of her house and rang the doorbell, he told her that she was the dumbest girl in the whole world and if she were his kid, he'd kick her butt good and hard.

At first her parents were almost hysterical, but once they got her dried off and warmed up, her butt got spanked good and hard, and the skates were taken away for the rest of the winter. By the time her tenth birthday rolled around, the skates were too small and her younger sister, Bernice, inherited them. Charlotte had to settle for a pair of used skates from the thrift shop. And she never again had the courage to skate in the middle of the pond, no matter how thick the ice was.

Stan's family moved away shortly after the rescue—to Des Moines, where his dad got a job in a bank. It was years later that Stan returned to Newberg to become editor of the town's weekly newspaper. By then he was twenty-six years old with a degree in journalism from the University of Iowa and a failed marriage under his belt. Charlotte had had to remind him that she was the little girl he'd saved from the pond.

Stan never talked much about his first wife. All Charlotte knew was that she had walked out after little more than a year of marriage. Mark, Vicky, and Suzanne didn't even know their father had been married before. There seemed to be no reason to tell them. The bedtime story was better without that particular fact. And by the same token, Charlotte never told them about the boy from Pender.

All Stan knew was that there had been someone. They kept that part of the past to themselves, accepting each other as they were—bruised but ready to get on with their lives. It wasn't a bad start for a marriage. They had no great expectations. All they wanted was a family and constancy.

With time there came love.

❧ When Charlotte told Suzanne that she hadn't thought about Cory Lee Jones in years, it wasn't exactly the truth.

Any mention of the town of Pender still brought thoughts of Cory. Whenever she drove by the farmhouse where his grandparents had once lived or saw movies about Vietnam, she thought about him. Boys with ponytails made her think of him, as did hearing the songs they'd listened to on the radio that summer: "Strangers in the Night," "Cherish," "Up, Up and Away."

Thoughts of Cory Lee Jones had become fleeting things, however, nothing she dwelled on at any length. Mostly she would wonder how he was. If he was even still alive. If he'd married, had children. Then she'd shake her head, put wondering aside, and go back to mothering, teaching, cooking, cleaning.

But those first years after he had left for Vietnam, she'd thought about him more waking minutes than not. She thought of him while she drove her car, when she bathed, while she waited for sleep, when she woke in the night—always asking the same question. *Why hadn't he come back to her?*

The letters he wrote from Vietnam became spaced further and further apart. The last one said he wouldn't write to her anymore, and that she should forget about him.

Charlotte hadn't known that Cory had come to see his grandparents until he'd already left again. The war had been hard on Cory Lee, his grandmother explained. The boy wasn't himself. He had moved to Texas and was being treated at a veterans hospital down there.

It had taken years for the pain to go away. Years for Charlotte to stop praying that it was Cory calling every time the phone rang, even after she was a married woman who by then surely would never leave her husband. She'd cried the night that Mark was born because he was Stan's baby and not Cory's. The thought had made her feel so ashamed that she had cried even more.

Sometimes she wondered if she was mistaken about the source of the pain. Maybe it had nothing to do with Cory. The pain was too heavy and real to be caused by emotions. She felt as if she could put her hand over it—right in the middle of her chest. A tumor maybe or a defective heart valve.

Eventually it was weariness that cured her. She didn't want to hurt any more. She wanted to put her arms around her husband and feel joy when they made love. She wanted to live in the present, delight in their children. She didn't want to speculate how her life would have been if Cory had returned. Finally she simply shut the door on him. It was so easy she wondered why she hadn't done it before. The door had a window for looking back, but she only allowed herself an occasional glimpse. The door itself remained firmly closed.

After Charlotte dropped Suzanne off at the drugstore for her Saturday job, she stopped by to have coffee with her mother and listened patiently while Hannah described her hands from yesterday's bridge club meeting and discussed the aches, pains, and family happenings of each of the club members in turn. Edna Mueller couldn't decide about bunion surgery. Doris Peterson's granddaughter—her son Phil's girl, who lived over in Blair and had almost died from a sledding accident when she was ten—had run off and married a divorced man from Chicago with two children. Charlotte remembered Phil, didn't she? The oldest of Doris's three sons—the boy with thick glasses who'd gone to optometry school and married that Otis girl with all that frizzy blond hair.

"Did you ever think about doing something after Daddy died?" Charlotte asked abruptly.

"Like what?" Hannah asked, frowning at the unexpected shift in conversation. With her carefully coiffed hair, rouged cheeks, and plump little body, she'd changed very little in the years since her husband died. Then as now, she was busy with her clubs and church activities. And more recently, she and her friends had discovered slot machines on the riverboat casinos at Council Bluffs. Charlotte couldn't remember her ever regretting anything about her life.

"Oh, get a job," Charlotte said. "Or start a business. Travel. Go to college. Write a family history."

"Now when would I ever have the time to do things like that!"

After she left her mother's house, Charlotte did her weekly grocery shopping at the Jack and Jill, then stopped by the liquor store
for a couple bottles of wine.

Back home, alone again in the big silent house, she put away the
groceries and carried a load of laundry to the basement. Delaying a
return to the attic, she dusted the living and dining rooms and
sorted through a stack of magazines.

But after fortifying herself with a bowl of soup, she put on a
sweater and headed up the attic stairs again, pausing on the top step
to take it all in. God, still so much stuff. Too bad a stray bolt of
lightning didn't come along and set the place on fire. What a blessing that would be. A clean break with the past, that's what she
needed. No disgruntled offspring expecting her to be the keeper of
the family shrine until she died or was shuttled off to the nursing
home. Nothing to throw away. Nothing to drag along. No guilt.
She'd save a couple of token photographs and let the rest burn.
Even her grandmother's china and silver.

She tried to imagine that—standing outside the house, watching it go up in flames, the children arriving the next day to sift
through the ashes in hopes of finding some memento to keep.

But then they would mourn for their father all over again. She
shook her head. Not a good idea. No fair wishing the house would
burn down. No easy out.

She glanced at the trash bag where she'd tossed the photograph
Suzanne had found this morning. She'd been a bit flustered when
Suzanne handed it to her and hadn't taken the time really to study
it. She'd forgotten about that bathing suit—the only two-piece
she'd ever owned. The only time her midriff had ever been brown.

She carried four bulging trash bags filled with old financial
records out by the garbage cans for pickup on Monday morning.
Before she tied the fifth bag closed, she dug around for the photograph. When she found it, she slipped it in her pocket to look
at later. Downstairs, where the light was better. Over a glass of wine.

Charlotte worked until dark, filling trash bags and pushing over
by the stairwell the furniture and boxes of items to be donated to

the next church sale. Mark could carry it all downstairs Sunday—after he discussed pros and cons.

Suzanne called to say she and Brady were driving over to Sioux City for dinner and a movie. She wouldn't be in until late.

Charlotte ate at the kitchen table, half-watching a documentary about the Florida Everglades while leafing through a magazine. Then she made a cherry pie for tomorrow, folded the laundry, paid a few bills.

Finally, leaving on the porch light for Suzanne, she carried her nightly glass of wine upstairs. She sat on the side of the bed and had just pulled the photograph from her pocket when the phone rang. It was her sister asking what she was doing.

"Actually, I'm having a glass of wine and looking at an old photograph of Cory Jones."

"Cory Jones?" Bernice chuckled in that warm, deep way of hers. "Now there was one fine-looking boy. God, that was a long time ago."

"Tell me about it," Charlotte said, holding the picture under the lamp. "I'm in the picture, too. In a two-piece bathing suit, no less. Before cellulite. I almost forgot—I used to be young."

"Ah, sounds like one of those life-has-passed-me-by moments."

Charlotte laughed. "More like a life-*is*-passing-me-by moment. I'm still hopeful I can jump on board."

"And go where?"

Charlotte put the photograph down and leaned against the headboard, stretching her legs out in front of her. They ached. Her whole body ached. "Someplace," she answered. "In this day and age, to have been no further from home than Kansas City seems pathetic, but it probably doesn't have to be a geographic destination. Just climbing out of the same old rut in the road might be enough. Not having everything in my life be automatic. Waking up in the morning and feeling excited about the day."

"And all this was brought on by a photograph of Cory Jones?" Bernice asked.

"Heavens no. Suzanne just happened to find it up in the attic, stashed away in an old yearbook. I've been working up there, dealing with the flotsam and jetsam from too many years of living in the same house—so I can move on. So, what's going on in Norfolk?"

"Oh, the usual—symphony openings, polo matches, debutante balls. But right now, I'm enjoying a rare Saturday night at home. The lord of the manor is snoozing in his recliner in front of the television, and I'm sitting here at the kitchen table looking over a set of house plans. I thought I might run over after church tomorrow and show them to you."

"You have house plans?"

"Yeah. I ordered a set from a magazine. With his and her bathrooms—can you imagine?"

"You think you'll really build it?"

"I don't know, Sis. I need to talk about it."

"Not tomorrow afternoon. Mark and Vicky are driving up. They want to talk me out of selling the house."

"You still sure that's what you want to do? There's a lot of good memories in that old house."

"What about the memories in your old house?"

"We were going to live here for just a couple of years. Remember? While Donald got his car dealership going? Well, he's added onto the business three times, and we still live in this old barn. It's not the same."

"I suppose so," Charlotte said. "The girls are worried that I want to move to another house so I'll feel more comfortable searching for my next husband."

Bernice chuckled. "And they wouldn't like that, would they? It would dishonor their sainted father's memory?"

"Something like that."

"Dear Stan," Bernice said with a sigh. "Problem was, he was a bit of a saint. You'll never find another man like him. Do you think you'll ever get married again?"

"Probably not. But I do think about sex sometimes," Charlotte admitted. "My kids wouldn't like that either."

"You suppose that Mama ever thinks about sex?"

Charlotte laughed. "God, what a thought."

"When she spends the night with us, I hear her talking to Daddy."

"Really?"

"Yeah. Harry this and Harry that. Not just mumbling in her sleep. Whispering. Giggling. Like he was right there in bed with her. Can you imagine—after all this time."

"That's so sweet it makes tears come to my eyes."

"What would you think if Mama got married?"

"Jesus, Bernice, she's pushing seventy."

"It happens. Now that she and the bridge club ladies have discovered the casinos at Council Bluffs, she might meet some dashing old geezer propped up at the next slot machine. Or suppose it was twenty years ago. How would you have felt?"

"She was so wrapped up in her grief it never would have happened. Then she started getting off on being the widow lady, like she'd been granted membership in some sort of exclusive club."

"But you're not listening. Suppose she had been more like you, wanting to move on?"

"So what are you saying?" Charlotte said, sitting up straight, swinging her legs back off the bed. "That I should be more like Mama?"

"No. I'm just trying to point out that having a widowed mother move on is hard for kids."

"I don't like this conversation," Charlotte said, picking up the photograph again, staring at it.

"Sorry. I didn't mean to upset you. Look, Sis, let's do something wicked next weekend—like checking into a hotel in Omaha and indulging ourselves with a weekend of shopping and girl talk. I could bring my house plans."

Charlotte smiled. "Sounds wonderful, but I can't afford anything like that."

"My treat."

"No way."

"I need this, Sis. Do it for me, okay?"

"Are you all right?"

"Depends on what you mean by all right. But don't work up a case of worry. Donald and I are healthy. The kids are fine. Noreen is pregnant. Business is great. I just need to think out loud with the only person in the world who won't give me a bunch of platitudes."

◆❧ Bernice hung up the phone, rolled up her house plans, and walked into the living room. The sound was muted on the big-screen TV, the football players silently cavorting about. She stared down at her husband—beefy face, mouth hanging open, eyes closed, the channel changer resting on his belly.

Donald Swenson used to be one fine-looking boy, too. Big and strong and blond. Sexy. Funny. He'd written, "Will you marry me, Bernice?" one hundred times on the sidewalk at NU—all the way from the Theta House to Bessey Hall where she had her first class. It must have taken him half the night. There'd been a picture of it in the student newspaper. "Football player puts it in writing," the caption said. He gave her a ring at the Pillars. In the moonlight. And promised to love her forever.

She looked above her husband's reclining body at her reflection in the mirror over the mantel. She'd changed, too. But not like Donald.

◆❧ Charlotte leaned back against the headboard and sipped her wine while she studied the boy and girl in the photograph, with their young flesh, sparkling eyes, windblown hair, laughing lips. His arm was wrapped around her body with his hand clasping her just above the waist, his thumb straying to the lower edge of her right breast. Maybe even touching it. Had Suzanne noticed that— a boy's thumb touching her mother's breast? But Charlotte hadn't been Suzanne's mother then. She hadn't been anyone's mother.

Still, she felt exposed—as though her daughter had caught her doing something indecent.

Charlotte reached under her shirt and placed her own hand where Cory's had been, imagining how she had felt to him. But the girlishly slim waist was gone. The taut skin. Her breasts were lower on her chest. And there was a bulge of extra flesh below her bra that she could no longer make go away by sucking in her breath.

She'd first seen Cory on the diving board, showing off a bit. He was more daredevil than diver. And gradually Suzanne became aware that his antics were being performed for her benefit. He would position himself on the board, then look to see if she was watching. He'd look her way again when he surfaced.

"You'd better speak to him before he kills himself," Bernice had said, giggling.

Charlotte would have noticed him anyway, without all the failed double gainers. First of all, she knew everyone in town, if not by name at least by sight, and he wasn't from Newberg. And he had to be the best-looking boy in the entire state of Nebraska. Tab Hunter with a ponytail. No boy in Newberg wore a ponytail. If he did, someone would have told him to cut it off—his principal or pastor or father. Back then, at least in Newberg, long hair for a boy seemed rakish or even immoral. Of course, the residents of Pender probably had pretty much the same opinion of long-haired boys, but Cory Jones was somewhat of a rebel. He questioned the war in Vietnam. He wasn't sure what he would do if he were drafted.

But they were young. And it was summertime, with all its associated freedom from school and overcoats. Vietnam was far away. And warm honey flowed in Charlotte's veins.

chapter three

When it was just her and Suzanne at home, Charlotte never bothered with a full-blown Sunday dinner. Usually they had grilled cheese sandwiches and a bowl of soup before Suzanne caught the two-thirty bus back to Lincoln.

But with Mark and Vicky driving up, Charlotte put a roast in the oven before church. Over dinner, she listened patiently while her law student son went through his arguments. He'd written it down, made a list on a yellow legal pad.

He talked about the tax implications of selling the house. She would be taxed for substantial capital gains. And if she were no longer a homeowner, she would lose her primary tax deduction.

She would lose the feeling of permanence and belonging that came with home ownership.

All his and his sisters' memories of their childhood and their father focused on the house. They'd been a family here—a good family.

As for the loneliness of living alone, she would just have to face that all over again in the next house.

"And if you're worried about the future, you know that we'll always take care of you, Mom."

Charlotte felt her spine stiffen. She didn't want to be taken care of. She just didn't want to spend the rest of her life taking care of their childhood home.

"When do you get to the pro list?" she asked.

"Well, there is the condition of the house to contend with," Mark allowed. "But the house is structurally sound, and you could get a home-equity loan to fix it up."

He paused and checked his notes to make sure he'd covered everything. Then looked up to make his closing point. "You are making a decision that affects Vicky, Suzanne, and me without taking our wishes into consideration. Once the house is sold, it will be gone from our family forever."

Vicky waited to make sure Mark was finished, then turned to her mother. "I still think that you and Grandma should live together. You could sell *her* house," Vicky said, as though that would satisfy Charlotte's urge to make a real estate transaction.

"That house is where *I* grew up," Charlotte reminded them. "According to Mark's reasoning, your grandmother should stay there until she dies so I can roam through the rooms remembering *my* father. You get over that, kids. I know you don't think so now, but you do. That house over on Iowa Street is my mother's house. Every time I walk in the door, I am not automatically filled with memories of my father. I know you kids don't remember him, but believe me, your grandfather was as good and gentle as your father. I don't need that house to remember him."

"Well, if you're really going to move, could you wait until after Christmas?" Suzanne asked. She'd been quiet throughout the meal, not quite paying attention to her brother's presentation.

"I hope the house has sold by then," Charlotte said. "Several people are interested."

"Brady and I are getting married," Suzanne explained, lifting her chin, as though fortifying herself for the maternal challenge she knew would follow. "I'd like to get married here—a Christmas wedding. It would seem more like Daddy was a part of it."

"Oh, Suzanne, you can't be serious," Charlotte gasped. "What about college?"

"I don't need a college education to get married and have children," Suzanne said.

"That sounds like Brady talking," Charlotte countered. "I thought you were going to medical school."

Suzanne shrugged. "Half the kids in the world say they're going to be a doctor when they grow up."

"Most of them aren't smart enough. You are."

"There are more than enough smart people to go around, Mom. And Brady doesn't want to wait that long to get married."

"What about what Suzanne wants?" Charlotte challenged, knowing she was going about this all wrong. Saying the wrong things. She looked to Vicky and Mark for support. But they were studying their empty dessert plates.

"It's what I want, too," Suzanne said. "I'm tired of all this back-and-forth every weekend. Tired of working part time for chicken feed so I can buy a new outfit every now and then. Brady's folks have offered to build us a new home out by the John Deere dealership."

"I didn't think I needed a college education either," Charlotte said, telling herself to stay calm, not to raise her voice. To reason with Suzanne. "I had to return to college with three young children at home."

"That's because Daddy got sick. If that hadn't happened, you wouldn't have needed to finish your degree," Suzanne said.

"How do you know Brady won't get sick or divorce you?"

"Mom, don't say things like that. You're supposed to be happy for me, and get all excited about helping me plan a wedding."

"You have a full scholarship. For God's sake, Suzanne, don't throw it away. You have the opportunity to really make something of yourself."

"It's what you did."

"Yes, but your father wanted me to continue my education," Charlotte said, hearing her voice become more strident. She had to clutch her hands together to keep from pounding on the table. "Remember when I finally got that degree? Mark was already in high school. Your father was so proud, I thought he'd bust his buttons. Brady wouldn't be proud. He wants to bury you here in Newberg. He doesn't want you to be more educated than he is."

Mark put his hand on his mother's arm. "Mom, don't. Let her be happy."

Charlotte pulled her arm away. She felt sick at heart. Angry. Betrayed. Suzanne had the second highest scores in the whole state on her college entrance exam. How could she settle for being an uneducated housewife in a town that didn't have a public library or a bookstore—no matter how wholesome and safe that town happened to be. Wholesome and safe didn't enrich one's soul. It would be different if Brady were like Stan. But Brady was more like Bernice's husband: two-dimensional; business and sports. Bernice joked that she'd have to bury Donald with the channel changer in one hand and a beer can in the other, just so the good Lord would recognize him.

Brady wasn't special enough for Suzanne. Did all mothers think that about prospective sons-in-law? Or maybe it wasn't his lack of specialness so much as the way he expected Suzanne to jump when he barked. Except that probably was Suzanne's shortcoming, not Brady's. Suzanne needed a different sort of man. A sweet man. Because she was a sweet girl.

And a brilliant girl. Brady had made fun of her when she was named valedictorian of their graduating class. He would ask for "the Brain" when he called on the phone. When Brady dropped out of college after one semester, Charlotte wasn't surprised. She'd had him as a student in the eighth grade. Not that he was dumb—he could recite stats for sports figures and car engines till the cows came in. He could cram for a test with the best of them. But he had no intellectual curiosity. He read magazines, not books. He had no desire to know anything except what applied to his daily life.

Other mothers might be pleased that their daughter was marrying a young man whose future was assured. The John Deere dealership in Newberg served a large area. The family was wealthy, by town standards anyway. Brady and his sister would inherit the business someday.

Brady was the only boyfriend Suzanne had ever had. What did she know about life? She was a baby. Only twenty years old, for God's sake! As Charlotte herself had been when she married Stan. Too damned young!

Vicky was giving her sister a hug. "My baby sister is getting married first," she said. "Imagine that."

Mark got up and came around the table to kneel by Suzanne's chair and plant a kiss on her cheek. Suzanne threw her arms around his neck. "Will you give me away?"

"I'd be honored," Mark said, his voice breaking.

"And you'll be my maid of honor," Suzanne told her sister. "No bridesmaids. Just you."

Charlotte watched her three children in their group embrace. A tender moment, and she wasn't part of it.

She had to do something, of course. Make some gesture of reconciliation. She would be good old mom and see this thing through. *I will not cry*, she told herself. *I will not cry*. "If it's what you really want, I'm happy for you," she said with what she hoped was a warm smile. "A Christmas wedding will be lovely."

She rose from her chair to stand behind her youngest child, to put her arms around Suzanne's slim shoulders and rest a cheek on her smooth head. She smelled of shampoo and youth. Her baby girl.

❧ Mark apologized for their having to hurry off right after dinner. A snowstorm was predicted for most of the state. He hadn't carried the things down from the attic for her, but it didn't matter so much now. She wouldn't be moving before Christmas.

A wedding. In this house. She'd have to at least paint the living room and entry hall. Have the rugs cleaned. God knows what else.

Why couldn't Suzanne get married in church with the reception downstairs in the fellowship hall? It would be so much easier. Did she think Stan's ghost was going to be hovering about, offering his blessing if she got married in the living room?

Charlotte waved good-bye from the front porch and watched Mark's car drive to the end of the street and turn onto the boulevard. Snow flurries were already swirling about.

She shut the front door behind her. Leaned against it—and felt her knees go weak. She stumbled forward and half-fell onto the stairs. Now she could cry.

She let herself go. Great, painful sobs racked her chest. She'd failed the child she needed to protect the most. Suzanne was giving up on her dreams, on herself. Charlotte lifted her head and howled her protest into the quiet of her big, empty house.

When she stopped, the stillness pressed against her ears and chest. If she were a stronger person, she would conjure up the sounds of family past to ease her through the void. Children running up and down the stairs, radios blaring, Stan calling out that he was home. But even her memories were silent.

"Okay, Charlotte, what now?" she said out loud.

And suddenly she was grabbing her coat. Pulling on her boots and gloves. Searching for her car keys.

The cemetery gate was locked, so she climbed over it and hurried across the frozen ground to her husband's tombstone. "I'm so sorry, Stan," she said. "I know you had such high hopes for her, and now I've let you down."

The snowflakes were bigger now, falling soundlessly around her as she knelt in front of her husband's tombstone. She traced his name with a gloved fingertip. Stanley Darnell Haberman. No one had called him "Stanley." He never used his middle name or initial. He signed his name "Stan Haberman." She should have buried him with that name—in a wooden casket, even if it meant delaying the funeral.

Charlotte put her arms around the shaft of granite and embraced it. "I'm glad Cory didn't come back. Glad I married you."

From the cemetery, she drove out Schoolhouse Road, to the farm where Cory's grandparents used to live. Mr. and Mrs. Hausman. Nice people. He was quiet. She was a pretty little woman with a southern accent. They'd met during World War I, when Mr. Hausman was stationed in Georgia. They called their grandson Cory Lee. Except for his mom, everyone else called him Cory, he'd explained. But Charlotte loved saying both names when they were alone. "Cory Lee." Together the words had a lilt she found pleasing; an intimacy, even. A name for a mother to whisper to the baby boy at her breast. Or to be whispered in the night by a woman in love.

The house was deserted now; a weathered FOR SALE sign hung from the fence. She pulled in the driveway and shone the car lights through the falling snow to the bunk house where Cory had lived that summer. The windows were boarded shut.

She had crept out of her house in the night and walked out here—a warm night with an almost full moon so bright she could have read a newspaper by its light.

She could see him through the screen door, asleep in his bed, a book on his chest, the lamp still on. She'd opened the screen door and tiptoed inside. The book was *Exodus*. She'd given it to him so they could talk about it. Talk about war, religion, patriotism, civil disobedience—things in his own life that confused him. She'd given him other books to read. And college bulletins. He'd been out of high school for a year, doing not much of anything. If he were a college student, he wouldn't have to worry about the war.

Cory's eyes fluttered open, and he saw her there.

He watched while she took off her clothes. No person had seen her naked in years—not even her own sister. She hadn't known she would do that. Hadn't rehearsed it in her mind. Hadn't known for sure what was going to happen. All she'd thought about was kissing him and touching him and feeling his hands everywhere on her body—as they had been hours before.

Or maybe she had known. For as she pulled her T-shirt over her head, she realized that she had never wanted anything in her life the way she wanted Cory Lee Jones to be the first boy to see her naked and make love to her. She wasn't even sure why. "Orgasm" was only a word she'd read in books. She knew only that her body felt hollow inside, and she would have walked over hot coals to get in that bed with him.

Charlotte leaned her forehead against the steering wheel of her Pontiac station wagon. She shivered. It was getting cold. Really cold.

Cory had thought she was beautiful. She had seen it in his eyes, heard it in his voice. No man would ever look at her like that again.

With a deep sigh, she turned the car around and headed home.

Back at the house, she abandoned the guest room and crawled into the bed she'd shared with her husband, searching for the comfort of his presence. The first and the last time they'd made love had been here in this room, in this bed. Their children had been conceived here. She wanted to believe all those soothing words about Stan looking down on her and making a place for her. She reached a hand out into the darkness. "I miss you so," she whispered.

Close to the end, he had dictated a list of the people she should notify. Relatives. Family friends from his childhood. Special friends from college. Former colleagues.

"What about Elizabeth?" she'd asked. His first wife.

"She knows," he'd said.

She knows? Had he called her? Written?

Life was so untidy. Nothing was ever all one way or the other.

❧ The Yocum family had lived in the house at the corner of Washington Street and Schoolhouse Road the whole time Charlotte was growing up. They owned the Dairy Dream. The Yocum children were older than she and Bernice—four of them, working at the drive-in after school and on weekends. The older three moved away when they graduated from high school. The youngest, Johnny, had Down's syndrome and stayed on with his parents. The

three of them died in a car wreck on the way to California to see one
of Johnny's sisters.

Soybean prices were at rock bottom, and the house stood empty
for almost two years. Anxious to settle their parents' estate, the
three surviving children accepted Stan's low-ball offer the month
before he and Charlotte got married.

Her mother and sister helped them clean it from top to bottom.
Charlotte's dad helped Stan replace the rotted boards in the front
porch and back stoop and tear down a dilapidated chicken house.
Stan had been living in a furnished apartment over the doctor's office, Charlotte with her parents, so moving in hadn't taken very
long. Charlotte put away the wedding presents. Sears delivered the
bed. Mr. Patterson brought over the kitchen table and chairs and
the chest of drawers they'd bought at his secondhand store. Stan's
parents gave them a sofa and easy chair, Charlotte's parents a May-
tag washing machine.

Charlotte still had the kitchen table—down in the basement by
the dryer. She used it for folding clothes. But that first night, she
had covered it with a lace tablecloth. Stan put a stack of records on
his portable player and opened a bottle of wine. Charlotte lit a pair
of candles and turned out the light. She remembered how strange it
had been, sitting down at that table over a meal she had cooked, two
married people beginning their life together. Any money they
might have used for a honeymoon had been swept into the down
payment. Instead of a hotel dining room in Omaha or Kansas City,
they were in the kitchen of the big, empty house that was now their
home. "Someday I'll take you to Paris," he promised.

"That would be wonderful," she said. "But this is wonderful,
too." And it was. They were both nervous but the wine helped.
"Let's be happy," she said.

Stan lifted his glass. "To happiness."

Later, as she lay beside her sleeping husband in their brand-new
bed, she vowed to be a good wife to him. And never to hurt him. He
would never know how much she wished he were someone else.

She'd gotten over that eventually. The years between getting over Cory and Stan getting sick had been the best years. Sometimes on a summer's evening after the children were in bed, they'd take their beer or wine or iced tea and go sit on the porch swing and talk about what they had to be thankful for. She would put her head on his shoulder as they swung back and forth and feel content.

There'd only been the two men in her life. Cory had vanished. Stan had died. If she could have had one of them back, it would be Stan. He was a part of her. But nothing again in her life would ever be like that sweet summer with Cory Lee Jones. And she did wonder whatever happened to him.

chapter four

Suzanne emerged from the dressing room, the saleswoman following behind her, fluffing the ruffled skirt of the wedding dress.

"Too fussy, huh?" Suzanne asked her mother and sister as she examined her reflections in the three-way mirror.

"Well, I like it better than the other ones," Vicky said.

Which wasn't saying much, Charlotte thought. The dresses all seemed overdone and chintzy—more like costumes for a school play than something to get married in.

Even with their modest budget, Vicky had been certain they'd have no trouble finding a dress worthy of her sister's wedding day. Suzanne had suggested a suit with a lacy blouse, but Vicky insisted she needed a real wedding dress, something appropriate for a home wedding—understated and tasteful. Think of the pictures. Did Suzanne want to be wearing a suit in her wedding photographs?

The saleswoman—a tiny woman named Wanda with overdyed black hair—stood on a small stool to fasten a shoulder-length veil to Suzanne's hair, then picked up her stool and backed away with a look of rapture on her face. "Lovely, my dear," she said reverently. "Absolutely lovely."

Once again, Suzanne scrutinized her images in the mirrors, then shook her head and pulled off the veil. "I haven't worn ruffles since I was three years old," she told Wanda.

Vicky nodded her head in agreement. No ruffles.

The day wasn't working out at all as Vicky had envisioned. They were supposed to find the perfect dress, have a lovely lunch at the Red Lion, then drive out to Westroads Mall and help Suzanne select china and silver patterns at Younkers Department Store. It was to be a day for mending bridges and getting on with the program. The wedding was less than five weeks away.

Vicky had made the appointment at the Omaha bridal boutique. And rather than meet her mother and sister in Omaha, she had confiscated the car from Mark and driven home on Friday night so she could ride with them to Omaha Saturday morning, knowing they needed her presence in the car to ease the tension. On the way back to Newberg, however, there would be talking and laughter. Wedding plans being made. Vicky even stuck a tablet in her purse so they could make lists.

Not that she didn't understand her mother's disappointment; she felt it herself. A brainy girl like Suzanne should finish her education. Vicky had been certain that her sister and Brady would break up when they went to college. Most high school sweethearts did. But Suzanne had gone with Brady since the ninth grade, and loyalty was her long suit—or downfall. She kept taking piano lessons long after old Miss Jonson was so hard of hearing her other students had abandoned her. Suzanne could have gotten a better-paying part-time job than the one she had working in Mr. Pratt's dingy drugstore, but she'd worked for him all through high school and didn't want to hurt his feelings by quitting to work for someone else.

If there was any breaking up to do, Brady would have had to do it. And he never would. Suzanne Haberman was a prize. Any boy would want to marry such a smart, pretty girl.

Vicky assumed her sister loved Brady. But she didn't believe that Suzanne was *in love* with him—certainly not the way their parents had been in love. There had been an equity about their parents' marriage, and Brady was too insecure for equity. His car had been the most expensive one in the high school parking lot, but he was a mediocre student and a mediocre athlete in a town that revered athletics. He was too short and stocky to be considered handsome and derived whatever popularity he enjoyed from being Suzanne's boyfriend.

Unlike her sister, Vicky had had lots of boyfriends over the years. She'd thoroughly enjoyed lengthy necking sessions with a number of them but never allowed any boy to touch her below the waist and never thought she was in love with any of them.

Vicky wasn't as smart as her sister and had never made straight A's, but she knew what she wanted out of life and didn't plan to settle for less. She would live in Newberg or some other small town and run the newspaper, as her father had done. Maybe her husband would be a journalist, too. Or he might be the high school principal. The town doctor. Someone respected in the community. A handsome, intelligent man with a kind heart, who would love and value her the way their father had loved and valued their mother.

Their parents' marriage had been perfect—a lovers-and-best-friends kind of marriage. Vicky never heard them say a cross word to each other. They hugged and held hands. They looked at each other. Complimented each other. Had long discussions about all manner of things—not just gossip or what to have for dinner. And they'd made love—during all those Sunday afternoon "naps" with the bedroom door locked—until her dad was too sick.

Vicky refused to believe a good marriage depended on the luck of the draw. When someone as fine as her father came along, she would recognize him. She would marry him in a beautiful ceremony at the First Lutheran Church and love him until the day she died. She couldn't understand why her sister was settling for less.

Poor Suzanne. She looked discouraged, standing there in that stupid dress, with her shoulders drooping, circles under her eyes. She gathered up the skirt and was heading for the dressing room when Wanda accosted her, triumphantly carrying yet another dress.

And suddenly their mother was on her feet, thanking Wanda for her patience, but she had decided to make her daughter's wedding dress.

"*Make a wedding dress?*" Wanda said incredulously, looking down at the beaded bodice of the gown she was carrying.

"Oh, Mom, would you?" Suzanne said, clasping her hands together.

Charlotte smiled and took her younger daughter's face in her hands. "It needs to be ankle-length—a tea gown. Ivory satin. Very simple. Straight skirt. V-neck. Long fitted sleeves. No overskirt. No ruffles. You'll look like Grace Kelly."

"But when would you have time?"

"I'll just have to find time. I won't have my daughter getting married in a dress with unfinished seams," she said.

With a sigh of relief, Vicky closed her eyes and sagged against the back of the loveseat she'd been sharing with her mother. Everything was going to be all right after all.

But when she opened her eyes a second later, everything was changing once again. Like a rag doll that had suddenly lost its stuffing, Suzanne was crumpling to the floor, taffeta ruffles pooling around her, her face as white as the dress.

Wanda gasped.

Charlotte dropped to her knees and gathered Suzanne in her arms.

And what had only been a nagging doubt for Vicky became a reality. She knew why her sister wanted a Christmas wedding.

Wanda had figured it out, too. The look on her face changed from shock to disgust, as though the store were suddenly filled with a foul odor.

❧ "Why didn't you just tell me, instead of spouting all that nonsense about one more Christmas in our beloved home so you could feel like your father was with you when you got married?" Charlotte gripped the steering wheel so tightly her knuckles were white. Her empty stomach was churning, her head pounding. "Why didn't you just explain that you didn't want a big church wedding because you're pregnant? Jesus, Suzanne, surely you knew I was going to figure it out eventually."

"Come on, Mom," Vicky pleaded from the back seat. "She just wanted to give us time to get used to the idea."

Charlotte had called Dr. Linderman from the bridal store to hear him say not to worry, to bring Suzanne on home and have her come in the office Monday morning. Dr. Linderman's office nurse was a mouth with legs. By next week, the whole town would know. Charlotte's mother would be hysterical.

"You don't have to marry him," she said. "If you want the baby, I'll help you raise it."

As she said the words, though, Charlotte thought about what they meant—starting all over again with a baby. A return to selflessness.

But if it would save her daughter from this marriage, did she have any choice?

Charlotte braked behind an ancient pickup truck crawling down the two-lane highway. Some old farmer with nothing on his mind. She felt a surge of anger at him. At the world. She wanted to honk the horn to let him know how she felt.

At the first opportunity, Charlotte sailed around the truck faster than necessary, then forced herself to let up on the accelerator—and glanced over at Suzanne. Vicky had reclined the passenger seat back to its lowest position and covered her sister with her coat.

Suzanne's eyes were closed, her face pale. She was very thin, Charlotte realized. She'd lost weight. Morning sickness, probably. Did all the girls in her dorm know what Suzanne hadn't bothered to tell her own mother?

Or should she have guessed without being told? Certainly she'd wondered over their five years of dating if Suzanne and Brady had sex. In the beginning, she'd worried a great deal about them spending so much time together and fretted about what her responsibility was. Birth control for a fifteen-year-old? Preaching about chastity? Extracting promises she had no power to enforce?

Finally, Charlotte had called the office of a female OB-GYN in Norfolk and given her permission, should her daughter ever come asking, for her to be examined and given a prescription for birth control pills. Then she told Suzanne what she had done. Suzanne acknowledged the information with a nod. Nothing else had ever been said. And now Suzanne was twenty. Not a child. Had this pregnancy been deliberate on her part so she could drop out of college and get married? In her heart of hearts, did Suzanne really love Brady that much? Did she even love him at all? And if she didn't love him, what in the hell was she escaping from?

Her mother's expectations perhaps?

No, damn it! Suzanne herself had established the expectations years ago. She wanted to be a physician. To help people. That was why God had made her smart.

And suddenly, Charlotte couldn't see the road for her tears. She pulled onto the shoulder. "You drive," she told Vicky.

Then she crawled into the back seat and pulled her coat over her face.

❧ Suzanne called Brady the minute she walked in the door. By the time he pulled in the driveway, she'd changed into her jeans and was racing out the front door.

Vicky found her mother standing at the kitchen sink, staring out the window. Vicky embraced her from behind. "I don't have to go back to Lincoln. Do you want me to sleep over?" she asked.

"No, I know you have plans," Charlotte assured her, telling her what she wanted to hear.

"But you're upset."

"Yes, I'm upset. But I'll get over it."

After sending Vicky on her way, Charlotte went up to the attic.

The culled pieces of furniture were still waiting for Mark to carry them down to the station wagon.

Stan's dust-covered yearbooks from the University of Iowa were stacked on top of the hutch.

The few times Stan had spoken of his first wife, she'd been simply "Elizabeth," but Charlotte discovered the rest of her name in an old newspaper clipping she'd found in a box of Stan's miscellaneous papers. The clipping was an announcement of the engagement of Elizabeth Patricia Easterling and Stanley Darnell Haberman.

Armed with a name, Charlotte had been able to find Elizabeth in his college yearbooks. God, how she had studied those pictures, each one in turn, over and over. Examining Elizabeth's smile, the tilt of her head, the curl in her hair.

Also a journalism major, Elizabeth Patricia Easterling had been a year behind Stan. She was a Delta Gamma from Fort Dodge, sang in the university choir, and belonged to the Young Republicans, the Spirit Council, the French Club. But the yearbooks couldn't tell Charlotte how much Stan and Elizabeth had loved each other and why they hadn't stayed married.

And now, years later, Charlotte was asking the same questions. Once again, she was thumbing through old yearbooks, looking for the face of the woman Stan had loved before her. Maybe had never stopped loving.

❧ Suzanne didn't come home until the next morning. Charlotte had spent the night imagining all manner of things—almost all of them bad. She met Suzanne at the door with a relieved hug. "We need to talk."

Suzanne was wary, but she allowed herself to be led to the kitchen table. "No coffee," she said, making a face when Charlotte picked up the pot.

"It made me nauseous when I was pregnant, too," Charlotte said, reaching for the tea bags.

"I've decided to go back to plan one and wear a suit when I get married, so you don't have to make a wedding dress," Suzanne said, watching her mother bustle about putting the kettle on the stove, getting cups from the cupboard, putting the sugar bowl on the table.

"Whatever you want. But you definitely are getting married?"

"I want this baby to have a mother and a father—as I did. I am sorry, though. I didn't mean to get pregnant. It just happened, Mom. I know Grandma will freak. People will look down their noses."

"None of that matters," Charlotte said. "What matters is that you get married for the right reason."

"Why did you get married?"

With her back to her daughter, Charlotte had to stop breathing for a minute to absorb the question. To formulate an answer.

Her first impulse was to revive the fairy tale. *She'd always known she would marry Stan. A love that was meant to be.*

But the fairy tale had been a lie, at least that part.

She sat across the table from her daughter. "Not because I was pregnant," Charlotte said carefully, "but because I'd had my heart broken, and your father was a safe harbor. In time, I came to love him very much."

"If I didn't marry Brady, I'd break his heart," Suzanne said.

"I got over mine," Charlotte said.

chapter five

It was only a five- or six-hour drive to Topeka—not a great journey. But Charlotte had never driven further than Lincoln by herself, never driven alone outside the state of Nebraska, and the thought of doing so made her feel adventurous. Not that Kansas was different in any significant way from its neighbor to the north. After she'd sold the house, she would take a trip to someplace that was different, some place far away and unfamiliar. She wanted to wake up in the morning and know by the smells and sounds that she was someplace other than the windswept prairie where she'd lived her entire life. She wanted to experience ethnic food and lofty heights. To taste salt air and hear foreign tongues.

But none of that would happen on the way to Topeka. Not that it wasn't beautiful, this Midland of hers, with its husbanded landscape and tidy farms, its vast space and open roads, and most of all, a sky that went from horizon to horizon and put forth sunrises and sunsets that made her spirit soar, and awesome thunderheads, followed by miraculous rainbows. But this land had begotten a homogeneous race of people. Conservative. Hardworking. Mistrustful of anyone who wasn't smugly satisfied with life as they knew it. Arrogantly worshipful of a God created in their own image.

It had snowed during the night, but not enough to make driving a problem. She fixed a thermos of coffee and wrapped foil around a couple of muffins before heading down the empty highway. Yes, definitely an adventure of sorts. Breaking the mold. She had listed her house with a realtor, and now she was driving to Topeka by herself. She'd feel excited if she weren't so nervous about meeting her husband's first wife.

Finding an address for Elizabeth had been easy. Five Easterlings had been listed with Fort Dodge information. The first number Charlotte tried was busy. She went on to the second, and it was answered by a man who acknowledged he had a niece named Elizabeth Easterling—his brother's oldest girl. And yes, she went to the University of Iowa in the late 1960s or thereabouts. Charlotte claimed to be an old college friend of Elizabeth's, a sorority sister. She wanted to invite Elizabeth to a reunion of their Delta Gamma pledge class.

William Easterling explained that his niece now lived in Topeka. Her married name was Kline. Charlotte waited while William rummaged around for a phone number and address, and listened patiently while he tried to figure out how long it had been since he'd last seen Elizabeth. Probably not since his wife's funeral. Pauline, God rest her soul, had died of a massive stroke five years back come February twelfth. Since the death of Elizabeth's parents, she didn't get back to Fort Dodge very often.

When she hung up, Charlotte wiped her sweaty hands on her jeans. She'd lied to get information from a nice old man, and she didn't like the way it made her feel. She didn't even bother with rationalization; it had been a tacky thing to do. But the next phone call would be truthful—painfully so.

Before she lost her nerve, Charlotte picked up the receiver and dialed the Topeka telephone number William Easterling had given her. A man answered. When Elizabeth came to the phone, Charlotte almost hung up. It was so stupid to be doing this; she should let sleeping dogs lie, leave Elizabeth alone. But she cleared her throat and began.

"This is Charlotte Haberman—Stan Haberman's widow. I'm planning to drive to Topeka next Saturday and wondered if I could drop by and see you?"

"See me? Whatever for?" Elizabeth asked.

"I'd just like to meet you. Now that Stan is gone, I'm having a hard time sorting things out."

"What sort of things?"

"If he really loved me. If we were happy. Stuff like that."

Elizabeth didn't say anything for a time. Charlotte listened to the silence, waiting, almost hoping Elizabeth would say no. But she said for Charlotte to call when she got to town. She'd meet her someplace.

Friday evening, Charlotte told Suzanne she would be gone all day Saturday—to a teachers' workshop in Lincoln. Another lie. Suzanne looked tired and wanted only hot tea and toast for dinner. But Charlotte had known better than to suggest she call Brady and tell him she needed to stay home this evening. He would come for her as usual, and they would go off to wherever it was they went. Sex in the pickup, she supposed. Except it was cold outside. Damned cold.

On the outskirts of Topeka, Charlotte purchased a map of the city at a service station and asked the attendant to show her the best way to get to Woodring Avenue. She needed to see where Elizabeth lived first. Then she'd call her.

The traffic was intimidating, and it took her almost half an hour to correct a wrong turn, but shortly after noon, she turned onto Woodring and drove slowly by the Klines' white frame house. The front door was flanked by narrow windows with leaded panes, but otherwise it was an ordinary house on an ordinary street. A faded blue Chevrolet sedan was parked in the driveway.

Charlotte called from a convenience store. Elizabeth told her to drive to a Holiday Inn on the highway. She'd meet her in the coffee shop.

Charlotte arrived first and went immediately to the ladies' room—to see if she looked old. The lighting was poor. She decided she didn't look so much old as drab.

She brushed on some blush and smoothed her hair.

Elizabeth was slightly plump, graying, her face an older but still attractive version of the woman in the yearbook pictures.

They ordered coffee. Then Elizabeth folded her hands on the table, waiting for Charlotte to explain herself. Her hands looked older than her face. She wore a plain gold wedding band much like Charlotte's.

"What did he tell you about me?" Charlotte asked.

Elizabeth looked surprised.

"Stan told me that you knew he was dying," Charlotte said by way of explanation. "I assumed that you'd been in touch."

"Yes. We talked occasionally over the years. I knew about his illness."

"What did he say about me?"

"He said he felt lucky to have you. That you had a good marriage. Wonderful children."

"Did he love me?" Charlotte asked.

"Oh, yes. I'm sure he did."

"But he never said so?"

"I'm not sure," Elizabeth said. "He talked about you in a loving way."

"Did you see each other?"

"No, never. Not since I asked him to pack up and leave."

"What happened? Why did you split up?"

Again Elizabeth looked surprised. "He never told you?"

Charlotte shook her head.

They waited while the waitress placed their coffee cups on the table. Elizabeth added sugar and cream and took a sip. "I can't believe he didn't tell you. We had to get married, which was embarrassing but not a big problem for either one of us since we'd planned to get married after I graduated the following year. But there were problems with the pregnancy. An x-ray showed the baby's

guilt? Surely. After twenty-seven years of marriage and three children.

Her life seemed to be composed mainly of loose ends; even her marriage, which had lasted "till death do us part" but was more unresolved now than when she had watched Stan's casket being lowered into the ground. She had raised her children only to discover there never would be a moment at which she could figuratively brush the dust from her hands and set the task aside. What did she owe them all—her children, mother, sister, and the people with whom she worshipped and worked in the town where she had lived her entire life? Not living up to expectations sent shock waves through the lives of others. Did that mean that one should live in as small a space as possible, never exploring, never lusting, never questioning?

But eventually she became bored with such weighty musings and turned her thoughts to more comfortable things—what to have for dinner, her glass of wine, the book waiting on her bedside table.

And she turned on the radio to a golden-oldies station and sang along with the Beatles, Roberta Flack, Mama Cass. The singing made her feel better. And the driving. In the car, driving down the highway, she was in charge of her own transient little universe. If she ever did go on a trip to someplace else, she wanted to drive there in a car.

chapter six

I know you think I'm not good enough for her," Brady said, his tone matter-of-fact, as he put the paintbrushes in a jar filled with turpentine.

Sitting back on her haunches, Charlotte pushed a strand of hair from her forehead and surveyed the hallway floor they had just finished varnishing. She realized Brady had been working up to saying those words for days, ever since he'd offered to help her get the house ready for the wedding.

His words stung. *Not good enough.* How arrogant that made her sound.

"I was bitterly disappointed when Suzanne first told me you were getting married," she admitted, putting a tentative hand on his arm. She tried to remember if she'd ever touched him before. Maybe years ago when he was migrating through her classroom.

"Even if she never went to medical school, I wanted her to finish college," she went on. "But it's not a matter of who's good enough for whom. I just don't think you and Suzanne are right for each other, but I hope you prove me wrong."

Over the Thanksgiving holiday, Mark and Vicky had wallpapered the dining room. Suzanne was either nauseated or so sleepy she couldn't hold her head up, but she and Brady did go house-hunting and found a small furnished house near the park. Charlotte half-expected Suzanne not to finish out the semester at NU, but she'd returned to Lincoln with her brother and sister after the four-day break.

Early the next morning, Brady had come to the junior high and visited with Charlotte in her classroom, sitting in the same desk he'd occupied in the eighth grade. "I know you have a lot to do to get ready for the wedding," he said. "I told my dad I'll be needing some time off to help you and to get the rent house cleaned and painted."

His offer flustered her. She didn't want to accept—after all, he was the guy who was ruining her daughter's life—but she could use his help.

When the weather allowed, Brady worked outside, washing windows, painting the front porch, raking leaves. Inside, he helped Charlotte paint the living room, hallway, and stairwell. This weekend was dedicated to varnishing the downstairs floors. The floors really should have been sanded first, but a coat of varnish was all they'd get.

Most of the work would have gone undone without Brady. Charlotte didn't have the money to hire someone to do it, and didn't have the time to manage on her own. But then none of it would have been necessary if Brady weren't marrying her daughter.

He pressed the lid onto the varnish can, then offered Charlotte his hand and pulled her to her feet. A second touch in the same day. They were both feeling their way into a relationship that was being imposed on them. If Brady hadn't been her daughter's boyfriend, she would have been well on her way to forgetting him. Just another lackluster student. A little obnoxious at times.

Brady shook the kinks out of his legs and leaned against the sideboard. Charlotte pulled a chair out from the table and gratefully sank into it. Her poor knees would never be the same.

Brady was better-looking than he used to be. Always a little on the soft side, his body was more defined now, his face less boyish. He'd given up on styling his thin, baby-fine hair and wore a burr, which suited him. "Maybe you hope things will work out for Suzanne and me now that there's a baby on the way," he challenged, folding his arms across his chest. "But before, you kept hoping we'd break up. You couldn't stand the idea of her being married to me and never leaving Newberg. You wanted her to leave here and do all the things you never did."

"And what things would that be?" Charlotte asked.

"Oh, I don't know," he hedged. "Travel maybe. Go to graduate school and become a college professor. Hang out with people who talk about books. I remember when we'd be studying some story in English class and you'd try to get us to talk about it, and Carl Schneider and Sylvia Daunsbach kept raising their hands and saying insightful things. You'd talk to them like the rest of us weren't there."

"Yes. I do get excited when students learn something. You can't imagine how much that means to a teacher. You could have been like that. You were as smart as Carl and Sylvia, but you'd roll your eyes when Carl raised his hand. I hated it when you did that. I wanted to throw something at you and your buddies. You boys didn't read the assignments and made fun of students who did. You made me feel so inadequate."

"The only students you cared about were the ones who read all the time and were in the Honor Society," Brady challenged. "My dad says back in high school you always had your nose in a book and made straight A's. Everyone thought you'd go out of state to some fancy Eastern college and never come back."

"No, I didn't have the courage for that," Charlotte admitted.

During her senior year in high school, she had applied to several out-of-state colleges along with NU and Drake—but not an eastern college. She'd been offered a scholarship to a number of schools, including Luther College in Iowa and the University of Iowa where her father had graduated, but she had to stay close to home because of Cory. She didn't want to be someplace else when he came home from the war. After Cory left for Vietnam, she hardly read anything at all.

At NU, she went through the motions of being a student, but mostly she lived inside of her head, conjuring up images of Cory, reliving every minute they'd been together, imagining how it was going to be when he returned, even wondering if she could go on living if he died over there. Sometimes she'd wake up in the night, certain she'd heard his voice or felt his touch.

But she couldn't tell Brady any of that. Couldn't tell him that she'd married Suzanne's father because she didn't know what else to do after Cory Jones was lost to her and she didn't have the heart for another wasted year at college.

Cory. Why in the hell was she thinking about him again?

"I wasn't all that smart either," she told Brady. "I was just bashful and didn't know what to do with myself except study. Suzanne is ten times smarter than I am, and I'd always thought she had the courage to go along with it."

"Doesn't it take courage to have children and raise a family?" he demanded.

"Not really. Having children mostly just happens. Raising them takes strength and incredible patience, not courage. What about your baby?" she asked. "What do you want for him or her?"

"To be the next generation," Brady said.

"Don't kid yourself," she said, heading for the kitchen to fix their lunch. "I wanted Suzanne to finish college, not drop out like her mother did. And you'll want this baby to be the superstar athlete or brilliant student that you never were."

Brady followed her. "You think I don't appreciate Suzanne," he accused. "Well, I know she's a lot smarter than I am. And she was always more popular. People kind of put up with me because of her. I wouldn't be anything without her."

"Don't put that burden on her, Brady," Charlotte said, as she pulled the makings for sandwiches from the refrigerator. She was out of lettuce.

They varnished the dining-room floor after lunch, and he waxed the kitchen floor. He offered to paint the kitchen next week while she was at school, but she turned him down. "You've done enough. You go paint the kitchen at your own little house." And she gave him an awkward hug. Poor Brady. He would grow as fat and boring as his father. And one day, Suzanne would look at him and try to remember if she'd ever really loved him.

After Brady left, Charlotte went upstairs and rummaged around in the bedside table drawer for the picture of Cory. She wished Suzanne had never found it. She thought about tearing it into small pieces and throwing it in the wastebasket. But instead, she put the picture back in the drawer, under Stan's old Bible.

❧ The Christmas tree lights were reflected in the freshly washed windows. A fire burned in the fireplace. The house smelled of fresh paint, evergreen, and freshly baked stollen bread. The draperies were newly dyed a rich hunter green, the white sheers freshly starched. Every surface was waxed; the rugs and upholstery shampooed. When Charlotte heard the car pull into the driveway, she rushed around lighting candles. *Her children were home for the holidays.*

Suzanne walked in the front door, took one look around, and burst into tears. Behind her, Vicky gasped, "Oh, Mom, it looks absolutely beautiful." Mark, laden with suitcases, let out an admiring whistle.

Charlotte looked around, trying to see through their eyes. She decided it looked as nice as their old house could possibly look. Getting the place ready for a wedding hadn't been in her game plan, yet she couldn't help but feel proud at how it had turned out. "I couldn't have done it without Brady," Charlotte said, hugging her three children each in turn.

Her children. Would this be the last time she had them all at home like this, all still hers? In three days, Suzanne would be married and have a home of her own. Vicky and Mark would soon be embarking on careers, and eventually marriages of their own.

In spite of the late hour, they had a snack in the refurbished dining room—hot cider, baked apples and cream, stollen bread warm from the oven.

"I can't get over how great the house looks," Suzanne said. "As soon as I start feeling better, I'll help you fix up the kitchen and upstairs."

"And this summer, I'll find the time to paint the outside and work on the roof," Mark said.

"Hey, kids, I'm still selling the house," Charlotte said.

Later, as she locked up for the night, she took another look around before turning out the lights. It was a good old house.

"I'm sorry, but I can't stay," she whispered into the dim silence and climbed the stairs, her hand trailing along the smooth wood of the banister.

From his bed, Mark heard his mother's footsteps on the stairs, then walking down the hall to the room she'd shared with his father, where his father had died.

Maybe that was why she was selling the house, so she wouldn't have to be reminded of her husband's illness and death every day and night of her life.

His mom was still a pretty woman—a little thick in her waist but not bad. Lots of women her age married again. But he hoped she never would—out of respect for his dad. It probably wasn't fair of him to think that way. In fact, if it were his mother who was dead and his father living on, he'd be inclined to condone a second marriage; old widowers got seedy and forgetful.

But it wasn't just the thought of a second marriage that bothered him. He didn't want his mom getting involved with a man either. And it wasn't just some Freud thing. His sisters felt the same way. Somehow she would seem less their mom.

❧ Halfway through the ceremony, the color left Suzanne's face, and she slumped against Brady. Mark rushed up with a chair, Charlotte with a glass of water.

Pastor Jenson knelt beside the chair and took Suzanne's hand. "It's okay for you to get married sitting down," he assured her.

"No, I'll be okay. Just give me a minute," she insisted, accepting a dampened napkin for her forehead from Brady's mother. Brady looked as though he were about to cry.

Suzanne took another sip of water and, with Brady's help, stood. He tucked his arm firmly around her waist and pulled her close. Vicky moved in on the other side and took her sister's arm.

Afterward, with Vicky, Bernice, and Hannah's help, Charlotte served a buffet lunch, and Suzanne held court from the living-room sofa, an afghan over her legs, Brady sitting on a footstool beside her.

Hannah kept muttering about the disgrace. She'd never be able to hold her head up again at her club meetings and at church. Anyone in town who didn't know Suzanne was pregnant would after hearing she collapsed in the middle of her wedding.

"At least her father was spared seeing his pregnant daughter get married," she said with a shake of her head. "Stan was always so crazy about Suzanne. She owed her father's memory better than this sham of a wedding."

"It was a wonderful wedding," Vicky said, putting her arm around her grandmother's shoulders. "Everyone here loves Suzanne and Brady and is excited about the baby."

"It's your very first great-grandchild, Mama," Charlotte reminded her. "And Suzanne is not the first pregnant bride this town has ever seen."

Charlotte could have ended up pregnant herself—with no one to marry her. And Suzanne's own father had had to get married. But Charlotte wouldn't tell her mother those things. Or her children. Not today anyway. Maybe never. They had enough to deal with. Or maybe she just didn't have the courage.

When it was time to cut the wedding cake—a gift from Bernice—Suzanne made her way to the dining room leaning on her new husband's arm. Mark offered a toast, wishing his sister and her bridegroom the kind of marriage their parents had shared: happy, complete, lifelong.

Charlotte wondered why everyone thought her marriage had been so perfect. It had probably been better than most, she would give them that. But "complete"? It was good and bad, happy and unhappy. After Stan became ill, they became so cautious. No cross words. No arguments. The air never got cleared. They talked about all manner of things but had trouble opening their hearts.

With Suzanne not up to a wedding trip, the newlyweds went home to their little house, the tin cans tied to the bumper of Brady's truck rattling along behind.

❧ Brady had put up a little Christmas tree and had a bottle of champagne cooling in the refrigerator. Suzanne told him he was sweet and headed for the bathroom. He sat on the bed listening to her retch for what seemed like a long time. When she finally emerged from the bathroom, she fell across the bed in her clothes. Brady pulled off her shoes, eased her out of her suit jacket, unbuttoned her blouse, and covered her with a comforter. "I'll be good to you, Suzanne," he said, bathing her face with a warm washcloth. "I promise I will."

"I know," she said, hugging a pillow to her middle. "You can turn on the TV if you want. It won't bother me."

He watched two movies, then went to lie beside his wife. For years, he'd imagined how it would be to make love in a bed. To have nightly access to Suzanne's body.

He wondered if she was asleep. If she was feeling any better. Maybe he could at least curl his body around hers.

She really did have a great body. He hoped the baby wouldn't change that. She wasn't showing yet. The only change was her breasts, which were larger.

His hand strayed to one of them—yes, definitely larger.

Immediately she rolled away from him. "I'm sorry," she said. "I just can't."

The John Deere dealership was closed until after Christmas, and Brady knew he was expected to spend the holidays at home with his new wife. He was giddy with gratitude the following morning when Suzanne said he should go ice-fishing with his dad and uncles up in the Idaho panhandle. She could be sick at her mother's house.

❧ Christmas Day, Mark and Vicky went with Charlotte to the nursing home to see their grandmother Haberman. Charlotte managed to get her to open her eyes. "It's Charlotte, dear. Vicky and Mark have come to see you."

Nellie stared at her grandchildren blankly. "Did you bring me chocolate candy?" she asked Charlotte.

"I don't want to come back here," Mark said as they left.

"I don't either, but I do twice a week," Charlotte said.

As it turned out, though, her last visit came two days later. In the middle of the night. Dr. Linderman asked if she wanted him to intervene; she'd told him no, it was past time. She wouldn't want to live on like that herself. She and the doctor stayed with Nellie until she drew her last breath. Charlotte kissed her forehead. Dr. Linderman covered her face with the sheet and whispered, "Go with God."

Nellie had been a quiet, undemanding woman, too easy to neglect in those years after her husband died and Stan became sick. Stan called her every few days, and Nellie always insisted she was fine. But one weekend, Charlotte had driven to Des Moines to check on her. She'd found her mother-in-law half-starved, with no food in the house. She had wrecked her car, and the police had taken away her driver's license. She hadn't thought of taking a cab to the grocery store—she'd never taken a cab before. She didn't know if there was a bus. "Why didn't you call me?" Charlotte asked, exasperated. Nellie shrugged. "Stan's sick. I didn't want to bother you."

That was when Charlotte moved her to the nursing home in

Newberg. Charlotte often brought her over to the house to sit with Stan, until eventually she too was bedridden. Nellie never did understand that Stan had died.

Charlotte, Mark, and Vicky buried Nellie in Des Moines next to Stan's father. Charlotte was surprised at how many of Nellie's old friends braved the cold to attend the brief graveside service. Women mostly. Two couples. Frail old people not long from the grave themselves.

chapter seven

Bernice pulled a bottle of Canadian Club from her suitcase and fixed them each a drink—hers with water, Charlotte's with Seven-Up. Now that the wedding and Christmas were over, Bernice finally had talked Charlotte into a weekend in Omaha. Her treat. None of that poor-but-proud stuff. She wanted to spend some quality time alone with her sister.

"I haven't stayed in a hotel in years," Charlotte said, wandering over to the window, drink in hand. "Not since Stan and I drove over to the hot-air balloon race in Indianola and spent the night at the Savery in Des Moines."

"I don't remember your doing that," Bernice said, standing beside her sister, linking arms. The fifteenth-floor window of the Red Lion offered a fine view of Woodman Tower and downtown Omaha, illuminated by the waning rays of January sunshine.

"It was just for one night," Charlotte said. "I really didn't think Stan would feel up to it, but he did just fine. We sat on the hood of the station wagon and watched the balloons sail across the bluest sky I've ever seen. It was filled with hundreds of silent, majestic balloons. A magical day. That night, we ate at a beautiful French restaurant complete with candlelight and harp music. Stan even managed a little wine. I think we both knew it probably was the last time we'd ever do anything like that."

"You had a wonderful marriage," Bernice said, squeezing Charlotte's arm. "I know that seems like an odd thing for me to say, with Stan so sick all those years. But you were good to each other. You have a nicer memory of that one little overnight trip to Iowa than I have of all those trips to Nebraska football games or playing on yet another of America's greatest golf courses."

"Oh, Bernice, you love football and golf as much as Donald does."

"I used to," she admitted. "But it's all starting to run together—for me, at least. Donald remembers every round. Every damned game. Give him the year and the opponent, and I swear the man can give you a play-by-play. It's gotten boring."

"Have you told Donald?" Charlotte asked. "Maybe it's time you take a trip someplace else—to Europe perhaps."

"I suggested that once."

"What did Donald say?"

"That he didn't like soccer. But enough of discontent. Let's enjoy the moment. Do you like the room? Can you believe we're actually here—just us sisters coming to the big city all by ourselves?"

"I kept thinking we should invite Mama," Charlotte admitted.

"Oh, come on, Charlotte. Haven't you heard enough of how Suzanne has disgraced the family? How Mama can never hold her head up in public again? She called last night to tell me she's thinking about resigning as chaplain of the Garden Club. A chaplain's family should be above reproach."

The lights were coming on now, giving the city a more festive look. Enchanting, even. Their mother would have been too busy talking to take notice. Sometimes Bernice wanted to tell her to hush, as she would with one of her children. But she never did. It would be disrespectful.

As children, she and Charlotte had mothered each other to make up for Hannah, whose notion of motherhood revolved around grooming and having meals on time. Hannah had doted on their father but never seemed to know what approach to take with two daughters. She was an intuitive bridge player, almost as though she had X-ray vision and could see into other players' hands, but she hadn't an inkling what was going on in her own daughters' minds. Their mother was of little use to them, so they simply didn't bother her, leaving her to her card games and club meetings.

Charlotte had been a constant in Bernice's life as long as she could remember. At times her need to pick up the phone and talk to her sister was almost physical. Not that they shared every thought. Bernice had not yet admitted how depressed she was with her marriage. But she would, probably tonight over dinner. And she hoped Charlotte would explain why she didn't want to talk about Stan. Bernice enjoyed talking about him, even getting a little maudlin. Stan had been a wonderful human being. He *looked* at her, talked to her, cared about what she had to say. When she called, he didn't automatically say "Just a minute" and call out for Charlotte, as other husbands would do. Sometimes they talked on and on. Bernice would even call during the day under the pretext of leaving a message for Charlotte just so she could talk to Stan. Sometimes he put what she said in his weekly column—"I was talking to my sister-in-law Bernice about how much harder it is to raise kids these days." Even Donald got along with Stan and had sobbed like a baby at his funeral.

When Charlotte married Stan, Bernice had been appalled—he was gangling, owlish, already losing his hair. But in the long run, Stan had turned out to be the catch, and not big, good-looking Donald, the football hero. Every man and a lot of women in the state of Nebraska still remembered All-Big-Eight center Donald Swenson, the big Swede who might have had a chance at an NFL career, who could have been the next Mick Tingelhoff if it hadn't been for a bunged-up knee. Bernice often thought of that long-ago Donald—how it felt to be his girlfriend and walk into a bar or restaurant at his side, with heads turning, people smiling and waving. How it felt to be loved by him. And he *had* loved her. He had filled her up with his love. But Donald wasn't like that any more.

Dear Stan was gone. Someday Donald was going to keel over from a heart attack, and then the two widowed sisters would grow old together, maybe even live together, traveling some, going to estate sales and craft shows, fussing over grandkids, going to movies, reading the same books, having conversations that began with "Remember when." Bernice almost looked forward to that time.

Standing close like this, shoulder to shoulder, Bernice was acutely aware of how much larger she was now than her sister. Two dress sizes at least. As young women, they had been the same size and even looked alike. People were always asking if they were twins. The family resemblance was still evident, but now Bernice looked like the older sister, her face and body sagging ungraciously into middle age.

She would have felt more comfortable around her sister if Charlotte had gotten heavy, too. If Charlotte hadn't had the perfect marriage. If she hadn't returned to college and finished her degree. If she was still just an ordinary housewife and not a schoolteacher.

"I'm glad we're here," she said, squeezing her sister's arm.

"Me, too," Charlotte said. "Thank you for making it happen."

Bernice sipped her drink and allowed the sweetness of the moment to settle into her bones. "I love you, Sis," she said.

"I love you, too, Bernie. What would we have done without each other?"

Bernice felt the sudden sting of tears. "Perish the thought," she said brusquely, putting down her drink. "And now, it's show time."

She pulled her house plans from a shopping bag and unrolled them on the table. "I trashed the plans I ordered from the magazine and hired an architect in Lincoln," she explained. "This will be a custom house, built to my specification with every amenity and geegaw I can think of."

She watched anxiously while her sister studied the floor plan, giving her time to take in the scope of the project. Charlotte wouldn't understand, not at first—Bernice wasn't sure she did herself—but perhaps explaining it to Charlotte would help firm up her decision to build the house or give up on the idea altogether.

"My God, Bernice," Charlotte finally blurted out. "This house must have over five thousand square feet!"

"More like six thousand," Bernice said.

"But why?"

"To make a statement. If Donald and I build this house, it means we are staying together."

"Was there ever any question?" Charlotte asked.

"Not for him, I guess. But we'll discuss that at dinner. Right now, you're supposed to ooh and aah. Let me give you a guided tour. The whole back of the house is floor-to-ceiling windows and will have an unhampered view of the river. The kitchen has a walk-in refrigerator and an institutional range. The entry hall is an atrium complete with trees and a fountain. The lower level has a rec room, kitchenette, and dormitory for the hordes of visiting grandchildren I plan to have someday. The master bathroom has a sunken eight-foot tub and a skylight. And look at the exterior drawing. The cupola is big enough for a bench all around and a telescope. It looks like Tara, don't you think, with the columns and veranda across the front for drinking lemonade of a summer's afternoon? Me and Rhett and the grandkids."

❧ Bernice's face was flushed, her voice girlish and breathless as she described her dream house, pointing out feature after feature. Charlotte was stunned. The house would look like a sorority house, not a home, not a place for a family.

Should she have known Bernice was that restless, that unhappy?

Charlotte thought of the little yellow house across from the high school that she'd had her eye on. The whole house would fit in the rec room of the home detailed in the blueprints. Yet both houses represented change. A future deliberately made different from the past.

The yellow house had been rented, just before Christmas, and

Charlotte no longer had in mind a specific place where she would move after her present house sold. But she knew it would be small, modest, cozy—the exact opposite of what Bernice wanted. Of course, their circumstances were different. Charlotte was a widowed schoolteacher with limited means, and she had no children at home. Bernice still had Clive and Paul in high school; Jake was in college, Noreen married and expecting a baby. But still, these plans were for an enormous house. With a house this grand, Bernice would be putting distance between her family and the others in their lives. Great distance. Friendships would be altered.

Charlotte sipped on a second drink and listened while Bernice explained every nook and cranny of the house. Obviously she'd been mentally escaping into an imaginary dream house for months—maybe years. Cedar-lined closets. Formica covering every shelf in every cupboard. A screened-in porch off the kitchen that would serve as a summer dining room. A heated garage large enough for three cars and a boat. Built-in, big-screen televisions in the family room, rec room, and master bedroom. Telephones in the bathrooms.

"What does Donald think about the house?" she asked.

"He says it will break him."

"Will it?"

"Donald makes money while he sleeps. But I wouldn't care if it did. Then we'd have to start over. The best time was when we were just starting out, dreaming the dreams."

"Are you sure you want responsibility for a house like this?" Charlotte asked.

"I need *something*, Sis. And I figure my choices are leaving Donald, becoming an alcoholic, having one last baby, or building a house that will make me feel like a queen. Of the four, I'd rather have one last baby, but since we never have sex, and now the doctor tells me the old uterus has got to go, I'm going to give birth to a tastelessly expensive house instead." Bernice held up both hands to ward off Charlotte's next question. "Don't ask. We'll talk about my marriage later. This conversation is about the house."

"But a house can't make you happy—if that's what you're looking for."

"Then just what would you suggest," Bernice said, her tone testy.

"Well," Charlotte began carefully, "you could go back to college. Take up a cause. Or adopt a baby, if you really want another child."

"I take it that you don't approve of the house?"

"I just don't understand why you want it."

"And I don't understand why you want to erase Stan." Bernice's hands flew to her mouth. She hadn't meant to say that, but the words had already escaped and hung there between them.

Charlotte sat perfectly still, not breathing. Then she crumpled into a heap on the bed and began to cry—hard, with her face buried in a pillow. She wasn't sure exactly why. Probably because her sister had hurt her feelings. Terribly. But there were other things, too. She was emotionally and physically drained from Suzanne's wedding and the holidays. She couldn't bear the thought of Suzanne being married and pregnant. She didn't know what she was going to do with the rest of her life. She didn't want to get old. She didn't know how she was supposed to remember her husband and their life together. And when she woke in the night, she wanted a man.

chapter eight

"Christ, Sis, I'm sorry," Bernice said, offering Charlotte a glass of water. "I didn't mean to set you off like that."

Charlotte sat up and took a sip of water. Bernice sat beside her and began rubbing her back and neck. "Talk to me," she demanded. "Are you okay?"

Charlotte shook her head. She wasn't. Not yet.

Had that really been her, losing control like that? She never lost control, never wept and carried on.

She listened while her sister apologized again for upsetting her—but not for the words themselves. A nice bath would make her feel better, Bernice went on. Their dinner reservation wasn't until eight.

Charlotte allowed herself to be led into the bathroom and watched while Bernice fussed about, filling the tub, adding bath salts, unwrapping a bar of soap.

Charlotte waited until the door closed behind her sister before she pulled off her clothes. She stepped into the tub and sank back into the water. It was very hot. Soothing. She let out a deep sigh. Closed her eyes. And heard her sister's words again.

Erasing Stan.

But that was unfair. Untrue. Charlotte sat up and held a wet washcloth over her face, letting the moist heat seep into her skin and eyes.

Sometimes she avoided talking about Stan because everything had already been said. Over and over. So many conversations she had endured since his death—well-meaning people saying how much she must miss him, what wonderful memories she must have of their life together, what a wonderful man he'd been, the impact he'd had on their lives and those of others. Family and friends wanted to share their favorite Stan story, or tell her about their favorite Stan column from the newspaper that they still had displayed on their refrigerator or bulletin board.

Last Sunday at church, Pastor Jenson related a discussion he'd had with Stan about blind faith, how it went against the grain for intellectual folks like Stan Haberman to embrace such a momentous concept with no logical basis for acceptance. How Stan had wrestled with this and realized that other things—such as love, friendship, altruism, courage, patriotism—often weren't based on logic. And with a smile in Charlotte's direction, the pastor read Stan's column on the topic of blind faith, while Charlotte remembered the discussion she'd had with Stan about that very column. Almost an argument. It was all well and good for him to report on newsworthy religious topics, she claimed, but he was overstepping boundaries by professing his own religious beliefs in the newspaper. That wasn't journalism, it was preaching. "But who in this town would protest?" he'd asked. "We all think pretty much the same way."

Charlotte avoided talking about her dead husband because she was confused and didn't know what to say. She didn't know what meaning to attach to their marriage—to having been Stan's wife all those years and taking care of him and having everyone still think of him as a saint and her as the saint's widow. She felt as though she were the one who had been erased. But that was unkind of her. Stan was dead. She still had a life. Except it was hard to go forward with that life until she better understood the past. After years of simply doing what needed to be done, she now had time to consider essential questions about herself. Like who she really was and what she really wanted. Examine her unexamined life.

No one had talked about Cory when she lost him. Not Bernice, or their parents—not even her friends. If anything was said at all, she was told it was "for the best." Better to know sooner than later if a man was untrue. She suffered humiliation and pain beyond measure in wretched silence. All by herself she'd had to decide if she wanted to go on living. No one ever acknowledged her suffering. No one said they were sorry and offered comfort.

But Cory had chosen not to come back to her, and his place in her life had long ago slipped from relevance. Stan's death had been a tragedy. He hadn't wanted to leave her and their children, and they would always miss him, always mourn him.

She dried herself as best she could in the steamy bathroom, then wiped off the mirror and regarded her not-young, not-old self. A woman in the middle. But the mirror quickly fogged over again, leaving only an undefined presence on the other side of the looking glass.

❧ While Bernice was taking a shower, Charlotte called the hotel desk and asked for the phone number of the closest beauty shop.

The woman who answered at Cut and Curl sounded weary. She was locking up for the night. But she reluctantly agreed to stay just a little while longer—for a haircut only. Charlotte left a note for Bernice and raced out the door.

She closed her eyes while the woman cut away the first lock of hair. She felt a little ill—maybe this wasn't such a good idea. Her no-nonsense ponytail had been a part of her for her entire adult life.

The hairdresser seemed pleased with the results and decided to blow-dry her handiwork. "Honey, you should have come to me years ago," she said.

Back in the hotel room, Charlotte knew what Bernice's reaction would be before the words were out of her mouth. "Oh, Sis, Stan loved your beautiful hair!"

"You got tired of football. I got tired of a ponytail. A person is entitled to change."

"Your kids won't like it," Bernice warned.

Charlotte made up her eyes with more than the usual touch of mascara and applied lipstick with a heavier hand as well. She'd brought her aqua mother-of-the-bride dress to wear to dinner but decided against it—it looked like a mother-of-the-bride dress. Instead, she wore her black pants suit without a blouse. Bernice suggested she wear a pearl choker or scarf to soften her bare throat, but she decided pearl earrings were enough. She looked good. Ten years younger. Chic even, without all that hair. She desperately wanted Bernice to say so, but she didn't.

❧ Maxine's, the restaurant on the top floor of the Red Lion, was Bernice's favorite in Omaha. The food and service were excellent, and people dressed up to dine there. Bernice had reserved a table by a window, not too close to the piano, in the smoking section so she could have a cigarette with her coffee.

Bernice knew what a rarity a meal in an elegant restaurant was for her sister and hoped the unpleasantness in the hotel room wasn't going to ruin the evening. She was shocked at how Charlotte reacted to her remark about Stan, but sometimes the truth hurt. At Suzanne's wedding, Bernice had noticed that Charlotte would drift away when the conversation turned to Stan. Everyone was sad that he wasn't there to see his daughter get married. He'd been such a devoted father, a sensitive man. He was the only person Bernice ever told about her unhappy marriage. Stan wanted her and Donald to seek professional help. "You are too loving a woman to live in a loveless marriage," he'd told her.

Charlotte looked so different with her hair short. Younger, Bernice supposed, maybe even prettier, but less like Charlotte. Bernice found it hard to look at her.

Charlotte seemed willing to let her set the agenda for their dinner conversation, and she kept to safe topics—family, friends,
books, current events. Bernice ordered a second and then a third
cocktail, leaving the wine to Charlotte, which she seemed to enjoy
more than the food.

Finally, over coffee, Charlotte said, "I want you to know, Bernice,
that I loved my husband very much. But just because he was a fine
person, I don't have to make the rest of my life a tribute to his memory. Whenever people start talking about him—you included—I
feel as though I have no significance to them except as Stan's wife.
It's starting to bother me."

"Is that why you're selling the house?"

"Partly. And financial reasons. Now what about you? What's going on with you and Donald?"

Bernice stared at the window—at her own reflection superim-
posed over the lights of the city. She was no longer sure she wanted
to discuss her marital problems with her sister. Charlotte had
changed since Stan died. Their paths no longer seemed quite so
parallel. But now that Stan was gone, who else did she have to talk
to? It was Charlotte or silence, and silence was wearing her down.

"I've thought about leaving him for years," Bernice admitted,
still looking at the window. "Sometimes I even wished he would
leave me so I wouldn't have to be the one to break up the family."

"Why haven't you ever said anything?"

"As long as I didn't say it out loud, I didn't have to deal with it.
It's like going on a diet. When you tell people you're going to lose
weight, you feel as though they're watching every bite of food you
put in your mouth. I didn't want you or anyone else to turn into ob-
servers of my marriage—in case I decided never to do anything
about it. Which I never will. Besides our kids, the one thing Donald and I have in common is inertia."

"So, why are you talking now?"

Bernice shrugged. "I need for you to understand why I have to
build that house. I couldn't bear knowing you were appalled every
time you set foot inside my door."

"But can a house make up for a worn-out marriage?"

"No, but I'm damned sure entitled to that house if I stick it out till death do us part. I want to drink my morning coffee sitting on a terrace overlooking the prettiest stretch of land in Madison County. I want my children to be proud to bring their friends home from college. I want my grandchildren to think that coming to Grandma's house is a treat. I want people to be impressed with me because I'm the lady who lives in that big house. And if Donald dies first, it would be a hell of a house for enjoying my widowhood. Maybe I'd lose weight then. Find a man who can still get it up, in spite of what the kids would think."

"Is that the problem with Donald?"

"Hell, Sis, I don't know," she admitted. "Maybe he still can and doesn't want to."

"Haven't you talked about it?"

"Not really. I suggested separate bedrooms in the new house, and he begged me not to do that—actually got down on his knees and *begged*. He said the kids wouldn't understand—and claimed that he needs me there at night beside him. Like always."

"How do you feel about it?"

"Not good. Rejected. A failure. After the kids came, the sex was never all that good. Originally, that's what all those trips were about—at least for me. In hotels without the kids, we still had good sex. Then the kids got older, and we started taking them along. Sports became something Donald shared with his sons. Noreen got to drive the golf cart and keep score. I was along to keep everyone on schedule and look under the beds and make sure no one left their shoes."

❧ Bernice had been nineteen when she first met Donald at a highway tavern on the Wahoo highway. She'd gone there with three pledge sisters even though the place was on the sorority's off-limits list. Donald had been in the back playing pool with two other NU football players. He was big, blond, and boyishly handsome. When he looked up from his shot and smiled at Bernice, she forgot about broken rules.

They only had time for one dance out on the deck before Bernice and her friends had to head back to campus and closing hours. But it was long enough for them to establish that he was from Norfolk and she was from Newberg, that they both adored John Denver and weren't sure about Vietnam. Donald was in ROTC and worried that he'd have to go on active duty when he graduated and would miss out on the NFL.

Back at the dorm, Bernice stood at a lavatory in the second-floor bathroom and alternately stared at herself in the mirror and applied a cold washcloth to her feverish skin. She couldn't decide if she was pretty or ugly. If she was in love or sick. If she was happy or scared.

The next day, she called her sister, who was a married woman now with a baby on the way.

"I think I'm in love," Bernice said, telling about the smile, the dance. "I'll die if he doesn't call me."

"No you won't. Just hang loose, honey, until you're sure he's for real. I don't want you getting your heart broken."

Bernice wondered if her sister was thinking about Cory Jones. Cory had broken Charlotte's heart when he didn't come back from Vietnam to marry her—even after she'd slept with him.

Donald Swenson was far more wonderful than Cory Jones. And Stan Haberman. Donald was a star.

He didn't call her that day, or the next. But Tuesday afternoon when Bernice returned from her botany class, a message was waiting in her mailbox: Donald Swenson had called and would call back. Bernice kissed the blessed piece of paper.

Donald was the only man Bernice had ever made love to, and she didn't do that until their wedding night. She'd always been smug about that—she'd been a virgin bride and her sister had not. Charlotte had never told her that she'd had sex with Cory Jones, but Bernice knew. Charlotte hardly had seemed to know the rest of the world existed during that summer of Cory Lee Jones.

When Donald took Bernice back to the dorm after their first real date, he held her close and said he wanted to do things right with her. Bernice assumed he meant that he hadn't done things right with other girls, that he wouldn't push her into sex if she wanted to set limits. Which she did. At first it was nothing below the waist. They evolved to touching everywhere but no penetration. She would smuggle a towel out of the dorm so she could clean up when he came between her breasts or against her belly. Not in her mouth, however. She wouldn't do that. Not then or after they were married, even though he sometimes asked that of her.

Did it matter that she had refused him? Did other women really enjoy doing that? Bernice wished now she'd been more experimental. She sometimes imagined ending their moratorium on sex by going down on him in his sleep, getting him hard with her mouth—not so much that she wanted to commit that particular act as wanting to lure him back inside of her, to be complete with him again. Not having sex was ominous. It made the future seem murky. If he'd had an accident and couldn't have sex, she would be quite comfortable with cuddling only. If he was impotent, she wished he would tell her. That would be almost the same thing— a real reason why they never made love. As it was, she felt like she had been neutered, and she didn't even have the memory of another man to comfort her.

Donald had had affairs—the first one while she was pregnant with Noreen. Bernice knew about two others. She would never forgive him and told him so at one point, even threatened to pay him back. But, of course, she wouldn't begin to know how.

There hadn't been another woman for years. Bernice was certain of that. She was married to a celibate man.

chapter nine

The next morning, while Bernice finished dressing, Charlotte visited a travel agency across the street from the hotel and picked up an assortment of brochures featuring the national parks, the Texas Gulf Coast, the Florida Everglades, raft trips on the Colorado, bus tours of Georgia's antebellum homes, hiking in the Ozarks. This summer she would go someplace, she promised herself, tucking the brochures in her purse. A short trip if the house didn't sell, a longer one if it did. But not for the whole summer as she had once planned. Not with Suzanne's baby due in July.

They spent the day shopping, going first to Westroads Mall. Charlotte followed her sister around while Bernice bought clothing for herself, her sons, pregnant daughter, unborn grandchild. And Donald. She bought him three golf shirts and a bathrobe. For her unbuilt house, she bought a pair of ornate lamps and a candelabra. Charlotte's only purchase was a single delicate crystal wineglass that was on sale for half price but still cost a wasteful twenty dollars plus tax. It pleased her, though, to think of drinking her evening glass of wine from such a glass. A goblet. A bit of perfection.

Throughout the day, Charlotte's thoughts would turn to the

travel brochures tucked in her purse. Tomorrow evening when she was back at home, she would spread them out on the dining-room table and savor their promises.

Mid-afternoon, the sisters headed back downtown to browse through the Old Market shops that now occupied the vintage buildings in the former warehouse district. Charlotte enjoyed the art gallery, giftshops, and bookstore, but decided to walk back to the hotel while Bernice investigated the drapery and upholstery material in a large fabric store. They would meet in the lobby bar at five.

She fished her gloves from her pockets and put her head down against the biting wind. Tiny particles of sleet picked at the skin on her face. She wished for a scarf or hat to protect her ears. And to think that on Padre Island, at this very minute, people were walking on the beach, barefoot.

Charlotte carried her purchase to the room and dialed Suzanne's new phone number. Brady answered. Charlotte could hear the television in the background. Suzanne was resting, he told her. She'd managed to keep down some clear broth that his mother brought over. Mildred had cleaned the house, too, and taken the laundry home with her.

Charlotte wanted to point out that Brady could have cleaned the house himself, and done the laundry, but she didn't. Mildred probably wouldn't have let him.

She ordered a glass of wine at the lobby bar and settled in for a half hour or so of people-watching while she waited for Bernice. An elegant white-haired woman in a flowing red dress was playing the piano: "The Days of Wine and Roses," "Catch a Falling Star," "Stranger in Paradise."

Charlotte wondered if the well-dressed people lounging in the handsome wingback chairs and enjoying the music and conversation over cocktails could tell that she was an impostor in their up-scale world. What would give her away? Not her hair, she thought with an inward smile. Every time she'd walked by a mirror today, she was taken aback by how much better she looked. And realized how dowdy she'd been before.

Her gray wool pants suit and black turtle-necked sweater were okay, she supposed. The jacket was a bit oversized to be stylish, but it wasn't frumpy. Her loafers were, however. If the house sold, she'd buy some good shoes, with leather lining and real stacked heels.

She was startled when an attractive, middle-aged man in a western-cut suit asked if he could join her. "I'm expecting my sister," Charlotte said in a rush, before realizing the last two unoccupied chairs in the bar area were facing her little table. "But please sit down," she added, smiling. "She's a real shopper. No telling how long she'll be."

He was from Alliance. A rancher in town for a meeting of state cattlemen. He had a pleasing smile, with even white teeth that contrasted nicely with his tan skin. He asked if she'd always lived in Newberg, if she liked teaching school. A nice man, Charlotte decided. She found herself glancing at his hand to see if he was wearing a wedding band. He was. But the fact that she had checked made her smile. When he asked why she was smiling, she told him. "Well, I'll be damned," he said with a chuckle and a grin. "That does make a man feel good." And he ordered another round of drinks.

He thought she was attractive, Charlotte realized. She could see it in his eyes, hear it in his voice. What a nice feeling—to be admired. She hadn't felt this good in ever so long.

By the time Bernice arrived, they were on first-name basis—he was Joe—and discussing a mutual friend, the editor of the Alliance newspaper who had served on the board of the state press association with Stan.

Bernice sat stiffly on the edge of her chair and quickly drank her Manhattan. Then stood abruptly and announced that she and Charlotte had to get dressed for dinner.

"You were rude," Charlotte said on the elevator.

"You were flirting with him," Bernice accused.

"I was not. But I might have been if he hadn't been married."

"Twice you referred to Stan as your 'late husband.' "

"Stan *is* my late husband, Bernice."

"Vicky's right. You're looking for a husband."

Charlotte sighed. "I'm not sure what I'm looking for, but if it turns out to be a husband, I do have that right, you know."

They walked down the hall in silence. Bernice unlocked the door and headed for the bathroom, which she occupied for a good long while. When she finally emerged, she said, "You're right. I was rude, and I'm sorry. It's just that sometimes I think I don't know you anymore, and it scares me."

Charlotte put her arms around her sister. "We're both changing, honey, but we'll always be sisters."

❧ Late Sunday afternoon, when Charlotte pulled into her driveway, she sat in the car for a time, staring at the plain white house that had been her home for almost the whole of her adult life, at the trees that had grown stately in those twenty-eight years, at the FOR SALE sign in the yard. Change was indeed scary. But at this point in her life, it actually seemed less ominous than staying the same.

After she'd unpacked her suitcase and eaten a sandwich, she filled her elegant new wineglass with some table red and spread the travel brochures across the dining-room table. Then she just sat there, sipping the wine, staring at the brochures, not opening them. Part of her wanted to gather them up and throw them away, forget the whole thing. She was setting herself up for disappointment. What if she did take a trip? She would feel self-conscious every place she went—a middle-aged woman, traveling by herself. Seeing Old Faithful or picking up seashells wasn't going to be a life-altering experience.

But the fact that she went at all could be.

Without thinking, she had spread the brochures at Stan's end of the table and was now sitting in his chair. Strange. She never sat there. She wondered if one end of the table would always be considered Stan's place, even after she had moved to a different house. Should she be wishing he was here with her and they were planning this trip together? If he had lived, they probably would be looking forward to traveling some, after getting the children through college, of course. But as things turned out, any trip would be hers alone, and she didn't want to feel guilty or sad because she was alive and Stan wasn't. She put down the glass of wine and picked up the brochure with the Colorado Rockies on the front.

✜ Vicky came home the following weekend and wanted to know about the travel brochures stacked on the sideboard. "But why would you want to go on a trip now—with Daddy gone?" She sounded genuinely puzzled.

✜ Suzanne had recovered from the unrelenting nausea she experienced in her first months of pregnancy. Her color was better. She took long walks when the weather permitted and was conscientious about her diet. She didn't look pregnant yet, but her waistline had lost definition. Her in-laws had given her a generous gift certificate from a Norfolk maternity shop, but she hadn't used it yet. "I think I'll let the ink on the marriage license dry before I show up in smocks," she told her mother.

Most afternoons, when Charlotte arrived home, Suzanne was sitting at the kitchen table, crocheting a yellow crib blanket, the television tuned in to a talk show.

Charlotte would fix them hot tea or hot chocolate. Suzanne would crochet while Charlotte went through the day's mail and graded papers. Shortly after five, Suzanne would go home to prepare dinner. Charlotte found it so strange to hear her daughter refer to someplace else as "home."

By her own admission, Suzanne was bored. As a college student there had never seemed to be enough hours in the day. Now, by noon she'd usually accomplished whatever cleaning, shopping, and cooking needed to be done that day. The months until her baby would be born loomed endlessly in front of her. Not until July.

She looked forward to a sonogram. She wanted to know what color to paint the baby's room. Then she could start thinking of it as little Stan or Edna, or whatever name they chose.

She and Brady were having trouble agreeing on names. "If I thought it would ease things with Grandma, I'd try to talk him into naming the baby Hannah if it's a girl," Suzanne told her mother, her eyes filling with tears.

But Hannah hadn't seen Suzanne since the wedding. She was waiting for Charlotte to beg her to forgive Suzanne and for Suzanne to court her. Always before, Charlotte had indulged her mother's pettiness with good humor. Now she resented it. But for Suzanne's sake she would patch things up before the baby was born.

Charlotte looked forward to the sweetness and wonder of having a baby in her life once again. She thought of baby skin and baby hair, of first smiles and first steps. Already she loved this child-to-be and could feel the seductive power of that love eroding her will and filling her life so completely that there would be no room for other living, just as her own children had done. Already her awareness of this baby was stealing away her resolve to take a long trip this summer. Maybe she'd take a couple of short ones instead.

Brady's parents were already grandparents. His sister Trish had two children, and Mildred and Andy were facing the birth of their third grandchild with unabridged zeal. Andy was making a cradle. Mildred was knitting a layette, and she had already purchased a sweatshirt that declared her to be a THREE-TIME GRANDMA.

Charlotte had no desire for grandma clothing and realized she was a bit superstitious about preparing for a baby so early. But feeling the need to demonstrate her own devotion, she bought books for Suzanne—on pregnancy, parenting, naming a baby.

The middle of February, Suzanne began to bleed—just spotting really, but certainly worrisome. Dr. Linderman put her to bed, and Charlotte started going by every day after work to clean and cook.

Brady should do more, but he probably wouldn't, and Charlotte didn't want his mother looking after Suzanne, a reaction she realized was probably petty. Mildred certainly had more time.

Charlotte usually ate dinner with Suzanne and Brady before going home to her own chores and some time to herself, which she had come to regard as an essential ingredient of her life.

After two weeks, the spotting subsided, and they all relaxed a bit, thinking the danger to be over. But a few days later, when Charlotte's phone rang in the middle of the night, she knew there would be no baby. "We'll pick you up in ten minutes," Andy said. "Suzanne's bleeding a lot, and Brady has taken her to the Oakland hospital."

In the back seat of Mildred's Cadillac, Charlotte was grateful that Andy was driving the twenty miles to Oakland. She wouldn't be able to see the road for her tears.

She wept for the baby she would never know, but mostly she cried for her own baby—for Suzanne and her loss. When they arrived at the hospital, Andy and Mildred rushed to their son. Charlotte went to Suzanne, so white and frail on the hospital bed, her pretty face contorted with grief. She reached her arms around Charlotte's neck and drew her close. "Oh, Mom, why did it have to happen?" she sobbed. "I tried to do everything right."

Charlotte's heart lurched painfully for her child. Her little girl. "Oh, honey, it's not your fault. It's nobody's fault. I am so sorry, so very sorry," she said, kissing her daughter's forehead, smoothing her hair.

"Do you think it had a soul?" Suzanne asked.

Charlotte pulled back and looked into her eyes. "Oh, Suzanne, I don't think so. It was so tiny. Not really a baby yet."

"I want it to have a funeral and be buried in the cemetery near Dad."

"I'm not sure we can do that. I don't think it's far enough along to warrant a casket and a cemetery plot."

"Andy and Mildred will pay for it," Suzanne said, hysteria creeping into her voice. "I don't want it just flushed away."

Charlotte gathered her daughter in her arms and gave Andy an imploring look. "Will you see what they've done with . . . with the baby?"

Andy nodded, wiping away the tears that were streaming down his face. "I'll see to it."

When Suzanne was released from the hospital the next day, they went directly to the cemetery, meeting Pastor Jenson and the undertaker for a short graveside service. The baby-sized casket was white. Charlotte wondered if it contained the actual fetus, or if they were just going through the motions for Suzanne's sake. At Suzanne's request, the yellow blanket she'd been crocheting had been placed inside.

Charlotte had suggested the service be limited to Suzanne and Brady, his parents, and herself. But Mark and Vicky drove over to be with their sister. Bernice came too, and a very pregnant Noreen. And Hannah was there, dressed in black, self-righteously announcing that she'd given up a casino trip with the Garden Club in order to attend. Afterwards, Charlotte put a hasty funeral lunch on the table—just sandwiches and canned fruit. Suzanne went upstairs to take a nap in her old bed.

Just before midnight, Bernice called. Almost apologetically she said that Noreen had given birth to a healthy, seven-pound girl. They'd named her Michelle.

chapter ten

The hospital room grew very quiet as Suzanne approached the bassinet holding her cousin's baby. Noreen's husband, Rusty, stood by his wife's bed. Bernice and Hannah were there.

Charlotte's chest felt as though it were about to burst open as she watched her daughter pick up the tiny bundle. She put a hand against the wall for support. Her poor Suzanne. It was too soon for her to be around a newborn.

"She's so beautiful," Suzanne said reverently.

Noreen was crying, grabbing Rusty's hand. "Oh, Suzanne, you didn't need to come."

"I wanted to," Suzanne said, not taking her eyes from the sleeping baby's face. "They could have grown up together—like we did." She sat on the edge of the bed and pulled aside the blanket to touch the baby's tiny hands. She rubbed her finger along the baby's cheek. Kissed her forehead, her chin, the top of her head. "I love you, little baby Michelle," she cooed. "Welcome to our world."

"Our children *will* grow up together," Noreen said, touching Suzanne's arm.

Suzanne nodded, then leaned forward to kiss her cousin's cheek.

"She looks a little like her daddy, don't you think?" she asked with a smile in Rusty's direction. "Our first baby, Noreen. Can you believe it? Michelle will be the leader of the pack and boss all the other cousins—like Mark always did. He and Vicky will be over this evening. They're so excited."

Charlotte put a hand to her mouth, stunned. When had her daughter turned into this valiant young woman? She was celebrating the arrival of her cousin's baby, not allowing the occasion to be marred by her own tragedy. Charlotte knew that the image of Suzanne holding Noreen's baby would be one she would carry with her always. Stan would have been proud of her after all.

Noreen and Suzanne were undressing the baby now, admiring her scrawny little body, her tiny shoulders, her miniature feet. Wordlessly, the rest of them filed out of the room, leaving the two cousins to their baby.

Charlotte made it halfway down the hall before she reached for her sister's arms, her sister's embrace.

Bernice understood. "Dear God, I've never seen anything like it," she said.

Hannah made a point of sitting by Charlotte in the hospital cafeteria, where they went for coffee and pie. "Suzanne looks like she's doing just fine," she said. "Maybe now, this family can get itself straightened out."

"I'm not sure what you mean by that," Charlotte said.

"Well, it has been embarrassing, Charlotte. At least, now when she has a baby, it will be more respectable."

Like many of her peers, Hannah wore too much makeup, thinking it made her look younger. But powder settled in her wrinkles. The patches of rouge looked almost clownlike. Lipstick bled into the lines that radiated from her upper lip. Yet she still had a plump prettiness about her that heavy-handed makeup didn't conceal, like a painted doll. Under the mask was a self-righteous creature who considered herself to be a "good Christian woman," but who had spent her life in judgment of others. Who thought it God's blessing that they had no Jews, "coloreds," or foreigners living in Newberg—even though her own forebears had immigrated from Germany just two generations before.

Charlotte had always regarded her mother with tolerance. Stan had helped her, reminding her that, after all, her mother had grown up in another time and had led a sheltered life. She wasn't blessed with Charlotte's intellectual curiosity. She was too old to change. She meant no harm. Underneath it all, she had a good heart.

But Charlotte felt that tolerance cracking now. Had her sweet father really loved this petty woman? She wasn't sure she still did. Maybe she never had.

"If you can't feel proud of Suzanne after what she just did upstairs, I feel sorry for you, Mama."

❧ On the first of March, Charlotte accepted an offer on the house from a young veterinarian and his wife. Starting with Mark, she telephoned each of her children—and listened while they said they wished she hadn't. Vicky cried. The dastardly task over with, Charlotte sat on the bottom step and cried herself. Suzanne found her like that. "If it makes you sad, why are you doing it?"

"We've already had that conversation, honey. You just have to accept that it's what I need to do."

The following Saturday, Charlotte drove to Pender, Cory Jones's home town. She'd gone there once with Cory, to pick up a registered letter from the Selective Service—his draft notice, of course. His parents had been stoic; a man had to do his duty.

Charlotte remembered that the house was across from a grade school, and she found it without too much trouble. The woman who answered the door said the Joneses were both dead—she and her husband bought the house ten years back. It was a nice old house, but it needed new plumbing.

No one had seen Cory in years, the woman explained through her screen door, not since his father's funeral. His sister had moved away. She didn't know where.

At a nearby convenience store, the clerk suggested that Char-

lotte check over at City Hall. The city clerk had been best friends
with Cory's sister, Cynthia, back in high school. If anyone knew
how to find her, Millie Sampler would.

The city clerk had lost touch with Cynthia since Mr. Jones's funeral. Cynthia's husband was from someplace in northern Missouri, and they'd bought a farm down there. His name was Robert
Stevenson, like the poet. His middle name was even Louis.

On the way out of town, Charlotte once again drove by the
house where Cory had grown up. She remembered sitting on the
porch swing with him that night, discussing the future. He
wouldn't go to Canada—he didn't want to go through life as a draft
dodger. But he sure as hell didn't want to kill anyone either. "Don't
look for me to be a hero," he'd told Charlotte.

She'd been given Cory's bed, and he was supposed to sleep on
the sofa. But he'd come to her in the night, and with his parents
sleeping on the other side of the thin bedroom wall, they made
silent, desperate love, then clung to each other until dawn. Their
summer had ended.

❧ Charlotte rented a small house next door to the Methodist
church—a narrow, two-story house with an entry hall, living room,
dining room, and kitchen lined up on the first floor and three small
bedrooms and an old-fashioned bathroom on the second. She
threw herself into making a new home, painting, papering, making
curtains. After a lifetime of dutiful housekeeping, she was amazed
at how much pleasure she took in making the house cozy and pretty
and her very own. She was constantly walking through the rooms,
dustcloth in hand, assessing the position of a picture on the wall or
the placement of a piece of furniture, making small adjustments
here and there, having to go back a few minutes later to admire the
results. Even in the night, she would wake up and pad through her
house.

The new math teacher at the high school showed her how to use a software program to search nationwide for telephone numbers. Using one of the school's computers, Charlotte was able to locate four Robert L. Stevensons in Missouri. The third one she called was married to the former Cynthia Jones. Cynthia and Robert lived in Amity.

"I never met you," Charlotte explained to the woman on the telephone, "but I dated your brother before he went to Vietnam."

Cynthia remembered her brother having a girlfriend the summer he worked for their grandparents in Newberg. She hadn't seen Cory in years. She wasn't even sure if he was still alive. "The last time I heard from Cory Lee, he'd been living in New Mexico. I tracked him down when Daddy died. He was out in the desert, near a town called Peyo. Why are you trying to find him?"

"I'm not quite sure. Maybe I just need a mission. My husband died last year, and I've been doing a lot of thinking about why my life turned out the way it did. Cory didn't come back to me, so I ended up marrying Stan, whom I came to love very much. But I guess it always bothered me that life turned out to be a crap shoot."

"Cory is not the man you remember," Cynthia said. "You wouldn't have wanted him back."

"Did he ever mention me—after he came home?"

"No. Not that I remember. Of course, I'm fifteen years older than Cory, and we were never that close. You aren't still in love with him, are you?"

"No. The present-day Cory—if he's still alive—doesn't really exist for me. I just wonder about the boy I knew back then. Or thought I knew. I realize that war changes people. That war especially. But how could something that seemed so genuine and good turn out to mean nothing at all?"

"I wondered about my high school boyfriend to the point that I bought a new dress to wear to a class reunion so I'd look good when I saw him again," Cynthia said. "I lost five pounds, got a permanent and a professional manicure. I even made my husband buy a new suit. Then our little girl broke her leg, and I didn't get to go. When the next reunion rolled around in five years, I was fat and didn't go."

❧ The high school math teacher was Colonel Eric Grimmett. He was new to town this semester, having replaced old Mr. Schwartz, who'd taught Charlotte and Bernice and almost everyone else in town.

Colonel Grimmett, a widower, was recently retired from the Army Corps of Engineers after thirty years of service. He'd grown up in Nebraska but had no family left there except for a second cousin in Columbus.

While he was teaching her to use the phone-search software, he had asked her about the churches in town. He'd grown up Episcopalian, but since he had been an army Protestant for years, he had no real denominational preference.

So Charlotte invited him to church.

When they sat in the back of the sanctuary, a ripple went through the congregation as people became aware that Charlotte Haberman was with a man. If the colonel was aware of the whispering and surreptitious glances over shoulders, he didn't let on. Thank goodness her mother was in Norfolk this weekend, Charlotte thought.

With a visitor sitting beside her, Charlotte found herself also slipping into the role of observer, as the congregation dutifully followed the order of service, reading their assigned responses, thumbing through the hymnal in search of the selected hymns, sitting quietly while Pastor Jenson delivered his sermon. Eric seemed familiar with the hymns, and the Apostles' Creed. He seemed to listen as Pastor Jenson discussed Abraham and Sarah's readiness to do God's will and challenged the congregation to lead a life shaped by faith in God's mercy.

"Are we ready to follow Jesus through the Lenten journey wherever he leads us?" the pastor asked in conclusion. The organist began to play. Everyone stood and reached for the hymnal. Number two hundred thirty—"Lord Keep Us Steadfast." The service concluded with the offering, a lengthy prayer remembering all those who were in the hospital and had suffered bereavement. The closing hymn was number two hundred fifty-nine, "Lord Dismiss Us."

Not exactly an uplifting experience, Charlotte had to admit as they bowed their heads for the benediction and threefold amen, but nonetheless comforting in its familiarity. And they could all file out feeling godly.

They drove over to Columbus afterwards for dinner at the Husker House. Eric did most of the talking. He'd served all over the world, building roads, bridges, dams. He and his wife had visited most of the great cities of the world. His son was career military, stationed in Guam; his daughter worked for a congressman in Washington. Charlotte's small-town life seemed boring by comparison. Still, it would have been polite if he had asked about it, had pretended to show interest. She thought of the cattle rancher in the hotel bar in Omaha—Joe. They had talked to each other. Charlotte grew weary of hearing about Eric's fascinating life and was relieved when he finally delivered her to her little house by the Methodist church.

"I talked too much," he said on her front porch.

Charlotte smiled. "A little. But it was all very interesting."

He winced. "May I have a second chance? I make a delicious Indian curry, if I do say so myself. I'd like to fix dinner for you and learn how you spent the last thirty years of *your* life."

The phone was ringing when she opened the front door. Her mother, back from Norfolk.

"Where have you been with that man?" she demanded. "I've been calling and calling."

Charlotte took a deep breath. "Did you have a nice time in Norfolk? I understand they're digging the basement for Bernice's new house."

"I can't believe you went out with a man and didn't even tell me!

Three different people have called to tell me. Can you imagine how embarrassing it's been to hear about this from someone else!"

❧ The sign in front of the building said: VETS CENTER—a shabby brick building in a run-down industrial area in south Omaha. Charlotte parked next to a pickup truck with military insignia on the back window.

The smell of stale cigarettes hit her as soon as she opened the door. Charlotte explained to a matronly black woman at the front desk that she'd called for an appointment. Carl Welbourne, one of the counselors, had agreed to talk to her.

"I'm looking for an old friend who disappeared after he came back from Vietnam," Charlotte said to Welbourne, a ruddy-faced man in his late forties.

He nodded, waiting for her to explain further before he commented.

"I wondered if your organization has any way to locate veterans," she went on. "I'm not a relative, but we were good friends once. I don't know if he ever came here, but he might have. But in general terms, how would one go about finding a lost veteran?"

"Veterans Affairs facilities are bound by confidentiality restrictions," he explained. "We don't give out any information on our clients, past or present."

"Is there any place I could write for information?"

"Not unless you're a relative."

A collection of bumper stickers decorated a bulletin board across the room: *"Boycott Jane Fonda"*—*"Jane Call Home 1-800-Hanoi"*—*"Jane Fonda—American Traitor Bitch."* Hardly healing fare.

"Do they still hate her?" she asked, nodding toward the board. Obviously Mr. Welbourne did, to have such a display in his office.

"Yes, ma'am," he acknowledged. "Some do."

"The veterans who need help—are they pretty good about asking for it?"

"Yes, ma'am. Between twenty and thirty thousand Vietnam vets suffer from post-traumatic stress syndrome to the extent that it interferes with their lives. I'd say that most of them seek counseling." He handed her a brochure, *Readjustment Problems Among Vietnam Veterans*.

"Do they get disability payments?" she asked, putting the brochure in her purse.

"Many do. The amount depends on the extent of their disability."

"What do they do when they come here?"

Welbourne showed her the room where he conducted group counseling sessions. The furnishings consisted of ten swivel chairs arranged in a circle. A large map of South Vietnam dominated one side of the room. The other walls offered amateur paintings and photographs, all war-related, and a poster with a poem—"The Long Journey Home."

"Do most of the men with post-traumatic stress syndrome come to vet centers on a regular basis?" Charlotte asked.

"Some have been coming regularly for years. Others only come at the bad times—like when they lose their job or their wife kicks them out. Some come on the anniversary days."

"Such as?"

Welbourne shrugged. "The anniversary of an ambush maybe. Eighteen guys on a hill—three came back. Stuff like that. Or maybe he was smoking a cigarette and his buddy's head gets blown off and lands in his lap."

Charlotte cringed. Had those kind of things happened to Cory?

"Help me," she said. "How can I find my friend?"

"Probably you can't if he doesn't want to be found. But sometimes there are personals in veterans' magazines. Or people tack messages up on the doors and bulletin boards at centers like this one. There are centers all over—in every state."

"Do you have copies of any of the magazines?"

He led her back to his office and gave her copies of *VFW, Saber,* and *Purple Heart.* "There are others," he said. "Every division has an association magazine. Do you know his division?"

Charlotte shook her head.

"That's important. Some of them still wear division patches on their jackets. It's their identity. But you've got to realize we're not talking about the majority of the vets. Most of them have gone on with their lives. Some of them just can't."

"Yes, I understand that. Apparently, my friend wasn't able to."

"Why do you want to find him—after all these years?"

"I'm not really sure. I should have to tried to contact him back then, but I was pretty gutless. I guess I'd just like to tell him I understand. And I'm sorry."

"You're not looking to save his soul, are you?"

She smiled. "No. Nothing like that."

She thanked him for his time and walked back down the hall. Two men were coming in the door—bearded; division patches on worn fatigue jackets. Neither was Cory. They stood to one side to let her pass.

That's how he would look, she thought. Like those men.

Back home, she called Cory's sister again, to ask if she knew his division.

Cynthia didn't know the name of the division, but the patch on his jacket had a silhouette of a horse's head. He wore that jacket to their daddy's funeral. He said he didn't own a suit.

"What about your mother's funeral?"

"When the doctor said she was dying, I left a message with the postmistress in Peyo, but apparently Cory drifted in and out. Mom asked for him toward the end, so we contacted the Red Cross, and they tried to find him. I got a postcard from him about a year later to let me know he'd heard. I told my husband not to bother with Cory when my time comes."

꒰ The brochure from the veterans' center described the symptoms of post-traumatic stress syndrome—depression, isolation, rage, alienation, survivor's guilt, anxiety, nightmares, flashbacks.

Stimuli such as the sound of a helicopter flying overhead or even a grove of green trees could put a vet back in the Vietnamese jungle. An account by one veteran said that he hiked only above the treeline and avoided situations in which people were behind him. He always sat with a wall to his back. Corners of the room were the most comfortable. Loud noises were a problem. He would grab his wife's neck during nightmares. She was thinking about leaving him.

Charlotte wondered if life with Cory would have been like that. She wondered also at what point you stopped loving the man you used to know and began to fear the one beside you.

chapter eleven

She would always be grateful to her mother-in-law, Suzanne reminded herself as she took her seat at Mildred's dining-room table for Sunday dinner. Mildred had diffused the gossip about Suzanne's pregnancy by disseminating the news herself. She all but went down the Newberg phone book, calling folks and telling them about the baby, making it perfectly clear that she and Andy were delighted, were more amused than upset about the hurry-up wedding, and thought Suzanne was the best thing that ever happened to their family.

So how could Suzanne mind that her attendance was required at Sunday dinner, along with Brady, his sister Trish, and her family?

In the past, Suzanne had often joined the family for Sunday dinner and taken delight in being treated as one of them. Now that she actually was a member of the family, she found herself resenting the obligatory gatherings around Mildred's overladen table, with Mildred circulating the food long after everyone had declared themselves full, the conversation dominated by Andy, Brady, and Ted discussing sports and tractor sales.

Like Brady, Trish's husband Ted worked for Andy at Brammer's Farm Implements, the sprawling John Deere agency located just across the road. Trish and Ted lived next door to Mildred and Andy. Suzanne and Brady were supposed to build their home on the other side, and Mildred was eager to get the project underway. She was having matching mailboxes made for the three houses, each decorated with a miniature replica of a John Deere tractor. And she was planning matching archways to go over the three driveways.

"Once in a while, I think we should eat Sunday dinner with my mother or drive over to Norfolk to be with my relatives," Suzanne told Brady.

He agreed. But somehow, every Sunday for the three months of their marriage, even while Suzanne was too sick to eat more than a few soda crackers, they'd been at this table in Mildred's formal dining room, with its crystal chandelier and flocked wallpaper.

Suzanne liked Mildred, even admired her in a way. But she wished she lived the next county over from her in-laws. Or better yet, in the next state.

Mildred was one of those women whose self-image was based on well-fed guests, an immaculate home, and helping out whenever she could. If someone died, Mildred had a meal at the bereaved family's house within hours. She took jars of homemade preserves and tins of homemade cookies to elderly shut-ins. No friend, acquaintance, or family member ever passed so much as a night over in the Oakland hospital without Mildred dropping by.

She was a pretty little lady with beauty-shop hair and vivid blue eyes that always seemed to be on the lookout for a coffee cup that needed filling or a tabletop that needed dusting. Her public persona was that of "the little woman." Andy was in charge at their house, as a husband should be.

But in fact, Andy Brammer had long since capitulated to his strong-willed wife. Once he might have protested when Mildred told him to run to the store for a bag of ice in the middle of a snowstorm or to go outside and cut that dead branch off the tree just when it was the ninth inning with the score tied and bases loaded, but now he simply got up out of his recliner and did her bidding. He didn't even sigh or mutter.

And Mildred had decided long ago that her son needed to marry Suzanne Haberman. If Brady were married to a pretty, smart, well-raised girl like Suzanne, he'd settle down and work hard. He'd stop biting his fingernails and driving too fast. His children would be more attractive and smarter than if he married some other girl. Mildred had courted Suzanne, lavishing her with compliments, buying her expensive birthday and Christmas presents, inviting her along on family excursions, and always telling her about the beautiful home that she and Brady could someday build right next door.

"Have you had a chance to look through that book of house plans?" Mildred asked Suzanne, handing her the bowl of mashed potatoes.

Of course she'd had a chance. What else did she have to do all day long? She just hadn't bothered to look at it. "Brady and I really don't need another house right now," she said, handing the bowl to her husband, who passed it on to Billy, the younger of his two nephews.

Brady was frowning. He didn't like the way Suzanne had responded to his mother's question. Suzanne knew he was debating whether or not he should contradict her in front of his parents. *Of course he and Suzanne wanted the new house for which his parents were generously providing the land and the down payment.*

She fully realized that her mother-in-law could not fathom lethargy. Mildred found it disturbing that Suzanne lay around all day long watching television and reading magazines. She needed to get with the program, to be purposeful—make lists, take up a craft. But Suzanne had fallen into a funk and hadn't the will to crawl out of it.

Mildred had probably never experienced a funk. She was a perpetual-motion machine, a whirling dervish of busyness. Even when she watched television, she was crocheting, knitting, clipping manufacturers' coupons, or copying recipes onto file cards.

"Surely you don't want to stay on in that little rental house any longer than you have to," Mildred said, passing Suzanne the bowl of creamed corn. "A woman needs a house she can make pretty, and when a baby does come along, you'll need more room. That house where you are now doesn't even have a place for a washer and dryer."

"Grandpa says when you and Brady move out here, he'll build a family swimming pool," said Bobby, Trish's nine-year-old son. He was a cute kid, more outgoing than his brother, who was always crawling into someone's lap and didn't talk much.

Mildred waited until after dinner, when the three women were in the kitchen doing dishes and the men had their feet up in the family room, to ask Suzanne about her mother and the new math teacher at the high school. "Do you think it's serious?" Mildred asked, as she poured the left-over gravy into a Tupperware container. Mildred was big on Tupperware. She'd bought a complete set for Suzanne and instructed her on how to burp it before sealing the lid.

"All they did was go to church together," Suzanne said. "He asked about the churches in town, and Mom invited him to visit First Lutheran."

"I understand they drove over to Columbus for dinner afterwards," Trish interjected. "At the Husker House." Trish was an older, slightly plump female version of her brother, with pale, fine hair.

"I hear his wife died a few years back," Mildred said, putting the skillet in the sink to soak. "It might be nice for your mother to get married again, although I doubt that I ever would if anything happened to Andy. It gets so messy mixing families all up together— you know, who goes where for holidays and which father walks a daughter down the aisle on her wedding day."

"I can't believe you're talking about my mother getting married when she hardly knows the man!" Suzanne said, not caring if her irritation showed. She'd had this same conversation with her grandmother. And with Mrs. Koch at the dry cleaners and Mrs. Bruner at the dentist's office.

"I'm so sorry, dear," Mildred said with genuine concern. "I didn't mean to upset you."

"It's okay," Suzanne said, not really meaning it. It wasn't okay. But she accepted her mother-in-law's embrace. "It just bothers me that everyone's making such a big deal out of it."

"No one means any harm, honey," Mildred said. "Folks just want your mother to be happy."

After the dishes were done, the three women joined the men in the family room, where the Sunday afternoon sporting event was occupying the big screen. The Lakers were playing the Rockets. Mildred worked on a half-finished needlepoint table runner. Trish played cards with Billy and Bobby. Suzanne just sat.

She didn't realize she was crying until she felt the tears falling onto her hands. How weird. Postpartum depression, she supposed. Or was it post-something-else when there was no baby? She was still bleeding. She could actually feel it at times, great clots of blood being passed. Wearing oversized pads for six weeks had left her horribly chafed down there. The doctor said she would need to have a D&C—whatever that was—if the bleeding didn't stop.

At least she had an excuse not to have sex. Brady was horny all the time, pawing at her, wanting her to jack him off, wanting to know the exact day and minute when they could screw again. He couldn't understand why she was so turned off to sex. "You're not going to stay like this, are you?" he'd asked last night. She'd told him she didn't know. As soon as he fell asleep, she carried a pillow and blanket to the sofa. She slept better there.

She used to look forward to sex. During the Friday afternoon bus ride from Lincoln to Newberg, she grew more aroused with each mile. *Soon*, she'd think, closing her eyes, getting turned on by her own mental images. But invariably the next morning, she wished she were back in Lincoln, studying at the library or hanging out with her sister.

The doctor had cautioned her to wait at least six months before she tried to get pregnant again. He seemed to assume that she would want to try again at the first possible opportunity. And she did want another baby. Someday. But shouldn't she grieve more for this one first? People kept telling her there would be other babies. But she couldn't accept that one pregnancy was just like another. Her baby had been unique and had a soul and was now in heaven. That was what the Methodist minister had said at the funeral. Her baby was in the arms of Jesus. But what would it be in heaven: a baby, or a four-inch-long fetus, or the person it was going to be? It had lived only in darkness, never uttering a sound, knowing nothing. Not love or sadness. No sense of family. Not even hunger or cold or pain. Did a being have to experience humanity before it could be a human?

She'd wake up in the night soaked in sweat, certain she could feel the baby still moving inside her. She even thought that maybe she had been pregnant with twins, and one baby was still in there.

Her daddy used to tell her that nothing was ever all one way or the other. She cried at night for her baby and felt a great emptiness. But in the light of day, she felt as if a door had opened. Since there wasn't going to be a baby, she once again had choices. Maybe she didn't have to build a house next door to Brady's parents—at least not yet.

The tears were coming faster now, and her nose was running. Sobs were forming deep in her chest, trying to force their way out.

The men were whooping it up over a half-court shot. Mildred was smiling indulgently at their antics while she stitched away. Trying to make herself invisible, Suzanne picked up her coffee cup and carried it to the kitchen. From there, she escaped out the back door and headed down the driveway.

She walked past the acreage where she and Brady were supposed to build a house and settle in and raise a family and live for the rest of their lives. Half a dozen Herefords were there now, gathered around a freshly broken bale of hay. Andy had built fences around three scraggly little trees to protect them from the cattle. She walked past rows of shiny green tractors, harrows, back hoes, combines, thrashers. She walked down the country road toward town.

She didn't have a coat on, but it didn't feel too cold. In fact, the air felt clean and good. It dried her tears, cleared her head.

Silhouetted against the flat pewter sky, she could see the hilltop cemetery where her father was buried. And her baby. And there on the very edge of town was the house where her father had died, where she and Mark and Vicky had grown up, and Tiger the cat was buried out by the shed.

The new family had already moved in. She had no home any more.

She cut behind the shed and down the driveway. The window where Daddy used to sit looked blankly down at her. She wished she could go back to the time when he was still alive and they all lived together in their big old house. Life then had seemed so full of possibilities.

She hadn't wanted to be pregnant. She hadn't even wanted to be Brady's steady girlfriend and come home from college every weekend. She would have liked to join Vicky's sorority and have girlfriends and go to Saturday night parties. But she hadn't known how to break the pattern without hurting Brady, and there had been something incredibly seductive about his need for her.

She usually took birth control pills. But sometimes she ran out, and Brady would use a condom. Still, it had happened. She had prayed continuously that she wasn't pregnant, and she made all sorts of solemn promises about how she would lead her life if only her period would start. Between classes, she hurried into the restroom, praying with all her might that there would be blood on her panties, blood on the toilet paper. She'd wrap a piece of toilet paper around her finger and jab it high inside her in hopes there would be at least a pinkish tinge, something to say that this wasn't happening to her, that she didn't have a baby growing inside of her after all. Outside the stall, girls who weren't late with their period would be talking about what they would wear to the dance and what classes they were taking next semester.

She thought about abortion but wasn't sure how she'd feel about it afterwards. At that point, it seemed a stretch to call doing away with a cluster of cells murder. But she just didn't know, and probably no one could tell her for sure. Not Brady or her mother or even Pastor Jenson. So she didn't ask. She alone had to decide.

And there was the other issue—the high expectations her parents had always had for her, and her own high expectations for herself. She was going to make her mark, not have the biggest decision of a day be whether to cook a roast for dinner or make a casserole. But what if it turned out she was ordinary after all? As ordinary as Brady?

Perhaps not having an abortion was the coward's way out.

The week before she lost the baby, she'd felt it move. Or thought she had. She had learned to want it. She would be a good mother. She would love her baby as much as her mother loved her. She would make up to it for those early dark thoughts about flushing it away.

Now, that baby was not to be. It had been living, but it hadn't been alive. Was it taken away because she wasn't worthy? Was there really a god in a distant heaven who arbitrated such things?

If she'd had an abortion, she'd be in Lincoln now, going to college as though nothing had ever happened. As it was, she was married and sentenced to eating dinner with Mildred every Sunday until one of them died.

She walked down the boulevard toward her mother's new house next door to the Methodist church that Suzanne now attended with her husband and his family even though she was a Lutheran. Three different people stopped to ask if she wanted a ride. Mrs. Worten from the flower shop insisted on loaning her a jacket. "You sure you're okay, dear?" she asked. Nice people lived in this town— they just gossiped too much. Tomorrow they'd be gossiping about her walking around without a coat on such a cold day.

When she put on Mrs. Worten's jacket, she started to shiver. By the time she reached her mother's front door, her body was shaking with the cold, her teeth chattering so she could hardly speak.

Her mother called Mildred so they wouldn't worry. Then she

put Suzanne in a warm tub and fixed her hot chocolate; held her close while she cried and bled into a towel between her legs. Charlotte was out of Kotex; she'd go buy some as soon as Suzanne calmed down. Tomorrow, she said, Suzanne would have to have that D&C. And yes, she'd go with her.

"You won't marry that man, will you—the math teacher?" Suzanne asked before she drifted off to sleep in her mother's bed. "It wouldn't be fair to Daddy."

chapter twelve

During his first semester of law school, Mark sat three rows back and directly behind Sarah Grigsby in constitutional law, but in property, he sat two rows back and six seats over—just the right angle to watch her in profile without seeming to stare. He became quite familiar with the tilt of her nose, the curve of her chin, the line of her throat, the arch of her eyebrow, her halo of outrageous red hair. He admired her smooth white skin, her vividly green eyes, her slim wrists. He liked to watch her jeans-clad fanny as she lowered it into her seat and the way her hand sometimes rested contemplatively on her breasts.

He knew that when she became very still, with a frown creasing her forehead and her lips pressed together, she was formulating a question and about to shoot a hand in the air. Her questions were often probing, making the professor pause, frown, answer with care. When the first-semester grades were posted, no one was surprised that Sarah Grigsby was in the top ten. Mark wasn't. Not that first semester.

He was intrigued by her wonderful red hair and wondered what it would feel like to put his hands in it. And his face. He would draw in his breath, inhaling the imagined perfume of Sarah Grigsby's hair.

What intrigued him most about her, however, was her lower lip, which was fuller than her also-full upper lip and curled itself over her chin in a manner that was both sweetly innocent and incredibly seductive. Mark had always considered himself a leg man. He'd never had sexual thoughts about a girl unless she had long, sleek legs that he could imagine wrapped around his bare thighs. But on numerous occasions lately, Sarah Grigsby's mouth had taken a starring role in his bedtime fantasies.

There was a problem, however. Sarah Grigsby was engaged—to an assistant district attorney in Omaha.

But even if she hadn't been engaged, Mark wasn't interested in a serious relationship with a fellow law student. Not that he had a problem with women entering the law; some of the law school's best professors were women. He fully expected over the course of his career to work with or even under female attorneys and argue cases before female judges. But he couldn't imagine being married to an attorney. *Maybe* to some other female professional; but what he really wanted was a devoted wife whose primary job in life was taking care of him and their children, which he fully realized was a chauvinistic attitude and definitely not in keeping with the times.

Mark's notion of family had been formed during those years before his dad got sick and his mother became a schoolteacher. Of course, he admired his mother for doing what needed to be done, holding down a job while she took care of Dad and managed their home. But life had been nicer before. She'd always been there in the kitchen when he got home from school. She'd cooked wonderful meals instead of rushing around to get something on the table. Back then, home-baked pies and cakes weren't just for Sundays and special occasions. The house had a polished look about it. Houseplants flourished in sunny corners. Flowers grew in the front yard, vegetables in the back. Clean clothes magically appeared in his closet and bureau drawers, clean sheets on his bed.

Then everything changed. His mother was always tired, always behind. She came home at noon to feed Dad, even ran home between classes if he wasn't doing well. Finally, she took a leave of absence and cashed in savings bonds to make the house payments and buy groceries. Toward the end, she had to feed Dad like a baby. When Mark was at home, he would help bathe his father in his bed. He was so frail Mark could pick him up as though he were a child. Those were hard times. Heart-wrenching. And oddly satisfying— the way they united as a family, spending every minute they could at their father's bedside.

Yet the picture of family that Mark carried in his head was not of them in a sickroom, but of the five of them sitting down to a meal, his father saying the blessing, passing the bowls and platters of food, their mother going back and forth to the kitchen, their father engaging them in discussions about politics, theology, history, current events, what happened at school that day. Above all, Mark wanted his future family to gather around a table for their evening meal. His mother had made that happen for their family. He wanted a wife who would repeat the scenario for him and his children. He couldn't imagine that as a role to be played by a female attorney.

Mark had reached the stage in life when dating became deadly serious. A mating game. He didn't want to end up like his sister Suzanne—married without really planning to be. Dating a woman he wouldn't want to marry was asking for trouble.

For almost four years, Mark had assumed he would marry Molly Maycomber from Beatrice. He'd known her since high school through statewide speech tournaments and church activities. Her father, like Mark's, was seriously ill. Other than Mark's sisters, she was the only person in his life who understood how having a dying parent set one apart and made it impossible for him to joke around or cut up like other guys his age. Molly was pretty, had great legs, wouldn't let him go all the way, and aspired to be a homemaker. She would be a supportive wife, a stay-at-home mother as her own mother had been. Her senior year, Molly won first in extemporaneous speaking at the state speech tournament. Even back then, it occurred to him that she would be a wonderful asset on the stump if he went into politics.

Molly's father died shortly after their graduation from high school. Mark and his mother attended the funeral—a preview of the heartbreak that awaited their own family. It tore him apart. He wanted to run away and not come back until his father was safely dead and in the ground. How did Molly bear it? Maybe she hadn't loved her father as much as Mark loved his.

Molly expected to get married the June they graduated from NU. Mark wanted to wait until he'd finished law school. He pointed out that they had no money and couldn't expect any help from their widowed mothers. Molly insisted she didn't mind working for three years. He argued that their whole future depended on his doing well in law school. He'd be a terrible husband, studying all the time. She promised to be the most undemanding wife possible.

Before he headed back to Lincoln for his senior year, his mother bluntly told him it was time for him to fish or cut bait; he needed to formalize his relationship with Molly or end it. A girl like Molly expected to find a husband at college and marry him shortly thereafter. He must not keep her dangling if he had doubts.

Mark assured his mother that Molly was the only girl for him, that he had no doubts. He just didn't want to get married for a few years. But the truth of the matter was that he was wavering. How was a man to know? On paper, Molly was perfect. But what if, by marrying her, he missed out on someone more wonderful, more exciting? Someone who wasn't so unrelentingly nice? Someone who didn't always agree with him?

Then Molly informed him that, since they were not engaged, she planned to date other boys during her last year in college. He wanted to rage, to tell her she was doing no such thing. He even thought about borrowing some money from his grandmother to buy a ring. But he didn't.

Before Christmas break, Molly called to tell him she was engaged. Mark hung up the phone and cried. He'd really screwed up.

Molly was a prize, the perfect girl. And she'd been a part of his life for such a long time. He thought longingly of her thoughtfulness, her purity. Some other man would have the privilege of marrying her. She would never be the mother of his children.

But he didn't call her back, didn't beg her to change her mind— he felt as much relief as agony.

Frequently other girls would show an interest in him, letting him know by their eyes and smiles that they would say yes if he asked them out, but he didn't follow through. He felt too old for the dating game. In fact, if it weren't for occasional sightings of Sarah Grigsby, he felt above sexuality. He was an ascetic and a scholar, disciplined and focused.

Then the week after Suzanne lost her baby, he realized Sarah Grigsby was no longer wearing an engagement ring. He asked her out.

She let him go all the way on their first date.

She lived in a garage apartment behind her aunt's house. She went into the house to distract her aunt while he sneaked up the stairs. Mark had had sex with his high school girlfriend before Molly—a girl who was now married and had three children—and he'd had sex with a girl his freshman year during a brief breakup with Molly. A dozen times all total. A novice.

Sarah Grigsby kept condoms hidden under her mattress. Sarah Grigsby had a pierced navel. He felt the navel ring before he saw it. She laughed when he asked what it was and wanted her to remove it. She refused. But it was pagan. It spoiled her nakedness. What sort of a girl was she, anyway?

She didn't turn off the lamp. There she was naked but for a navel ring, with a body straight out of a centerfold. Even her pubic hair was red.

"Keep it quiet, okay," she said. "My aunt sleeps with her windows open."

"It's ten degrees outside."

"She's Norwegian. I want you to go down on me before we kiss."

She took the lead. Mark fought desperately for control, and it became a game. She won. He felt as though he were being turned inside out. He had to bury his face in the pillow to keep from crying out.

Sneaking back down the wooden steps, he felt not so much like a thief in the night as someone who'd suffered a loss. He'd left a part of himself up there. He hated Sarah Grigsby, hated the men who'd felt their way down these stairs in the dark before him. He wished he'd married Molly and was now leading a safe, sane life. Molly was dear and good. He was suddenly filled with missing her. And he wondered when he would again be allowed to climb back up these stairs to Sarah Grigsby's bed.

With the gift of a warm April day, Rollerbladers and cyclists were darting about the campus. On Greek row, frat guys were playing touch football in the street. Pansies were blooming in front of the student union.

Vicky loved the campus, loved the life there. The university was a place for learning and being young and making memories. She had a sense as she was living them that these were the best years of her life.

"Do you ever think about coming back, about being a part of all this again?" Vicky asked her sister as they strolled by the Bell Tower.

"I never was a part of it. Maybe if I'd been in a sorority or joined some clubs; but I had to go home on weekends. It just wasn't in the cards."

Vicky wanted to point out that Suzanne had not had to go home every weekend. She had *chosen* to go home. Instead, she said, "But you liked your classes."

"Yeah. I liked them. A lot."

Vicky glanced over at her sister—her changed sister. Suzanne was more self-contained, more serious. She was wearing an unfamiliar navy jacket—probably one of Brady's—and setting the pace, striding out so that Vicky was having to hurry to keep up with her. Mom said she walked by herself all the time now, up and down county roads. People would tell Mom they'd seen her all the way to Gurneysville, or up by Wilson Creek.

Vicky wondered if insisting Suzanne come for the weekend was such a good idea after all. Mark wanted them to meet his new girlfriend, and Vicky's roommate was away for the weekend. She and her sister hadn't spent much time together since Suzanne's marriage. She felt a distance. Her sister was a married woman, and had suffered a miscarriage. The relationship between them wasn't the same any more. It was both strange and sad.

She should have confronted her about Brady, about her rush to marry him. If Suzanne wanted to be a doctor, what the hell was she doing going home every weekend to spread her legs for a boy like him? Brady wasn't the sort to have a physician for a wife. Vicky should have insisted Suzanne pledge her sorority, be a part of things.

"I've missed you," Vicky said. "I get scared sometimes that I'm losing you. I don't quite know what to say to you anymore."

Suzanne moved closer and linked arms. "Naw. You're stuck with me. Are you really coming home this summer?"

"Looks like it. I've petitioned the journalism department to approve a summer internship at the *Record.* Otherwise I'll try for one at West Point or Columbus. Either way, I'll live in Newberg—in Mom's new house. Which will be weird. I think I'll always have to look the other way when I drive by the old house. It makes me too sad."

"They took off the front porch," Suzanne said.

"Grandma told me. I loved that front porch. God, all the time we spent on it—or under it. I'll never think of the house where Mom lives now as my home. Even Mom isn't the same. All that talk about a trip. I was looking forward to having a resident mom again, but when I told her I was probably moving back this summer, she said it would be nice to have someone look after the house while she was gone. I'll tell you, Suzanne, it really hurt my feelings. I thought she'd want to stay home if I were there. Do you think she's really going?"

"Yeah, I do, now that there won't be a baby. She pores over maps and travel magazines and says she wants to go places that everyone should go to once in their lifetime—like the Grand Canyon and the Rocky Mountains."

"But what is she really looking for?"

"Maybe she's just bored. With Daddy being sick for such a long time, she was pretty tied down."

"So was Daddy. So were we all," Vicky said. "I'm sure he would have liked to see the Grand Canyon and the Rocky Mountains. It bothers me that she gets to go places because he's dead. It doesn't seem fair somehow."

"I doubt if she'll stay away long. I can't imagine it being any fun, driving all that way by herself."

"It's embarrassing. Women her age just don't go off on their own like that. What if she has car trouble or gets in a wreck? What if some man tries to pick her up?"

Suzanne shrugged. "She's not helpless, Vicky. She broke it off with the high school math teacher."

"She didn't sleep with him, did she?"

"I don't know."

"I wonder if she's gone through menopause."

"Why?"

"What if she could still get pregnant? Remember when Sharon Mueller's mother came up pregnant. She was about Mom's age. Sharon was mortified. But at least her mother was married."

"Getting pregnant out of wedlock isn't the end of the world," Suzanne said dryly.

"Oh, for God's sake, Suzanne, you know what I mean! Screwing around—at her age."

"She's not *that* old. I suspect that math teacher won't be the last man to come sniffing around."

"God, Suzanne, that's disgusting," Vicky said.

"What do you know about Mark's new girlfriend?" Suzanne said, changing the subject.

"Just that she's a law student. He's been pretty close-mouthed. I think he fell for this girl in spite of himself. Law school doesn't usually prepare a girl for dutiful wifehood."

Mark was waiting in front of Devaney Center. The girl with him had vividly red hair.

Vicky watched while Mark engulfed Suzanne in a bear hug. "I'm so glad you're here," he said. Suzanne looked as though she were about to cry.

chapter thirteen

Charlotte sat at the kitchen table, a map of the southwestern United States spread out before her, a half-eaten sandwich on a plate at her elbow. Her collection of travel brochures, clippings, books, and relevant volumes from her set of twenty-year-old encyclopedias were stacked on the windowsill.

Most evenings, she would sit there for an hour or so, CNN or *Dateline* playing in the background, while she imagined her journey, taking notes on locales in a spiral notebook on which she'd written lines from Bert Leston Taylor:

. . . blest is he who follows free
The road to anywhere.

Across the map, she'd marked possible itineraries with various-colored Magic Markers. The map had been folded and refolded so many times, it was beginning to give way at the creases. She'd bought a new role of Scotch tape last week with the thought of making repairs, but she hadn't gotten around to it. Actually, she was thinking about putting the map away and signing up to teach summer school.

Doubt was back and threatening to engulf her like night fog on a low-lying stretch of country road. First it had been thoughts of Suzanne's baby that made her hesitate; now it was Suzanne herself.

Charlotte finished her sandwich, more out of habit than hunger, and carried the plate to the sink—a different sink and a different view than the one that had greeted her for the last twenty-eight years. It still seemed strange to look out at the white-painted walls and stained-glass windows of the Methodist church after all those years looking out at the same backyard, with corn fields beyond, the expanse of sky, the passing seasons leaving their imprint on the land. Now her view was limited.

The Methodist church was prettier than the more sedate Lutheran church where she'd spent so many hours of her life, where she'd taken her children every Sunday morning. Even during blizzards, they went. Because she had made their attendance non-negotiable, they considered their mother to be a religious woman, but it was their father who answered their questions about heaven and hell and what God expected of them.

She had tried to think what Stan would have said about her plans. Would he tell her that she deserved the trip after all those years of never going any place? That of course she was now free to go anywhere she wanted? Or would he counsel her to watch over their children? Trouble was, she could envision him going either way, even though he knew that Charlotte had long ago vowed that she would not be like her sister.

Bernice hovered about her children like a mother hen trying to keep a coyote at bay. She'd been one of those mothers who always had Band-Aids, Kleenex, and packets of disposable towelettes in her purse, granola bars in the glove compartment, and extra jackets in the trunk. Bernice had gone with Noreen to the obstetrician's office throughout her pregnancy and now accompanied her daughter and grandbaby on visits to the pediatrician. Bernice spent as much time at Noreen's house as she did at her own—"helping out," she called it. And she still made her sons' beds, cleaned their rooms, packed their suitcases, paid their speeding tickets, reminded them to do their homework and take their medicine. Once, when Charlotte suggested that Bernice did too much for her children, she had taken it as a compliment.

Charlotte couldn't remember ever buying disposable towelettes, and she hadn't cleaned her children's rooms for years. She would always be there for her children if they needed her, and she would do what she could, but she didn't want their need to become a habit.

Stan had depended on her for every bite of food, for a clean bed and body, for companionship, entertainment, love. Charlotte had given without hesitation. Endlessly. After all, look at what was being taken from him. Any sacrifice on her part seemed insignificant. Sacrifice became a way of life. She lived for her dying husband—for his voice, his touch, for providing whatever comfort she could. The children, in their pain, became *his* children. The house became *his* home. She hadn't known what to do with herself in those months after his death. Her grief had been mingled with the throes of withdrawal. She'd wept as hard when the hospital bed was taken away as when the undertaker carried off Stan's body.

In many ways, the years of her husband's illness had been elevating. But she didn't want ever again to be that responsible for another life—not a husband's, not a child's, not even a pet's.

What she wanted was a go at selfishness. Surely she'd earned the right to wish her children well and march off into her own sunset. But how could she leave when Suzanne was floundering, even if ultimately she must solve her own problems?

Charlotte sighed out loud in her silent kitchen, put the few dishes in the dishwasher, folded up the map, put on a jacket, and headed out for an evening walk—a habit from long ago that she was trying to reestablish now that spring was making its presence felt.

In those years between small children and Stan's illness, she and Stan had often walked after dinner, briskly or leisurely, depending on the weather. The muscles in her legs had been wonderfully firm back then. She'd like them to be that way again. And her body. No roll of flesh below her bra.

She thought of a firm body while she walked with long strides, chin up, arms swinging at her sides. Across town and back. Not by the old house. She needed for it to stay frozen in time, forever in her memory as it had been when her family lived there.

By the time she returned from her walk, the choir had gathered in the sanctuary for Tuesday night practice, their voices lifted in a triumphant anthem, the stained glass glowing from within. Pretty damned beautiful, inspiring even, with the backdrop of a nighttime sky so full of stars they seemed to merge into clouds of stardust. "Are you up there, God?" she asked as she studied the sky from her front step.

A dog would be nice at moments like this, she admitted to herself. A living presence at her side. But then she wouldn't be free. She'd have to worry about his habits and health. She'd cry when he died.

Softly, she sang along with the choir—"A mighty fortress is our God/A bulwark never failing"—and thought of the lines from Robert Browning: "God's in his heaven/All's right with the world!" Tonight, it almost felt that way. If only she wasn't so worried about Suzanne.

She stretched her legs out in front of her and reached down to feel her flexed calf muscles. Definitely harder. And maybe she was a bit leaner, not much, but some.

Later, before she took a bath, she examined her body in the mirror, running her hands up and down her sides, lifting her breasts. It was a lived-in body, with the stretchmarks of pregnancy, the relaxing skin of middle age, the freckled white flesh that once had been the color of honey. But when she stood up straight and turned off the overhead light, the womanly reflection in the mirror was almost pleasing. When she closed her eyes and imagined a man's gaze on her, she felt a tingling in her nipples, and longing stirred deep inside.

For so long, she'd been asexual. Sex was not a possibility in her life, so she simply stopped thinking about it. But now, although she couldn't imagine being married again, she would like to be with a man. Arousing thoughts would flit around her consciousness. Not full-blown fantasies but rather bits and pieces of erotica—a man's mouth at her breasts, her legs locking around a man's thighs as he entered her, her hands kneading a man's buttocks. But the man himself was a nebulous shadow with no identity. Not her dead husband. Not the math teacher. Not even Cory Lee Jones, although she'd half-expected his face to appear.

Her thoughts of Cory dealt only with the moment of seeing him once again. Of asking him why. And understanding finally why her life had turned out the way it had.

She hadn't tried to put the math teacher's face on the shadowy male form. Eric had put his hand on her thigh, and she pushed it away. He was tired of frozen dinners and was looking for a wife.

She thought of seeking out a one-night stand—just so she could find out if sex was even worth bothering about after all this time. But there were diseases and crazy men to worry about. And besides, she'd forgotten how to flirt.

With Cory, there had been no flirting. The attraction had been there from the very first. She was hot for his touch by the time it came. Could she ever experience that heat with another man? And the astounding passion. The completeness. They talked about it afterwards, their discussions of how it had felt almost clinical. Sex had been a shared adventure, an exploration of their carnal selves. If they weren't experiencing it, they talked about it. Endlessly.

She and Stan had enjoyed good sex on occasion, but good or otherwise, they never talked about it. They each retreated into their private selves when they were finished. She and Cory never really finished. They just ebbed and flowed. The sex had been with her every minute. In her mind—on her skin—in her soul.

Instead of her usual tub bath tonight, Charlotte showered, turning the showerhead to its most forceful setting. The water felt as though hundreds of tiny needles were pricking at her skin. She inhaled the steam into her lungs, made a lather of the soap to rub over her flesh.

Still damp from the shower and wrapped in a towel, she sat on her bed and took out the picture of Cory. She studied his face and body. A beautiful body.

Then with the picture back in its hiding place, she turned off the lamp, opened the towel, and lay back on the bed. But images of Cory still did not come into her mind. Just the shadowy lover. And he couldn't satisfy her the way Cory once had. She remembered the lovemaking more than the boy.

❧ Suzanne walked in the afternoons—almost every day, except when she drove over to Norfolk to see Noreen and the baby. When the weather was bad, she walked in town. Other days, she walked for hours out in the countryside.

She'd found an abandoned mangy, half-grown dog during one of her walks, and he became her constant companion. She named him George—a long-legged, skinny black dog that looked to be part Lab. Brady couldn't understand why she didn't buy a good dog—a pedigreed collie maybe or an Irish setter.

Suzanne was lean and tan, her demeanor solemn. There was no sparkle to her eyes, but there were no tears either. Charlotte wanted to encourage her to at least finish an undergraduate degree—she could commute to Wayne State or Midland Lutheran. She had sacrificed everything to have a baby, but the baby didn't happen. Now Suzanne had an obligation to herself.

But Charlotte said nothing. If she did, Suzanne would have someone to argue with. As it was, she had to argue with herself.

All Charlotte could do was ache for her. Vicky and Mark were in Lincoln, studying, being young, working toward degrees, excited about the future. Mark even seemed to be in love—or at least involved. Suzanne had nothing to do but clean her little house and walk with her dog. By her own admission, she seldom cooked any more. Mostly Brady ate at home with his folks, and Suzanne lived on hamburgers or chili dogs from the Dairy Dream.

She still had Sunday dinner with the Brammers, but she no

longer accompanied Brady's family to church. If she went at all, she joined her mother at First Lutheran, and Charlotte herself wasn't going regularly these days. She still loved the music but tuned out the sermons. And knowing that the pastor, her mother, and others in the congregation were scanning the pews, taking note of who was and was not in attendance, no longer motivated her as it once had. She enjoyed Sunday morning at home watching the news shows on television and drinking too much coffee.

Suzanne had begun lunching with her mother almost daily, either in the school cafeteria, with George waiting patiently by the bicycle rack, or at home, with George under the kitchen table. But that routine had ended a few weeks back.

Charlotte hadn't planned to invite Suzanne along on her summer journey. That's how she thought of it—a "journey." A trip was just going from one place to the other. A journey seemed more open-ended. Sharing it with another human being had never been a part of her plan. It was to be a time of self-examination and learning—even if all she learned was that she was a homebody. She'd been showing Suzanne a newspaper article about the ancient Santa Fe pueblo, and the words just came out of her mouth. Why didn't Suzanne come along? Get away for a while. Just to get her bearings.

"I'm a married woman, Mom," Suzanne said indignantly. "I know I'm not doing a very good job of it right now, but I'm not going to run away."

Charlotte was hurt. Her magnanimous gesture had been rebuffed.

The next day, Charlotte had her lunchtime bowl of soup alone. Suzanne had been there earlier and left a note, explaining only that she'd borrowed the electric mixer.

The following day, the mixer had been returned, and Suzanne left a note saying she'd borrowed a muffin tin and the recipe box.

The next day she'd returned the muffin tin and left two oatmeal muffins on the table. Her note said she'd return the recipes later. She wanted to copy some of them.

The day after that there was no evidence that Suzanne had been in the house, nor in the following days, except when she left the recipe box inside the front door.

Without the impetus of a child to feed, Charlotte put off trips to the grocery until she was out of coffee and milk. Otherwise, she made do on what was there; often just a bowl of cereal. She found it a bit frightening—was this a glimpse of her future alone? Cheerios at twilight?

Charlotte missed their lunches and the pleasure of seeing one of her children on a daily basis. Suzanne's distance was painful, but ironically it eased Charlotte's doubts. She taped together the tattered map and began to count the days. Just another month. She really was going to do this thing. She was both afraid and excited.

Mid-May, Mark helped Vicky move home for the summer before moving himself to Omaha in preparation for his summer job at an Omaha law firm.

Charlotte had cooked a real meal in honor of Vicky's homecoming and Mark's visit. Such a production, and to think she used to cook every day, week in, week out. Year after year of "What's for dinner, Mom?"

Mark was helping himself to a second serving of mashed potatoes when he addressed the car issue. "If you take this trip, Vicky won't have any transportation this summer."

"It's only a five-minute walk to the newspaper office," Charlotte pointed out. "When she needs a car, she can borrow her grandmother's Buick. Or Brady's truck."

"I don't understand why Andy and Mildred haven't bought Suzanne a car," Vicky said.

"She doesn't want one. She and George walk."

"Aren't you worried about her?" Mark asked, lines creasing his forehead. His father's forehead; his father's voice.

"Yes. But there's nothing I can do for her."

"I don't like the idea of you setting out in a seven-year-old station wagon," he said.

"I've joined a car club and had the engine tuned up. If it dies along the way, I'll trade it in. If it makes it back, I'll have the engine rebuilt and drive it for another year."

"Why didn't Suzanne and Brady come to dinner?" Vicky asked.

"Your sister didn't offer a reason. She wants you both to come by for breakfast in the morning."

"Aren't you and Suzanne getting along?" Vicky asked.

Charlotte was unprepared for the spasm of emotion that welled in her throat and brought tears to her eyes. She turned her face away, embarrassed. No, she and her youngest child were not getting along. And it hurt.

Vicky came around the table and knelt beside her. "I'm sorry, Mom. Anything I can do? Or need to know about?"

Charlotte took a deep breath and a sip of water. "I made the mistake of asking her to go with me this summer. I thought it might be good for her to get away for a while, but she interpreted the invitation as an editorial comment on the state of her marriage. Or something like that. And maybe it was, I don't know. Certainly it wasn't calculated. Anyway, she's started keeping house and stopped dropping by. I've hardly seen her since."

Her explanation made, Charlotte hurried to the kitchen to slice the pie while Vicky and Mark cleared the table.

"Now, tell me about this new girlfriend," Charlotte said as she placed a piece of pie in front of Mark. "How come your sisters got to meet her and I haven't?"

"She's okay. Just someone to go out with. Nothing serious."

❧ Vicky's summer internship at the *Record* was front-page news, along with a picture of her sitting at her father's old desk. Hannah was thrilled. Her friends had all called to say they'd seen her granddaughter's picture. "With Vicky at the newspaper and Bernice's mansion going up, maybe people will stop talking about Suzanne," she told Charlotte. "But promise me that you're not really taking a trip all by yourself. Good grief, Charlotte, people will think you've lost your mind."

"Well, you'll just have to tell them I'm off looking for it," Charlotte said.

"I don't know you anymore, Charlotte. What happened to that good little girl who never gave me a minute's trouble?"

"She grew up," Charlotte said flatly.

The last two weeks of school, Charlotte was as restless as her students. At best, teaching literature and grammar to junior high school students was a challenge, but as summer vacation drew near, they grew bolder with their note passing and smart remarks. Inattention became chronic. Charlotte would find herself wishing she'd earned a degree in elementary education.

Of course, her degree wasn't in English either. She'd majored in history with the intention of replacing old Mr. Marx, the junior high history and social studies teacher, when he retired, but the school had hired a young man fresh off the Drake basketball team to teach history and coach the boys' team. Charlotte had taken a sufficient number of electives in journalism and American lit to qualify for a teaching certificate in language arts, and she was offered a position teaching English and advising the newspaper and yearbook staffs, which she accepted rather than face a commute to West Point, Norfolk, or some other town. She needed to be as close to Stan as possible. That's why she'd wanted to teach secondary school in the first place. The building that housed the junior and senior high was less than a block from their house.

Her first years as a teacher had been a nightmare. Now they were just difficult. She wasn't a gifted teacher, but she did the best she could.

The last week of school, out of desperation, she asked her eighth-grade classes to pretend they were eighty years old and write their life stories. Only two of the girls wrote about marrying hometown sweethearts and raising their children in Newberg. The other students mentioned children and spouses only incidentally, focusing instead on exciting lives as entertainers, sports superstars, musicians, or television news anchors. Gretchen Guiterman wrote about becoming a famous mystery writer and a U.S. senator. Sickly little Toby Schwartz planned to become a missionary. Beautiful, blond Stevie Stevenson wrote of being the first man to set foot on Mars and being elected President of the United States when he got back home.

The last day of school, Charlotte handed out report cards and a reading list for the summer that most of her students would never look at. Most, but not all. There were always the few who made her efforts seem almost worthwhile. Betty Monroe, who'd written about spending her life in Newberg, was such a student. She was brilliant and a voracious reader, but with no plans for college, she'd end up like Suzanne. Stan would say that Charlotte was judging other people by her own prejudices. Who was to say what was best for the girl? Maybe when she was eighty, she'd look back on her life with great contentment.

As Charlotte pulled up in front of her house, she was surprised to see Suzanne and George sitting on the front steps. A wave of nervousness swept over her. And hope.

She got out of the car and advanced carefully, as one would approach an injured bird.

"Still leaving in the morning?" Suzanne asked.

"Bright and early."

"The invitation still open?"

Charlotte nodded. "What made you change your mind?"

"What you said about getting my bearings. Can George come along?"

A most amazing feeling of joy washed over Charlotte, so sheer and pure it made her lightheaded. She put a hand on the newel post to steady herself and stood there for a minute, aware of the rustling of the tree branches, a chirpy bird in the oak tree, the organist practicing next door, her beloved child sitting on the front porch with her homely black dog.

So much for self-discovery, Charlotte thought as she sat beside Suzanne—close, so their shoulders touched. The summer wouldn't be as she had planned, but she didn't care. She could take her youngest and most fragile child away from here for a time at least. George stuck his nose under her hand, and she obligingly scratched his ears. "You sure?" she asked.

"Is that ever possible?"

"I guess not. What does Brady say?"

"He cried."

chapter fourteen

The fertile rolling farmland of eastern Nebraska gave way to the harsher Sand Hills region as Interstate 80 made its way along the Platte River, following much the same route as the Oregon and Mormon trails a century and a half before. Western Nebraska was cattle country, its arid, treeless landscape crisscrossed with mile after mile of wire fences.

Suzanne was a quiet passenger, reaching over the seat from time to time to pet her dog and listening politely as Charlotte rattled off stories about frontier life and building the railroad across the prairie. Charlotte had never seen this part of her state firsthand, but she had studied its history. And she had written her senior research paper on the women who came west with their restless men and found themselves isolated in the middle of a vast treeless prairie, raising their children in sod houses with dirt floors and grass growing from the roof, going months at a time not seeing another adult female, helplessly watching children die for lack of a doctor or food. "Sometimes the loneliness and hunger got to them," Charlotte said. "A man would come home after months on a cattle drive and find his family dead, their bodies rotting inside the soddy. His wife would have killed her children, then herself. One woman left a note explaining that back in Boston she'd had a piano and neighbors, but out here there was only wind, dirt, and emptiness."

"You really should have taught history," Suzanne said. "If Mr. Stuben ever leaves, maybe you can move over into the social studies slot."

"That might be nice. I've enjoyed teaching literature, but I've never done a very good job inspiring my students to be better spellers or to learn the difference between the objective and the nominative case. Actually, I'd like a more drastic change than switching from junior high language arts to junior high social studies."

"What else could you do? Career opportunities for women don't exactly abound in our little town. I can't see you waiting tables or opening a beauty shop."

"Probably I'll just teach until I'm old enough to retire, then shuffle off into my dotage and ride on the nursing home float in the Old Settlers Day parade."

Suzanne was silent for a time, her attention devoted to the passing landscape. Then she asked, "If a fairy godmother came along and offered you the perfect job, what would it be?"

"The perfect job? For that I'd need an advanced degree, and at my age, I don't think I have either the desire or the energy to go back to college for the years and years it would take to get a Ph.D. in history or archeology so I could teach at a college instead of a junior high school."

At my age. Where had those words come from? Limiting words. Did that mean she had already resigned herself to a different station in life? Had she become the aging widow lady?

She knew she wasn't old—not yet, anyway—but she was aware of a shrinking number of years remaining to her for learning new things and experiencing different vistas. Henry David Thoreau thought one needed to go no further than a nearby pond to suck all the marrow from life. But Charlotte had already experienced the quiet life. Now she needed to separate herself, at least for a time, from her own Walden Pond and from people like her mother, who for whatever reasons had opted for a tidy, safe, and therefore what seemed to Charlotte a limited life.

They spent the night at a motel in eastern Colorado and saw their first mountains about noon the next day. At first Charlotte thought she was looking at lofty cloud formations, but gradually she realized they were the snow-covered peaks of the Rockies.

Suzanne leaned forward. "My God, Mom, *mountains*," she said. "They go up to the sky!"

Charlotte smiled at the excitement in Suzanne's voice—it was something she hadn't heard for a long time.

Suzanne took over the driving after lunch, and they watched the wondrous mountains grow ever closer. In Loveland they bought groceries, then headed west along the Big Thompson River.

They stopped at Paradise Bend Fishing Camp, perched on the side of the river and surrounded by mountains. The sound of rushing water and the scent of pine filled the air. Their log cabin had a deck that jutted out over the water. Suzanne stood at the railing, looking at the river below, the mountains beyond.

Charlotte came to stand beside her and realized her daughter was crying. "Oh, honey, are you sorry you came?" Charlotte asked, slipping an arm around Suzanne's waist.

"It's all so beautiful it makes my chest hurt," Suzanne said. "But I should be back home, cooking dinner for Brady."

"You're only twenty years old, Suzanne. You have lots of time to cook dinner for Brady. Can't you just live in limbo for a little while? See things you've never seen before? Feel what it's like to be out in the larger world?"

"You don't want me to stay with Brady, do you?" Suzanne asked, pulling away from her mother.

Charlotte leaned against the railing, turning her back on the mountains. "I wish you'd waited to get married. But I can accept your staying with him if you're doing it for the right reasons."

"Which are?" Suzanne asked. She knelt beside George and took his head in her hands, not looking at her mother.

"That you can't imagine life without Brady. That you truly believe you both will have a better life if you stay together."

"I can make him happy," she said, laying her cheek against the top of George's head.

"People have to be responsible for their own happiness, Suzanne. You'd probably make Brady *un*happy if you left, but staying—in and of itself—doesn't guarantee anything."

"Maybe," Suzanne said, getting to her feet. "We need to get the car unloaded and cook dinner."

With their belongings and the groceries put away, the two women cooked hamburgers and carried their plates and cans of beer out on the porch. George dutifully followed and stretched out beside Suzanne's chair. "Tomorrow night we'll eat fresh trout," Charlotte promised.

The sounds of the river and night birds seemed magical as darkness descended around them. The sunlight lingered on the mountain peaks, however, tinting the snow with an amazing palette of golds and pinks and purples. When the sunlight finally ebbed away and the peaks were bathed in darkness, the massive mountains remained a formidable presence, darkly silhouetted against the starry sky, dominating even the night. The mountains were humbling, but with humility came a sense of peace. Charlotte felt at the same time inconsequential and liberated. Newberg, Nebraska, seemed very far away.

"I wonder what it would be like to live here all the time," Suzanne said. "Would the awe go away?"

"I don't see how it could," Charlotte said. "Maybe you wouldn't be constantly aware of it, but surely there would be times, like when the light strikes the mountains a certain way or everything is covered with fresh snow or springtime is pushing buds from the tree branches, that even the old-timers have to stop and feel the splendor."

"Do you believe that God made all this?"

"Is belief in God a necessary ingredient in appreciating the wonders of nature?" Charlotte responded, rubbing her arms against the chill that had descended with the darkness.

"I guess not, except it's easier for me to believe that God made it happen than to believe it happened all on its own over billions and billions of years."

Suzanne went inside for their jackets and two more cans of beer. Charlotte didn't usually drink beer and was surprised how satisfying it was tonight—as cold and clean as the evening air.

"I like this place," Suzanne said when she returned. "How long can we stay here?"

"As long as you want. You kids always loved to go fishing, and according to the brochures, the fishing here is fantastic."

"Yeah, but Daddy always cleaned what we caught."

"Just imagine that we've gone back in time. There are no supermarkets. No fish fillets in Styrofoam trays covered with cellophane."

"And no telephones," Suzanne said, glancing at her watch. "I've got to go call Brady, Mom. I promised him I would—at ten o'clock Newberg time."

She'd called him last night, too. Charlotte realized phone calls to Brady would be a nightly occurrence, designed to keep Suzanne firmly tethered. Newberg wasn't so far away after all.

They stayed at Paradise Bend for eight days. Mornings, they fished, George sitting patiently on the bank. Afternoons, they hiked in the national park, following a different nature trail each day. Flowering plants and small wildlife were everywhere. One morning before dawn they left George in the cabin and went on a bus tour of the park. They saw deer and elk materialize out of the morning mists.

Evenings, legs aching from hiking up and down rocky trails, they grilled the morning's catch and ate on the deck, drinking beer or wine, the sounds of the river and night surrounding them, a star-filled canopy above. At quarter of nine each night, Suzanne would drive off to make her phone call.

Even with Suzanne checking her watch, evenings were the best time for Charlotte, as she sat with her youngest child on the deck, watching night fall on the Rockies. And to think she could have lived out her years on this earth without ever seeing mountains, without feeling them in her marrow. Thoreau should have come here, too.

"Remember when I asked you if dogs and cats had souls?" Suzanne said one evening, her booted feet propped on the railing, George's head resting on her lap.

"No. What did I say?"

"That you were going to be mad at God if our Tiger didn't get into heaven. I'd like to believe that Tiger's up there now, sitting on Daddy's lap, keeping him company. God, I loved that old cat. And I love George here," she said, stroking his head. "He's my buddy, and he's got more soul or character or whatever than a lot of people I know." She fell silent for a minute, then said, "You never gave us yes-and-no answers. I thought you were just trying to make us think for ourselves."

Charlotte smiled. "Now you know I have no answers. Does that bother you?"

"Yeah. Parents are supposed to know everything."

"Sorry."

❧ After their time along the Big Thompson, they wound their way southwest, stopping at Central City, Leadville, Silvertop, and other old mining towns that reflected Colorado's past. Some of the towns had been converted into tourist traps. Charlotte preferred the out-of-the-way, rustic communities inhabited by aging hippie types in beards and boots.

They crossed into Arizona at the Four Corners. Charlotte took a picture of Suzanne and George standing on the flat, square monument, the endless expanse of the high plateau surrounding them.

They'd been away from home two weeks when they reached the Grand Canyon. Intentionally, they arrived after dark and drove straight to the motel, wanting their first sight of the canyon to be at daybreak.

The motel was an old-fashioned tourist court left over from the 1950s—a time-warp kind of place, complete with an ancient window air conditioner that spat out droplets of water. At dawn, they drove to the South Rim to watch the sun come up over the canyon.

No other sight on earth could match it, Charlotte thought. It was more—much more—than she'd thought it would be.

"I want to remember this moment always," Charlotte said. "I'll pull it out and think of it on my deathbed—standing here at dawn, arm-in-arm with my darling Suzanne, seeing all this for the first time."

The two women sat side by side on a large boulder, watching the canyon change as the sun inched its way higher in the sky. "Your dad and I wanted to bring you kids here," Charlotte recalled. "We were going to take a major family vacation—stop at the Grand Canyon and head down into Old Mexico. We'd even started saving a little money each month in a vacation fund at the bank. But it always got used for something else."

"I think I appreciate it more now than I would have back then," Suzanne assured her. "You and Daddy always made the trips we did take seem special, with all the planning and history lessons. The rodeo in Ponca. The Swedish Festival in Stromsburg. Fishing up at Lewis and Clark Lake. I thought staying overnight in a motel when we went to the state fair was the coolest thing going, and we loved camping at the state parks. We never felt deprived, Mom. Even when Daddy got sick, we were okay. We wouldn't have traded places with anyone."

"I know, honey. Your dad and I thought we were the luckiest people in the world to have you kids."

They stayed at the Grand Canyon two days, hiking, watching the sun rise and set. They took snapshots of each other on the rim but made no real attempt to take pictures of the canyon itself, knowing their point-and-shoot camera was unworthy of the task. At nine o'clock both nights, Suzanne went over to the pay phone by the office to call Brady in private.

They took four days driving to Santa Fe, stopping in Flagstaff with its soaring pine trees, at the Petrified Forest, and the Painted Desert, the Continental Divide, the Acoma Indian Reservation. Suzanne always seemed interested when her mother shared the knowledge she'd acquired about these places during her evenings at the kitchen table. Charlotte would take in each vista, then close her eyes to imprint it on her memory. She wanted to mesh the story of a place with the look and feel of it, with its smells and sounds and the emotions it evoked.

Perhaps it wasn't the travel itself, however, but the fact that she'd actually done it. No one wanted her to fulfill this promise to herself. Many people would never feel the same about her because she had done what they would never do. Maybe she could go back home and live the rest of her life with a sense of fulfillment. It wouldn't matter that no one else understood or cared. *She* would know.

❧ Charlotte was enchanted with Santa Fe. It was another world, another time. George had to wait in the motel room while mother and daughter visited every gallery, every museum. The third night, over margaritas in a wonderful little bar with adobe walls and an ancient tree that grew through an opening in the roof, Charlotte told Suzanne about the next destination.

"Remember the man in the photograph you found up in the attic? In one of my old yearbooks?"

Already looking wary, Suzanne nodded.

"That man once lived off and on in Peyo, New Mexico. Maybe someone there knows something about him."

Suzanne said nothing for a long minute, her face a mask. "Is that what this trip is all about?" she finally asked.

"This trip is about being with you and seeing some of the world outside the state of Nebraska and figuring out some things about myself."

Suzanne sat with her hands in her lap, looking down at her empty glass.

Charlotte felt a wave of panic. She could feel Suzanne retreating from her. "Imagine if Brady disappeared," she went on, talking too fast. "Wouldn't you always wonder about him, even if you'd gone on with your life and he was no longer a part of it? If given the chance, wouldn't you try to find out?"

"I don't know. Maybe so. Maybe not. What if I tell you I don't want to go to that town? So far, we've followed your itinerary. What if I want to go to Old Mexico like you and Daddy had planned? A foreign country. That would be memorable, too."

"I'm game for that. But I want to go to Peyo first. If you don't want to do that, you can wait for me here, or I can put you on a plane for home."

Suzanne pushed her chair back and headed for the rest room— and the pay phone. It was ten o'clock in Newberg. Charlotte paid the check and went to wait in the car.

She'd assumed too much. After the last two weeks, she thought that Suzanne now saw her as a real person who struggled with conflicting emotions, like Suzanne herself. But mothers were not allowed complexity. Mothers must be forever simple—fountains of love with no other need than to live up to their children's expectations.

Suzanne said nothing when she got in the car. Charlotte started the engine and drove back to their motel on the edge of town.

"I called for a plane reservation," Suzanne said as she got out of the car. "My flight is at ten o'clock in the morning, out of the Albuquerque airport. I can rent a carrier for George."

Other than fitful dozing, Charlotte didn't sleep. She considered her options. She could wake Suzanne and beg her not to go. She could offer to forgo Peyo. She could even apologize. Tell her she realized it wasn't an appropriate thing for a mother to ask of her daughter. But the next morning, all she said was that she wished

Suzanne would reconsider and that the last weeks had been among the best of her life. Then she put her daughter and George on a plane back to Nebraska. Brady would pick them up in Lincoln.

Charlotte walked though the airport parking lot crying. Once in the station wagon, she blew her nose and checked the map. She could be in Peyo by late afternoon. Cory wasn't there, she knew that. But he'd been there. Maybe he'd left a clue.

chapter fifteen

Charlotte stopped in the middle of the road to study the map. She looked in both directions—her dusty station wagon was the only vehicle on the gravel road. In fact, from her vantage point atop a small rise, she couldn't see a house, barn, fence, or even a utility pole. The only sign of civilization was the road itself.

She'd definitely come too far, she decided. That cluster of buildings twenty miles or so back must have been Peyo.

But there'd been no sign. And it hadn't even occurred to her that such a tiny place warranted a dot on a map. But then De Baca County needed all the dots it could get. Only three other communities were shown on the map in an area larger than some states.

She turned around and headed back up the road, hoping the station wagon wouldn't select this desolate stretch of roadway to die. The emptiness was intimidating.

She drove for almost thirty minutes before reaching the cluster of buildings scattered about the intersection of the gravel road and a dirt one that headed up into the foothills. The only indication that the tiny community was indeed Peyo was a faded sign over the door of the sole business establishment, a combination post office, general store, and service station. The rest of the town consisted of a tiny, boarded-up church; an untended cemetery with a dozen or so lopsided tombstones; three vintage house trailers, each with its own satellite dish; half a dozen houses, just one of which appeared to be occupied; foundations where other buildings had once stood; and two windmills. The only trees were stunted mesquite.

Peyo used to be a real town with more than two hundred folks living thereabouts, explained the postmistress/proprietor, an angular, graying woman with two missing fingers on her left hand. Forty years ago, there'd been a brief flurry of oil activity; the town had even been incorporated. But the oil gave out, and most people moved away. The ones that stayed tried to dry-farm or raise cattle. It took forty acres to support one head, but land was cheap. There were some flocks of sheep back up in the hills. Scary people, the shepherds, she said, with their matted hair and hunting knives. All total, seventy-seven people received their mail and bought supplies at her establishment.

Had there been a Vietnam vet named Cory Jones? Charlotte asked. The woman vaguely remembered the name. There had been men like that over the years. Dropouts or outcasts. Squatters mostly. A few would buy land. "Help me remember," Bessie said. "What'd he look like?"

"Blond hair. Blue eyes. Average height. Nice broad shoulders. Before the war, he was a beautiful young man. I don't know about after. He grew up in Nebraska."

"Nebraska. Yeah. He had a three-legged dog named Cornhusker. His sister called when their old man passed on. Most people out here don't have phone service and give this number for emergencies. That must have been fourteen, fifteen years back. They were going to wait the funeral so he could get home. He never came back after that. I thought maybe he'd stayed up there."

"Where did he live when he was here?"

"Lord, I haven't the faintest. All I know is folks' box numbers," Bessie said, tilting her head toward the corner of the store set aside for a post office. "Some of the loners drag an old trailer out in the backcountry. Some of them build a shack or find an abandoned one."

"Is there anyone around here who might have kept up with him?"

"I doubt it. Folks just come and go. Hardly anyone leaves a forwarding address. But you might try the VA hospital over in Albuquerque. He'd drive over there for treatment. The last time I kept his dog for him, but it ran off. I felt real bad about that."

❧ "I could claim to be his sister," Charlotte told the admissions clerk at the veterans hospital. "I'm sure her name is listed on his records as the next of kin. Cynthia Stevenson of Amity, Missouri. But the truth of the matter is, I used to be his girlfriend."

The woman pecked away on her computer. "Look, dearie, I don't care who you are or who you claim to be. I can't give out any information on patients, past or present."

"I just want to know what happened to him," Charlotte explained. "I drove all the way from Nebraska."

The clerk stared pointedly at the gold band on Charlotte's finger. "My husband died," Charlotte explained. "I didn't really drive all this way just to find Cory Jones. I came down with my daughter on vacation. His sister told me he used to live down here. She hasn't heard from him in years."

"Well, you might check at that boardinghouse out by the Vet Center. A lot of the vets used to stay there when they were in town for treatment or counseling."

The landlord remembered him. He used to pay Cory to do odd jobs; he was good at fixing things. "Guys like him drifted into town because of the Vet Center. I don't know if the counseling helped or if they just needed to hang out with other guys who couldn't let go of the war. I was in Korea, and some of us got messed up pretty bad, but nothing like Vietnam. I figure it was the drugs. I suppose there were drugs in Korea, but I never knew anyone who took them. We just drank beer when we could get it."

"Did he ever talk about his life before the war?"

"About Nebraska? Not that I can remember, except once he told me that there was no such place, which struck me as a strange thing to say."

"Did he say where he was going after New Mexico?" Charlotte asked.

The man shook his head. "He may have told me, but I doubt it. Cory didn't talk much."

❧ Every few days, Charlotte called home. The purpose of these phone calls was make sure everyone was all right and to put her mind at ease. But the phone calls were never that simple.

Vicky was having second thoughts about small-town journalism. The biggest story she'd covered to date had been a barn fire. "Did Daddy ever wish he worked for a real newspaper?" she'd asked.

"He did that in Des Moines. Your father preferred managing things. And he loved writing his column."

"I always thought I wanted to come back home and work here. If I don't do that, I'll feel like I'm letting him down."

"Your father would have wanted you to find your own way in the world, Vicky. To spread your wings. You can always come back home if it doesn't work out. Think of Newberg as your safety net."

Mark was finding his summer internship stressful but had figured out that he could make a six-figure income within five years if he was invited to join the firm. He had broken up with Sarah Grigsby and was dating a nursing student named Faith.

Vicky approved of Faith. Sort of. She was a bit uptight. "I knew he'd break up with Sarah sooner or later," she said, adding that Sarah had "been around a lot."

Shortly after Suzanne returned to Newberg, Vicky reported that her sister had moved in with her. "But she and Brady are trying to work things out," Vicky said. "They've had their first counseling session with his minister."

Charlotte's mother was a broken record, still carping about Suzanne's "shotgun wedding" and Charlotte being off God-knows-where. Bernice's house was taking forever to build. And now Suzanne wasn't even living with Brady.

"You've been gone more than a month now, spending all that money you should be putting away for your old age," Hannah chastised. "Suzanne says you're trying to find that long-haired boy you dated before you went off to college. That's not true, is it, Charlotte? That boy broke your heart."

"I had no idea you realized that," Charlotte said. "You never offered a word of comfort."

"My goodness, child, if I'd told you it was for the best, you would have gotten mad at me. If I'd told you I was sorry, you would have told me to leave you alone. So I didn't say anything. I told your father we should just let you be, and you'd get over it. I was right, wasn't I? You married Stan.

"Now, when are you coming home? I'm tired of Vicky using my car all the time. She goes to the newspaper office down in Fremont because they give her better stories to write. She hasn't driven over to see Bernice or Noreen once. And Noreen's baby is the most precious thing. Bernice is absolutely crazy about her. I keep telling Vicky she could write about things here in town. Why, only last week, the Daughters of the American Revolution had an auction to benefit their scholarship fund; but Vicky wasn't interested. She said that a fly passing wind makes news in Newberg—only she didn't say it that way. I was shocked. You didn't bring that girl up to say things like that, Charlotte. I want you to talk to her."

❧ Charlotte stayed in the Albuquerque area for three days, visiting the Pueblo ruins at Coronado State Monument, the Church of San Felipe de Neri, museums, the campus of the University of New Mexico. She liked the Old Town area best; it reminded her of Santa Fe.

Her itinerary called for her to drive south to Carlsbad Caverns, which was to have been one of the stops on the family vacation they never took. Kids love caves, Stan had said. But Charlotte decided to forgo Carlsbad this time. Her next phone call home she almost promised her mother that she'd be back within the week. Her wanderlust was lessening. Maybe she'd accomplished enough for one summer.

She drove north instead, heading for Taos, planning just to spend a day or two visiting the artist colony there that she had heard so much about. One last hurrah.

Taos somehow managed to feel authentic and be a tourist haven at the same time. The rustic little town had surprising art galleries filled with western and Native American art. Much of it was quite good; all of it was quite expensive.

She singled out a painting displayed in the window of a small gallery just off the brick-paved plaza as the one she would buy if she had the money. The painting was an impressionistic view of the Grand Canyon with two lone figures standing on the rim. Yes, if she could have one perfect memento to represent the best of this summer, it would be that painting.

The sign over the shop window promised: *Affordable Western and Indian Art.* A help-wanted sign was posted on the door.

She came back the next day to look at the painting again. The two figures were female, or at least in Charlotte's interpretation they were. Her and Suzanne—before things went bad.

She should have put off the trip to Peyo until next summer—or forgotten about it altogether. Then she and Suzanne could have gone on trekking until Charlotte had to return to her teaching duties. She would never have another chance like that with one of her children.

Only time would tell how high a price she had paid for the image Charlotte now had of an older, probably bearded Cory driving down a gravel road in an antiquated pickup with a three-legged dog at his side. She still didn't know if Cory ever thought about the long-ago summer he'd shared with her.

Cory had told his landlord in Albuquerque that Nebraska didn't exist. Was Charlotte herself included in that sweeping dismissal? She wondered if he attached any significance at all to the time he spent in Newberg. Maybe that summer hadn't been real for him, either.

Cory had backed away. Suzanne had backed away. Maybe Charlotte herself was the problem. She expected too much. Maybe it was best to float along the surface of life as her mother did, best to play bridge and be happy.

She heard the door to the gallery open. A man came out to stand beside her. "I saw you here yesterday," he said with a tentative smile and a soft drawl. "I like that picture, too. The artist isn't well known. She's only been painting for a few years—didn't start until she was past sixty. A natural. No training at all. She just picked up a brush one day and started experimenting."

The man was about Charlotte's age, maybe a little older. He had a friendly, weathered face, brown eyes, graying hair, a lean body. Clearly he hadn't spent his life indoors.

"No, she'd had training," Charlotte responded, looking back at the picture. "Sixty years' worth."

"Are you interested in buying it?"

"No. Everything in this town is too rich for my blood. But that painting is my favorite of all the ones I've seen. It's me and my daughter. It's the summer I dared to go someplace."

"Where's your daughter now?"

"She went back home."

"Where's that?"

"Nebraska. Where's yours? You sound Southern."

"I'm from Georgia. My wife and I came out here five years ago. To start anew."

"How's it been?"

"Good until she got sick. We both love the art of the region and get a kick out of finding new talent. The fishing and skiing are great."

"I noticed your help-wanted sign. I have to go home the end of the summer, but I could work until then."

"You know anything about art?"

"Not really."

"Neither do most of the tourists. What do you do back in Nebraska?"

"Teach language arts to junior high students."

"I can't pay much."

"It doesn't matter. I've lived in the same little town my entire life, and I'd like to see what it feels like belonging someplace else—even if it's just for a little while."

He reached out to shake her hand. "I'm Lonnie Daniels. My wife is Marie. She still comes in when she can."

❧ Marie Daniels made a few phone calls and found Charlotte a place to stay nearby—an upstairs room with its own outside door, a hot plate, and small refrigerator. A previous occupant had been an artist, judging from the splatters of paint on the floor by the room's only window, which offered a fine view of the mountains. The *Sangre de Cristo* range, the Blood of Christ—arid, rocky mountains with no pine trees or grassy meadows to dress them up, yet they were stately and stunning in their own harsh way.

Charlotte put away her clothes, pushed the furniture into an arrangement that suited her, with the table in front of the window. She bought a flowered tablecloth and a pot of ivy to make her residence for the next six weeks seem more homelike. That night, she ate a peanut butter sandwich and drank wine with a book propped in front of her. All that was missing was a radio. She'd buy that tomorrow.

She left the window opened and slept under a blanket. Back home in July, she'd be sweating. She felt good about being here, good about Taos and the Daniels.

Marie was dying. Charlotte could see that in her ashen skin, her wasted body, her thinning hair. Watching Marie and Lonnie was like watching herself and Stan—the hovering spouse, the dying mate. Maybe it was crazy for her to subject herself to that all over again, but she was not uncomfortable around them. She didn't have to look away. Didn't get tears in her eyes.

Marie sensed her acceptance and asked why.

"My husband was sick for a long time," Charlotte explained.

"Did you mind taking care of him?"

"No. We got through it together."

Every day at the gallery meant different faces—a continual parade of tourists from all over the country and even the globe. It was incredibly strange and exciting for Charlotte after a lifetime of seeing the same people day after day, year after year. At first, heavy accents and foreign tongues intimidated her—she was too provincial, too monolingual—but she soon learned to relax and watch the faces that spoke to her, pay attention to body language. She was able to understand whether they were looking for something grand or just a souvenir. She could read their tastes and sensibilities from their clothing and jewelry, from the way they gravitated to certain pictures.

"I like to watch you with people," Lonnie said. "You're more interested in the people themselves than in selling them something, but you sell them something anyway. It's amazing."

Charlotte felt a flush rise in her neck and cheeks. She liked Lonnie. His praise felt good.

He spent afternoons in the store, and Charlotte looked forward to seeing him, to talking with him. She asked questions about the artists and the art; he brought her books to read. He asked her about Stan; she was able to tell him things she'd never told anyone. That she wasn't a saint, that at times she'd wanted him to die and get it over with. But there were other times, when she crept over to his bed in the night to make sure he was still alive, and she would be weak with relief that he was still with her.

Lonnie was healthy. His thighs and buttocks were firm under his jeans. His arms and hands were tan and strong. In her bed at night, Charlotte read herself to sleep rather than allow her mind to stray into thoughts of Lonnie.

During her free time, she visited the other galleries. And

walked—morning and evening, quickly learning her way around. At night, she read the books Lonnie had loaned her. She learned about Western art and its icons; about Remington and Russell, Hurley and Bierstadt. She loved sleeping in the cool night air, loved getting up in the morning. She didn't want the summer to end.

chapter sixteen

At first glance, the young man made her think of Cory, but later she realized it was just that he wore his blond hair pulled back in a ponytail, and his body was long and lean. Unlike Cory, this man had brown eyes, and his cheekbones were more prominent, his mouth fuller.

He was an artist, wanting to show some of his work. He would need to talk to one of the proprietors, Charlotte told him as she bustled about the store, closing blinds, getting ready to lock up for the night.

The young man showed no sign of leaving. He leaned against the counter and chatted. His name was Jason Piper. He taught junior high art in Shreveport and had spent last summer in Taos—he and his wife. She hadn't come this year. His dream was to someday support himself painting. "I don't want to do tourist stuff, but I don't want to spend the rest of my life in a junior high school, either," he told her. His drawl was less pronounced than Lonnie's. He offered to buy her a drink.

Charlotte had to replay his words. *He wanted to buy her a drink?* "You don't need to do that," she said. "Just tell me how to get in

touch with you, and I'll set up an appointment with one of the own-
ers."

He gave her a phone number, then said, "I know I don't *need* to
buy you a drink, but I'd like to. I've told you all about me. Now it's
your turn."

He was Mark's age—maybe a year or two older—not someone
she'd feel comfortable with in a bar. "I have plans," she announced
and pulled her purse from under the counter.

He opened the front door and waited while she turned off the
lights. "Just one drink," he said with a lopsided smile. "I know
where they make the best margaritas on the planet."

Charlotte felt stiff walking along beside him and kept switching
her purse from one shoulder to the other. *Calm down,* she told herself. *He's just being nice—probably killing time until he meets
some friends.*

The bar was little more than a shack, with board tables and the
floor littered with peanut hulls. The margaritas were not so much
extraordinary as large, served in tall, heavy glasses. He asked her
about herself. Charlotte made her answers brief: a recently widowed
schoolteacher from Nebraska, three grown children, her first real
vacation.

"You must be older than I thought," he said, giving her face a
careful appraisal.

Charlotte resisted the urge to fluff her hair, to pull out a com-
pact and put on some lipstick. "Yes," she acknowledged. "Unless
you're a lot older than you look, I'm old enough to be your
mother."

"And it bothers you to be sitting here with me?"

"A little," she admitted. "I'd hate for anyone to get the wrong
idea."

He flashed a mischievous grin. "And what idea would that be?"

Charlotte reached for a peanut. "You know good and well what I
mean. I'd hate for anyone to think I was . . ." She paused, not sure
how to phrase the statement. "I'd hate for anyone to think I had de-
signs on you."

"Do you know any of these people?" he asked, indicating the bar's other clientele with a wave of his hand.

Charlotte didn't bother to look around. Of course, she didn't know anyone. But it would make her uncomfortable even for strangers to think that a woman her age was coming on to the young man sitting beside her. Her entire life had been spent caring about what people thought. Every choice she made was filtered through that overriding concern. Even when she decided not to go to church, she had to weigh her desire to stay home with her concern for what people would think. "If I were back home I wouldn't be sitting in a bar with you," she explained. "Why should I break the rules now just because I'm away from home?"

He shrugged. "Because they aren't your rules?"

"Ah, but some of them are. Look, I'm sure you are a nice young man, but I don't feel comfortable being here with you. So I am going to finish my drink and go home. And you are going to go out into the night and be young."

He shook his head. "Sometimes I don't feel so young—not anymore," he said, suddenly serious.

"Problems at home?" Charlotte asked.

He nodded. "My wife found someone she likes better."

"And you're still in love with her?"

"I'm not sure," he said, absently picking the encrusted salt from the rim of his glass. "I just wish I could stop thinking about her."

Charlotte sighed and offered a sympathetic nod. She knew how that was. "I was jilted once, and it took me years to get over him," she said, then paused and regarded the young man sitting beside her. "You remind me of him. When you first came in the store, I had to catch my breath. But of course, he'd be my age now."

"Did he find someone else?" Jason asked.

"I'm not sure. I think he just got messed up in Vietnam. But whatever the reason, it was a bad time for me. Even after I got married, I had a hard time not thinking about him."

"Did you love your husband?"

"Oh, yes. A great deal. Stan was a wonderful man."

Jason leaned forward. "But now you get to take a vacation for the first time in your life," he challenged.

"Hey, you've got it all wrong," she said, bristling a bit. "He was sick for years. Vacations were out of the question."

Jason sat back in his chair. "That must have been rough for both of you. But now you are spreading your wings."

"Yes, and it's been lovely," she admitted. "I've lived in the same town my entire life, and now I'm living someplace else. It's just for a few weeks, but I feel myself changing. My children think I should stay home and grieve. They think it's not fair that I'm getting to do things their father never could do. And I do feel guilty some of the time."

He lifted his glass. His eyes were deeply, wonderfully brown. "Life is complicated," he offered.

Charlotte smiled. "I'll drink to that," she said and took a sip of her drink. She didn't object when he ordered a second round.

Such a shabby little bar. Such an unlikely companion. But she felt herself relaxing—this woman living someplace else. *Spreading her wings.* She liked the analogy and the young man. He was easy to talk to, easy to be with. She risked a glance around the bar. Not one single person was paying a bit of attention to them. They were just a man and a woman having a drink.

They talked—on and on they talked. She told him about the first time she saw Cory at the local swimming pool, how they spent a glorious summer together, how his letters stopped coming. She told him about driving out to Cory's grandparents' house in the middle of a snowstorm to revisit that other place and time. She was amazed at all the things she told him. She realized with a start that she'd never told her husband the things she was now telling a stranger in a bar.

And Jason told her about Tessa. They had gone together since the sixth grade. She wanted him to be a doctor or a lawyer, but she married him anyway, thinking he would eventually come around. She said she wanted a showplace home and financial security, but in the end the guy she left him for was a tennis bum.

Charlotte told him about marrying Stan on the rebound, about the years of his illness, about driving to Topeka to meet his first wife.

Jason's surgeon father wanted him to go to medical school and was embarrassed to have an artist for a son. He didn't know how his mother felt about him. She never offered an opinion on anything.

They switched from margaritas to beer, and about ten o'clock they ordered hamburgers. She told him about Suzanne's marriage and selling the house. He said he was losing faith in his talent—maybe teaching junior high kids and judging the annual senior citizens' art show was the best he'd ever do.

The bar closed at two A.M. Charlotte was almost too tipsy to walk. Jason couldn't remember where he'd parked his Jeep. They helped each other up the stairs to her apartment, and she gave him a pillow and a blanket before falling across her bed.

She awoke to sunlight streaming through the window and an unbelievable headache. It hurt to open her eyes, to move, to think. She'd had too much to drink before, but the effect had been nothing like this.

With a minimum of movement, she carefully looked over the side of the bed. Jason was still there, a pillow under his head. A sleeping boy. Even with her throbbing head, she could appreciate the youthful beauty of him.

She knew she couldn't possibly go to work. If she got out of bed, her head was going to burst open. But she had to go to the bathroom, and Lonnie was counting on her to open the gallery.

When she emerged from the bathroom, still in bad shape but more able to function, Jason was curled in her bed, a blanket over his head. She left him there.

Lonnie showed up at the gallery about noon. His face was drawn. Marie had had a bad night, he said. The doctor had diagnosed her with pneumonia and put her in the hospital for a few days.

"You don't look so hot yourself," he commented.

"I went drinking. Remind me never to do it again."

"Anyone I know?"

"No. He's an artist who came in yesterday. I told him you'd look at his pictures. I hope that's all right?"

"I suppose. Is he any good?"

"I haven't the faintest idea."

Charlotte went out briefly for lunch and brought back a sandwich for Lonnie. Then she tidied the small room he used as an office and fixed him a cup of tea. She wanted to do more—like massage away the tightness in his neck and shoulders, smooth the furrows in his brow. She wouldn't let herself think of him alone in his house tonight, with Marie in the hospital.

Jason stopped by about four, looking even younger with his hair hanging loose about his shoulders. He'd brought two paintings and photographs of other works. The paintings were too stark for Charlotte's taste, but they did capture the color and sweep of the landscape. "Not bad," Lonnie commented and asked what price range Jason had in mind. Jason left the paintings; Lonnie would take others if they sold. The two men shook hands. Jason smiled shyly at Charlotte as he left, going only as far as a bench across the street.

Lonnie noticed. "Looks like you've made a conquest," he said.

Charlotte shook her head. "He's just a kid."

"And you're a lovely older woman. It's not unheard of."

Charlotte busied herself with cleaning fingerprints off the showcase of Indian jewelry. "I'm not interested in an escapade with a younger man, but I can't wish for what I want," she said.

"I know," Lonnie said softly, coming closer, putting a hand on her shoulder. "It's the same for me, Charlotte."

She stopped dusting and met his gaze. They were so alike—two people who had put living and passion on hold for a very long time. She wanted to take his careworn face in her hands and kiss his eyes, his forehead, his lips. She wanted to soothe and succor him, to be with him in every way that she could. This was a man she could love, but that was a threshold she would never allow herself to cross.

"Maybe I should just pack up and go home," she said.

"No. Please, don't do that. Marie would wonder why, and you can't imagine what pleasure it gives me just to be with you a few hours every day."

She looked out the window at Jason sitting on the bench, his impossibly young face lifted to the sun. Lonnie followed her gaze. "Go with him," he said, his voice little more than a whisper. "It will makes things easier for both of us."

Then he left the shop—to be with his wife, whom he loved, just as Charlotte had loved Stan. She stood in the middle of the gallery and began to weep. Then she shook herself. This was her summer away from home, and she'd had enough of tears and tragedy.

Jason was still there an hour later when she locked the door. She walked over and stood in front of him. "I've been thinking about you all day," he said softly. "I'd like to spend what's left of the summer with you."

Charlotte shook her head. "I can't."

"But why? What would be the harm?"

She touched his cheek, and he wrapped his arms around her thighs, burying his face against her belly. She stroked his fair hair. Clean hair. Had he washed it in her shower? With her shampoo? How long had he lingered between her sheets?

She sat down beside him and took both his hands in hers. "You don't understand," she explained. "You're the same age as my son. And you're too much like that boy from long ago. Besides, I couldn't bear to have you look at me. I have stretchmarks and sags."

"I have an appendicitis scar and a hard-on," he responded. He looked like an earnest schoolboy who had come up with the correct answer for his teacher. Charlotte giggled. Then laughed. He was laughing, too. The laughter felt delicious.

"Let's have dinner," she said, putting off a decision about what, if anything, would come later. "But not so much drinking tonight."

"Yeah. No hard stuff."

"And food. I just realized my headache finally is gone, and I'm actually hungry."

But over dinner she grew reticent.

"What are you thinking about?" Jason asked.

Charlotte had put down her fork and was staring at the candle flame inside its hurricane chimney. The restaurant was housed in an ancient adobe building, their table in one of a maze of small dining rooms. "Lots of things," she answered, "like is it right for me to be with one man when I would prefer another, and what my children would think, and how long it's been."

"Since you had sex?"

She nodded.

"How long?"

"More than three years."

"Too long," he said and ran his fingers over the back of her hand.

She closed her eyes to relish the shiver that ran the length of her body. "All my life I've thought that sex had to mean something," she said. "It had to be about everlasting love and fidelity and family."

"Don't you think that once in your life you're entitled to do it just for fun?" he asked.

"I think I'd like that, but maybe it's too late for me."

"You're not going to eat the rest of that, are you?" he said, nodding at her plate.

She shook her head, and he called for the check. They stopped at a liquor store and bought a bottle of Merlot, which they drank sitting on the top step of the stoop outside her second-floor apartment. The moon was huge and orange, with stars scattered about like glitter spilled on a navy carpet. They speculated about life in the universe and what they would take along on a space voyage. He would take a sketchpad and charcoal. She would take books and an empty journal.

His arm was around her shoulders; her hand was resting on his thigh. The wine made the blood in her veins feel warm. She wanted to ask him if he'd ever made love with an older woman before. But what if he said, yes, dozens of them? What if he said he did it all the time? Then she'd have to send him on his way. Maybe sex didn't have to be profound, but she didn't want it to be trivial, either. And she did want to have sex with him—very much, she wanted to.

When the bottle was empty, they floated inside to her bed. Oddly enough, she took the lead, caressing him endlessly, taking his hand and placing it where she wanted it, kissing and touching him at will. "Are you having fun yet?" he asked.

Was she? She was never going to marry this man, never have his children, never have a committed relationship with him, or even see him again after summer's end. Her family would be appalled at what she was doing, but they were almost a thousand miles away. Pastor Jenson would say they were committing adultery, which they probably were since Jason was only separated from his wife and not divorced. And having sex with this man was certainly the single most outrageous act of her entire life. "Oh, yes," she told young Jason Piper from Shreveport. "I'm having the time of my life."

Their third night together, he insisted on turning on the lamp and examining her stretchmarks. They weren't so bad, he told her, and in what was supposed to be a tender gesture, he began kissing the web of silvery lines that had erupted across her belly when she was pregnant with Mark. But the kisses tickled. She squirmed away from him and demanded to see his appendectomy scar, only to discover that his flat belly was seamless. "You lied to me," she said indignantly. "Only about the scar," he pointed out.

&❧ They had a month together.

When she had the afternoon off, they bought picnic fare and drove into the mountains, where he would select a vista, and she would watch while he sketched and took photographs.

Evenings, they sometimes went to the crumbling, two-room adobe house he had rented on a hillside east of town, and he would show her what he'd painted that day. Then they would climb the ladder to the flat adobe roof and drink Mexican beer while they watched the sun sink behind the mountains.

Sometimes they ate out, but often they went to her place, where they would eat carry-out meals and talk and make love and then talk some more.

As delightful as the sex was, for Charlotte the talking was just as exhilarating in its way. She hadn't talked this intently with anyone since Cory. She and Jason talked mostly about themselves, which was narcissistic, Charlotte supposed, or perhaps just therapeutic. She even told him about her feelings for Lonnie. Jason said he couldn't decide if he ever wanted to see his wife again. For this brief period in time, they became as close as two people could be. Maybe such intimacy was possible only because it wasn't expected to endure. For the most part, Charlotte accepted their time together as a lovely gift.

The only flaw was Jason's tardiness.

One night she waited for more than an hour on the bench across the street before giving up. Obviously he'd forgotten. Or maybe he'd fallen off a mountain.

He rounded the corner in his Jeep just as she reached the end of the block. He hopped out and opened the door for her. "Great evening, isn't it?" he said. "What should we do for dinner?"

Charlotte stood on the sidewalk, waiting for him to explain why he'd been delayed, waiting for him to apologize.

"Something wrong?" he asked.

She walked away. He followed, of course. They talked about it. He said he was sorry that she was upset. He hadn't realized she was such a stickler for punctuality. "You mean, other people don't mind if you keep them waiting one hour and ten minutes?" she asked.

"Look, I came, didn't I?"

That night she sent him on his way and ate cheese and crackers for dinner. The next day, they started anew. He was never an hour late again, but he was never on time, either. She refused to meet him places, knowing she'd find herself sitting in a bar or restaurant by herself, feeling conspicuous.

"Then don't be so punctual," he said when she complained, which struck Charlotte as ridiculous. What was the point of establishing an appointed hour when he was going to ignore it? Perhaps it was the difference in their ages. Or maybe it was a cultural thing. In Nebraska, people were punctual. Maybe in Louisiana, time didn't matter so much. And after all, Taos was a timeless sort of place.

Still, his tardiness felt like disrespect. He didn't have enough regard for her to keep track of the time, to put away his paintbrushes and show up when he said he would. Maybe his wife felt the same way and went off with a man who didn't keep her waiting.

As Charlotte waited for him one evening on the stoop, she tried to convince herself that she was enjoying this time of solitude, that she could rise above the irritation that buzzed about her brain like a bumblebee.

In an attempt to even the score and make his shortcoming more palatable, she tried to think of things she did that probably irritated Jason. She was impossibly tidy. She had no appreciation of the Rolling Stones. She walked too fast.

And there in the middle of her musing, thoughts of Cory abruptly pushed their way into her mind—irritating thoughts. Every minute of that long-ago summer had not been perfect.

Yes, there was lots of talking that summer, but she had done most of it, planning their future together, imagining their future home and family, with Cory only half-listening. Maybe not listening at all, she realized now.

And Cory almost never said her name. He called her "kid" or "kiddo." Not even when they made love had he said her name, even after she asked him to. She'd told herself it didn't matter, that it was kind of cute.

But it was never intimate, she realized all these years later. Consciously or subconsciously, Cory had felt the need to depersonalize her, to make her just another girlfriend. Even his letters from Vietnam addressed her as "kiddo." And they weren't love letters. They were about food and buddies and the countryside, the kinds of letters that he could have copied over and sent to anyone, even his parents. Or maybe it was the other way around. Maybe he'd copied their letters to send to her. Only at the end would he write endearments, saying that he thought about her at night, saying that she was a wonderful girl.

By the time his first letter had arrived with an address where she could write to him, she had a packet of letters waiting to send. Hers were nightly letters filled with passion, graphically spelling out her need for him. She told him how she wanted to make love to him. How she touched herself every night in her bed, imagining that he was there with her. She lived for the minute she would be in his arms again. She loved him more than life itself. All she wanted in her whole life was to make love to him every night and to have his babies—she told him all that.

After reading that first letter from Cory, however, she destroyed those letters and began writing chatty ones more in keeping with the tone of his. Only at the end would she tell him of her undying love, of her total inability to love any boy but him.

Now it was thirty years later, and here she was in Taos, New Mexico, waiting for a tardy young lover and remembering how she had longed to hear her name coming from Cory's lips and how disappointing his letters had been.

But she was certain that she had loved Cory and knew she had suffered for years from the pain of losing him. For so long, even after she was a wife and mother, she had prayed he might still come back to her. Later she'd simply hoped that someday she would see him again.

Suddenly dizzy, Charlotte leaned forward to put her face in her hands. If Cory hadn't been as wonderful as she remembered, then how could she have suffered so when he didn't come back? How could her heart have been so completely broken? Had it never been real? Had she done that to herself?

With time she had exorcised the ghost of Cory from her marriage and had learned to love her husband, but she had never adored Stan the way she had Cory, had never wanted to open him up and live inside of him.

And Stan had lived under the shadow of his lost Elizabeth. In all that time they had never crawled through the brambles and found their way to each other's souls.

She stayed hunched over for a long time, adjusting her image of that other time, feeling again the small but real hurt of a boy who would not say her name, of the long-awaited letters that didn't fill her up.

After a time, she realized that Jason was standing at the bottom of the steps, looking up at her. "Are you okay?" he asked.

She nodded and smiled.

"Sorry I'm late," he said.

"That's okay. And actually I need to sit here for a minute more. Would you go inside and get me a glass of wine?"

chapter seventeen

Jason was leaving Taos first. His father wasn't well, he explained. He needed to get organized for the upcoming school year, and he might try to arrange an exhibition of his Taos paintings at a Shreveport gallery, although he wasn't sure they were good enough.

"Your wife called, didn't she?" Charlotte asked. They were sitting in the square, people-watching. It was a beautiful evening, just cool enough for a sweater.

"How did you know?"

Charlotte shrugged. "You got distracted." She touched his cheek. Such a nice face. "I hope it works out for you—and Tessa."

He left two days later, stopping to say good-bye on his way out of town. They stood by his Jeep, searching for words to fit such an occasion. "It's been quite a summer, hasn't it?" he said. "Will you come back next year?"

"I don't know," she said, putting a reassuring hand on his arm. "It's okay that it's over, Jason. It's supposed to be."

"No regrets?" he asked, a frown creasing his young brow. He looked at her intently, her answer obviously important to him.

"No regrets," Charlotte said.

"I'm going to miss you," he said.

"And I will miss you. I wish you love and success, Jason Piper. Someday, I want to pick up a magazine and read about this incredible landscape artist from Louisiana who has taken the art world by storm."

He smiled, and they embraced one last time. She waved as he backed out of the driveway. She could feel herself tearing up just a bit. Jason was a sweet, worthy man. She hoped that Tessa had figured that out.

It was early, so she took the long way to work. *An uncomplicated summer romance,* she thought as she strode along, smiling. She hadn't realized she was capable of such a thing, and with a younger man, no less—a *much* younger man.

A week later, saying good-bye to Lonnie and Marie was much more difficult. She probably would never see Marie again. She was confused about Lonnie.

As a parting gift they gave her the painting of the Grand Canyon that she had admired that first day, and she choked up with emotion.

"Go," Marie said, pointing toward the door. "Take our love and thanks and go back to your Nebraska."

"I'll never forget you both," Charlotte said, hugging Marie's frail body. It was just skin over bones, as Stan's had been.

Lonnie carried the painting out to the station wagon.

"I've been in touch with a doctor at the Baylor Medical Center in Houston," he said. "There's an experimental program there that Marie may be eligible for, and I'm trying to talk her into one more try. Maybe we can buy a few more years." He paused, looking back at the gallery. "It's just now starting to pay off. Some of the artists we've found are starting to make a name for themselves. She deserves the chance to see it all happen, and I refuse to imagine life without her." He abruptly ran out of words and lifted his hands in a helpless little gesture.

They shook hands. He opened the car door for her. Then she drove away.

She watched him in the rearview mirror until she turned the corner. Then she pulled over and put her head against the steering wheel.

"Live on, dear Marie," she whispered. "Don't die yet if you can help it."

❧ She allowed herself three days for the drive home. She needed transition time between Taos and Newberg, time to leave summer behind.

She connected to Interstate 40 at Raton, stopping to spend the afternoon at the race track and eat one more meal of hot and spicy New Mexico cuisine before returning to blander midwestern fare.

Everything had been different in Taos—the food, liquor, music, architecture, people, weather, scenery. And the freedom.

The second day, she drove only as far as Colorado Springs, visiting the futuristic campus of the Air Force Academy. She was fascinated by the young men and women marching about with their military bearing and uniforms. They had opted for a carefully orchestrated world, full of rules and regulations, which, as Charlotte thought about it, wasn't all that surprising. Except for two widely separated summers, she'd lived a pretty uniform life herself.

The next afternoon she spent at the Denver Museum of Art, gravitating to the art of the American Southwest, viewing firsthand some of the paintings pictured in the books Lonnie had loaned her.

Then it was time to head home.

As she crossed the state line, she was greeted by a sign welcoming her to "the good life," and she burst out singing the NU fight song: "There *is* no place like Nebraska . . ."

Indeed, her state was special. Not majestic and mysterious like the mountains and desert perhaps, but an open, honest land where people put down roots and got to know their neighbors.

❧ Late that afternoon, however, as she drove into Newberg, she felt as though she'd been away for years. The town seemed smaller, plainer, even a bit alien. A man waved from his truck, and it took Charlotte a full minute to realize it was Sam Haag, the custodian at the high school for as long as Charlotte could remember.

On a whim, she drove by the old house—the first time she'd done so since she'd moved out. With the porch gone, it didn't look like the same house. But she decided the new windows and paved driveway were nice. She wondered if they'd redone the kitchen.

She looked up at Stan's corner window and felt a swell of emotion. Dearest Stan. She really had loved him. She just wished they could have known each other better.

At her little house by the Methodist church, George was doing sentry duty on the front porch and watched intently as the station wagon pulled into the driveway. The instant that recognition dawned, he raced down the steps barking, his tail wagging furiously. The screen door flew open, and Mark and Vicky came rushing out. Hannah followed.

Mark was an unexpected pleasure. He'd driven over to welcome his mother home. Charlotte was touched.

The mother in her came flooding back as she embraced her two older children. How beautiful they were. How much she loved them. How good it felt to have her arms around them.

Then she saw Suzanne, standing on the front porch with her grandmother and another girl. Mark's new girlfriend, Charlotte supposed. Warily, Charlotte approached her youngest child. Suzanne stayed put, making her mother come to her.

She did not return Charlotte's embrace, did not respond as her mother touched her cheek and stroked her hair. Charlotte felt the heavy pain of rejection.

"Well, you finally came home," Hannah said when her turn came for an embrace. "I hope you got whatever it was out of your system."

Mark's girlfriend, Faith, was a nursing student. Mark was nervous, apparently concerned about the meeting between his unconventional mother and the wholesome-looking blond beauty with a dainty gold cross at her throat.

They all helped carry Charlotte's things inside. Nothing was said about Brady.

Charlotte lingered upstairs to freshen up and snoop around a bit to see if Suzanne was still living in the house with Vicky. She was. In the third bedroom she spotted a wicker dog basket in the corner.

Vicky's possessions were boxed up and waiting to be carried downstairs. Suzanne was driving her to Lincoln Monday morning to begin her senior year. Mark was moving back to Lincoln from Omaha to begin his last year of law school.

Vicky had cooked dinner: chicken and dumplings, green beans, tossed salad; even a rhubarb pie. Suzanne sat quietly by, allowing Faith to help her sister serve the meal. "Is this a serious relationship?" Charlotte asked her son while Faith and Vicky were in the kitchen dishing up dessert.

Hannah sat up straighter, awaiting her grandson's answer.

Mark nodded solemnly. "She's a wonderful girl—almost too good to be true."

"Which means she won't let him go all the way," Suzanne interjected. "He screwed his brains out with sexy Sarah, then dumped her because she wasn't pure. God, what a hypocrite my brother turned out to be. But at least we don't need to worry about a hurry-up wedding with our virginal little Faith, do we? Her tummy will be flat as a pancake inside her bridal finery."

Hannah gasped.

"Good grief, Suzanne, what's gotten into you?" Charlotte demanded.

"You wouldn't talk like that, young lady, if your father were still alive," Hannah informed her granddaughter.

Suzanne shrugged. "You're probably right, Grandma."

After dinner, Charlotte gave each of her children a different framed print by the same well-known Navajo artist; she gave her mother a small turquoise broach. Mark helped her hang the picture of the Grand Canyon over the mantel. "That's you and me, Suzanne," she said proudly. "I fell in love with the painting the first minute I saw it."

Suzanne was sitting cross-legged on the floor with George. "Did you find your old boyfriend?" she asked.

Faith looked to Mark for explanation. His expression was stricken. Vicky stood abruptly, dropping her gift, the glass shattering. "I'll get the glass replaced," she told Charlotte, kneeling to pick up slivers of glass. "Right away. It's a great picture. Come on, Suzanne. It's time to do the dishes."

Charlotte waited until her daughters were out of the room before turning to Faith. "I went to a town where a man I once knew lived back in the eighties. Suzanne didn't approve. That's why she came home before I did. And no, he doesn't still live there. I don't know where he lives. I haven't seen or heard from him in thirty years."

Faith nodded and glanced over at Mark.

"Come on, Grandma," Mark said, standing. "Faith and I will take you home and head on back to Omaha."

❧ "I thought you were going to show me the house where you grew up," Faith said.

"Some other time," Mark said as the Newberg city limits sign flew by.

"Are you upset?"

"Yeah, you might say that. My family has gotten a bit dysfunctional."

"I'm sure everything will work itself out," Faith said soothingly, reaching over to pat his arm. "Vicky says that Suzanne and her husband are seeing their minister once a week for counseling. And now that your mother has gotten this trip out of her system, she'll settle down again. You'll see. You told me yourself she's a very devout woman." Faith paused a minute before continuing, as though debating her next words. "Was he really an old boyfriend—the man she was looking for?"

Mark glanced over at her—pretty Faith, with her peaches and cream complexion and smooth blond hair. Her lipstick and fingernails were pink. Her dress was blue. She wore blue a lot, he realized. Baby blue, the color of her eyes. And he'd never seen her without the gold cross at her throat. He wondered if she wore it to bed, if she would wear it the first time she went to bed with a man. But of course she would. It would be her wedding night. A sacrament. He thought of Sarah, who engaged in lust, not sacraments. "I don't think it was her only reason for taking the trip, but yes, I guess my mother was looking for an old boyfriend. Does that bother you?" he asked.

"A little. Of course, she is a widow, so it's not immoral or anything like that. Just a little strange. A woman her age. She seems more normal than that."

"What's normal?"

He felt her gaze but kept his eyes on the road. "Are you teasing me?" she demanded.

"No. Just curious. What is your perception of a normal woman?"

"Well, you know. A woman who doesn't do weird things."

"Maybe what my mom did isn't so weird. I have an old girlfriend I think about sometimes. Maybe in thirty years I might want to find out what happened to her, especially if I wasn't married anymore."

"But you're a man. That's different."

"Why?"

"Women are wives and mothers. They have to be better than men. Holier."

"Faith, I'm not sure I'd be comfortable around a holy woman."

She sat up straighter, her hands clutched more tightly in her lap. "Then why are you going with me?"

Mark felt ill. Why indeed?

But then he knew exactly why. He was ambitious. He had a specific goal that he'd never told to anyone, not even Sarah—most of all Sarah. She would have laughed at him and called him a silly boy. He wanted to be a United States senator by the time he was forty. Sarah was beautiful and smart, but she drank too much and laughed too loudly. Sarah believed first and foremost that life should be enjoyed. Sarah liked to tell bawdy jokes and go without a bra. Sarah was outrageous and sexy. Sarah had a past. She was not the right woman for him, not for a man with his ambition. Faith was the right woman. Faith was impeccable.

But he knew that marriage to Faith would not put an end to thoughts of Sarah. No other woman would ever excite him the way Sarah had.

Was that how it had been with his mother? She married the good man but never forgot the other guy? Mark wanted to deny that. Except for his father's illness, he'd always thought his parents had had the ideal marriage.

He didn't want to think of his mother as a sexual being. Probably no son did. He wanted her to be a saint. But could he have loved a saint the way he loved his mother? When his dad died, Mark had been overcome with grief. His only comfort was that at least it hadn't been his mother who died.

❧ After the dishes were washed and put away, Charlotte insisted that Suzanne join her for a walk. George came along without being asked.

They walked down Main Street through the deserted downtown and circled the football stadium in silence before Charlotte asked, "Are we going to be enemies?"

Suzanne leaned against the stone wall that had been built around the field back in the WPA days. George went sniffing around in the grass. The single pole light cast a yellowish glow. "I've been tending Daddy's grave," she said.

"And you think I should have stayed home all summer to trim

the grass around his tombstone and keep it supplied with floral tributes?"

"Grandma tends to Grandpa's grave."

"Yes. Between the card games and the trips to Council Bluffs, the widows in her crowd all check up on each other to see if anyone is shirking their duty. How's Brady?"

"Mad at me."

"What's going to happen with you two?"

"I don't know. I thought I wanted to have a marriage just like you and Daddy. Then I find out your marriage wasn't so great after all."

"On what do you base that opinion?"

"If you'd really loved Daddy, you wouldn't have sold our home. You'd want to put flowers on his grave. Did you ever think about him while you were running around looking for that man? All that time Daddy was sick, were you hoping he'd hurry up and die so you could go find your old lover and get laid?"

For the first time in her life, Charlotte slapped one of her children. And the world stood still for a ghastly, sick instant. Her cheek already turning red, Suzanne looked triumphant. Her mother was indeed a wicked witch. Charlotte's hand stung. She wanted to die.

Then the instant passed. Suzanne took off running, George chasing after, barking gleefully. And Charlotte fell to her knees in the dusty grass.

Brady was pulling into the driveway by the time Charlotte got home. Suzanne was already piling her possessions on the porch for him to load into his truck.

Charlotte walked around the house and sat on the back stoop. She'd wait there until Suzanne was gone.

In the night, Charlotte went downstairs to look at the painting over the mantel. Mother and daughter at the rim.

For a time, she and Suzanne had connected. Delicately, like a kite tethered with a gossamer thread. But it had been real.

Now, at this very minute, Suzanne was in the arms of a man she didn't love but felt responsible for, telling him she loved him, promising she would never leave again and would live in a house next door to his parents, go to his church, cook his meals, raise his children, and never want for more.

chapter eighteen

To whom it may concern:

I saw your personal ad in the classified section of the VFW magazine. I knew a Cory Jones back in the early 1980s. He fought with the First Cav down in the Delta. Seems to me he was from Nebraska or someplace up north like that. If you find him, tell him if he ever shows his face in Provost again, Big Foot is waiting.

❧ Charlotte's classroom was dusted and tidy. A bulletin board display featured the parts of speech as cartoon characters, and a message on the blackboard welcomed the students back to school. Student desks were arranged in four neat rows.

Little had changed since Charlotte herself had taken seventh-and eighth-grade English in this very room, taught by her predecessor, Miss Clara Gertsch. The students' desks had been nailed to the floor back then, the walls painted a limey shade of green. Otherwise, it was a room in a time warp.

Charlotte sat at her desk, surveying her domain. Tomorrow

morning, there would be students seated out there—new faces in the seventh-grade classes, and familiar ones among the eighth graders, back for a second year under her tutelage.

Junior high students were often human beings at their most awkward. Adolescent feet grew faster than adolescent bodies. Libido grew faster than intellect. Coolness was more prized than grades. Athletic prowess was as important to the boys as good looks, while for the girls, how they looked was everything.

Miss Gertsch had taught adolescent children for—to Charlotte's mind, at least—an incomprehensible forty-four years, but cool hadn't been invented back then, and she had managed to discipline through fear. Still Charlotte wondered how she had lasted so long.

She got up and walked around the room where she'd spent the last nine years and probably would spend many more. But she was losing energy. She hadn't bothered with potted plants this year, and she'd left the windows unadorned, deciding that the curtains she'd made five or six years ago were too faded to bother with again. Once she'd even painted the walls, and they needed it now. However, she wasn't even tempted to undertake the task.

Charlotte realized that if she had any sort of integrity at all, she would resign. A teacher should have some degree of anticipation about the beginning of a new school year and be filled with resolve to do a better job than she had the year before—not just take out the same tired lesson plans and put up the same old bulletin board displays. A teacher should want to teach and not have arrived at the profession because it offered the best opportunity for a reasonable salary in the tiny rural community where she lived. She couldn't resign, of course. She had to support herself and maintain her pension plan and health benefits.

Not that she didn't take the job seriously. What she lacked in innate teaching ability, she tried to make up for with organizational skills. She never walked into a classroom unprepared and always graded papers promptly. But she was also never spontaneous, never asked the kids what they wanted to learn. As a result, she seldom learned from them.

For the past three months, Charlotte had scarcely given a thought to her job, to facing another crop of students, putting out the biweekly school paper, supervising another yearbook staff, compiling yet another stapled-together "poetry anthology" compiled from mostly coerced, unmotivated efforts. And now, after that horrible scene with Suzanne, she felt defeated and completely devoid of the kind of enthusiasm she needed to teach her students.

What she wanted to do was get into her station wagon and drive someplace where she had no students and family, where she could once again experience life without the restrictions she felt here in Newberg, life as she had experienced it in Taos.

Charlotte realized that for the rest of her life, Taos would symbolize freedom for her. It was where she dared to take a young lover, where she learned that it was possible—at least for a time—to escape from the ties that bind.

But she would never go back there.

She had slapped Suzanne for accusing her of waiting for Stan to die so she could search for Cory Jones. Of course, she hadn't done that. Not ever. And no matter how much she cared for Lonnie Daniels, she would not allow herself to imagine a day when his wife was dead. She genuinely wanted Marie to live on into a ripe old age. Marie and Lonnie loved each other. Their love had been a beautiful thing to see. Ironically, Lonnie's love for his wife was part of what attracted Charlotte to him. It was why she could never return to Taos.

Next summer, she would take a northern route to the Pacific Ocean and avoid the temptation of New Mexico altogether. But first, she had a school year to get through, a first day to get through. She opened her lesson plan book and picked up a pencil.

She couldn't do it the same way she always had because she wasn't the same person. While she had never been so unimaginative as to ask her students to write about how they spent their summer vacation, always before she'd had them write a two-page paper about the most unforgettable day of their summer—using at least two complex sentences, two compound sentences, one compound-complex sentence, and one rhetorical question.

Last year Mildred Lamb wrote about receiving Jesus Christ as her Saviour. Billy McCurtain wrote about his grandmother's funeral. Rusty Marshall wrote about the day his parents told him they were getting a divorce. Most wrote of less remarkable happenings, like breaking a toe, or catching a big fish.

Tommy Braunsmeyer wrote about the day he saw Elvis Presley at the local swimming pool. According to Tommy's fanciful paper, Elvis had been living in a Canadian monastery learning how to chant and make sandals. The paper showed marked originality and Charlotte gave him an A, even though he had ten misspelled words and three run-on sentences, infractions that would have gotten him an F under Miss Gertsch.

Most of the children who would file into this room tomorrow were sitting in church pews right now, singing hymns and listening to sermons that emphasized blind faith, with no questions allowed. The only time Charlotte felt as though she was succeeding as a teacher was when her students challenged her, when they asked questions and demanded to know more.

She should have taught history. She'd been so pleased when Suzanne made that observation on the first day of their journey. Charlotte had enjoyed sharing her knowledge with her daughter, remembering things she thought she'd forgotten.

Even though she hadn't been given the opportunity to teach history, perhaps she could use history to bring literature alive. There was no need to separate the two. Literature, and indeed all art, was created within a historical context.

Charlotte put her lesson plan book aside and let that thought germinate while she wrote the students' names in her attendance book. Except for some of the rural children, she already knew most of them, or at least she knew the family name. Newberg was a stable community; families occasionally moved away, but not many new ones arrived.

She had started entering the third-hour names when she decided on her lesson plan: she'd have them write about an imaginary house guest who stayed with their family this summer—a figure from American history, either famous or not. A private from the Revolutionary War would be fine, or Betsy Ross, or a pioneer woman—any historical figure they wanted. What had they learned from their guest? Who was his or her favorite author? What had their friend thought of Newberg? Of the student's family? Of football and MTV? Of McDonalds and space stations? Of Stephen King and rap?

On a whim, she rearranged the student desks in a circle. No more rows. No more doing it the same way year after year.

Monday morning, while she was explaining the assignment to her first-hour class, they paid attention. It was something different. What *would* Abe Lincoln have thought of MTV? Clark Gregory asked Charlotte who she would write about if she were given this assignment. Without thinking, she said Sacagawea, the American Indian woman who led Lewis and Clark to the Pacific, a woman who had dared.

"But she never went to school," Clark pointed out. "She wouldn't have had favorite authors or poems."

"You're exactly right. The Revolutionary War soldier might not have known how to read, either. But he had favorite stories and songs. His literature was passed on by word of mouth, as Sacagawea's would have been. I would have to find out about the myths her tribe passed down through the generations."

Tommy Braunsmeyer wanted to know how long they had to complete the assignment.

"As long as it takes to get it right—within reason, of course," Charlotte said, surprising herself. Assignments were supposed to have due dates, with grades lowered for late papers. "I'll help you," she said. "We'll go to the library together. If our school library doesn't have the right books, we'll get them on interlibrary loan from other libraries."

She told them to take a week deciding who their house guest would be. "Talk to your friends or your parents or grandparents about it if you like. And your other teachers. Find a historical figure you'd like to get to know."

Tommy had decided by the next day to write about his adventures with an imaginary runaway slave named Moses. Tommy was a slight boy with freckles, crooked teeth, and a voracious appetite for books. His final book report last year had been on *War and Peace*. A thirteen-year-old who read Tolstoy deserved a brilliant teacher, Charlotte thought, not one who just went through the motions.

❧ Charlotte missed Suzanne terribly, thought about her constantly. Her longing for her daughter was a physical thing. She needed to see and touch her, to hear her voice.

Charlotte understood why her sister was so enchanted with her grandbaby. Bernice could kiss and touch the baby, feel its warmth, nuzzle its neck.

Charlotte touched Mark and Vicky more now when she saw them. She saw Vicky more frequently than Mark. In his last year of law school, he was preparing to take his bar exams and was again dating Sarah Grigsby, whom Charlotte had yet to meet. "A wild girl," Vicky said, but with less censure in her voice than before. Now in her last year of college, Vicky suddenly seemed older, more mature. Instead of moving into the sorority house, she and her roommate from last year had moved into an apartment. And she came home more often. She seemed at the same time suddenly older and more in need of her mother's presence.

The last Sunday in October would have been Stan's fifty-fifth birthday. After church, Charlotte drove to the cemetery. She had sensed that Suzanne would be there, and indeed, there she was, standing in front of her father's tombstone, crying.

"Will you talk to me?" Charlotte asked.

Suzanne's nod was almost imperceptible.

They sat on the grass, using Stan's monument as a windbreak. "I loved your father," Charlotte began. "Very much. But before him, I loved Cory Lee Jones. Cory was the first boy I'd ever loved, and I was certain I would never love anyone else in my entire lifetime. I didn't meet your father until a year after Cory had disappeared, but still I held back a part of myself from your father because of Cory. And now I realize that your father did the same—he'd been in love with someone before he met me. Our marriage was more about respect and family than passion, and we both allowed ourselves to be slightly disappointed."

"Are you still going to look for the other man?"

"I may, but only because I started something and want to finish it, not because I want to start up again with a lost love. Maybe I need to find out some things about myself. Or maybe it's just rest-lessness—an excuse to go someplace. I may never find him. It's go-ing someplace that matters. The trip this summer changed me, Suzanne. I feel like my skin has stretched to make room for all the things I've learned and felt. I want to finish the journey, my search for Cory, and maybe see what else I find out along the way."

"Do you want to marry him?"

"No. I just want to know what happened to him. Maybe he's dead or in prison. Maybe he's married with six kids."

"But Daddy had to die for you to be able to sell the house and go off like that."

"I didn't want him to die, Suzanne. You know that. I would have done anything to keep him with us. Except in passing, I hadn't thought about Cory for years, not until that picture fell out of the yearbook. I'd decided to sell the house and do some traveling long before then. But then I did start thinking about him. I needed to figure out some things so I could go forward. I'm not buried in this grave. I get to go on living, and I'm very grateful for that. I can taste life on my tongue and in my veins, and it's wonderful. Don't deny me that wonder. And don't deny yourself. If you decide to stay with Brady, you must learn to really love him. If you stay out of a sense of responsibility or sacrifice, you will be sad for the rest of your life."

Charlotte studied her daughter's face, searching for any sign of softening. "I do love him," Suzanne said, her chin high. "I just don't like being married. I miss college but know it wouldn't be the same if I went back. He wants me to get pregnant again, but I'm not sure."

"May I put my arms around you?"

Again, the little nod. And Charlotte pulled her daughter close, kissed her forehead. "Oh, God, Suzanne, my darling girl, I've missed you so!"

chapter nineteen

Hannah's quavery soprano voice rose above the others as they sang "Happy Birthday" to Donald, who stared impassively at the large cake with its fifty candles. *He could at least smile,* Bernice thought with annoyance, and transferred her gaze to her granddaughter's face. Sitting on her daddy's lap, Michelle was wide-eyed as she took in the proceedings.

No other sight brought Bernice so much pleasure as her eight-month-old granddaughter. She was captivated by the changing expressions on her precious little face. Watching her crawl about like a puppy dog, her diapered rump moving back and forth, never failed to make Bernice smile. Or watching her splash in the bathtub. Play with her toys, eat, sleep. She was so innocent. If it weren't for Michelle, Bernice wouldn't have bothered with the balloons and streamers and all those candles.

Bernice sensed her sister's eyes watching her watch Michelle and flashed Charlotte a misty-eyed smile. Bernice suspected that Charlotte thought she had crossed the line into obsession when it came to Michelle. And her new house. Maybe she had. She didn't care. If she wasn't thinking about Michelle, she was daydreaming about her wonderful house, arranging furniture in her head, visualizing window treatments, counting the days until she could finally move in. By Christmas, the contractor had promised. Almost daily, Bernice made him repeat that promise.

Bernice returned her attention to her husband as the song ended, watching him lean forward to blow out the candles. It took him two tries, but Jake whistled, and the others clapped: Noreen and Rusty; Clive, Paul, and Paul's girlfriend Missy; Hannah and Charlotte. They'd all gone to church together this morning for Michelle's christening and gathered afterwards to celebrate her granddaddy's birthday.

When the singing ended, Donald rewarded them with a quiet smile. Bernice remembered another birthday when he initiated a conga line around the table. One birthday he ate some of the candles just to make the kids squeal.

"What did you wish for, Daddy?" Noreen asked.

Donald looked puzzled. *Wish for?* Then he smiled again. "A new car," he said, which brought laughter all around. Donald drove a different vehicle from the agency almost daily.

Bernice had cooked all of Donald's favorites—pork roast, stewed apples, mashed potatoes and gravy, homemade rolls, Waldorf salad, chocolate cake. The children expected it of her. Donald had actually complimented her on the meal. "You're a wonderful cook, Bernice," he'd said. "You could have owned a restaurant." She'd felt herself blushing with the pleasure of his words.

Donald was doing better. His doctor had prescribed an antidepressant right before Michelle was born, after he'd gone days without sleeping and barely speaking, just sitting in his chair staring at the television screen. At first he refused to take the medication, but he finally agreed only if Bernice promised the children would never know. It had taken weeks, but gradually the pills began to make a difference. Donald was playing golf again; returning phone calls; cutting his toenails. He'd even suggested they all go out and look at the new house after the birthday dinner—which also pleased Bernice immensely.

She visited the house two, three, sometimes four times a day. She couldn't stay away from it. She had found every stage fascinating: excavation, pouring the foundation, framing, roofing. She read books in the subjects, and bombarded the workers with questions. She knew about studs, headers, floor and ceiling joists, top plates, ridgepoles.

She pored over wallpaper, paint, and carpet samples into the night. She'd driven all over Lincoln and Omaha, viewing houses made with this or that style, size, and color of brick—dozens and dozens of different kinds of brick. Selecting the brick had been one of the most difficult choices she'd had to make. She'd finally settled on a queen-sized, tumbled, dark red brick laid with light weeping mortar.

She hated weekends when no one was working—when nothing got done. But even on Saturday and Sunday, she would visit the construction site, inspecting every board, every nail. More than once, she insisted that subgrade lumber be ripped out. Her house was going to be perfect in every way.

Bernice wasn't alone in her fascination. The house had become a favorite stop for Sunday drivers. A photo of the half-finished hilltop house had appeared in the *Daily News* two Sundays ago, along with the architect's drawing of how the finished house would look. "Plantation House Going Up on Nebraska Prairie," the caption read.

Bernice knew that people were gossiping about the house, wondering at her excess. She didn't care. She could hardly wait to live there, to cook in the state-of-the-art kitchen, bathe in the sunken bathtub, warm herself in front of the three fireplaces, enjoy music piped throughout the house onto the terrace via a twenty-thousand-dollar sound system.

She had thought they would be living in their new home by now, but there had been weather-related delays last winter, and a delay as well in shipping the heavy steel beams needed to support the massive roof. But the house was now enclosed. She could see where the rooms would be. The windows and outside doors would be installed next week. Soaring windows. Magnificent hand-carved doors. Leaded-glass transoms and sidelight sashes. Imagine being able to open the front door and walk into the two-story entry hall! Already the carpenter was framing the curving staircase—he promised a masterpiece.

Noreen came with her sometimes; her boys less often. Donald seldom, and when he did accompany her, his only comment was that the house sure was big. He took little interest in her samples and didn't seem to care what kind of brick and flooring she used. He referred to it as *her* house. Everyone did, even Bernice herself. And it *was*. She wouldn't be earning the money to make the considerable payments, but she had conceived it and mothered it. It filled her up: the house and Michelle. She loved the rest of her family, but she was smitten with her house and her grandbaby.

Once everyone had arrived at the building site, Hannah insisted on leading the home tour, with Bernice filling in the details. Hannah was as taken with the house as Bernice. Two of Hannah's clubs—the Garden Club and the PEO—were going to have their Christmas party in Bernice's new house. Donald was sending vans from the car agency to transport the ladies from Newberg.

"Mama is so thrilled," Charlotte told Bernice as they walked out to the cars. "I think she feels like your house compensates for her embarrassment over Suzanne, which—mind you—still irritates the hell out of me."

"You still think I'm crazy?" Bernice asked, linking arms with her sister.

"I never thought you were crazy. It just wasn't something I would have done. But you're doing a splendid job. It's going to be a wonderful house," Charlotte said, looking back at the unfinished structure.

"You and the kids will come for Christmas, won't you? I want you to come as soon as school lets out to help me cook. I've already ordered a fifteen-foot tree for the entry hall. Can't you just see it standing there in the curve of the staircase? It will be the best Christmas ever."

"Without a doubt," Charlotte said.

"What would Stan have thought?" Bernice asked, glancing over her shoulder, her tone unsure.

Charlotte regarded her sister's face. The soft glow of the late afternoon sun made her look almost young again. Or maybe it was rapture over her house, or her pleasure over the improvement in Donald. Bernice hadn't looked this good in a long time. "I imagine Stan would want the Newberg Lions Club and the *Record* staff to have their Christmas parties here, too," Charlotte said. "And he probably would have written a column about his sister-in-law's fabulous house and the principle of *carpe diem*."

Bernice smiled. "I would have liked that. He was the nicest man I've ever known."

Charlotte agreed. He was that.

She and Hannah told the others good-bye at the building site. Charlotte hugged Donald last, wishing him one last "Happy Birthday."

"I'm glad Bernice has a sister like you," he said.

Hannah did most of the talking on the way home. About the house. Updates on her friends. Local politics. How Suzanne could have a new house too, if she'd get her head screwed on straight.

"Don't get started on Suzanne," Charlotte warned.

They finished the hour-long trip in silence. At first Charlotte thought her mother was angry but then realized she was just dozing.

Charlotte dropped her mother off and headed home to grade papers and enjoy a few hours of solitude. The phone rang about ten, just as she was heading up stairs. It was Noreen.

"Mom's all upset," she began. "Daddy dropped us all off after we came back from the new house, and we haven't seen him since."

"Did he say where he was going?"

"No. We got out of the van, and he just drove off. The guys are out looking for him."

"It's still early. Maybe he just went to a bar or took a drive."

"That's what I said. But Mom is certain that . . ." Noreen started to cry.

"Certain of what?" Charlotte demanded.

"Oh, God, Charlotte," Noreen sobbed. "One of Daddy's hunting rifles is missing from the gun cabinet."

Charlotte called Suzanne. "Will you go with me?"

"We'll be right there."

Then Charlotte called Mark and Vicky and told them to sit tight. She'd call as soon as she had anything to report.

Brady drove fast. Charlotte held onto Suzanne's hand. No one talked. Giving voice to their fears might make them come true.

Brady and Suzanne joined in the search, and Charlotte stayed at the house throughout the night with Bernice, Noreen, and little Michelle, making coffee, cleaning up from the birthday party. She wanted to say that surely Donald wouldn't do anything so drastic as what they were all thinking, but she didn't know what Donald would do. During the endless hours of waiting, as she thought about her brother-in-law, she realized she really didn't know him well at all. They would hug at comings and goings. Compare notes on the kids. Occasionally, they'd joke a bit privately about how Bernice spoiled the kids.

He'd been closer to Stan. They shared their love of sports, especially the state high school and college teams. After Stan was bedridden, Donald would call often to discuss this or that game and sometimes drive over to watch a special game with him on television. They talked politics some, and even got into religion on occasion, but mostly it was sports.

Donald had offered on more than one occasion to pay for a nurse to help look after Stan. And he wanted to buy a big-screen television for the bedroom. Charlotte and Stan always refused. His friendship was enough. Toward the end, Stan asked Donald to make arrangements for him: the cemetery plot, a suit of clothes for the funeral that would fit his wasted body.

Donald had grieved sincerely for Stan. And for his father, who had died not long after. But as Charlotte and Bernice talked into the night, Bernice insisted that he had started to withdraw before their deaths. Years before.

After Noreen had stretched out on her parents' bed with her fretful baby, Bernice and Charlotte sat at the kitchen table to wait. "He put up a front for the kids and relatives," Bernice said. "The rest of the time he just sat in that damned chair with a beer can and the remote control. Every time I'd suggest we talk to someone— you know, a marriage counselor or a psychiatrist—he'd get mad. That was the only thing he ever got mad about. The rest of the time, he didn't seem to have the energy for anger."

"But he ran the business. My God, Bernice, how many years now has the car agency been one of the top three in the state?"

"Yes, he ran the business. I think he must have had a remote control down there, too. Punch a button and watch something happen. But he was doing better. I swear he was, Sis. He didn't want anyone to know, but he'd been taking an antidepressant. It was working, too. He'd signed up for the annual country club golf tournament. He even patted my fanny a few times. Things were getting better. The kids are getting older. The boys haven't wrecked any cars in over a year. With the pills and the new house and Michelle, I thought everything was finally going to be okay."

"It may be yet," Charlotte said. "We don't know where he is, Bernice. Maybe he just needed to be alone."

"I hope so, Sis. If I get him back, I'll make him better, I swear I will. I'll make him see a psychiatrist. I'll push those damned pills down him like they were candy. The kids need their father. Michelle needs her granddaddy. Just think how awful that would be for him to . . ." She couldn't say the word. Charlotte didn't blame her. Such an ugly word. Unlike any other. Humanity at its most hopeless.

The sun was coming up when Charlotte heard a car door open and close. She stepped out on the front porch. The car was from the county sheriff's office. A solemn-faced deputy was coming up the walk. With a sinking heart, Charlotte knew the waiting was over.

"I'm Charlotte Haberman, Mrs. Swenson's sister. Have you found her husband?"

"Yes, ma'am. He'd driven out to the state park. One of the rangers found him. The coroner says he died yesterday evening sometime."

"Do you need to talk to my sister?"

"I'd appreciate it, ma'am."

Charlotte showed him into the living room and walked down the hallway toward the kitchen. Her feet felt as though they were made of lead.

Bernice and Noreen were feeding Michelle. Mother and daughter turned to look at her. Charlotte put a hand against the door frame for support. "A deputy is here from the county sheriff's office," she told them. There was no need to say anything more. They could see it in her face.

Charlotte kneeled between her sister and her niece, put her arms around them. "I am so sorry. So very sorry."

Noreen drew in a deep breath, then jumped up and ran out the back door. The door slammed behind her. Michelle, in her high-chair, began to cry. Bernice stood, straightened her blouse, and headed down the hall. Charlotte picked up Michelle and carried her to the sink to wash the oatmeal and applesauce from her face and hands. The water seemed to distract her, so Charlotte pulled off the little girl's nightie and diaper and sat her in a sinkful of warm water. "It's okay, sweetie," she soothed while she watched her splash. Such a pretty baby. So absolutely perfect.

Other car doors were slamming now. Bernice's boys. Rusty, Suzanne, and Brady. Mark and Vicky would be here soon. Donald's cousins. Charlotte would need to cook breakfast. Call her principal, tell him to get a substitute. And call Hannah, send someone after her.

Eventually, the whole family had assembled in the living room. Food and flowers began to arrive. The funeral director and the minister came together. The regular minister and his family were in their motor home heading for Disneyland, but the retired minister who'd baptized Donald as a baby would fill in. An appointment was made for tomorrow morning at ten to select a casket and plan the service.

Clive took the call from the towtruck operator. "He wants to know what to do with the van," he told his aunt, his voice breaking. "He said it's a real mess."

Charlotte felt a wave of dizziness and rubbed at her forehead. "Tell him to call the assistant manager at the car agency. He can figure out something."

Bernice and Noreen were able to cry. But Clive, Paul, and Jake had been taught by their father since childhood that only girls and sissies cried and were desperately trying to gulp back sobs. Their grief was more painful to watch. Finally they drifted upstairs, each to his own room, to deal with their grief in private.

Later, Jake came back downstairs and sought out Charlotte. She led him into the family room, and they sat side by side on the sofa—facing the trophies, an entire wall of them, documenting the family's achievements. "I thought he loved us more than that," Jake said. His eyes were swollen and red, the skin on his face and neck blotchy.

Charlotte reached for his hand. Dear Jake. She'd always had a soft spot in her heart for the lanky red-headed boy who wasn't athletically gifted like his father and brothers but so bright. And funny. He could do a perfect imitation of his grandmother Hannah singing "In the Garden." He insisted that football should be the official state religion in Nebraska, with beer and peanuts replacing wine and wafers as communion fare.

"Your father loved his family with all his heart," Charlotte told him, "but someplace along the way he got discouraged or disheartened. Or maybe it was a chemical imbalance in his head. We'll never know for sure. But you can't let what happened today alter the memory of all the other days you had with your father."

"I'm surprised that old twenty-two didn't misfire," Jake said, staring at the gun cabinet. "I'm sure he hasn't used or cleaned it for more than four years—when we took it on our last hunting trip. Remember how he used to take Paul, Clive, Mark, and me out all the time? He coached our Little League teams and taught our Sunday School classes. He made waffles every Sunday morning. I used to think he was the greatest dad ever."

"He was," Charlotte said. "Remember him like that."

"Is it our fault? Should we have shamed him into getting out more? Should we have taken an ax to the television?"

Charlotte put a finger to his lips. "None of that, Jake. Hindsight is never just. If any of us had seen this coming, we would have tried to do something."

Bernice refused to rest. Throughout the day, she greeted those who came to pay their respects: Donald's employees, family friends, neighbors, people from their church.

That evening, Charlotte and her daughters set out the food that had arrived during the day. Mark said the blessing, asking God to take good care of his uncle Donald and to help them through their grief.

People were starting to help themselves to the desserts when Jake began reminiscing about the hunting trips. The spitting and pissing contests. The ghost stories around the campfires. "One night Dad started pointing out constellations," Jake said. "He knew the names of constellations none of us had ever heard of and the Greek mythology behind each one. Finally he pointed to this cluster of stars and said that was the 'Wishbone' constellation and was named for an offensive maneuver the Greeks first used during a football game with the Persians—and we knew he'd been making it all up."

Then the others began telling Donald stories. His exploits on the college gridiron. How he once sold a red Cadillac convertible to a rich farmer who'd come in to buy a tan pickup truck. The way he used to dress up as Santa Claus for the school carnival and slip ten-dollar bills into the poor kids' pockets. Only Bernice had no story to tell.

After the dishes were done, they sorted out where everyone

would sleep—Vicky and Hannah would go home with Noreen and Rusty. Mark, Suzanne, and Brady would find a spare bed or sofa. And finally Charlotte was able to lead her sister up the stairs.

Bernice sat on the side of the bed. "Damn him to hell," she said.

"You don't mean that," Charlotte said, kneeling to pull off Bernice's shoes. "I'll run you a bath and find something to help you sleep."

"I do too mean it. I hate him. He couldn't even stay alive for our children. My poor babies have to go through life knowing their father blew his brains out. What kind of a man would do that to his kids?"

"A sick one," Charlotte said, sitting beside her sister, putting an arm around her broad back.

"I don't think I ever really loved him."

"Oh yes you did. You were head over heels in love with him." Bernice's wedding portrait hung by the dresser. Her dress had been snow-white. The proud virgin bride. She'd loved Donald then.

"Once maybe," Bernice said. "But it all dried up. The part of him I loved died a long time ago."

Charlotte shushed her "You're so exhausted, you don't know what you're saying. Come take a bath and let me tuck you in bed."

Bernice shook her head and stretched out on the bed. "I can't take another step. Stay here with me, will you, Sis?"

Charlotte kicked off her shoes and laid down beside her sister. Just for a minute, she thought. She'd been wearing the same clothes for more than twenty-four hours. She wanted a bath. A glass of wine. Some time to herself.

She pulled the comforter up over their legs and thought about turning off the lamp. Every bone in her body ached with fatigue. What a nightmare. It seemed worse even than when Stan died. Stan hadn't wanted to die.

"We're both widows now," Bernice said. "At least we have each other."

"Always," Charlotte said and reached for her sister's hand.

As she felt herself drifting into sleep, she thought about the huge, unfinished house presiding over its hillside south of town. A monument to nothing. She started to ask Bernice if she still wanted to live in the house but didn't have the energy. Bernice probably hadn't sorted that out yet anyway.

Charlotte awoke in the night with a start. The lamp was still on. Bernice was gone.

She got up and searched through the house, in the backyard, finally in the garage. Bernice's car was gone. It was then that Charlotte heard the sirens.

She prayed that Brady had left the keys in his truck. He had. Under the mat. Charlotte headed south, toward the glow in the sky.

The sight that greeted her was like something out of a Gothic film. There stood the manor house on the crest of a hill, engulfed in flames.

Bernice was leaning against the front of her car, at a safe distance from the inferno. Even so, the heat was intense. Sweat was running down her face. "He never wanted the damned house anyway," Bernice yelled over the roar of the flames. She smelled of gasoline.

"But you did," Charlotte yelled back.

"Not anymore."

Charlotte took her sister's arm and led her further down the slope, away from the radiating heat. They sat on the ground and watched while the roof caved in, sending a blaze of sparks to the heavens. The firemen also retreated and turned to watch the blaze.

"Do you think he killed himself so he wouldn't have to live there?" Bernice asked.

"No. I think he killed himself because he didn't want to live anywhere."

Already, a river of car headlights could be seen coming from town. The citizens of Norfolk were coming to see the "Plantation House on the Prairie" burn to the ground.

"And I'm not supposed to take it personally that he didn't love me or our children enough to hang around?" Bernice said. "I think of Stan, who would have given anything to stay with you and his kids, to watch his grandkids grow up. But Donald couldn't be bothered."

"Cut out the crap, Bernice. It's not that simple, and you know it."

"I'll never forgive him."

"That's up to you."

"I wasn't like you. There was only Donald. I never even had fantasies about other men."

"Except for Stan."

Bernice sucked in her breath, then she rolled back on the ground and began to pound the earth with her fists. "I don't understand anything!" she wailed.

Charlotte gathered Bernice in her arms just as the front wall of the house came crashing down. Charlotte could feel the impact in the ground beneath her. She watched as another spectacular display of sparks fanned out across the night sky, the heat from the blaze tightening the skin on her face. Charlotte didn't understand, either. Not anything.

Her poor sister. Her poor, poor sister.

chapter twenty

Charlotte called the house on Bernice's car phone and woke Suzanne. "Bernice and I are out at the construction site. The house is on fire."

Suzanne gasped. "On fire? I heard all those sirens. Bernice's new house? My God, what happened?"

"We'll talk about it tomorrow. I just didn't want you to worry if you realized we weren't there."

"Is it a bad fire? Will they be able to save the house?"

"No, the house is a total loss."

"Should I wake everyone?"

"No. There's nothing anyone can do. Go back to bed."

"Is Bernice okay?"

"I think so."

"What about you?"

"I will be if I ever get to take a bath and get some sleep," Charlotte said.

"Grandma will be devastated. Bernice's house was all she ever talked about." Suzanne paused. "Bernice started the fire, didn't she?"

"What makes you say that?"

"The sound of your voice. The way she didn't say anything at dinner. Why, Mom? Why would she do such a thing?"

"She didn't want the house anymore, I guess. And she didn't want anyone else to have it."

Which was only part of the truth, but Charlotte could never tell the rest. She could never explain that the house was to be her sister's reward for staying in a tired, sexless marriage. But now there was no marriage, and no husband. And Bernice couldn't bear to leave the house standing out there as an obscene reminder of the bargain with herself gone bad.

The last wall of the burning house had just collapsed when Charlotte noticed a man in jeans and a tan jacket walking toward them, his stride full of authority. She and Bernice scrambled to their feet. Charlotte knew he was a police officer before he showed his badge and introduced himself.

"Excuse me, ma'am, are you Mrs. Swenson?" he asked Bernice, his tone deferential. He was a young man but already going to fat, his shirt straining over his belly.

Bernice nodded, her gaze still fixed on what was left of the burning house—two chimneys presiding over a heap of burning rubble.

Cars and trucks were parked haphazardly about the hillside. People were sitting on hoods or wandering around, gossiping with other spectators, their faces illuminated by the fire. The scene had an oddly festive air about it. Charlotte noticed that a nearby couple had broken out a six-pack of beer.

"Is that your car?" the police officer asked, pointing toward Bernice's Cadillac.

Again she nodded.

"Do you have a car phone?"

Another nod.

"The farmer who phoned in the fire said your blue Cadillac was parked out front. He said it was the only vehicle on the property. He gave us your license number."

"Is there something you want to know?" Bernice asked.

"I was just wondering why you didn't phone in the fire and if you know anything about how it got started?"

"Yes, I know," Bernice said. "But I don't want to talk about it now."

"Yes, ma'am. I'm sorry about your husband. But I'd like for you and your attorney to come by the police station tomorrow and tell us what you can about the fire." He handed her a business card and headed back up the hill.

"But it's your house," Charlotte protested.

"No, it's not," Bernice said. She sounded exhausted. Her shoulders were slumping. "All we owned was a construction loan."

Charlotte took her sister's arm, trying to lead her away, but Bernice refused to leave until the fire had burned itself out. A funeral pyre. Charlotte was cold now, aware that she was shivering. Cold and tired—God, she was so tired.

A man took Bernice's picture as she sat on the ground watching her dream house burn. It probably would appear in the local paper tomorrow.

᪲ Donald's funeral started well enough, with the organist playing a medley of songs his family thought appropriate—including the NU fight song, "Take Me Out to the Ball Game," and "The Battle Hymn of the Republic." The service began with the reading of Donald's favorite psalm: "I will lift up mine eyes unto the hills . . . "

But when the elderly minister began his sermon, Charlotte stiffened. His tone wasn't right. He was challenging in his remarks about salvation and thou shalt not kill, quoting from Romans about the wrath of God for the unrighteous, how the just must live by faith. "And die without faith," the minister added ominously.

And now he was reading Donald's biography like an indictment, emphasizing how Donald had been given every blessing in life. His fine Christian parents had raised him well. He had remarkable athletic talent. He'd been provided with a good education. He'd married his college sweetheart, had four healthy children, enjoyed tremendous business success. Had the love of family and friends, the respect of his community.

"But such blessings mean nothing when one has no faith," the minister said from his pulpit, a nimbus of fine white hair floating around his head. Then he paused, looking down at the congregation, his sweet, old-man countenance gone, replaced with the damning look of an old-time New England Calvinist. "And Donald Swenson lost his faith," he called out, his voice reverberating from the vaulted ceiling. "Only those who refuse to place their trust in the Lord take their own life. The only sin worse than taking one's own life is taking that of another. Those who commit this grievous affront to the Lord do so at the risk of their eternal soul."

Horrified, Charlotte gasped and grabbed her mother's hand. This could not be happening.

She looked down the pew toward Bernice and realized that Jake was standing, his anger apparent in his posture, in the vein throbbing in his neck. All sound seemed to have been sucked from the sanctuary, leaving it submerged in a sea of deafening silence.

Charlotte held her breath and knew that all around her, others were doing the same.

The minister had stopped in midsentence and was staring down at Jake.

Charlotte jumped when Jake's clear voice cut through the silence. "Thank you very much, Reverend Henshaw," he said, and began edging his way past his mother and brothers. "I think we can handle things from here."

The robed clergyman hesitated. Was he actually being dismissed? He looked over at the organist as though searching for guidance. A fiery orator no more, the frail old man descended from his perch, hesitated again, then sat in the thronelike ministerial chair to the left of the altar.

Standing beside the oversized bronze casket, Jake faced those who had gathered to mourn his father. Charlotte could see the

Adam's apple in his neck move up and down as he swallowed back his nervousness. He looked at his mother and nodded.

"I want everyone to know what kind of man my dad really was," he said, and began retelling the stories about Donald that had been told at dinner two nights before. He even included the pissing contest. People began to relax, even laugh—except for Hannah, who sat staring down at her lap. Charlotte felt a wave of irritation. She knew her mother too well. Hannah's grandson was being magnificent, but all she could think about was "what will people think?" Charlotte tried to feel more charitable, to put herself inside her mother's skin. But at that moment, she would have liked to shake her.

She let go of her mother's hand and devoted her full attention to Jake. The stream of sunlight from a high transom window had captured his red hair, turning it gold. Charlotte's heart filled with admiration and love. She prayed that Bernice was feeling the same.

"Well, I guess that's it," Jake said when he ran out of stories to tell. He regarded his family in the front row. "Except that I'm sure I speak for my brothers and sister, and for my mother and the rest the family, when I tell you that my father was a good, decent man. I don't know why he killed himself, but like my aunt Charlotte told me the other night, we have to remember him for the sum total of his life, for the days he spent loving and helping us, not for that last sad day when some sort of despair took him from us. I'm sorry he didn't ask for help. I'm sorry as hell we didn't guess how much he needed it. But I just can't believe that the God my parents taught us kids to believe in would choose to bar my dad from heaven because of the one day he fell apart. That God wouldn't erase from the ledger all the other days he lived. No way. If there's a heaven, Donald Swenson is in it. If there isn't, then all that's left of him is our memories. And I for one have damned good memories."

Jake put his hand on the casket. Again, Charlotte could see the Adam's apple bobbing as he fought back the tears. "I love you, Dad," he said in a voice that all could hear.

Bernice rose, her shoulders back, head high, and went to join her son. Paul, Clive, and Noreen followed. They stood there, united at Donald's casket. The organist began playing the final hymn, and a young baritone in a choir robe stepped forward to sing "Nearer My God to Thee."

Blinded with tears, Charlotte reclaimed her silly mother's hand. The sound of sobbing was all around her. How proud Donald would have been of his oldest son, she thought. How very proud.

✥ "Why does all this keep happening?" Hannah whispered while they waited for their turn to file by the casket.

"What keeps happening?" Charlotte whispered back, knowing very well what she meant.

"Embarrassing things. This funeral was a disgrace."

Hannah's eyes were red, and she was fighting back tears, but they weren't being shed for her son-in-law. The tears were for Hannah herself.

Fortunately, at Bernice's request, the graveside service was for family only. They gathered under the green canopy and watched while Donald's sons, nephew, and son-in-law helped the funeral director move the casket into place. With no minister, Bernice led them in the Lord's Prayer. Then Noreen gave each family member a rose to place on the casket. Bernice went first. When it came Hannah's turn, she seemed confused. "The flower," Charlotte said. "Don't you want to put the rose on Donald's casket?"

Hannah took a step forward. Then her knees gave way, and she sank to the ground. At first Charlotte couldn't react. Was it theatrics, or was something wrong? Vicky and Noreen knelt beside their grandmother. "I don't want to go home," Hannah said.

Helped back to her chair, Hannah fixed her gaze on the casket and began her own funeral litany. She was a good Christian woman. She went to church every Sunday. She was a fifty-year member of the Lutheran Church Women. Why was all this happening to her? She used to be so proud of her family. Vicky was homecoming queen. Stan was the editor of the newspaper. Donald made all that money. But now she would never be able to hold her head up in public again. Her life was over. She might as well die. First Suzanne had to get married. Then Charlotte went running off looking for an old boyfriend. Her son-in-law committed suicide like some criminal or crazy person. And Bernice burned down her own house—that wonderful house. The most wonderful house in seven counties. Everyone in Newberg knew about Bernice's house. Her friends could hardly wait for Christmas to see it. Now she couldn't have her Christmas parties there. She'd looked forward to that more than anything in years and years. Then there was that picture of Bernice in yesterday's newspaper and a story saying that the fire was being investigated as arson, that a man who lived near the house said Bernice's car was there when it started. And today, the embarrassment of this hideous funeral. Funerals weren't supposed to be like that. It was all too much. Too much. "I don't want to go home," she said again. "I'd never be able to hold my head up in Newberg again."

❧ The ladies from church had lunch ready when the funeral home limousines delivered them back to Bernice's house. Hannah said she was too tired to eat, so Vicky and Suzanne helped their grandmother to the guest room for a nap.

Noreen sent Rusty to pick up Michelle from the baby sitter's. When Michelle arrived, she held her arms out for her grandmother. The look of such absolute love on Bernice's face made Charlotte turn away. She didn't know whether to be jealous of her sister or to pity her. Bernice would devote the rest of her life to running her family, loving them at times to the point of alienation, serving them in whatever way she could. Her individual life was over, but at least Bernice had no doubts. Her path was clear. She would live through her family.

Later, Vicky went to check on her grandmother and returned quickly. Hannah was unable to walk to the bathroom; she couldn't even hold a glass of water.

Charlotte and Bernice decided against an ambulance and drove their mother to the hospital themselves. She had had a stroke, the doctor explained. There was a decided weakness on her right side, some palsy in her face and slurring of her speech.

Fortunately, by the next day she was already showing improvement, and the doctor predicted she'd continue to recover. Of course, she would need physical therapy, and someone would have to stay with her for a few weeks and make sure she took her medication.

"She's getting on, you know," the doctor told the two sisters. "It might be the time to start thinking of alternative living arrangements for her."

Bernice and Charlotte sat whispering by their stricken mother's bedside. The right side of Hannah's face sagged noticeably, the corner of her mouth drooping. Bernice suggested that, for the time being, Hannah could stay with her in Norfolk during the week, and with Charlotte in Newberg on the weekend.

Charlotte agreed reluctantly, hating to sacrifice her precious weekends. But then what else was there to do? Bernice was making the greater commitment, even though at the moment she had so much to deal with, like settling Donald's estate, solving the legal problems stemming from the fire, and deciding the future of the car agency.

On Sunday evening after the funeral, Vicky and Mark headed back to Lincoln, while Charlotte, Suzanne, and Brady prepared to drive back to Newberg. Bernice held Charlotte tightly when they said good-bye. "I don't know what I'd do without you," she said. "You're the only person in the world who knows my heart."

Charlotte promised she'd come back Friday evening and spend the night; then she would take Hannah home for a few days.

On the way back to Newberg, in the cab of Brady's truck, Suzanne reached over and patted her mother's arm. "It will be all right, Mom. I'll help you with Grandma."

Charlotte managed to say "Thank you" before putting her hand to her mouth in an attempt to control the flood of conflicting emotions that welled inside her. Family was the most important thing in her life, in everyone's life. She should feel grateful, not trapped. Was it possible, she wondered, for a woman to worship at two altars—the altar of family and the altar of self? Or did one have to bury self to be worthy of the other?

Charlotte watched as a red-tailed hawk took off from his perch on a fence post and rose in lofty circles, finally visible only as a speck against the golds and pinks of the twilight sky. She thought of next summer, of the trip she was already planning, of three months of freedom. What would happen to that? She felt as though she were watching her summer and perhaps all the other summers of her life sail away with that hawk, now vanished in the western sky.

Stan used to say that planning was the secret of life, that the day you stopped planning was the day you died. He'd even written a column about it. So when his life was ending, he had planned his funeral.

Charlotte wondered if Stan had ever watched a red-tailed hawk and wished he could go along for the ride.

She had done that in Taos, with Jason. Darling Jason. She had loved both him and the moment, then let him and the moment go without a backward glance. Which was pretty damned remarkable. Women like her didn't do things like that.

chapter twenty-one

"At least your house is paid for," Charlotte said, looking around her sister's large kitchen. Bernice had lived in the rambling old house for more than twenty-five years, adding on to it as her family grew.

"Yes, this old house is paid for," Bernice agreed, stirring a generous portion of cream into her coffee and helping herself to a second cookie. "But it needs a new roof and a lot of other things I probably can't afford once I've settled with the insurance company for the other house. They filed suit, you know. It will take most of Donald's insurance money to pay off the construction loan and settle the rest of the outstanding debts against his estate. And their attorney made it clear that if I file for bankruptcy, they'll press charges. Arson is a felony, I'm told. They say I could go to jail."

The sisters were sitting at the large table that occupied a windowed alcove. Last night's early snowfall had blanketed the backyard with several inches of white. Sounds of the *Oprah* show drifted in from the family room, where their mother was ensconced in front of the television. They had invited Hannah to join them in the kitchen, but she had declined and asked for hot chocolate instead of coffee.

"Was it worth it?" Charlotte asked, letting the heat of the coffee mug warm her hands.

"Burning down the house? Of course not. But I wasn't thinking about financial security when I struck that match. All I could think about was making my own grand gesture to somehow even the score with fate—or whatever—for my husband blowing his brains out rather than living on with me and our family. I'm glad the damned house is gone, but now I'm afraid."

Bernice sighed and took a bite of cookie. She'd gained noticeable weight in the month since Donald's death, and was letting herself go in other ways. She needed a haircut. Stray hairs were growing between her eyebrows. Her sweater was missing a button.

"Given Donald's inertia for the last couple of years, I guess I should have known his business wasn't doing well," Bernice continued. "I wanted to believe he was still hauling in the money down at the agency, and that we would always be able to live well. On the other hand, now that I know the truth about the business, maybe I don't have to take his killing himself quite so personally. Maybe he did it because he couldn't face financial ruin and not because he couldn't stand me."

"Donald's problem was with himself," Charlotte reminded her. They'd been down this road numerous times, but Charlotte understood her sister's guilt, even shared it in a way. Donald had needed help. Dear Donald, who was such a good friend to Stan, had been in need of a friend of his own.

She sipped her coffee, which was strong and rich, clearly not store brand. Bernice was accustomed to buying the best of everything. It was hard to imagine her joining the ranks of frugal homemakers.

"He told me that we couldn't afford the house, but I didn't believe him," Bernice said. "What I don't understand is why he signed the construction loan. Why in the hell didn't he sit me down and show me the books? Why didn't he tell me that we were in trouble?"

"Pride, maybe," Charlotte suggested. "Or perhaps he thought things would turn themselves around."

Hannah called from the family room for more hot chocolate. Bernice sighed and pushed herself up out of her chair. "I'm getting tired of this," she admitted. "She could come in here and get it herself, but she won't."

Charlotte nodded. It was the same routine at her house—Hannah had assumed to role of invalid and expected to be waited on. Or maybe it was more the role of victim. If their mother went back to being the same indomitable Hannah, it would imply forgiveness on her part, and she apparently had decided never to forgive her family for not being perfect.

According to the doctor, Hannah was recovering nicely from her stroke. The only residual effects were weakness on her right side and some slurring of speech when she was tired. But whether it was from the stroke or her wounded pride, Hannah had changed. She no longer wore rouge and lipstick, and she refused to take phone calls from her friends or to see them when she was in Newberg. All she did was watch television, usually in her robe and slippers. During commercials, she'd sometimes wander about, looking out of windows, her right foot not quite keeping up with her left.

"Maybe you should think about moving into a smaller house," Charlotte suggested when Bernice returned.

"Perhaps after Paul and Clive start college. Right now, I've got to deal with the lawsuit and figure out what to do about the car agency."

"Why don't you run it?"

"Don't be ridiculous," Bernice said, her brow knitted with irritation. "I don't know the first thing about running a business."

"Come on, Bernice. You've been running things for years. Benefit golf tournaments, blood drives, the hospital auxiliary."

"Running clubs and benefits isn't the same as running a business. Even if it were, you forget that I'm now a local pariah—the crazy woman who burned down her own house. My presence behind the big desk would hardly inspire much confidence in the employees—or customers."

Charlotte opened her mouth to argue, but Bernice held up her hand, calling a halt to the discussion.

"Are you coming to Newberg for Thanksgiving?" Charlotte asked instead.

"No, Noreen's roasting her first turkey. The boys and I will probably go to her house for Christmas, too. It will be Michelle's first," Bernice said with a smile. "I'll tell you, Sis, I don't know what I'd do without that baby. She's the light of my life."

Charlotte looked at her watch and took a final sip of coffee. "Time to go," she said, hoping to escape before Bernice went off on a Michelle tangent. She'd already heard about the new tooth and peek-a-boo. "I've got stew in the Crock-Pot. Is Mama all packed up and ready?"

Bernice nodded. "I tried to get her to call some of her friends— to set up a bridge game or invite them to drop by your house—but she still insists she's too humiliated to see anyone ever again."

With Hannah and her suitcase in the car, Charlotte turned to tell her sister good-bye. "Get your hair done, Bernie. And pluck your eyebrows."

"What's the point?"

"The point is that life goes on. Donald's the one who's dead."

On the drive to Newberg, Charlotte tried to carry on a conversation with her sullen mother, pointing out the beauty of the snow-covered landscape and the progress on the new shopping center going up in the outskirts of West Point. Her mother's current silence was disconcerting, especially after a lifetime of so much chatter.

"Come on, Mama," Charlotte finally said. "I know you think you're punishing me, but you're only hurting yourself. You have more friends that anyone I know. You've always led a full life. You used to look forward to things. It could be like that again."

Hannah stared straight ahead. "They're all gossiping about me."

"So what! My God, Mama, you've gossiped about them. Gossip is the number one recreational activity with your set. What goes around comes around."

Charlotte felt her blood pressure rising. She wanted to blurt out that her father would have been appalled to see his beloved Hannah give up on life like this. She wanted to tell her mother to grow up, to stop acting like a spoiled child. She wanted to tell her that she'd never been a good mother. That she'd cared more about the lady friends she was now shunning than she'd ever cared about her own daughters. And she wanted to tell her that she was making it damned difficult for Charlotte to feel like a good daughter.

But she turned on the radio instead, and worked at calming herself. She thought about the mountains in New Mexico with their stark, barren beauty. They would be topped with snow now. She took a deep breath, imagining the desert air. And the space and the silence.

Since her mother had started spending weekends with her, they had lost their significance for Charlotte. No longer were they a time for solitude and catching up on chores. Was it going to be this way for years and years?

Hannah did indeed expect to be waited on, and she was impossible to please. Her tea was either too hot, too cold, too weak, or too strong. She whined if Charlotte didn't sit with her to watch the television programs she had selected, or if Charlotte forgot to cook her oatmeal with currants.

But as trying as the weekend arrangement was, it was the prospect of losing an entire summer that bothered Charlotte the most. She desperately wanted at least one more summer on the road. She had experienced so much during the last one, but the journey she had begun still was not completed. She hadn't gone all the way back to Cory Lee Jones. To bedrock. To where her journey through adulthood had truly begun.

The aroma of the stew in the Crock-Pot greeted them when Charlotte opened the back door. She turned on the gas log in the fireplace and installed her mother in front of the television, covering her legs with an afghan. "Dinner in twenty minutes," she said cheerfully.

She was surprised when Hannah grabbed her hand. "No one loves me anymore," she said.

Charlotte knelt and embraced her mother. "You're my mother. I'll always love you."

"Your daddy loved me."

"I know that. Do you want to go to the cemetery on Sunday? We could put some holly on his grave. And on Stan's."

"Not on Sunday. Someone might see me. Maybe tomorrow morning. Early."

"Sure. What would you say to eating in the dining room tonight, with candlelight and the good china?"

"No. I need to eat in here so I can watch Vanna."

The next morning, on the way back from the cemetery, Charlotte deliberately went the long way home, driving by her mother's house, stopping out front. "Do you want to go inside?"

Hannah shook her head, but later in the day she announced that she wanted to have Thanksgiving dinner at her house. She'd scarcely mentioned her own home since her stroke, and Charlotte allowed herself to hope. Maybe they could interest her in moving back there for a few more years.

The weekend before Thanksgiving, with Hannah looking over her shoulder, Charlotte cleaned her mother's house from top to bottom, polished the silver, hand-washed her grandmother's Spode, ironed a linen tablecloth. Sunday evening, she made her grocery list. Monday evening, she did the shopping. Tuesday, she made the dressing, cranberry salad, and green bean casserole. Wednesday evening, after Mark and Vicky had been welcomed home and fed, she baked the pies and made one last run to the grocery.

Thursday morning, she began transporting food to her mother's house, waiting until late morning to roust Mark and Vicky out of bed. Vicky was to set the table and help with the final meal preparations. Mark's assignment was to rake leaves and jump-start Hannah's car. Vicky might as well drive it back to Lincoln. The car wasn't doing anyone any good sitting in the garage.

Thanksgiving dinner was served in the evening to accommodate Brady and Suzanne, who had eaten earlier in the day with his family. Of course, neither one of them was hungry. When the meal was over, Mark and Vicky went off to visit friends home from college. Brady and Suzanne headed back to his folks for a poker game.

Although Hannah complained she was tired and wanted to go "home," Charlotte made her wait while she cleaned up the kitchen and loaded up the car to take all the food and utensils back to her own house.

Before she put things away in her own kitchen, she carried a cup of tea upstairs for her mother. "I'll never forgive Bernice for burning down that house," Hannah said. She was wearing her robe, and was seated on the side of her bed.

"Never is a long, long time," Charlotte said, sitting beside her. "And even if she hadn't burned it down, she wouldn't have wanted to live there. You wouldn't have been able to have your Christmas parties there."

"Donald was going to send over vans," Hannah said. "Why did he kill himself? I never did understand."

"Depression. He convinced himself that being dead was better than being alive."

Later, with all the food stored away, and her mother in bed, Charlotte curled up on her own bed with a glass of wine and dialed her sister's number. "You still awake?" she asked.

"Barely. Michelle's spending the night with me. I just rocked her to sleep and about put myself down in the process."

"How'd your Thanksgiving go?" Charlotte asked.

"Mixed. Noreen overcooked the turkey and got all upset about it. And it seemed like Donald should have been there for all the food and football. I'm glad we were at Noreen's, though. Otherwise there would have been that empty recliner sitting there. I guess I need to get rid of it. How about you? Did Mama say anything about moving back home?"

"Not a word. But now she wants to have Christmas dinner at her house, put up a tree in the front room, have all of you come over here." She paused. "I'm not going to do that, Bernie. I just don't have time to get two houses ready for Christmas. If she'd move back there, it'd be different. But from now on, if I have to cook the meal, we're going to eat it in my house."

"Maybe we should just move her back in her house and see what happens."

"Believe me, I've thought of that," Charlotte said, pulling the comforter up over her legs. "Other old ladies no worse off than she is manage on their own with a little help. But if we forced it on her and she fell down the basement stairs, it would be our fault. I really wouldn't mind the current arrangement so much if it didn't feel like punishment."

"You sound down."

"I guess I am a little. I haven't been able to get into the holiday spirit this year. When I was cleaning up over at Mama's house tonight, I found myself counting the hours I'd spent in the last week preparing for just that one meal. I figure it was close to thirty, with all the cleaning, shopping, and cooking. And then it took about forty minutes for my kids to eat the meal and rush off to be with their friends. Suzanne and Brady came from his mother's table and weren't even hungry. I found myself wondering if it was worth all the fuss."

"Well, your kids may not remember anything specific about this particular Thanksgiving in the years to come, but they'd damned sure remember if you hadn't celebrated it."

"I suppose," Charlotte said, looking at Stan's picture on the dresser, remembering the last Thanksgiving with him. Mark had carried his father downstairs—like a child. His last meal downstairs. Stan had offered a blessing that made them cry. "Everything is different now," she told her sister. "All my kids want is to have me around in case they need a little mothering—good old Mom to fix the holiday meals and be there in a crisis. That's fine, I guess. I get time off in between. But now my mother needs me more than my kids do. I've gone from child care to caring for Stan to caring for Mama. I thought there'd be more time in between for me."

"But just imagine what it would be like if nobody needed you for anything," Bernice said. "Besides, you'll feel differently about everything when you have grandchildren. Sometimes I wish Noreen and Rusty would just go off to China or someplace and leave Michelle with me all the time. You should have seen her today in the little outfit I made for her, with appliquéd turkeys on the skirt and vest. I'll tell you, Sis, that little girl has stolen her granny's heart pure and simple."

"No kidding," Charlotte said.

"Hey, if Suzanne had had her baby, you'd feel the same way. You wouldn't want a day to pass without seeing your grandbaby. You'd hate to leave town for fear you might miss a new word or trick."

Would she? Charlotte wondered. Would she now be as doting as Bernice, more in love with a grandchild than anyone else in her life? She did feel a need to hold her children's children in her arms someday, to love them and watch them grow and change. But she didn't want her relationship with her grandchildren to be the guiding influence in her life. Maybe that would happen someday, but not now—not before she explored other possibilities.

Bernice announced she was ready to get off the phone and into bed.

"What about this summer?" Charlotte asked abruptly. "I want to take another trip. Could we split the three months, and each take Mama for six weeks?"

"I thought you'd gotten that traveling stuff out of your system," Bernice snapped, irritation clear in her voice. "Why would you want to go off like that again?"

"Because there's a world out there."

"You just want to look for Cory Jones," she said, her tone accusing.

"Yes, but not for the reason you think."

"Oh, come on. You think you can take up where you left off. You must have had some steamy summer with that boy for you to carry the torch all this time. Sometimes I wonder if you really loved Stan at all."

Charlotte felt a wave of hot anger flush through her. She kicked off the comforter and sat up straight. "Damn it, Bernie, don't you *ever* say or even think anything like that again! If you do, I swear I'll never speak to you again. I loved my husband with all my heart. But that fact doesn't erase what came before—in my life and in Stan's. And I do not expect or want to take up with Cory where we left off."

"Then what's the point?" Bernice asked, spitting out the words, drowsiness gone from her voice.

Charlotte couldn't decide if she should end the conversation or try to explain. And if she did explain, would Bernice even try to understand?

She needed her sister, though. Her earliest memories were of Bernice—of crawling over the sides of the baby bed so she could sleep with her baby sister at night. Charlotte rubbed at her forehead, willing the right words to come. And if they did, maybe she would understand better herself why once again she had to load up her station wagon and head down the highway.

"It's just that all my life, I've gone along with things," she began. "When Cory didn't come back to me, I almost stopped living, but I didn't get on a bus and go looking for him. I didn't demand that his family tell me where he was. I didn't track down his friends. I just wallowed in misery like a pig in mud—like our mother is doing now. Then when Stan came along, we got married because being lonely with someone seemed better than being lonely without a warm body in the bed. We were lucky, Stan and I. We found love and respect and balm for our wounds. But now he's gone, and I want to do now what I didn't do before. I don't want to just wait around for something to happen, wait around until I get sick or old or bitter. Maybe if I find Cory, I can live the rest of my life more purposefully."

"Like having affairs," Bernice challenged. "You had one last summer, didn't you? With the man at the art gallery in Taos who gave you that painting? I could tell. You looked different when you got back. Your hair was even shorter. Plus you were brown as an Indian and thin enough to tuck your shirt in your jeans."

"No, you're wrong, I didn't have an affair with that man. But I did with someone else." Almost immediately, Charlotte wished she hadn't said that. The pause on the other end of the line was too prolonged, too ominous.

"What man?" Bernice finally demanded.

"An artist from Louisiana."

"And?"

"And what?"

"When will you see him again?"

"Probably never."

"Why?"

"When the summer ended, we just said good-bye. It was time for us to go our separate ways."

"And will you do something like that again?"

"I don't know, Bernie. Maybe, if the right nice, safe man comes along. It was lovely. Different from being married."

"Different in what way?"

"It had nothing to do with duty. We just enjoyed each other." With a sinking heart, Charlotte realized that Bernice was crying. "Why does that upset you?" she asked.

"I can't believe you spent the summer having sex with a stranger. What about Stan? What did you do with his memory while you were in bed with another man?"

"Are you saying that I should never have sex again because I might think of Stan? I probably did think of him. His memory comes in and out of my head of its own free will. I probably thought about you and my kids, too. All of you are a part of me."

"I thought we'd always be together," Bernice said, pausing to blow her nose. "Two widowed sisters living out their lives together. I don't want you going off to screw men. I don't know you anymore.

And no, I won't keep our mother for half the summer so you can go off and act that way."

The Musket Makers
109 E. Okmulgee St.
Anadarko, OK 73001

December 1

Dear Charlotte Haberman,

I am writing to you about Cory Jones. I saw the ad in *Purple Heart* that said you were looking for someone by that name who grew up in Nebraska and served in Vietnam with the First Calvary in 1967 and 1968. That's the guy I knew. We served in the same platoon.

After the war, Cory drifted through Oklahoma three different times and worked for us. He never stayed one place very long. Last time he was with us he got into a bar fight and had to split.

I hope you really are an old friend of Cory's and not from a collection agency.

Seems like the girl who wrote to him was named Charlotte. He said you were nice, but he wasn't ever going back to Nebraska. He didn't think he'd fit in back there anymore. He was probably right. Cory mostly hung out with other vets.

Last I heard of Cory, he was heading for Colorado with a black guy named Billy Birmingham, also from the 1st Cav. That would have been in the late 1980s. Cory thought it might be easier to get clean in the mountains.

If you find him, tell him that Bonnie and I just sent the last kid off to college, and the business is doing great. We've got three full-time employees—all vets—and sell muzzle loaders all over the world. None of them are as pretty as the ones he etched for us, though. Those guns are real collectors items now with the Revolutionary War buffs.

And tell him old Lem from Brooklyn finally wrote that book he was always talking about and actually got it published. We're all in there, apparently, pictures and all. I'm kind of scared to read it, but I guess I should. Maybe I'll have Bonnie read it first. It's called *Vietnam Diary*.

Don't expect much if you do find Cory. He was pretty scruffy last time I saw him. And strange. He wouldn't sleep under the same roof with anyone because of the nightmares. He had a little travel trailer last time he was here that he parked way out back.

Cory was like a brother to me. I served with him from the very first day, and we kept each other going. We saved each other's life more than once and took more lives than I'd care to count. He had a hard time shifting gears when he got back to the States. I did, too, and probably would have re-upped if it weren't for Bonnie.

Sincerely,
Billy Little Eagle

chapter twenty-two

On the Monday afternoon following Thanksgiving, a Christmas poinsettia was delivered to Charlotte's classroom just as her last class was filing out the door. The card was signed by Eric Grimmett, the high school math teacher.

Charlotte took a second look at the envelope to make sure the large, showy plant with a huge gold bow really had been intended for her. But why, she wondered. Other than a perfunctory greeting when they crossed paths at school events, she hadn't seen the retired army officer since she realized that twice accepting his invitation to drive over to West Point for a movie implied interest on her part. Of course, in truth, there had been a little, at the outset at least. But it vanished when she realized how easy it would be to slip into a pattern. Go to another movie with him, then to a high school play, then a basketball game—people would start thinking of them as a couple.

She and Jason Piper had been a couple in Taos. But that had been away from here. And it had been temporary—an island in time.

When she called Eric to thank him for the poinsettia, he asked if they could go out to dinner. "Just two friends," he added.

"Why waste time with me?" she said. "There must be widow ladies across two counties willing to bake you pies and gush."

He laughed. "Maybe just one county."

"And?"

"Well, they're looking for a replacement, preferably a man who doesn't snore too loudly and can fix drippy faucets—just like I was out looking for another Vera to serve me meals on time and put clean underwear in the bureau. When I figured all that out, it scared me to death. I'd rather stay single for the rest of my life than get married again just for the sake of having a wife around to look after me. In fact, the idea of staying single doesn't unnerve me the way it used to. But I would like sometimes to enjoy the company of an interesting woman."

"We live in a town where people our age don't just enjoy each other's company. You can't believe the grilling I got from the other teachers about that poinsettia."

"What did you tell them?"

"That it was from my sister."

"I suppose we could wear disguises when we go out," he said with a chuckle.

It was the chuckle that did it. Charlotte realized she was smiling, and suddenly she found the idea of sneaking off with the colonel rather appealing.

They went to dinner at the Vets Club in West Point. Most of the time was spent talking about teaching, which Eric described as a frustrating, daunting, and occasionally glorious way to make a living.

Charlotte explained how she was trying to make literature more meaningful for her students. "I realized how formulaic and boring my teaching had been. Of course, I'll probably get in trouble for taking liberty with the curriculum, but I want my students to understand that the sun doesn't rise and set in Newberg—that it's important for them to know there are other cultures and other ways of thinking that are just as valid as their own."

"I hope you're treading lightly," Eric warned. "Last semester, one of the football players in my algebra class asked me to show him where in the Bible it said he had to learn algebra, and I asked him to show me where in the Bible it said he had to play football. Next thing I knew, the football coach had accused me of saying that football was un-Christian. I made matters worse by saying that football seemed like a pretty pagan game to me—that's why we all like it so much. I halfway expected to lose my job over the ensuing flap. But apparently qualified high school math teachers are hard to come by in small towns, and the principal was able to keep Coach Kinder from taking the matter before the school board."

"Why did you come back here?" she asked. "Newberg must seem very provincial after your military career."

"The military is just as provincial in its own way. And Vera grew up over in Pender. I come from Wakefield. We'd decided a long time ago we wanted to retire where we could see the horizon in all directions, and where the only time we'd get caught in a traffic jam would be driving down to Lincoln on game days. Vera was a dedicated bird-watcher, and she wanted to look out her kitchen window and see the birds from her childhood. I wanted to keep a couple of retrievers and go pheasant hunting more than once a year. When I was offered a job in Newberg, it seemed like the perfect place. When Vera died, I came anyway."

"You must have had a good marriage," Charlotte said.

"Yes, and I miss my wife very much. I keep her binoculars and her copy of *Peterson's Field Guide to Western Birds* on the windowsill over the sink. It's taken me the last year and a half to learn to enjoy my own company. But now, I don't dread going home at night. When I open the back door, my little house welcomes me, and I'm glad to be there. I feed my dogs, putter around—not bad at all."

Charlotte nodded. "I feel the same way. Sometimes I like my solitude so much it bothers me. Shouldn't I open the door and feel sad because Stan isn't there?"

"Feeling sad gets old," Eric said, dividing the last of the wine between them. He was a nice-looking man with a strong jaw and hazel eyes with lots of smile lines. She liked watching him across the table, liked being here with him.

When she stood to leave, Charlotte realized she'd had too much wine and had to concentrate on getting herself out of the restaurant without bumping into something. The night air was absolutely still but so cold it took her breath away. It felt exquisite against her flushed face.

The car seemed warm, and she had to fight against dozing during the drive home. She was grateful when Eric turned on the radio and found a station playing Christmas carols. Enjoying their giddiness, they both sang along.

"Can we do this again?" Eric asked as he walked her to the front door.

"I really don't know. Weekends, I have my mother. Most school nights, I have to grade papers. I don't have much space in my life."

"Will you call me when you find a niche or two?"

She agreed reluctantly, not at all sure she really would. But when he gathered her in his arms, heavy coats and all, for a moment of closeness before she opened the door and went inside, Charlotte didn't object. As his lips brushed her cheek, she had to resist the urge to turn her face and find his mouth.

❧ Charlotte bought a cassette of seasonal music to put herself in the holiday spirit while she arranged evergreen branches and pinecones on the mantel, decorated the tree, canned jars of blackberry preserves as gifts for her fellow teachers, baked holiday goodies for her children, and strung lights around the living-room windows.

It felt strange to decorate a different house after twenty-eight years of Christmases in the other house. The ceilings were lower, the fireplace less significant, the stairway enclosed. But now that the decorations were up, she was rather proud of how the house looked. It was nothing grand, of course, but cheery.

Hannah said she wasn't up to Christmas shopping but perversely refused to delegate the task to her daughters. Charlotte found a picture of her parents taken on their honeymoon at International Falls and had copies made and framed for Hannah to present to each of her seven grandchildren. Bernice addressed Christmas cards to Hannah's many friends and told her mother she could either sign them herself or Bernice would do it for her.

When Bernice brought Hannah to Newberg the Sunday before Christmas, Charlotte switched on the Christmas lights and turned on the Christmas music. "What do you think?" she asked.

"You need more lights on the tree," Hannah said, making a production out of lowering her body onto the sofa.

"How about a glass of sherry in front of the fireplace while we listen to carols?"

"It would be nicer if you had a real fire instead of that gas log."

"You have a gas log at your house," Charlotte pointed out.

"That's because I don't have your papa anymore to bring in the wood and build the fire."

"Well, I don't have a man around either, so let's just be glad we have a gas log to warm us."

"Harry used to say that I looked beautiful in the firelight. He'd make hot spiced wine, and we'd watch that old black and white television after you girls were in bed."

Charlotte was surprised to see tears running down her mother's cheeks. She sat on the sofa and took Hannah's hand. "He always took such good care of me," Hannah went on. "That's what I miss the most—the way he fussed over me and wanted to know if I needed an afghan to put over my legs or for him to rub my shoulders. When we went upstairs, he would turn down the bed and plump the pillows. And come downstairs to get me hot milk when I couldn't sleep. No one fusses over me anymore. You girls never did that. You always had each other."

Charlotte examined her mother's hand. The skin lay loose like an oversized glove. Her rings were loose, held on by knobby knuckles. Hannah's hands had always been plump, like the rest of her—plump, pretty Hannah Vogel, her cheeks surprisingly unwrinkled under their rouge. But she seemed to be shrinking now. She was not so pretty any more: no rouge, no sparkle. She was paying them all back by giving up on life.

Hannah's status in the community had been derived, for the most part, from her family and their accomplishments. She'd had a good run. Her husband had been vice president of the bank. Charlotte's husband had been editor of the local newspaper, her son a football star, one daughter the high school valedictorian, the other homecoming queen. Bernice had two sons who distinguished themselves athletically, one son who won scholastic honors, a daughter who'd been named most popular by her senior class. But most importantly, Bernice's husband owned one of the most successful car agencies in the entire state. Her son-in-law's wealth had been the biggest feather in Hannah's cap. And because of that wealth, this was to have been her finest Christmas ever, as she entertained her friends in Bernice's glorious new mansion with a fifteen-foot-tall Christmas tree and holiday music piped into every room.

Now that would never happen. The good run had ended.

Charlotte began to sing along with "Hark the Herald Angels Sing." It was glorious music, even on her cheap Wal-Mart stereo. She squeezed her mother's hand, desperately willing her to join in. Charlotte remembered her father singing this very carol with her and Bernice, while Hannah played the piano. Why couldn't Hannah think of that time and sing with her?

Charlotte imagined her daddy standing in the doorway now, looking in at them—at his elderly wife and his middle-aged daughter, side by side on the sofa. He would want them to celebrate the season, to feel joy and remember fondly. Charlotte sang even louder on the second verse, but Hannah only stared ahead. Charlotte couldn't hate her mother. That was unthinkable, for her father's sake, if for no other reason. But she was finding it very difficult to feel any tenderness toward her. Or love. That realization made her sad. She didn't expect to be happy all the time—happiness was just pieces of fluff that drifted by from time to time—but a sense of well-being was nice, and she definitely wanted to keep sadness at a minimum.

❧ Charlotte counted the days until Mark and Vicky arrived. For two whole weeks, they would once again be under her roof and in her care. Suzanne promised she would spend as much time with them as she could. Charlotte had scrubbed and polished and cooked ahead with a vengeance, imagining long conversations with her children over the dinner table, watching football games on television, ice-skating in the park, maybe going to the after-Christmas sales in Omaha with Vicky and Suzanne, all of them spending New Year's Day with Bernice and her family.

Mark and Vicky arrived on the evening of the twenty-first to candles in the windows and the aroma of coffee cake baking in the oven. Charlotte remembered last year, when they walked in the door and were amazed at how she'd transformed the old house for Suzanne's wedding. She wanted them to tell her that this house also looked nice all dressed up for Christmas, but like their sister, Vicky and Mark had no comment. The familiar ornaments were decorating the wrong living room. The familiar aroma was wafting from the wrong kitchen. Their mother lived in the wrong house. And the people who'd bought *their* house had chopped off the front porch.

Suzanne stopped by for a while, then Mark and Vicky proclaimed themselves exhausted from final exams and headed upstairs to bed. During the next two days, when they weren't sleeping, they were rushing off to do the Christmas shopping they hadn't had time for before and to check in with their friends.

But on Christmas Eve, Mark and Vicky went to church with Charlotte, standing shoulder to shoulder as they sang the traditional hymns of the season and listened to the reading of the age-old scripture with its message of hope. She wished Suzanne and

Hannah could have joined them. But Suzanne was a Methodist now and was spending Christmas Eve with Brady's family. And not even Mark could talk his grandmother into venturing out. She didn't want to see anyone, she said. They'd left her in front of the television.

Christmas morning, Vicky passed out the presents, which were opened one by one with appropriate ceremony. Charlotte felt more like an observer in the ritual than a participant. Her children weren't children any more, but she felt toward them the same worshipful love she always had. And she couldn't protect them any more, which made her love for them all the more poignant. They were so young and beautiful, with their lives yet to lead, newborns yet to hold in their arms, joy yet to embrace—pain yet to suffer.

Then there was her mother, old and difficult. Charlotte knew her love for her mother had always been more dutiful than heartfelt. Now it was tainted with anger.

And lastly, there was Brady, whom she could now regard with affection, but she would always wish he hadn't married her daughter.

Charlotte wondered how many more years she would have them with her on this special day. Soon her children would have families of their own, and she would be the visitor in their homes, just as Hannah was now in her daughter's home. But the thought of passing the responsibility for Christmas to the next generation wasn't an altogether unpleasant one. Every year the decorations looked a bit shabbier. And she went about all the holiday preparations with less delight than she had experienced when Stan was on the ladder decorating the tree and three small children were clamoring all around.

Maybe she would find renewal, as Bernice did, through the eyes of grandchildren. No, that wouldn't be enough, she decided. Charlotte also wanted to find her own renewal, through her own eyes, just as she had done last summer with Suzanne, reaching out rather than waiting for.

Early Christmas afternoon, they went to the cemetery. Other families were there, braving the cold. The wind was so biting that

Hannah stayed in the car, watching while they went first to their grandfather's grave, then their father's, placing Christmas wreaths on each. Suzanne laid a holly spray in front of the tiny marker commemorating the baby she'd never had.

Everyone was silent on the way back to the house, each lost in private thoughts.

Stan had been dead for almost two years. Already Charlotte couldn't remember if he liked whiskey or brandy in his eggnog. Mark had asked her, and she couldn't recall. She tried once again, seeing Stan make his own special concoction, reaching into the cupboard for a bottle. She imagined the first taste. But all she recalled was its smoothness, the freshly ground nutmeg on top, the immediate rush of warmth from the liquor.

After dinner, they gathered around the piano to sing carols and drink Mark's very stiff eggnog—made with bourbon. Charlotte was surprised at Brady's wonderful baritone voice. "You should sing in the choir," she told him, and he actually blushed.

That evening they watched *It's a Wonderful Life* on television for the umpteenth time and got appropriately misty-eyed at the end—even Hannah, who said the smooth-faced Jimmy Stewart reminded her of Harry as a young man.

After taking Hannah her bedtime cup of tea, Charlotte sat with Vicky and Mark a little longer, finishing the eggnog, unwilling to turn loose of the day. But finally, she dismissed them, and they hugged good night at the top of the stairs—a three-way embrace. "Thank you, my darlings," she said. "It was a beautiful day."

She watched them walk down the hall, Vicky to tiptoe into the room where her grandmother was sleeping. Mark paused at his door, then came back for another hug. "Are you all right, Son?" she asked.

"Yes and no," he said, following her into her bedroom. He leaned against the dresser. Charlotte sat on the side of the bed and slipped off her shoes.

"I've fallen in love with the wrong girl," he told her.

"The girl from North Platte?"

"Yeah. Sarah."

"But if you love her, maybe she is the right girl."

"I don't think so, Mom. We don't agree on anything. She'll devote her life to getting murderers off death row and opening abortion clinics. I'd never have a chance for a political career if I married her."

"Maybe you need to rethink some of those things you're against. It might be good to have someone in your life who doesn't allow you to get away with the knee-jerk stuff."

"Maybe. But not Sarah. She got herself a tattoo for Christmas—a butterfly on her left thigh. Can you imagine Vicky or Suzanne doing such a thing? And I'm not even sure she'd marry me if I asked."

"Then just be with her for a time. See what happens."

"Yeah. I suppose. But sometimes I wish I'd never met her."

"No, don't think that. She's taught you a valuable lesson."

"What's that?"

"That nothing is simple."

Mark looked into his mother's face. "But you and Dad raised us to think it was. Just work hard and be good and everything will work out."

"I'm sorry about that," Charlotte said. "We should have taught you that working hard and being good are better than slacking off and being naughty."

The day after Christmas, Vicky went to Topeka to spend a few days with her roommate. Mark went back to Lincoln to work on a law review article; maybe he would drive over to North Platte to meet Sarah's family—or maybe not. Vicky promised to be back for New Year's; Mark said he didn't know.

Charlotte had hoped to have her two older children with her longer than just four days, and when they left, she felt herself hovering on the edge of a funk. She'd cooked all that food, expected too much of them. But she understood and forgave them. She would always forgive them anything.

🐞   🐞   🐞

❧ Vicky had known that Patty Dearing's family was rich, but when she pulled her grandmother's elderly Buick into the circle drive of their vast Topeka home, she had to resist the urge to keep right on going. The Tudor mansion was twice as big as the house her aunt Bernice had been building in Norfolk. It was hard to believe that sweet, unassuming Patty had grown up in such a dwelling. A house like that had a staff of servants. The people who lived there would dress for dinner.

Dress for dinner! Vicky had just thrown some things in a bag—to wear sightseeing and hanging out. If she'd had an inkling, she would have packed with care. She would have brought stockings and heels and borrowed her grandmother's garnet earrings.

She had tried to back out of the Topeka trip before they headed out for the holidays, but the crestfallen look on Patty's face had made her backtrack a bit. She'd see, Vicky said, maybe for just a few days. She really needed to spend some time with her family.

Which was the truth. Vicky knew that her mom was looking forward to having her and Mark around after Christmas. And she had a sneaking suspicion that Mark was going to head for North Platte. But she hadn't had the heart to pick up the phone and tell Patty she wasn't coming.

Now she wished she had been tougher. With a sigh, she reached over the back seat for her duffel bag and headed for the huge front door that looked as if it belonged on a medieval castle. The butler would probably take one look at her and direct her to the service entrance.

But before she reached the door, it opened and Patty appeared, squealing, "You came! You came!"

"Of course I came," Vicky said with a tinge of guilt, and dropped her duffel bag to embrace her friend. Strange how she'd come to think of Patty as a special friend. Unlikely, but nice.

Patty was plain and shy and had one leg shorter than the other, which made her walk with a decided limp. Last year, when she transferred to NU from a Topeka junior college, she'd been pledged by the sorority only because she was a legacy and her family was rich.

Vicky agreed to be her roommate because no one else wanted her. As it turned out, however, Patty was a perfect roommate—tidy, quiet, thoughtful. Vicky started asking her to come along when she went to the library or shopping. When Vicky decided to forgo the sorority house her senior year and rent an apartment, she had invited Patty to live with her and share expenses.

"I've been watching for you," Patty said, all breathless and aflutter. "I was so afraid the snow would delay you. Or there'd be a blizzard, and you couldn't come at all. I just can't believe you're really here. Come on in. There's someone I want you to meet."

Vicky stepped inside and found herself in an entry hall large enough to encompass her mother's entire house. Vicky had a quick impression of rich paneling, Persian rugs, a huge brass chandelier, and ornately carved balusters, before she saw the young man coming down the wide curving staircase.

"She's here," Patty called up to him. "It's my brother," she said to Vicky.

Vicky knew that Jonathan Dearing had been serving as a lay missionary in the Philippines, and this was his first Christmas home in two years. The picture of him surrounded by native children on Patty's bookcase hadn't done him justice; not that Jonathan Dearing was extraordinarily handsome. In fact, his face was a bit on the flat side—like Patty's—and he wasn't much taller than Vicky. But his eyes were a deep, velvety brown. And his smile was dazzling. Vicky realized that she was looking into the face of an extraordinary man.

Later, as she watched Jonathan over the dinner table and witnessed the adoration of his parents, sister, and the aging housekeeper who served their meal, she saw that her first impression had been correct. And she realized that in spite of their wealth, Mr. and Mrs. Dearing were nice people.

She felt herself relax. It didn't matter that she was wearing slacks and a sweater from JCPenney's or that she had never been in such a splendid house, never tasted fine wine, never dined among the truly rich. She felt at home with these people. And knew that something very special was happening between her and Jonathan Dearing. Mr. and Mrs. Dearing also saw it and conveyed their approval with beaming smiles, as did Patty, who apparently had planned that it would happen just this way. An aura of goodwill hung over the table, with its candlelight and crystal.

Only later, when Vicky lay in bed reliving the evening, did misgivings intrude. After last summer's disappointing internship, she had given up her someday dream of buying the *Newberg Record* and had set her sights on loftier goals. She knew she had the makings of a good journalist and had even won a state press association award for feature writing. Already, she had applied for jobs in Omaha, Kansas City, Cleveland—and New York City.

Jonathan Dearing was going to be a minister and would go where the Church sent him. His wife's place would be at his side.

But already, she could feel the first stirrings of love deep inside her. She thought of Jonathan in bed just down the hall, thinking of her. She knew that he was.

She stretched her body luxuriantly between the silken sheets, then turned on the light. Pulling her nightgown over her head and tossing it on the floor, she walked naked to the full-length mirror in the corner and examined her body from every angle. Pleased with what she saw, she imagined how it would be when Jonathan saw her for the first time. Then she closed her eyes and thanked God that He had given her the courage to remain a virgin.

chapter twenty-three

Port Sulphur, Louisiana
Dec. 26, 1990

Dear Mrs. Haberman,

I found a letter that you had written to my brother asking about PFC Cory Lee Jones. Your information was correct. Cory visited Frank and me right after he got back from Vietnam and for a long time showed up every year or two after that. He worked for us a few months in the late 1980s.

I am sure my brother would have written to you, but Mike passed on in November and had let things slide there toward the end.

Anyway Cory and Mike were in the same platoon in Vietnam. Frank had told him that if he ever wanted to work on a shrimp boat to come on down. But Cory did not take to the water and worked in a bait shop for a while till he got crossways with some of the boys from up bayou and took off. He was thinking about going someplace out West. He heard that some of the vets started their own settlement up in the mountains and thought that might be the best place for him. We never heard from him since.

I think it is real nice that you are trying to find Cory. He never talked about his people back home. I am not sure why. We all need our own people. If you find Cory, be sure and tell him that Frank died. He got cancer in his lungs and went real fast.

God bless you, Mrs. Haberman, and Happy New Year,
Claude Bouziden

❧ After Christmas, Suzanne decided to stay with her mother and grandmother while Brady went deer hunting in South Dakota with his dad and brother-in-law—which pleased Charlotte immensely, perhaps even making up for the early departure of Vicky and Mark.

It snowed off and on, but not so much that Suzanne and Charlotte couldn't bundle up and take long walks with George loping along in front of them. For miles and miles they walked, their feet crunching on the crusted snow as they wandered over the countryside, recalling the history of families who still owned or had once owned the houses and farms.

One glorious afternoon with the sunlight simmering on the snow and the air so still they could hear sounds of traffic from the state highway, they poked around the abandoned farmhouse where Hannah's father had lived as a boy after his family immigrated from northeastern Germany. Given Nebraska's more southern latitudes, they probably thought they were coming to a kinder climate, Charlotte pointed out. But they didn't know about the prairie. The women learned to make quilts out of rags and to insulate the walls with newspapers. The men learned to run a rope from the house to the barn so they wouldn't get disoriented in a blizzard.

Hannah's grandmother had carried with her to America the root stock of a climbing rosebush that had grown on their farm back in the old country. Bushes generated from that original stock had survived a hundred years on the prairie and still came to life every spring, producing masses of tiny white roses all along the fence row. Suzanne promised she would dig up one of them someday, to plant at her own home. She did not say where that home would be.

The house had collapsed, but the barn was still standing, although it leaned precariously. Even so, they went inside and marveled at its size and the churchlike feel with its soaring, steeply pitched roof. Suzanne found a rusty, oversized horseshoe hanging outside a stall and took it home to show her grandmother.

When she presented it to her, Hannah was unimpressed. "They were just big old draft horses. I never liked them," she said, refusing to reminisce about her father's family. "I've told you all about them before," she said impatiently. "My grandparents never had indoor plumbing or learned English."

That evening, after Hannah had gone to bed, Charlotte and Suzanne sat in front of the fireplace, drinking hot spiced wine and chatting.

"Grandma used to love talking about her papa and how he won a scholarship to Dana College and was mayor of Newberg for twenty years," Suzanne said. "I miss the way she used to be—when she still liked me. Do you think she'll ever be the same again?"

"Only if she wants to," Charlotte said. "Right now, she's getting some sort of perverse satisfaction out of being unpleasant."

"Are you angry with her?"

"Yes, I guess I am," Charlotte admitted, staring at the flickering gas flames. Her mother was right. Gas logs weren't as pretty as a real fire, but they were better than an unused fireplace. And they did cast a warm glow on the room, the same as a real fire. "Your grandmother won't look past her own nose. If your grandfather were still alive, he could cajole her out of it, but I'm afraid Bernice and I haven't found the key."

Tomorrow, Bernice would be driving over to get Hannah—finally. A week and a half with her mother was too long. Charlotte had found satisfaction and even joy in caring for her housebound husband, but tending to her petulant mother only brought out the worst in her. At times she even wanted to yell at her, to tell her she was an ungrateful, selfish old woman. She wanted to take her to the nursing home and push her out of the car. Never see her again. But the feeling would pass. Charlotte still longed for some sign of affection from her mother—be it a touch or a word—some indication that she was glad it was her own daughter preparing her meals and doing her laundry and not just any caregiver.

Charlotte wouldn't have Hannah again until the second weekend in January. Then they would be back on schedule: weekdays with Bernice, weekends with Charlotte—with no adjustments for summer unless Charlotte could change her sister's mind. Even if Hannah decided to return to her own home, she would need someone to keep an eye on her and help with chores. Whether the result of her self-enforced inactivity or the stroke itself, Hannah had declined over the past months. She was no longer robust and probably would never be as independent as she once had been.

Yet in Charlotte's mind, she still saw herself driving out of town the day after school ended. She could close her eyes and feel herself becoming more buoyant with each mile she put between herself and Newberg, floating really, her arms and legs light as feathers, the tightness gone from her neck and chest, her forehead becoming smooth and cool. For whatever time she could manage, she would push aside the mantle of family and become just Charlotte. The Charlotte only she knew. Lighter-than-air Charlotte.

Sometimes she envisioned Suzanne and George in the car with her, as they had been last summer. Other times not. Charlotte wanted Suzanne to come along only if she didn't call Brady every night at ten o'clock Newberg time. She wanted her to come only if she simply came. No expectations. No censure. Just floating.

Suzanne picked up the horseshoe that was supposed to have brought a look of nostalgia to her grandmother's face. "Grandma didn't really dislike the horses," she said. "I think I'll go over to her house tomorrow and bring back some pictures of her parents and grandparents and Grandfather Harry to put up in her room."

At least Suzanne was still trying with her grandmother, Charlotte thought, still trying to reclaim the fluffy, bustling woman who had been a fixture of her childhood.

"I wish I could remember my grandfather Harry," Suzanne said. "He sounds like such a sweet man. He and Grandma were really happy, weren't they?"

"Yes, your grandfather adored her, and she liked being his helpless little Hannah—which as I look back seems like a total joke. She was always in charge. Your grandfather either didn't realize it or didn't mind indulging her. But I think they had always loved each other and always known they would get married. Someday, you'll have to go up in her attic and look at the messages they wrote in each other's high school yearbooks."

"What about you and Daddy? How could you have married him if you were still in love with someone else?"

Charlotte drew in her breath, fearing a confrontation. But the look on Suzanne's face was earnest, no longer that of the challenging daughter indignant over a flawed mother.

"It broke my heart when Cory didn't come back after Vietnam, and I must have thought that getting married would be a cure. I remember being surprised that the pain went on and on. Then one day, I finally realized that even if Cory had shown up on my doorstep, I needed your father more than I needed him. Things changed for me after that. I didn't forget Cory, but I was able to put his memory aside and devote myself to your father. And I did come to love him—very much."

"But if Cory had shown up before you really fell in love with Daddy, would you have divorced Daddy and gone off with him?"

"I don't know. But I'm glad that didn't happen. Are you thinking about someone to go off with, Suzanne?"

Suzanne took a sip of wine before answering. "Not someone specifically," she said. "But I keep wishing Brady were different. We never talk—not like you and Daddy did. You and Daddy were each other's best friends. I know that Brady loves me, but he wants me to sit there on the shelf so he can take me down from time to time and feel good that he has me. His real life is what he does with men—

business, hunting, golf, talking about sports and politics. I like to discuss sports and politics, too. I like hearing about the business. But he tunes me out, and I don't know how to get to him. I'm lonely, Mom. I don't think you and Daddy ever felt lonely."

Never lonely?

Charlotte thought of Stan dialing Elizabeth's number, "occasionally over the years." She thought of herself rolling away from her husband after lovemaking and wondering why it was never as wonderful as it had been at eighteen with Cory Lee Jones. She and Stan had become friends to muffle the loneliness.

They had been able to do that, Charlotte realized, because they read the same books and had a shared interest in the world and raising their children. It was friendship, not passion, that gave their marriage substance. In the end, of course, it was friendship that made any marriage a successful one.

But friendship wasn't an option for Brady and Suzanne. They had too small a common ground.

"Brady can't understand why I'm not domestic like his mother, why I don't get off on cooking fabulous meals for him, why I don't want to build that house out there next to his folks," Suzanne went on. "And he can't understand why I'm not pregnant again."

"Why aren't you?"

Suzanne actually looked around before answering, as though she were searching for listening ears. "I got an IUD," she said softly. "I'd rather take pills, but I was worried that he might find them."

"Can't you just tell him you're not ready to have children yet?"

Suzanne shook her head. "It would make him afraid. If we have kids and a house, then he knows I'm not going anyplace."

"And where is he afraid you'll go?"

"Back to college," she said, not looking at her mother.

Charlotte knew Suzanne was remembering that awful scene when she announced she was going to get married. When Charlotte insisted she had to finish college first. When Charlotte said that Brady wanted to bury her in Newberg.

"The commute over to Wayne State isn't that far," Charlotte

said hopefully. "Maybe you could start slowly—just a class or two to show him that it won't interfere with your life together."

Suzanne shook her head. "What I really want is to go back to Lincoln—to finish my premed and go on to medical school."

"And where would Brady fit into such a plan?"

"It could be like before we were married. I'd come home on weekends."

"Do you think he would go along with that?"

Suzanne stared at the flames. The contours of her young face were so pure. Charlotte reached out and gently traced the perfect curve of her daughter's jaw.

"I don't know," Suzanne said softly, tears glistening in her eyes. "I keep thinking that maybe he'll see how unhappy I am and suggest I go back to school. It would be okay if the idea came from him."

"And if it comes from you?"

"He would be against it."

"So what will you do?"

"Nothing," she whispered.

Charlotte reached for the empty mugs, not knowing what else to say, not wanting Suzanne to see her despair. She couldn't tell her daughter to leave her husband. She couldn't tell her that, pregnant or not, she never should have married Brady.

New Year's morning, Charlotte and Suzanne loaded casseroles and pies in the back of the station wagon and headed for Norfolk. Brady was snowed in and would be watching Nebraska play for the national championship in a sports bar in Rapid City. It had snowed most of the night in Newberg but stopped by morning, and the snowplows had cleared the highway.

"Did you and Bernice have a fight?" Suzanne asked when they were on their way, seemingly the only inhabitants in an immaculate world.

"What makes you think that?" Charlotte countered as she slowed down for the Highway 77 intersection.

"When Bernice came after Christmas to get Grandma, the two of you were all business," Suzanne answered. "No sitting down for coffee and a chat. And I haven't heard you talking to her on the phone."

"I asked Bernice if we could each take your grandmother for six weeks this summer, instead of the weekday-weekend arrangement we have now. She said no."

"So, you're still planning to take another trip?"

"Yes, I'd like to."

"To look for Cory Jones?"

"Yes, but that's not the only reason, Suzanne. I need to get away again. Like last summer. Get some distance. See the world."

"And Bernice doesn't approve."

"Something like that. My sister thinks that she and I should live parallel lives—two widowed sisters with their families and their routines, getting old together, looking out for each other. It scares her that I want something more than that."

"Like what?"

"I'm still trying to figure that out. All I know is I'm not ready to hole up just yet."

"What about Colonel Grimmett? You seem to have patched things up with him. At least, you're nice to him when he calls on the phone."

"He's a nice man."

"If I hadn't been staying with you, would you have gone out with him last night for New Year's Eve?"

"I might have. More likely I would have sat on the sofa with him like you and I did, drinking hot chocolate and watching the ball drop in Times Square."

"It's hard to think of you dating."

"I'm sure it is. It's hard for me to think of you married."

❧ Donald's recliner was gone from the family room, which was only marginally better than having it still sitting there. Bernice had arranged the dining-room chairs theater fashion in front of the TV for the football games. Mark was already there, beer can in hand, talking football with the guys. He gave Charlotte his usual hug, but he seemed distracted and tired.

"Did you go see Sarah in North Platte?" Charlotte asked.

He nodded. "I drove six hours in a snowstorm to find out that she's run off to England. She never bothered to tell me that she'd accepted a scholarship next semester at Oxford. I'd say that's about as determined as a girl can be not to continue a relationship."

"Maybe she wants you to come after her."

"You don't know Sarah, Mom. It's all over. Which is just as well, I suppose."

"But you don't feel that it's just as well down here?" Charlotte said, touching his chest.

"No. I'm not sure I'll ever get over her."

Charlotte embraced him—her son with a broken heart—and felt his pain in her own chest. She could love him, but she couldn't protect him.

She watched while he opened another can of beer and rejoined his cousins. He looked over his shoulder at her, acknowledging her gaze, rewarding her with a small, resigned smile. Some things were not meant to be.

Charlotte turned away. She suddenly wanted to leave. To walk in the snow. Sit in a church pew. She wanted to be anywhere except here with her suffering son; her frightened sister; her mother who would rather punish them than enjoy what life she had left; Suzanne, who was sacrificing herself in the name of duty; and the ghost of Donald, who killed himself rather than try to rebuild his life.

She slipped through the kitchen door and went upstairs to Bernice's room, seeking seclusion in her bathroom. She splashed cold water on her face and stared at her image in the mirror. She could see glimpses of the girl she had once been and the old woman she would become—a woman in the middle. It had taken a lot of years to get to this point, years of simply going from one day to the next.

Now she wanted to feel each day, to choose what would be remembered and not just let life happen. But that meant not letting the rest of them drag her down. What if she didn't have the courage for that?

She turned to leave, then spun around and looked at her face again. She lifted her brows to smooth out the creases around her eyes. Lifted her chin. Fluffed her hair. Rummaged around for a lipstick.

In the kitchen, Bernice gave her a perfunctory hug. "Vicky called. She said not to wait dinner. She's bringing some boy."

"How's Mama?"

"The same. She's resting before dinner. The neighborhood kids had a New Year's Eve party last night, and she called the police because they were keeping her awake. I'm not too popular with the neighbors right now."

"Looks like you've been cooking for a week," Charlotte observed, taking in the counters laden with casseroles, homemade rolls, a chocolate layer cake, plates of cookies. Both ovens were on. Every burner of the stove was occupied by a pan.

"It's what I do," Bernice said.

"And you do it very well. Let's have a good day, okay? You look nice, Bernie. I like your haircut."

Vicky and her guest didn't arrive until late afternoon. Charlotte's heart contracted at the sight of her older daughter. Vicky's lush dark hair was dotted with snowflakes, her cheeks flushed with the cold, her green eyes dancing. She glowed. She was as beautiful as a human being could possibly be. A woman in love.

Charlotte met Mark's eyes across the room. He saw it, too.

In unison, brother and mother turned their attention to the man with Vicky—a nice-looking young man with a slight build and an expensive overcoat. He was smiling shyly as Vicky led him across the room, toward her mother.

"Mom, this is Jonathan Dearing," she said in a voice as proud and clear as a church bell.

chapter twenty-four

Mark was staring out the window of his apartment when his mother's station wagon stopped out front. He watched while she got out of the car and headed for the building entrance. She was wearing black slacks and snowboots, her beige coat unbuttoned, swinging about her legs as she walked. She was slim, he realized. When had that happened?

Not that she'd ever been fat. Not like Bernice. But he couldn't remember her ever looking as she did now. She even walked differently. More like Suzanne, with a long stride and her hands thrust in her pockets.

What motherly mission was she on, he wondered. Was she coming to cheer him? To fix him up with some friend's daughter?

He'd thought he'd done a splendid job yesterday, betting on the bowl games with his cousins, nibbling at his food, pretending to enjoy himself.

Other years, he had really cared about scores and national ratings. This year, he couldn't make himself concentrate and took clues from the cousins, cheering when they cheered, groaning when they groaned, doing just fine really until Vicky arrived with her new boyfriend, the two of them looking like poster children for true love.

His mother had watched him embrace Vicky, shake Jonathan's hand, then try to make himself invisible. She hadn't tried to stop him as he searched through the mountain of coats tossed on the stairs and hurried out the door.

She'd waited until this morning to call and announce she was coming to see him. He explained that there was nothing to talk about. Yes, he was devastated. But he and Sarah would have made each other miserable. "Can't you just say what you have to say over the phone?" Mark asked.

"No," she'd said. "I want to see you. I'm leaving now, and I expect you to be there."

She looked up and saw him at the window but didn't wave. He heard the front door open and close—her footsteps on the wooden stairs. The door to his apartment was unlocked.

She kissed his cheek and asked for a cup of coffee. His coffeepot was broken, he explained, as he microwaved two cups of water and stirred in instant coffee. "So what did you think of Jonathan Dearing?" he asked.

"He seems like a fine young man. And clearly they are in love. But he's going to seminary in the fall. Being a minister's wife is not something I would have chosen for Vicky."

"Why not?"

"She'll never be able to be herself," Charlotte said, accepting the cup of coffee. She took two sips and put the cup on his cluttered coffee table.

"I want you to go to England," she said. "I'll loan you the money."

Mark stared at her, stunned. "God, Mom, that's dumb."

"No, it's dumb not to fight for what you want."

"I don't want her. Not anymore. It never would have worked."

"That sounds like rationalizing."

"Look, I'm angry. Hurt. Sad. But aside from that, Sarah and I are as different as night and day. I can't make her change. She wouldn't be Sarah if she changed."

"Yes, I know. The two of you would fight all the time, and you'd never be elected governor or senator or whatever. So, you'll settle for safe and always wonder how it might have been."

"I wouldn't know where to look."

"Oh, come on, Mark. How many red-headed girls from Nebraska are studying law at Oxford this semester?"

"I don't have a passport."

"Then get one. Go to the federal building or wherever right now—this morning. Stand in line. Bribe someone. Call your congressman."

"Classes start a week from Monday."

"So take a quick trip. Or miss a few days. Miss the whole damned semester and make it up next fall."

"Would you have been happier with that other guy—the one you were looking for last summer?"

"Probably not. But I should have at least found out what the hell happened and not spend the rest of my life wondering how it would have been if I had gone after him."

"And Dad? Was there someone before you? What about him pulling you from the pond and always knowing you were the girl for him?"

"Your father had been married once before."

Mark stared at his mother for a long minute, his mind refusing to accept what she had just said. He realized he was holding his breath and let it out slowly. "I wish you hadn't told me that."

"I gather you don't want this," she said, holding out the check she had written to pay for his trip.

Mark shook his head. He watched while she tore it into the tiniest pieces possible and threw them on the floor.

❧ The subject of Sarah Grigsby was closed with Mark for all time, and Suzanne made it clear to her mother that she regretted saying anything about returning to college. It wasn't going to happen. End of discussion.

Vicky, however, wanted to talk all the time. She called her mother almost nightly to share her excitement. Jonathan sent her flowers. Jonathan drove to Lincoln every weekend to see her. Jonathan gave her a string of pearls. By Valentine's Day, she had a three-carat engagement ring.

Vicky seemed to be so much in love that Charlotte couldn't help but be happy for her. Of course, she wanted her to get married someday, but she also wanted more for her. She wanted her to experience some of the independence that she herself had never known. Marrying Jonathan Dearing would end all that. Minister's wives had no identity aside from being a helpmate to their godly husbands.

New Year's Day at Bernice's, Hannah had taken one look at Jonathan Dearing and recognized quality—at least, that was the way she told it afterwards. Her true conversion came when she discovered that Jonathan's mother was a Caldwell of the Topeka Caldwells, and his father was one of the richest men in the state of Kansas. Hannah didn't bother with subtlety. She simply announced that she was feeling better and wanted to resume her life. In one fell swoop, Vicky had erased Hannah's shame over Suzanne's marriage of necessity, Charlotte's wanderlust, Donald's suicide, and Bernice's fire.

By the end of January, Hannah had moved back to her house, which complicated rather than simplified Charlotte's life. Vicky returned her grandmother's car, but Hannah had no business behind the wheel, as testified by the deep ruts on either side of her driveway. She also could no longer carry sacks of groceries or manage heavier housekeeping chores. And going up and down stairs made her dizzy. She would have to stop every two or three steps and close her eyes to regain her equilibrium.

Charlotte suggested she turn the dining room into a downstairs bedroom, but Hannah wouldn't hear of it. Where would she entertain? She didn't want people to think she was an invalid.

So Charlotte stopped by every morning on the way to school to make sure her mother's broken body wasn't lying at the foot of the stairs. And she did most of her mother's grocery shopping, cleaned her house, did her laundry, ironed her clothes. But even with all the extra chores, it was better than before. Charlotte's own home was once again sacrosanct, her own little corner of the world. She found it strange how important a physical sense of privacy had become to her when most of her life privacy was something that existed only inside her head.

In February, she and Eric had dinner once again at the Vets Club in West Point. This time the glow from the wine and conversation was laced with possibilities. When they emerged into another bone-chilling night with a million stars overhead, Eric said, "Damn, I hoped for a blizzard. You know—impassable roads, immediate bivouac required."

"As in a nice warm motel room?"

"Yeah, something like that."

"We don't need a blizzard."

"You mean that?"

"I think so," she answered, not at all sure that was what she meant, wondering if it was the wine speaking.

"Would you rather go back to Newberg?"

"No, someplace neutral would be better."

In the car he kissed her. The kisses were wonderful, but coats, gloves, and scarves were in the way.

He drove half a mile to a generic motel. She started to protest as he turned into the parking lot. Not here, she wanted to say, someplace nicer. But she also didn't want to go driving around West Point looking for a motel.

She waited in the car while he went inside to get a room. Sitting there with the vacancy sign flashing on and off in her face, her ardor cooled considerably. Maybe they should have driven back to Newberg, except she didn't want to invite him to the bed she had shared with Stan. She wondered if he still slept in his marital bed, and if his wife's picture was on the bureau. No, a motel was better.

The motel room was plain, of course, and smelled of stale to-
bacco smoke. Once inside, Charlotte went directly to the bathroom.

Sitting on the toilet, she put her forehead on her knees to quell
a bout of dizziness. She hadn't had so much to drink since Taos,
since the night she first met Jason Piper. She shouldn't have let Eric
order a second bottle of wine, shouldn't have let him keep refilling
her glass. She reached up and turned off the light, enclosing herself
in complete darkness in the windowless tub-toilet cubicle, a nice
little warm cocoon.

She could hear Eric walking around the room. Probably he was
wondering what the hell she was doing in here. She knew she had to
get up off the toilet, to get on with it so she could go home and go
to bed.

She considered pulling off her pantyhose but pulled them up instead. She was too drunk to put them back on if they decided not to
go through with this.

"This doesn't feel right," she told him when she emerged.

"I know." He came across the room and embraced her. "Let's just
go on home. There'll be another night."

"Yes. Another night." She leaned against him, relieved. Such a
nice man. And he didn't have a paunch. So many men his age had
one. Eric was flat and lean, and he smelled good—like soap and af-
tershave. She nuzzled up against his neck and inhaled him. Then
she tasted him, and he began rubbing his hands up and down her
back. A small whimpering sound came up out of her throat. Immediately, she could feel his erection pushing against her, and she giggled.

"Sorry," she whispered.

"Is it funny?" he whispered back.

"No, just fun. I don't think I want to go home after all," she said
and lifted her face to be kissed. The kissing was good. The kissing
made everything all right.

His hand was at her neck, at the top of the zipper. "May I?" he
asked.

His question took her down a notch. My God, couldn't he tell?

Even with the lights out, more illumination than she wanted filtered through the draperies. She turned her back and stripped, tossing her clothes in the direction of a chair and hurriedly joining him between icy sheets. She realized that one of them should have turned up the heat.

"I haven't been with a woman for a long time," he said. She understood. He wasn't promising much.

He rolled over on top of her too soon. The sheets were still cold. "No, wait a while," she protested.

"I'm not sure I can," he said, pushing himself against her. She reached down to guide him. Once inside, he held very still, not even breathing.

She began gently stroking his back as she would to calm a child. He had a nice strong back. She told him so.

"Am I too heavy?" he asked.

"No."

"Are you sure? Vera always said I was heavy."

"You are not heavy."

Cautiously he settled into a rhythm, and Charlotte searched around in her head for desire, grabbing at random erotic thoughts, trying to find the right pathway. But she needed the fusion of kissing, and he didn't want to kiss for fear of falling over the edge.

Still, she was finding her way. Her body wanted it. She wanted it. She felt it kindling deep inside of her, radiating outward.

But once again he was asking if he was too heavy. And her mind slammed shut, leaving her body to close itself down as best it could.

On the way home, he asked when they could go out again, which she assumed was euphemistic for having sex. But she didn't want to do that again, at least not for a long time. The next time, she wanted less wine and a nice warm room with a fire burning. And she would find some gentle way to tell him to cool the questions.

"I don't know," she answered, which sounded dumb, but she had to say something.

"We do dinner well."

She laughed. "Yes, we do."

"How about dinner once a week?"

"How about dinner once in a while—Dutch treat?"

"Maybe sometime we can get drunk and talk about tonight."

"Maybe. But right now my head is starting to hurt, and I've promised myself that I'll never drink again."

❧ Vicky wanted to put seventy candles on Hannah's birthday cake, but Noreen insisted there wasn't enough room. They settled on one candle for each decade.

Hannah, with Michelle on her lap, beamed while her family sang to her. Jake snapped a picture as she leaned forward to blow out the candles.

It was a day of firsts, Charlotte thought. It was the first time the entire family had gathered since Donald's funeral, the first time Bernice's sons had been in her new home, and Jonathan Dearing's first visit to Newberg. Her little house was full to the seams. The ham and potato salad meal had been served buffet-style with people sitting where they could find a place.

After the cake was served, they presented Hannah with her gifts. Noreen and Bernice had made a beautiful piecework quilt for her bed. Charlotte had had a faded snapshot of her father standing in front of his brand-new 1938 Buick restored and framed. Suzanne had refinished her grandmother's favorite rocking chair. Bernice's sons gave Hannah an IOU that promised they would paint her house in the spring.

Hannah saved until last the large, elegantly wrapped gift from Vicky and Jonathan. She took great care not to tear the foil paper as she unwrapped it, and her hands shook as she lifted the lid from the box.

They all let out a collective gasp when Hannah lifted up a mink coat. Hannah stroked the fur in wonder. "This is the happiest day of my life," she said reverently. Then she cried a bit, had to blow her nose.

Vicky helped her into the coat, and everyone clapped as Hannah did a pirouette. "The Queen Mother never looked so good," Jonathan told her and planted a kiss on her cheek. When Jake stepped forward to take her picture, she linked arms with Vicky on one side and Jonathan on the other.

"The rest of us needn't have bothered," Bernice whispered to Charlotte.

Charlotte nodded, thinking of all the hours Bernice and Noreen had spent making the beautiful quilt that now lay forgotten in its box. She thought of the hours Suzanne had spent sanding and refinishing her grandmother's rocking chair and the hours her nephews would spend painting her house. All Vicky had done was select a coat that Jonathan's father would pay for. But it was most generous of the Dearings, she reminded herself, and they had made Hannah supremely happy.

When the doorbell rang, Mark was nearest to the entry hall and went to see who it was. Charlotte felt a rush of bitterly cold air. A minute later, Mark returned and sent a puzzled look in his mother's direction. Over her son's shoulder, Charlotte saw Jason Piper standing by the front door. And felt the room grow silent around her as all eyes turned to stare at the stranger.

"Excuse me," Charlotte blurted out, then rushed forward, grabbed her coat off the hall tree, and led Jason back outside to the privacy of the front porch. His Jeep was parked behind Brady's truck.

"I guess I caught you at a bad time," he said.

"What in the world are you doing here?" Charlotte demanded, pulling her coat close around her body.

"I missed you," he said, shivering. He was wearing only a thin jacket, no gloves, no hat, in the middle of a Nebraska winter.

"I can't talk to you now."

"When can you?"

"I don't know. Tomorrow maybe. Come back tomorrow. But I really have nothing to say to you, Jason. We said good-bye, remember?"

"Where can I go?"

"The closest motel is in West Point."

"Where's that?" he asked, before staggering backwards. He leaned heavily against the porch railing.

"Are you all right?" Charlotte asked.

"Just tired," he said. "I drove all night to get here. I had to see you again, Charlotte."

Then he began to cry. Charlotte put her arms around his shivering body and listened while he claimed to be in love with her, how their time in Taos had been the happiest of his life. "I want to be with you," he pleaded. "I know you won't marry me, but just let me be with you. Maybe I can get a teaching job up here, and we can live together. I want it to be like it was in Taos."

Finally, when he ran out of words and his exhausted body began to relax, she took him into the house. With her sister watching from the hallway, she led Jason up the stairs and down the hall to the back bedroom, told him where the towels were, brought a comforter for the bed. When she went back downstairs, her family was still crowded into the dining room, waiting for an explanation.

"I met him in Taos," she said. "He's not feeling very well."

"What's he doing here?" demanded Hannah, still wearing the mink coat.

"He came to see me," Charlotte said. "I'm sorry for the interruption. I had no idea he was coming. You really look beautiful in that coat, Mama. I'm so happy for you. All your friends will be green with envy. Now, how about another piece of cake for you boys? And there's more coffee."

But everyone began gathering up coats and carrying Hannah's gifts out to Jonathan's car. Vicky and Jonathan left first with Hannah. Bernice waited until her crew had said good-bye and gone to get in the van before she said her piece. "He has long hair, just like Cory Jones," she said. "And Mark said his Jeep has Louisiana plates."

Charlotte was very aware that Suzanne, Brady, and Mark were listening. "Go home, Bernice. We can talk about this tomorrow."

"He's the man you were involved with last summer, isn't he? An artist from Louisiana?"

"It's none of your business who he is," Charlotte said.

"My God, Charlotte, you're old enough to be his mother."

"Yes, I am. And I rather suspect that mothering is what he's looking for."

Bernice made a great show of hugging Suzanne and Mark and patting Brady sympathetically on the shoulder before she marched out the door.

"I think I should stay here," Mark announced, unbuttoning his coat.

Charlotte shook her head. "That's not necessary, Mark. You need to get back to Lincoln."

"Then I think Suzanne should stay," he insisted. "It's not right for you to be here alone in the house with a man."

"Grow up, Mark," Suzanne said, grabbing Brady's hand and heading for the door.

Then it was just Charlotte and Mark. "Whatever it is you are about to say, I don't want to hear it," she told him in the firmest tone she could muster. "You go on, Son. I'll take care of this."

With everyone finally gone, she went back upstairs. Still in his jacket, Jason was curled on his side with his hands between his knees. He murmured when she pulled off his shoes and covered him with the comforter.

It was an hour or more before she finished cleaning the kitchen and was able to put herself to bed. She didn't sleep well, acutely aware of the young man who had been her lover sleeping just down the hall. When she said good-bye to him in Taos, she truly wanted Jason to become just a fond memory. Now it seemed that her summer romance came with complications after all.

She got up early. When he came downstairs, she was having her second cup of coffee in front of the fireplace.

Without a word, he knelt in front of her and put his head in her lap. Automatically, she began stroking his hair. A part of her wanted to be angry with him, but she understood.

"Tessa left again, didn't she?"

He sat back on his haunches and nodded. "But that's not why I came. I never really loved Tessa, not like I love you."

She took his face between her hands. "You don't love me, Jason. We had fun, remember? We shared every secret we could dredge up. We trusted each other because we knew that when the summer was over, we would go back to our separate universes. And all that was wonderful, but it wasn't love."

"Then what was it?"

"We were lovers and best friends. But we were not and are not in love."

"You wish I hadn't come," he said, his tone accusing.

"Oh, yes, I wish you hadn't come. I really hadn't planned for my children to know that I'd had an affair with a member of their generation. God, Jason, when you drove up and saw the vehicles out front, didn't it occur to you this wasn't a good time for me? You could have at least called first."

"If I'd called, you would have told me not to come."

"You're right about that."

"Haven't you thought about me at all?" he asked, almost whining, a little boy with his feelings hurt. "Haven't you wanted to be with me again?"

"Of course I've thought about you, but not like that. I've moved on, Jason. If I get involved with another man, he's got to be my age. You know why I always got up so early in Taos? I couldn't bear the thought of you looking at me in the light of day without at least brushing my hair and putting on some makeup. I didn't like that. I don't want to be embarrassed about my age."

He got up and went to stand by the fireplace, looking at the picture that had once hung in the window of Lonnie and Marie's gallery. If he recognized it, he didn't say. "All I could think about after Tessa left was finding you. All those hours driving up here, I imagined how it would be when you saw me, how you would throw your arms around me and tell me how much you'd missed me, that you'd been hoping and praying I would come. I thought we'd be in bed five minutes after I got here. I went into your room this morning, but the bed was made. You were always making the bed. I never did understand that. We were just going to get back in it again."

He turned and stared at her. "You're going to send me away, aren't you?"

"Yes, you have to leave. You have to go back and finish out the school year. Then you can move someplace else if you want to. You can move to Taos, devote yourself to painting, find out if you can make a living as an artist."

"But what if I can't?"

"Then you'll know you have to do something else."

"Would you come with me?"

Charlotte laughed. "No, I will not come with you. I'll fix you some breakfast, then I want you out of here before you get snowed in."

Jason got his satchel out of the Jeep and showered and shaved while Charlotte put a slice of ham in the skillet and mixed waffle batter. When the phone rang, she knew it would be Bernice.

"Is he still there?"

"Yes."

"And his vehicle sat out in front of your house all night for the whole world to see?"

"I don't think the whole world drove by here last night."

"I feel so sorry for your children."

"*You* were the one who announced in front of Mark, Suzanne, and Brady that I'd had an affair with him. For God's sake, Bernice, they didn't need to know that."

"I have no secrets from my children," she said self-righteously.

"Oh? So when did you tell them about the last years of your marriage to their father? When did you tell them why you really built that house? I never would have betrayed your confidence, Bernice. Never."

Then she realized the line was dead. Bernice had hung up.

Denver, Colorado
April 17

Dear Mrs. Charlotte Haberman:

I am writing in regard to your letter of April 1. I have forwarded your request on information about a mountain community of Vietnam veterans to the previous director of this office, Mr. Miles Hamlin, who retired last year.

Yours very truly,
Hayes Dickerson
Director
Denver Veterans Center

chapter twenty-five

Charlotte tapped on the principal's open door. "You wanted to see me?"

Mr. Brothers was sitting with his back to the door, staring out the window at the scurry of students crossing the school grounds as they headed for home.

He swung his chair around. "Yes, Charlotte. Come in, please, and close the door, would you?"

Charlotte did as he asked, the skin on her forehead prickling with apprehension. Closing the door meant something serious. Her mother had fallen. One of her children had been hurt in an automobile accident. No, he would have come to her for family emergencies. This summons meant something else.

Was there a rule against teachers dating? Did they care that she and Eric went out occasionally?

Maybe she shouldn't have let the seventh graders read the William Faulkner short story "A Rose for Emily." But surely that couldn't be it—they saw stories just as macabre on television and at the movies.

"Tell me about Tommy Braunsmeyer's term paper," Mr. Brothers said, his hands carefully folded in front of him, his expression a studied neutral.

Ah, so that was it, she thought. Not good. Charlotte cleared her throat. "His paper compared the world's major religions. Tommy is a very bright boy, you know. Very well read."

"Yes, I realize that. Did you assign the topic?"

"No. The students were to choose an area of interest and write a simple research paper, with a bibliography that included at least three sources. Most of the students used encyclopedias and other reference books from the school library, but Tommy went far beyond that. He got books on interlibrary loan and wrote a paper that any college freshman would have been proud of."

"Did you make this assignment to both of your eighth-grade classes."

"No, just the third-hour class. The students in that class are more advanced."

"Did Tommy have your approval for this topic?" He was frowning now, his voice lower.

"Yes, they had to submit a one-page outline before actually writing the paper. Tommy's outline was five pages long. His paper was twenty-five pages."

"So, you knew the direction he was going with this paper before he actually wrote it?"

"Yes, I saw that he was going to compare the differences and similarities of the world's five major religions."

"What were some of the other students' topics?"

Charlotte stared at the picture of Abraham Lincoln hanging above Mr. Brothers's carefully groomed head of snowy-white hair. "Dinosaurs, Michael Jordan, cheerleading, raising pigs, the history of Nebraska, prehistoric horses. And a couple of others I don't remember. I can give you a list."

"Actually I'd like copies of all the papers, including Tommy's, of course."

"May I ask the nature of your inquiry?"

Mr. Brothers dismissed her request with a wave of his hand. "We'll get to that. I understand that each student read his or her paper to the class."

"Not exactly. They were to give a five-minute talk on their topic and explain how they did their research. The point of the assignment was research. They had to validate what they wrote. They couldn't just wing it or depend on what their parents knew."

"I understand that. And when Tommy gave his five-minute talk, did he say that Christianity was"—Mr. Brothers paused and glanced down at a tablet on his desk—"Did he say that Christianity was 'all made up'?"

"No, he didn't say that. He talked about religion in general terms. He may have said something about primitive people not understanding natural phenomena and gradually evolving stories to explain them."

Mr. Brothers leaned forward, his gaze intent. "And did you correct him?"

"How do you mean?"

"Did you point out the difference between Christianity and pagan religions? Did you point out that Christianity is based on the word of the one true God as reported in the Bible? Did you point out that the Bible cannot be refuted because it is divinely inspired?"

"No. I'm a schoolteacher, not a minister. Tommy cited various religious scholars to back up his statements. It wasn't something he was saying on his own."

"And what grade did you give Tommy on this paper?"

"I gave him an A-plus."

"Did you award such a high mark for any of the other papers?"

"No, I gave several A's, but only one A-plus. Tommy's paper was head and shoulders above those written by the other students."

"And I understand that you supplied some of the books he used in his research."

"Only one book. One of my old college textbooks. He got his other sources on his own."

"What sort of textbook?" he asked.

"An introductory anthropology text."

"Had this book been approved by the state schoolbook commission?"

"A dated college textbook? I doubt it."

"I see. You will have the students' papers on my desk by the time school is out tomorrow."

"I've already returned them."

"Then I suggest you notify your students and ask that these papers be returned to you. *Tomorrow*, Mrs. Haberman."

At home, Charlotte called each of the students in her third-hour class and asked them to return their term paper. None of them asked why. She wondered if they knew.

Tommy was already in bed. She left a message with his grandmother.

Then she sat with her hand on the phone, wanting desperately to call Mark and talk to him about what was happening. Had she broken a law? Maybe she needed to hire a lawyer. But she'd had little contact with Mark in the weeks since Jason Piper had shown up at her door. He'd left a message for her with the school secretary, saying that he needed a copy of his birth certificate so he could register for the state bar exam. And he'd asked Vicky to let her know that he wouldn't be home for Easter. Charlotte had written him a brief note saying that she was sorry he was upset and that she loved him very much.

She picked up the receiver and put it down again. Then she dialed Mark's number but hung up before it rang. *I am his mother,* she reminded herself. Who she did or did not sleep with could not alter that. She dialed his number again, this time letting it ring but halfway hoping he wouldn't answer.

She jumped when he picked up the phone, then took a deep breath and said, "I've got a problem."

When she finished explaining, she asked, "What's going to happen to me?"

"Well, first of all, you haven't done anything wrong, at least not

in the legal sense. Let's hope the principal just strongly suggests
you be more prudent in the future."

"And if it's more than that?"

"I don't know. It could get messy. Separation of church and state
may be the law of the land, but it isn't practiced in towns like Newberg. Good grief, Mom, you teach in a town that routinely sings
hymns at commencement and offers prayers before assemblies and
sporting events. Didn't any bells and whistles go off when that kid
handed in his outline?"

"I don't know. Maybe. I know how people are, but I didn't think
any of this would go outside my classroom."

"What kind of a kid is this? Comparative religions seems kind of
weird for an eighth-grader."

"His family is from Newberg, but he was born in India. His parents were medical missionaries. His mother died two years ago, and
he was sent home to live with his grandmother. He's bright and curious, and he's seen more of the world than the other kids."

"Well, I wished you'd encouraged him to write about the Hi-
malayas or the Taj Mahal instead."

"Am I going to lose my job?"

"I hope not," he said. "Don't talk to anyone about this, and keep
me posted."

"I've missed you, Mark," Charlotte said.

"I miss you, too, Mom, but I don't know what to say to you anymore. I wish you were still living in the old house and had never
gone on that trip."

"Oh, Mark, that's like me saying I wish you were still five years
old and carrying around that tattered old Teddy bear."

"I suppose," he allowed.

The following day, she gave the papers to Mr. Brothers's secretary. And then she waited.

With each day and week that went by, she breathed a little easier.
Maybe he had decided not to pursue the matter. Surely he had realized how thoughtful Tommy's paper was, not something to warrant
concern.

❧   Hannah thought they should entertain the Dearings at her house since it was larger and nicer than Charlotte's. But Charlotte felt the need to invite Vicky's future in-laws to her own home, modest as it might be.

Charlotte was pleased when Mark drove down the day before to paint the front door and wash windows. She found herself hovering, bringing him drinks of water and asking him questions about this and that. And much to Charlotte's surprise, Hannah spent the day polishing silver, peeling potatoes and apples. Brady raked leaves and hauled off fallen branches. Suzanne undertook the tedious task of ironing the Battenberg lace tablecloth and napkins and came back Saturday morning to help with the final preparations. Vicky and Patty were meeting the family's private plane at the airport in Norfolk and driving the senior Dearings and Jonathan to Newberg.

"I wonder if Vicky will show them the town before bringing them here," Charlotte said as she and Suzanne struggled to get a leaf in the dining-room table.

"I imagine," Suzanne said. "And she'll probably take them by our old house."

Yes, Vicky would do that, Charlotte thought. She would stop out front, point up to her father's window, explain that the house used to be painted white and have a front porch, and make absolutely sure they understood that the house they would be visiting was not the home of her childhood.

"Mark is still angry with me for selling the house," she said as they carefully spread the tablecloth over the table—a beautiful cloth that had belonged to Stan's mother. "What about you?"

Suzanne shrugged. "Maybe not angry. But it still makes me sad. Vicky, too. It's where we were kids and Daddy was still alive."

"Do you understand at all why I had to sell the house—aside from needing the money?" Charlotte asked.

"Sure. Keeper-of-the-shrine is a limited role. But that doesn't make me like losing it any better. I wish I could buy it instead of building a house out there by Brady's parents."

"Believe me, Suzanne, I struggled with my decision about selling the house every bit as much as you are struggling with deciding about building a house next door to Brady's folks."

"That much, huh? Then after you decided, was it easier?"

"Deciding is usually the worst part."

"Have you decided what to do this summer?" Suzanne asked.

"Well, I have to get Vicky married first. Then I'd still like to take a trip if I can work something out with Bernice about your grandmother."

"I could look after Grandma, I suppose. But I feel the same as Bernice. I don't want to be the one who enables you to go. I don't want you to find Cory Jones. You might never come back."

"I was sort of hoping you'd go along with me," Charlotte said.

"I'm still paying penance for last summer. It wasn't worth it."

❧ Charlotte found Angela and Charles Dearing easy to be with. They were a handsome couple who treated each other with respect and obviously adored their children. They asked Hannah about her family background, her childhood memories of Newberg. And they wanted to know about Stan. "Vicky is quite proud of her father," Charles told Charlotte. "She showed us some of the editorials he wrote. And I can see that she has had a wonderful role model in you."

"Are you happy about Jonathan's decision to enter the ministry?" Charlotte asked.

"Oh my, yes," Angela Dearing said. "We always knew that Charles's nephew Robert would run the company. Patty will run the family foundation. And Jonathan will be a minister. We are quite blessed, you see, especially now that your Vicky has agreed to join us. She is the perfect girl for Jonathan. Just perfect."

Charles Dearing agreed. "Jonathan will never make much money, of course. But we'll look after them and see they live well. Their children will have trust funds. Vicky, too, in case anything happens to Jonathan. For the rest of her life, no matter what happens, your daughter will never want for anything, Charlotte. That is a solemn promise that we make to you."

Charlotte thanked them and said how grateful she was. But was she really?

After dinner, Suzanne and Brady said good-bye, and the rest of them drove to the Lutheran church to meet with the minister. Next week's engagement party would be at the Dearings' home in Topeka and a wedding reception would be held the evening of the wedding at the Topeka country club, but the wedding itself would be a morning ceremony in Newberg—at the First Lutheran Church. Vicky stood her ground on that—she had grown up knowing she would someday walk down that aisle and stand at that altar to marry the man she loved.

Their footsteps on the wooden floors echoed in the empty sanctuary of the simple country church that had stood on its corner for more than eighty years, where Charlotte and her sister had been christened, where they both had been married and their parents before them. There was a dignity about the building that Charlotte loved. It was a place for meditation and singing. No distractions. No ostentation.

Stan had loved the church, too. He'd been a deacon for years. His funeral had been here, his casket in front of the simple altar.

Charlotte looked at her daughter's face, so full of love and joy as she stood with her husband-to-be, discussing their wedding ceremony. Stan would have liked Jonathan and would have been happy for Vicky, proud that she was marrying a man of God. Charlotte was trying to be happy about that, too, but it was a struggle. Vicky would never be a journalist now. She was turning her back on all those years of planning and study to become the good wife at her husband's side, always smiling, always agreeable, never drinking more than half a glass of sherry, dressing modestly, never raising her voice, never having an opinion of her own. Would all that restraint eventually diminish the love she now felt for Jonathan? He was sincere in his beliefs, of that Charlotte had no doubt. And he loved

Vicky. She didn't doubt that, either. But who would he love more—Vicky or his God?

She realized Mark was watching her, his expression puzzled. She was supposed to be overjoyed. Her daughter was marrying a man who would probably be a bishop someday.

While Pastor Jenson answered questions about the history of the church, Charlotte and Mark linked arms and walked back down the aisle to the vestibule. "She'll be okay," he said. "She and Jonathan will live their lives on a different plane than the rest of us, love and holiness all mixed in together. They'll build orphanages and save souls. Have a television program called *Fireside Chats with God*. Raise angelic children who never pick their noses. His folks will buy them a new car every year and turn the parsonage into a show home. And they'll be happier than the rest of us. Or maybe 'contented' would be a better word, since happiness seems to come in spurts. They'll be fine, Mom. You'll see."

Charlotte smiled and dared to lean her head against her son's shoulder. She knew she should be glad for her daughter, take pleasure in her good fortune, not try to negate it by looking behind it or down the road. Stan used to tell her to live more in the present, and he had been better at enjoying the moment. She used to always worry about tomorrow or next month or next year. But she was more relaxed now, able to take pleasure in small moments like this one with her son. Private moments with her daughters came naturally in the course of things. With sons, they were rarer and therefore more precious.

Mark had changed over the last months. He seemed older, quieter. She wondered if his failed romance continued to bother him.

"Are you content?" she asked.

"For the most part. I've got the bar exam hanging over my head, and now that I've got a job lined up with the best law firm in the state, I have nightmares about flunking the damned thing. It's happened, you know—people finishing in the top ten of their class and still not passing the bar. And with Carl Eshelman retiring, I may be running for the state legislature in the fall."

"Are you old enough to do that?"

He laughed. "Barely. But I think I'd have a good shot at it, un-less . . . "

"Unless what?"

The gathering in front of the altar was breaking up. Patty and Vicky were walking toward the door, Jonathan following with his parents. Mark and Charlotte walked outside and down the steps. "Has your principal said any more about that kid's term paper?" Mark asked.

"No. But there's a rumor floating around that I may have to ap-pear before the May school board meeting."

"I was afraid of that. Let me know, will you? We'll have to work out a strategy."

"Strategy for what?" she asked, but had to wait until they were back at her house for an answer.

Charlotte made coffee while Mark gathered up his things.

"About the school board," she said, filling a mug for him.

"Yes. If you're asked to appear, we'll need to decide how you should answer their questions."

"I'll answer with the truth."

Mark leaned across the table and put his hand on her arm. "What if they ask you about your personal religious beliefs?"

"They have no right," she said.

"Legally, that may be true, at least on the federal level. The Ne-braska constitution says, 'all public schools shall be free of sectar-ian instruction.' Of course, most of us who live here would hardly consider Christianity a sect. But regardless, Newberg isn't a town that would take kindly to a teacher who refused to answer a ques-tion about her personal religious beliefs."

Mark tilted his chair back and put his hands behind his neck. "I've been thinking about this a lot, Mom, trying to figure out how you would answer questions like that. And I realized how private you've always been on that front, which really surprised me. You got us to church on time and helped us learn our Bible verses, but you deferred to Dad when it came to doctrine. He was the one who related biblical passages to daily life. He even worked them into his weekly column. And when he said good-bye, he promised us that we'd all be together in heaven. With Jesus. But you never said anything like that. You never tried to make us feel better by telling us Dad was in heaven and thinking about us and waiting to be with us again someday. You'd speak up on political issues and tell us to be responsible citizens, but when it came to religion, you never had much to say."

"What does this have to do with Tommy Braunsmeyer's paper?"

The front legs of Mark's chair hit the floor with a thump. Charlotte jumped. "You let Tommy write it," Mark said, leaning forward, beating out the cadence of his words on the table with his index finger. "You didn't tell him that Christianity is *not* just another of the world's religions, *not* just another belief system."

"I've never told anyone what they can and cannot believe, not even my own children—as you have pointed out. I think everyone has to reason out things for themselves."

"What about faith, Mom? What about just *knowing* something is true, feeling it in your bones and in the air you breathe? Where does that fit in? How have you been able to live without it?"

"I love this town and our church, loved going there with my family on Sunday mornings, singing the hymns, hearing the scripture. I accept the teachings of Christ, but I've never been comfortable with the sermons. And the arrogance, with everyone thinking they have the keys to the kingdom and excluding anyone who didn't believe exactly as they do."

"But for the good people of Newberg, without faith, you're a heretic," Mark warned, "and they don't want heretics teaching their kids."

"*Heretic?* Isn't that a little melodramatic? This isn't the Middle Ages. Aren't you just worried that a controversial mother might hinder your chances for a political career?"

"I'm worried about us all, Mom. Vicky is marrying a minister. Suzanne has to live in this town. And Brady. Their kids. Your mother lives here. Bernice's family is just an hour away. I can just see the headline of the *Record*: 'Teacher Challenges Christianity.' You'll lose your job. The civil libertarians will get wind of it. They'll demand you fight against injustice and stand up for freedom of religion. The state press will pick up on it. Christ, Mom, you could take the whole family down with you."

"So, what am I supposed to say?" Charlotte asked, staring at the backs of her hands.

"Whatever those five school board members think is the right answer. Give witness. Tell them that you've accepted Jesus Christ as your personal saviour. That you let Tommy go too far, and it will never happen again. That you'll start every class with a prayer. Don't come off as different, Mom. It will cost us all."

"You want me to say those things even if they're not true?"

Mark shook his head back and forth. "I can't believe we're having this discussion. *You*, of all people."

The Dearing house was lit like a public monument for the engagement party. A tent with a dance floor had been erected in the backyard, with the music provided by a fifteen-piece orchestra. A disc jockey was installed in the basement rec room, a harp player in the solarium. There was a sushi bar by the pool. A Mexican buffet was spread in the den. A roasted pig presided over the dining room. A fountain bubbled with champagne in the entry hall, and strategically placed wet bars dispensed mixed drinks. Heaters had been installed outdoors to warm the spring evening.

As soon as they arrived, Suzanne raced upstairs to help Vicky with her hair, leaving the rest of the family to wander about the house before the other guests arrived. "*Rich* is an understatement," Bernice observed wryly.

A surprising number of people from Newberg were coming tonight—Pastor Jenson, several teachers, the newspaper staff, family friends, two carloads of Hannah's lady friends. Hannah actually got teary-eyed, thinking how they would see all this and report back to the rest of the town. "This is our family's finest hour," she said reverently. Noreen looked over her grandmother's head and rolled her eyes for her mother and aunt's benefit.

"All this, and she loves him, too, or so I gather from what Suzanne tells us," Bernice said, linking arms with Charlotte.

"Yes," Charlotte said, grateful for the physical contact. This was the first time she and Bernice had seen each other since the Jason Piper fiasco. Phone conversations had been cool. But tonight, for whatever reason, Bernice was being sisterly.

"You look good," Bernice said.

Charlotte didn't have anything elegant, so she had opted for simple, shortening a black, V-necked sheath she'd had for years that miraculously fit her once again. Her only jewelry was her gold earrings. She did buy a pair of open-toed pumps that looked like something the Andrews Sisters would have worn in the 1940s. She kept looking down at them, enjoying the way they looked on her feet.

Bernice was wearing a navy print dress she said was an original by Abdul the Tentmaker. Charlotte didn't laugh.

Elegant and gracious, Angela and Charles Dearing came downstairs before the other guests arrived to meet Vicky's aunt and cousins. And shortly Vicky, Jonathan, Patty, and Suzanne joined them.

Vicky's dress was of dark green strapless chiffon, worn with the pearls Jonathan had given her. Her hair was piled on her head, and pearl and diamond earrings, her engagement gift from Angela and Charles, dangled from her ears. Charlotte couldn't take her eyes off her.

The next hours passed in a blur of meeting hundreds of people, saying the same thing over and over again. Yes, Jonathan was a special person. The Dearings were a wonderful family. Yes, it would be wonderful to have a minister in the family. And thanking people when they said nice things about Vicky.

She would catch glimpses of Vicky and Jonathan, always together, always touching. Charlotte was amazed at how Vicky seemed to take all this wealth in stride. After their honeymoon in Paris, she and Jonathan would be moving into a nine-room home in Dallas, near Southern Methodist University, where Jonathan would be earning a doctor of divinity degree. The engagement ring on Vicky's finger was worth more than Charlotte's house. She couldn't even hazard a guess at the cost of the engagement party—equal to her annual salary probably, or maybe even more. She had no doubt that Vicky would have married Jonathan even if he were penniless but was somewhat bothered by the ease with which her daughter accepted all this grandeur.

Charlotte wondered if they had made love yet and decided not. Vicky had apparently stood firm this long and would want their wedding night to be the first time. Jonathan would invite God into their marital bed and proclaim their lovemaking a sacred rite.

Most of Patty and Vicky's sorority sisters were there, and after the toasts, they clustered around Vicky to serenade her with the songs of their sisterhood, some of them quite beautiful and poignant.

Angela came to stand beside Charlotte during the serenade. And they had a moment to lounge on the chaises by the pool and rest their feet. Charlotte's wonderful new shoes were turning on her.

"I want you to know that long before Vicky and Jonathan met, we'd come to think the world of your daughter," Angela said. "Before they became roommates, Patty had never really had a girlfriend, never had someone who called her just to chat. Vicky made Patty her sidekick, took her shopping, to the movies, studied with her, took her home to Newberg, and made our Patty a happier girl. My daughter would do anything for your daughter. And my husband and I already love her as our own."

Yes, Charlotte could see that. They loved her and doted on her. Their new child. They would not only love her as their own, they would make her their own. Vicky would be absorbed by this remarkable family, with her own mother and brother and sister existing only on the periphery of her life. This grand house would be where she came for holidays, not her mother's house. Charlotte had never wanted to cling to her children the way Bernice did with Noreen and the boys, but she'd never expected to give them away, either. Vicky would never be of Newberg and the Haberman family again. Her identity, her role, her ambition would all rest with Jonathan and his family.

Charlotte put her head against the back of the chaise, feeling warmth from the nearby heater, smelling the chlorine from the pool and the aroma of the hundreds of gardenias that were floating on its surface. She wished that Stan were here to hold her hand and tell her she was wrong, that Vicky would always be their little girl.

chapter twenty-six

"*B*ut Mrs. Haberman, why didn't you point out to this student that his term paper was blasphemous?" Warner Binford's tone was incredulous.

Mrs. Haberman. Charlotte had known Warner since kindergarten. As president of the school board, he was directing the inquiry. He had been a pallbearer at Stan's funeral. His wife taught the confirmation class at the Lutheran church. Their children had grown up together.

Charlotte looked back at Mark. He was sitting in the second row of the high school auditorium, his face in his hands. *Look at me, please. Tell me what to do.*

She'd wanted Mark to be up here with her, but having him act as a legal counsel would make the proceedings seem too adversarial, he pointed out. And besides, he wasn't yet a member of the state bar.

"You're my son," she protested.

No law had been broken, he kept reminding her. The school board knew that. They could only push this thing so far. And yes, she could refuse to appear, but that could jeopardize her job. They could claim her evaluations had fallen off, that her students weren't prepared for high school, that she assigned non-state-sanctioned reading material.

Fifty or sixty people were scattered throughout the auditorium. She recognized the parents of some of her students, and she saw Suzanne standing in the back by the door. Paul Lentz, who had covered school and church news for the newspaper since before Stan was editor, was sitting in the first row holding a tape recorder. Eric Grimmett was seated with a group of teachers in the middle of the room. He'd given her a thumbs-up when she came in.

"I never thought of the student's paper as blasphemous," Charlotte said, looking back at Warner. He was wearing a coat and tie, his bald head shining under the stage lights. The other men were less formally attired. Mildred Johnson was wearing a denim dress. The five board members were seated behind a table facing the audience. Charlotte was off to one side, sitting at a one-armed student desk, its surface covered with years' worth of graffiti—initials, hearts, GO BEARS, JESUS SAVES.

"But the writer of this paper suggests that all religions, including Christianity, are little more than folk tales," Warner said, holding up a copy of Tommy's paper. "Never once does he acknowledge the divine inspiration of Christian scripture as put forth in the Holy Bible."

"The boy was writing about religion in general terms," Charlotte explained, trying to sound reasonable, not upset. "The purpose of the paper was not to say that one faith is legitimate and others are not. He was looking for similarities and differences. Followers of every faith believe their doctrine comes either directly or indirectly from a deity or deities."

She could almost hear Mark's thoughts. She was saying too much. *Brief answers. Yes and no, if possible. Don't volunteer anything.*

Mildred leaned over and whispered something to Warner. He nodded. "Tell us what the student had to say about what he referred to as the 'Creation myth,' " he said.

"He simply pointed out that all faiths have a Creation story."

"And so, according to this student, the story of the Creation as put forth in the Holy Bible is a *myth?* It's made up, and therefore not true?"

"He explained that a 'myth' is not necessarily untrue—it just can't be proven. Even among Christians, some think the account in Genesis is to be taken literally, while others see it as allegory."

"And you didn't anticipate that some of the students would find the contents of this paper upsetting?"

"No, I didn't. I can see now that it was a mistake on my part to have him discuss it in front of the class, and I can understand why his comments might have been disturbing to some of his class-mates. They didn't understand what he was trying to do. They've never considered the historical basis of the world's religions, never contemplated why there might be different belief systems."

Mildred was whispering to Warner again. Her behavior irritated Charlotte—if she had a question, why didn't she just ask it her-self?

Warner cleared his throat. "Mrs. Haberman, are you a religious person?"

She wanted to ask him to explain his use of the word "religious." Was it someone who led a principled life or someone who was a member of a church? She looked at Mark again.

He nodded. She knew what she needed to say.

She faced the board members. "Yes. I've been a member of First Lutheran Church all my life."

"Do you attend services regularly?"

"I'm less inclined to attend every Sunday now that my children are grown and my husband has passed away, but church attendance is still a very important part of my life. Church membership even more so. I'll always be grateful for the way the church community rallied around me and my children when my husband died."

"Are you a Christian?"

"Yes."

"And you believe that Jesus Christ is the Son of God and died to save our immortal souls."

"Yes."

"Do you believe in the hereafter?"

She wanted to look at Mark again, to will him to put a stop to this. But she understood that he couldn't, and that she had to do it. The school board had no right to conduct this inquisition, and she was not obligated to answer these questions. But refusal on her part would label her as a non-believer.

She folded her hands in front of her. "Yes. I believe in the hereafter."

"How often do you pray?"

"Whenever I feel the need."

"Which is how often?"

She took a breath. "Daily."

"Do you revere the Holy Bible as the word of the one true God?"

"Yes."

Warner exchanged glances with the other board members, and they pushed their chairs back from the table for a huddled conference.

Five stalwart souls deciding her fate. Charlotte looked away. She was so tired. She hadn't slept well in weeks. Her head hurt; her body ached. Once again she was trying to get ready for a daughter's wedding, less than a month away. This time she really was making the wedding dress—that was what Vicky wanted. She had wept when Vicky asked her and relished the shopping trip with her to find just the right pattern and fabric. But now she was so tired, and there still was so much to do. A rehearsal dinner. Flowers. A brunch following the ceremony. A dress for herself. The trip to Topeka for the reception. And *her* trip. Her salvation. She planned to leave from Topeka. She wouldn't even come back to Newberg after the reception. Have the station wagon packed and ready to go.

The audience in the auditorium was getting restless, with much foot-shuffling and whispering. Charlotte looked around at the familiar old room. The flaking plaster and the faded curtain had been brand-new when she was in high school—when she acted in the senior play on this very stage. *I Remember Mama.* She'd played Mama. It seemed as though she'd been a mother all her life. She and Bernice had mothered each other growing up. She'd raised three extraordinary children. Now she was mothering her own mother. She didn't regret a moment of it, but she was so tired. She loved them all and didn't want to humiliate them, didn't want to become a pariah in their home town. She had done what she had to do. She couldn't have told the absolute truth, and shades of gray wouldn't do.

Finally, the board members were resuming their positions, the conference over. Warner was smiling. "That will be all, Charlotte. Sorry to have put you through this. We appreciate your willingness to answer our questions even though you were under no obligation to do so—as I'm sure young Mark there pointed out. This board certainly understands the concept of separation of the church and state. But we're all proud to live in a Christian community, and I'm sure you understand our need to deal with complaints about one of our teachers. As for the parents who brought the complaints, I hope they realize that you made some bad decisions but are a God-fearing woman who meant no harm."

"Thank you. May I go?"

"Certainly. But before you do, I'd like to recognize your son. Mark, stand up, will you? I'm sure all of you remember our All-State running back from a few years back. I guess he drove down tonight to make sure we didn't beat up on his mother." Warner chuckled and waited while the audience responded in kind. "I understand you've completed law school, Mark, and will be graduating next weekend. We'd like to offer our congratulations. It's always nice when one of our home-town boys makes good."

The other board members smiled and nodded their agreement. Mark stood and waved at them, then stepped up to take Charlotte's arm as she descended from the stage. Together, they walked down the center aisle. Charlotte leaned on his arm. Just a few more steps, she thought, and this will be over.

Suzanne followed them out. In the dimly lit lobby, lined with cases of dusty trophies, Charlotte slumped into the single chair holding vigil by the auditorium door and began to sob. "I'm so sorry," she said. "So sorry. How awful that was for you both."

"You did fine, Mom," Mark said. "Let's hope this is the end of it."

"Mark told you to lie, didn't he?" Suzanne said.

Mark scowled at his sister. "She had to say what they needed to hear. Otherwise it would have caused a real uproar, and God knows what the repercussions would have been."

"Did either of you ever tell Vicky what was going on?" Charlotte asked.

Suzanne shook her head. "And I made Grandma promise not to tell, but I needn't have bothered. She's petrified that something might jeopardize the royal wedding."

"Will one of you call your grandmother and tell her that it's over and I wasn't burned at the stake."

"I'll call her," Suzanne said. "Come on, Mom, I'll take you home. Our young attorney here is champing at the bit to be gone."

Charlotte stood and reached for Mark. "Thank you, Son, for your help." He stood stiffly for an instant, then returned her embrace.

She stepped back to look at his face. "I've disappointed you terribly, haven't I?"

"I thought you'd changed since Dad died. Now I find out you were different all along—not the person I thought you were."

"I've always been your mother and always loved my children more than anything."

"It all seems like such a charade. Our own mother, for God's sake. You even taught Sunday School!"

"Oh, Mark, I'm not a total disbeliever. I believe in the sanctity of life and something larger than us all. I loved the Bible stories and their intent. I just had a hard time with piousness and believing that never having doubts somehow made one more blessed. I feel blessed every time I look at your faces, every time I take a walk in the countryside or hear beautiful music. If that's not good enough for God or whoever, then so be it."

"Well, I'm just glad my father didn't have to live through this." And then he walked away.

❧ The next morning, a letter was waiting in Charlotte's box in the teachers' lounge. It was from Warner Binford. Due to a reorganization of the junior high and high school faculties, her contract was not being renewed for the upcoming year. Her many years of service to the Newberg school system were greatly appreciated. He wished her and her family well.

Charlotte walked down the hall in a daze, down to the room where she had spent the last ten years trying to be a good teacher, succeeding more this year, she felt, than the other nine. What would she do if she didn't teach? She was years away from any sort of meaningful retirement income. She wondered if she'd even be able to get another teaching job in the state. Would other towns contact Newberg school administrators and learn about the teacher who wasn't diligent enough in upholding the Christian standards of the community? A teacher whose beliefs were suspect?

Two teachers walked by her room without calling out cheery good mornings. Did they know? she wondered. Did the whole town know?

The door opened. She looked up, expecting to see an early student. Suzanne was standing there staring at her. "Are you all right, Mom? Oh, my God, they didn't fire you, did they?"

Charlotte could only nod.

"That really sucks," Suzanne said, slamming the door behind her, making the glass rattle dangerously. "I'd like to give them all a piece of my mind."

She took her mother's hands. "You are the most moral person I've ever known. I never cheated in school because I knew I would be letting you down. Daddy always spoke about what God expected from us, but you told us what *you* expected from us. I wasn't sure if I could hide from God, but I damned sure knew I couldn't hide from you."

Charlotte grabbed for her chair, lowered herself in it, not sure if she was crying because she'd been fired or because she was so touched by her daughter's words.

Suzanne knelt beside the chair, embracing her. "How did you know?" Charlotte sobbed.

Suzanne grabbed a handful of tissues from the box on the desk and handed them to her. "I didn't until I saw your face. I came up here to say that Mark is a butt-head and to tell you that he wasn't speaking for me last night. He wasn't speaking for Daddy, either. Daddy would have preached at you, but he would have stood by you, no matter what."

"Thank you," Charlotte said, blowing her nose. "Thank you from the bottom of my heart."

"Sure," Suzanne said. She got to her feet, took off her jacket, and hung it on the back of the door. "Now, we've got to figure out how to get you through this day."

Suzanne stayed with her mother the entire day, telling the students that she was practicing to be a teacher. In each class, she carefully reviewed the parts of a letter from the heading to the complimentary close. Then she had each student write a letter to the governor, offering him advice on some problem facing the state. And she warned them she was going to mail the letters, so they'd better use the correct format, spelling, and punctuations so he'd think kids in Newberg were intelligent. "Funny is okay, too. Anything to get his attention."

Charlotte sat off to one side, watching her daughter's impromptu teaching job, and thought how strangely life doled itself out, with pain and joy all mixed up together. She would remember this day always as the day she lost her job *and* the day Suzanne saved her from despair. Magnificent Suzanne, shining once again.

chapter twenty-seven

School was out, the accumulated paraphernalia of years in the classroom now boxed and stacked in Charlotte's basement. An open suitcase sat in the corner of the bedroom for her to pack things for her trip as she thought of them. Vicky's wedding dress hung on the bedroom door, and every time Charlotte walked by it, she marveled at how well it had turned out. The dress itself was an ankle-length, ivory-satin sheath, the bodice appliquéd with lace and cut to a deep V in back. For the wedding, it would be worn with an overskirt that formed a short train.

With the wedding in two weeks, she had put off dealing with her sister as long as she could. She had thought of begging or bargaining, but in the end she simply called Bernice and announced she was taking her trip and would be leaving the day after the wedding. Bernice could stay with Hannah in Newberg, or she could take her over to Norfolk for the rest of the summer.

"I've looked after her since she moved back into her house," Charlotte said, the phone tucked under her chin while she wiped the kitchen counters. "I go by there every morning to check on her.

And I run her errands and clean her house—never to her satisfaction, I might add."

"Did you really lose your job?"

"My contract was not renewed."

"I'm sorry. That must have been horrible for you."

"Yes, it was. But maybe it's a turning point."

"Shouldn't you be spending the summer looking for work instead of chasing around the country looking for men—and spending money you'll need to pay the rent and put food in your mouth?"

"Don't, Bernice." Charlotte threw the sponge in the sink and sank into a chair.

"What if *I* have plans?"

"I know you don't want me to go, Bernie. But it's your turn to look after Mama. And when I come back, we're going to have to make some adjustments. Her days of living in a two-story house are numbered. And she really has to stop driving a car. She forgets to look when she backs up. She's run into Mr. Cooksey's tree three times and almost hit his old deaf beagle."

"Then you are coming back?"

"Yes. Maybe not forever, but I'll be back."

"Can't Suzanne look in on Mama?"

"Looking in on aging relatives will come soon enough in her life. I don't care if she helps out some, but Mama is our responsibility."

"Noreen said she came over and helped appliqué the lace onto the bodice of Vicky's wedding gown."

"Yes, I appreciated her doing that. Michelle was a doll."

"I would have come if you'd asked."

"Bernie, I didn't *ask* Noreen. She called and asked *me* if I needed any help. She also offered to help with the wedding breakfast and decorating the church. Do we have to be like this? I miss having a sister I can count on. I'm always going to be your sister whether you like it or not. Whether or not I go on a trip or sleep with some man doesn't change that."

"Mama said you lost your job because you let a boy write a paper attacking Christianity."

"That's not true. He wrote a paper comparing religions, and in it he pointed out that everyone thinks their brand of faith is the right one. That upset some people."

"Do you believe in God?"

"I already answered that question for the school board, but they fired me anyway. And please don't tell me that I've changed, and don't tell me what Stan would have said or thought or done. This is my life, and I'm trying to live it the best way I can." She paused, took a breath. "I have to take this trip, Bernice. I have to get in my car and drive away from here. I know you don't understand, so please just trust me. I love you. I love Mama. But I have to go away. If you don't agree to look after Mama, then I'll just bundle her up and leave her on your doorstep."

❧ Jonathan, with his father, cousin Robert, and college roommate were waiting in front of the altar. Suzanne, Noreen, and Patty, in their attendants' dresses of burgundy brocade, made their march down the aisle, nervous little smiles on their faces. Charlotte stood as the organ burst forth with the "Wedding March," her heart soaring with the music as she looked down the aisle at Vicky on her brother's arm—surely the most beautiful sight of a lifetime.

Charlotte grabbed hold of the pew to steady herself as she etched this moment on her memory: The music. The look of her radiant daughter. The flickering candles. The church decorated with garlands festooned by Vicky, Suzanne, and Noreen from wild roses they had gathered at the abandoned farm their great-grandparents had homesteaded. Charlotte made a silent appeal to whatever forces in the universe might listen to the prayers of mothers that life would not disappoint her daughter, that Vicky would still look at Jonathan's face with love fifty years hence, and he would look at her and remember how she looked as she walked toward him on their wedding day.

Hannah was fumbling for her handkerchief. "Thank God I lived to see this day," she whispered.

Charlotte took Hannah's hand, feeling more kinship for her mother than she had in a long time as they shared their love for Vicky—and their shared widowhood, Charlotte thinking, of course, of Stan, and knowing her mother was thinking of her beloved Harry. *If only . . .*

Charlotte wondered if Suzanne was thinking of her own rushed little wedding in the living room at their old house. If so, no hint of disappointment showed on Suzanne's face as she attended her sister throughout the ceremony. Only love was there, tinged with the sadness of knowing Vicky was going to a different family, a different place, a different life. From now on, Suzanne's access to her sister would be limited.

During the brunch in the church basement, Angela Dearing came over to Charlotte and embraced her. "It was perfect," she said. "You've done a marvelous job." And that evening, at the reception, Angela Dearing told the guests in the receiving line that the wedding had been "charming, absolutely charming." Yes, Angela would say, she was sorry the wedding hadn't been in Topeka, but Vicky had grown up in Newberg. The quaint little church was dear. Vicky was the loveliest of brides. Imagine that her mother made her wedding dress! And the guests would express their amazement, glancing back at Vicky, bridelike in her satin gown even without the train and veil, with flowers in her hair, so young and joyous, her adoring young husband at her side.

Charlotte felt somewhat detached from the festivities. It was the engagement party revisited, only this time at the imposing country club rather than the Dearing home. So many people. An incredible array of food. Waiters constantly offering glasses of champagne. She exchanged pleasantries until the receiving line dissolved, then allowed herself to slip into the background, becoming more observer than participant, her mind drifting toward tomorrow, toward getting into her station wagon and driving away. Going west. All the way to the ocean. The mighty Pacific.

Bernice had insisted on bringing Michelle to the reception. All dressed up like a little pink doll, she toddled around collecting smiles, her doting grandmother close behind.

The toasts were made, Mark speaking for the Haberman family. But Charlotte found herself pushed to the forefront, saw faces turned toward her. She lifted her glass to Vicky and Jonathan: "My darlings, I wish you friendship as well as love."

Then in an upstairs ladies' room, she helped Vicky change into her going-away suit, even though the newlyweds were going no further than a nearby hotel for their wedding night. Tomorrow, they would fly to Paris. The suit was exquisite, a gift from Angela. Vicky looked incredibly chic, not at all like a girl from Newberg. A horse-drawn carriage awaited her and Jonathan out in front of the country club.

The rice was thrown. A sorority sister had claimed the bridal bouquet. Suzanne rushed forward to give her sister one last hug before she stepped into the carriage. "Don't forget your sister back home," she said.

"Never," Vicky said. "Never, never, never. You'll come to Dallas in the fall. Promise?"

"I promise."

Seated in the carriage, Vicky blew a kiss in Charlotte's direction. "Thank you, Mom," she called out for all to hear. "I love you."

The photographer raced after the carriage, taking pictures as the bride and groom waved merrily.

Suzanne waved back, longer than anyone, until the carriage had driven from view. Charlotte waited with her. "She doesn't belong to us anymore," Suzanne said.

"No, but we'll borrow her from time to time."

❧ Charlotte got up at dawn, tiptoeing about the hotel room, trying not to wake her mother. She'd said her good-byes last night—to Hannah; to everyone. She'd see them at summer's end. But her mother was awake. "Come sit down and talk to me for a minute before you go," she said.

Without her makeup, her hair wrapped in a turban to protect her hairdo, Hannah looked pitiful, almost genderless. Just a generic old person. Charlotte helped her to a sitting position, propped a pillow behind her back. She was frail. Charlotte could see it and feel it as she helped her about. Hannah was no longer the pretty, plump lady she'd been throughout Charlotte's memory.

"Your father said I needed to talk to you," she said matter-of-factly, "in case I die while you're gone."

Charlotte caught her breath. *"My father?"*

"Oh, I don't *really* talk to him," Hannah said with a wave of her hand. "I may be old, but I'm not crazy. But I do pretend sometimes. At night, mostly. That's when I miss him most, so I tell him things. And I know exactly what he would say back to me. I can almost hear him saying the words. Do you remember his voice? He had such a nice gentle voice." Hannah was smiling, absently patting Charlotte's hand. Yesterday, during the wedding, they'd held hands. Now once again there was physical contact that had nothing to do with rendering aid. Strange but nice—her mother never had been a touching sort of person.

"In the night, I told him about Vicky's wedding day," Hannah went on in the girlish voice she sometimes affected. Or maybe it wasn't an affectation, Charlotte realized. Other old ladies talked that way. Going full circle, perhaps.

"I talked in my head so I wouldn't wake you," Hannah said. "I told him yesterday was one of the finest days of my life. Right up there with getting married myself. That carriage was right out of a fairy tale. Our little Vicky riding away like a princess. And when I finished telling him all about the wedding, I told him you were leaving again. That's when he said I needed to make my peace with you."

"We're not at war, Mama."

"No, but I've been difficult, and I know it and I'm sorry. Always before, I was just thoughtless, which upset you. You wanted another kind of mother. And I wanted a daughter who wasn't so serious. I guess you couldn't help being serious, with Stan being so sick for such a long time, but even as a little girl, you always had your nose in a book and wanted to send food to starving children. And you were always asking questions I couldn't answer—like what holds up God's throne and if angels went to the bathroom.

"Lord, Charlotte, you were such a strange little girl," she went on. "Bernice, too. She got over it, though. You never did. But anyway, your father was better at dealing with you girls than I was, and if he were still alive, he'd tell me I have to patch things up with you before I die. I never even told you I was sorry you lost your job. I know that was hard for you. That little Braunsmeyer boy must be a lot like you—full of questions that other people never think to ask."

"I wish you wouldn't talk about dying. You're not sick."

"No, but I feel cold in my bones—even now that the weather's turned warm."

Charlotte took hold of her mother's ancient hands. "Do you want me to stay home this summer?" she heard herself say, while an inner voice protested, warning that there would always be some reason not to go.

"Your daddy says to send you on your way," Hannah said. "You need to get out there and figure out what you're all about."

"You're making me cry, Mama."

"Don't do that. It'll give you a headache."

"I can't leave you when you're talking like this."

"We all love each other, don't we, Charlotte? In spite of it all?"

Charlotte nodded.

"That's what I told your father. I'll tell you what, Charlotte, I won't die this summer—not if I can help it. I'll sit in the sun over at Bernice's and watch Michelle play. Such a pretty child—she reminds me of Vicky. I'm not sure I'll make it through another winter, though."

"I'll call you every few days." Again the voice protested. She was fettering herself when the whole point was to be detached.

"I know you will, dear. Go along now. I hope you find what you're looking for."

"Do you want me to call Bernice and tell her you're awake?"

"No, you'd wake up Michelle. I'll order coffee from room service. I'm fine. Really I am."

And so, Charlotte left as planned, but without the long-anticipated euphoria she had hoped to feel as she left them all behind. Her children: Mark, who decided not to risk all for love but live a sane, safe life; Vicky, who had love in abundance; Suzanne, who walked miles and miles every day with her dog because she had no real home. Her sister Bernice, who occupied her days by meddling in her children's lives. And her mother, who talked to her dead husband and perhaps knew herself better than anyone had ever realized.

Then there was Eric, who seemed content to wait around and see if they ever became more than friends. He had given her a beautiful little gold compass on a key chain, "To find your way home," he'd said.

She could always find her way home, would always think of Newberg as home. And someday she would be buried in the Newberg cemetery next to Stan. A person could never escape the place that had formed them. Life would always be lived either in accordance with that place or in rebuttal of it.

She would miss them all more than she wanted. But she wouldn't miss them every minute. Already as the miles of distance were increasing, she felt the knots in her stomach unraveling, her brow smoothing, her shoulders relaxing. She glanced at her reflection in the mirror. "How ya doin', kid?"

Along the highway the summer wildflowers were in bloom— blue flags, columbine, larkspur, poppies. Little patches here and there. Sometimes whole fields of color.

chapter twenty-eight

Her first glimpse of the Pacific came near Rockport. It was almost evening, and the sun was a great orange ball sinking into the horizon. Charlotte got out of the car, her chest swelling with emotion and pride. She'd kept this promise to herself.

The historian in her paid tribute to Lewis and Clark, who'd first seen the Pacific a few hundred miles to the north. Their journey took a year and a half. Hers took a lifetime.

She planned to stay two or three weeks in Northern California. Maybe longer. Long enough at least to explore the shoreline and take day trips up and down the rugged coast. She wanted to visit the artist colonies, see the seals and seabirds. Then she would head north into Oregon and Washington, crossing over into Canada, leaving the United States for the first time. She'd take a seaplane to Victoria Island, her very first trip in an airplane. Then she would see Yellowstone and head south into Colorado—where she might find Cory, if he was still alive.

She'd known how the ocean would look. What she hadn't realized was how it would feel and sound, how intimidating it would be to stand at its edge, like being on the edge of eternity. Was there a

God? Charlotte didn't know. But there was nature and beauty to inspire—and make humble. Perhaps that was enough.

She now understood that she was not one of those people who found solace in the ocean and needed to live out their life under its spell. Mountains were better for her. They were solid, more predictable. But the prairie with its distant horizon was home. That was nice to know. At heart, she was like Dorothy with Toto under her arm, like Edna Ferber and Willa Cather. She was a daughter of the wind and sod.

She called a family member every other night; sometimes she dialed Bernice's number; other times she would call Suzanne or Mark. Once she called Noreen, when no one else answered. Vicky would enter into the rotation when she and Jonathan returned from Europe. Hannah was with Bernice, doing fine, apparently. Almost resentfully, Charlotte made these calls. They pulled her back when she needed to be cut loose. But her mother had said she felt cold in her bones. And what if one of them was sick or in trouble? She thought of Elizabeth Montgomery's character in the old television series *Bewitched*. Samantha could twitch her nose and magically place those around her in suspended animation, leaving her free to roam about other realms knowing that nothing was going to happen to kith and kin in her absence. But Charlotte wasn't a witch, and real life was never free. So she would find a pay phone and begin dialing numbers until someone answered.

She didn't call Eric. She had told him she wouldn't. The only person she missed was Suzanne. Not that she loved her younger child more than the other two, but Vicky had moved into another world in which Charlotte would only be an occasional visitor, and Mark had pulled away—any love he now felt toward her was dutiful. Her connection to Suzanne, tenuous though it was, was stronger, went deeper. In Suzanne's eyes, she sometimes saw understanding.

On the first of July, she journeyed inland to visit Humboldt Redwood State Park and checked into a rustic bed and breakfast that was no more expensive than one of the usual motels and had a tiny deck off her room that offered a spectacular view of the mountains. She made her phone call home from a deli, where she planned to buy a meal to eat on the deck while the sun went down. She dialed Vicky's number first. She wanted to hear that she and Jonathan were back safe and sound from their honeymoon, that they had had a glorious time and were getting settled in their Dallas home.

Instead, she caught them on their way out the door to catch a plane to Nebraska. Hannah had died in her sleep the night before.

Charlotte hung up the phone and stared at the spanking clean deli with its display of cheeses and breads. Her mother hadn't kept her promise. But then it hadn't really been a promise at all. It had been a blessing. A setting free.

She called Bernice and was glad when Noreen answered the phone. She would have cried if she had heard Bernice's voice. She wanted to be home first, with her sister, before she cried. "Tell your mother I'll be there as soon as I can get a flight. I'll let you know when to expect me."

But she discovered it would be tomorrow before she could fly to Nebraska, and she couldn't possibly wait until then to leave. Without thinking, she threw her things back into the station wagon and started driving. All day and all night she drove, calling along the way. She was coming. Don't bury her mother without her.

The door opened the minute she pulled into her mother's driveway. Bernice had been watching for her.

On her mother's front porch—where they had spent many a summer day, sharing dolls, books, dreams—they sat on the glider and clung to each other and wept for the mother they loved more than they realized and whose passing would leave an everlasting void in their lives.

"She was different toward the end," Bernice said. "Nicer. She even thanked me for things. Do you think she felt it coming?"

"Maybe so. She told me the morning I left that she'd been thoughtless, but she'd always loved us."

"She said that?"

"Yeah. She said she'd been talking to Daddy, and he wanted her to make peace with me."

"I heard her talking to Daddy when I came upstairs that last night. The next morning she was dead."

"You had no idea that the end was near?"

"None. She was doing great. Taking little walks up and down the block. Even helping in the kitchen. When she didn't come downstairs for her morning television shows, I went up to check on her, and she was gone. I knew as soon as I saw her."

"That must have been awful for you."

"No, just a shock. She died in her sleep. We all should be so lucky."

Charlotte nodded. The tears were starting again. They cried a while longer, then dried their eyes. "I went ahead and made all the arrangements," Bernice said. "I hope they're okay."

"I'm sure they're fine."

"We can go to the funeral home after you've had a chance to rest. She's wearing the dress she bought for Vicky's wedding. I think she would have liked that."

"Do I have to go to the funeral home?"

"Please. For me. We have to see if her hair is done right. And her makeup. Remember how they had Daddy's hair parted on the wrong side? You know how proud Mama was. She'd want to look her best."

So Charlotte went, to please her sister. It wasn't so bad. Their mother looked pretty as ever.

The sisters buried Hannah the next day, by their father, saying farewell to the woman herself and to the generation. They had no parents. Now they were the family elders.

Charlotte stayed in Newberg throughout the month of July while she and Bernice saw to their mother's estate and got her house ready to sell. Most of their time was spent going through Hannah's possessions; in doing so, they relived the years they'd lived together in the house. Emily Dickinson had called the process "The Sweeping up the Heart/And putting Love away . . . "

Charlotte was surprised at how many of their grandmother's belongings Hannah's grandchildren wanted. "Don't let anything go," Suzanne insisted. And so, other than clothing and the mundane, they stored what wasn't claimed by Bernice and Noreen in Bernice's attic to be doled out as Hannah's grandchildren established their own homes.

Aside from the mantel clock and a few trinkets and photographs, Charlotte claimed little for herself. Her life was too uncertain to be adding more baggage.

Bernice was angry when she realized Charlotte planned to leave again, to take up her journey for what was left of the summer. "Damn it, Charlotte, your family needs you here." They were in Charlotte's kitchen, having a cup of coffee before Bernice left for Norfolk. "What's the good of having a sister if you aren't here when I need you? The first thing I thought of when I realized that Mama was dead was finding you, getting you home so we could face it together. But I didn't have a phone number, not even the name of a town. I thought we were going to have to bury her without you."

"You know I called in every other day. And I came as fast as I could."

"Always before, you were only an hour away."

"Nothing stays the same, Bernie."

"Was Cory Jones in California?" Her question was like an accusation.

"No. I think he's in Colorado."

"Are you still looking for him?"

"Yes, it's something I started. I'd like to finish it."

"Poor Stan. You didn't deserve him."

Charlotte closed her eyes, rebuffing the intended wound of her sister's word. "Stan had been married once before and stayed in touch with his first wife until the end," she said. "Yet I think he loved me. I know I loved him. Life isn't tidy, Bernie. Surely you know that by now."

"Stan was married before?" Bernice looked stunned. Charlotte couldn't be talking about the Stan she knew.

"Yes, to a woman named Elizabeth. I drove down to Topeka to see her last year. She was nice."

"Why didn't you ever tell me?"

"I'm not really sure. Stan and I were both pretty private about what came before. We ended up creating this fairy tale for our children—that people met and fell in love and lived happily ever after. We were wrong to do that. Our children have suffered because of it."

"I wish my children had a fairy tale," Bernice said, picking up her purse.

Charlotte walked her to the door. "Tell me good-bye, Bernie, and wish me well."

Bernice's hug was perfunctory. "I'm not going to take care of you if you catch a sexually transmitted disease."

"I'd take care of you," Charlotte said.

Bernice tried to look stern, but finally she had to smile. "Don't be a smart-ass."

The second hug was better. "Don't forget who you are," Bernice said.

"Never. I'm Bernice's big sister."

Later, as Charlotte was locking up for the night, she realized that Suzanne and George were sitting on the front steps. George's tail began to thump when he saw her through the screen door.

Charlotte went outside and sat beside her daughter. An almost full moon and millions of stars shone down on them. A cricket chirped under the steps.

"What time are you leaving?" Suzanne asked.

"First thing. The station wagon is loaded and ready to go."

"Are you going back to California?"

"No, just to Colorado. I think I know where Cory Jones is."

"What will you do if you find him?"

Charlotte shrugged. "Say hello. Let him know someone remembers him. Ask him why he never came back."

"What if he doesn't want to be found and refuses to see you?"

"That's okay. I'm not really looking for him, honey. I'm looking for me."

"Last spring, you asked if I'd like come to come along. Is the invitation still open?"

"Always."

"I need some distance."

"I understand. But does Brady?"

"No. He makes threats that he doesn't mean."

chapter twenty-nine

Charlotte was in no hurry. They drove evenly, poking along, enjoying the untouched world about them that was so vastly different from their prairie home.

This was a different part of Colorado than they had visited before. There were no ski resorts or quaint tourist towns here.

Star City, deep into Colorado's San Juan range, was not unlike other such places they'd seen along the way. The tiny mountain community stretched for two miles along a meandering stream.

Charlotte introduced herself to Mr. Simms, the proprietor of the town's old-fashioned general store. "So you really came," he said, shaking Charlotte's hand.

As he had told her on the phone, Mr. Simms explained, the place she was looking for was two ridges over—a primitive settlement inhabited by a group of Vietnam vets. About a dozen of them were there right now. The number changed as they drifted in and out. Some stayed through the winter; some didn't. He never knew for sure who was there until they straggled in to pick up their mail, cash their government checks, buy supplies.

"Cory Jones hasn't been in since you called. But one of his buddies was here. I told him a lady from Nebraska was looking for Jones. I figured he should have a chance to clear out if he didn't want to see anyone."

"Yes, certainly," Charlotte said. "Is Cory well?"

"Far as I know. They take care of each other. Still, one of them froze to death a few years back. Got lost in a snowstorm. When they brought him down, he was still frozen solid."

Mr. Simms's store was remarkable. "I wonder if he ever takes inventory," Suzanne said, as they took in the incredible array of merchandise stuffed onto shelves, piled onto tables, stacked on the floor. Groceries, car parts, fishing gear, guns, food, clothing, shoes, liquor, hardware, dishes, cookwear, books, radios, cassettes, pharmaceuticals—all mixed together. There was even a section for video rentals, a tiny post office, and a snack bar.

Mr. Simms showed them to a room upstairs—one of three he rented out, mostly to hunters and fishermen. The room was marginally clean, with a bathroom down the hall.

The next morning the guide he'd promised was waiting. Sammy White Feather, an Indian boy who couldn't have been more than fourteen. And so Charlotte, with her daughter at her side and George on a leash, began the final leg of her journey.

They walked for hours, following a narrow trail, stopping at midday to eat the lunch Mr. Simms had supplied—peanut butter and jelly sandwiches in the wilderness. Sammy was talkative. He went to a government boarding school. His mother wanted him to be a doctor, but he wasn't so sure. He was a pretty good roper and was thinking about trying the rodeo circuit.

The nameless settlement was composed of widely spaced log huts, seemingly one for each of the bearded, unkempt men who greeted them. A surprisingly well-kept garden occupied a clearing. One of the men pointed—Cory Lee's hut was the farthest up the mountain. He didn't talk much, Charlotte was told. Suzanne, George, and the guide waited below while Charlotte climbed up the steep incline. Cory was sitting on a rock, watching her approach.

She wouldn't have recognized him on the street. His hair and beard were long and gray, his skin old and wrinkled; his body was lean to the point of emaciation. He looked the way Charlotte remembered his grandfather looking back then. Older even. His eyes, however, were the same sky-blue as before.

"I heard you were looking for me," Cory said. "Couldn't figure out why."

"At first, it was just to find out what happened to you. But I kind of figured that out along the way. Yet I came anyway, so I guess I just wanted to see you again. Close the book, so to speak. You want me to leave?"

"Naw. That's okay. You went to a lot of trouble to get here."

Charlotte sat down on the rock beside him, turning her face to the sunshine. "I loved you, you know. And I had a terrible time getting over you."

She thought of the wall she'd built around herself, telling herself that she could never love another man the way she had loved Cory Lee Jones. It became who she was. The woman with the broken heart who could never completely love again.

"Yeah. I loved you, too. But you scared me, girl. All that talk about us going to college together and then settling down for the rest of our lives. I wasn't sure I wanted to go to college. I never did read all those books you gave me. I didn't need to. You told me what was in them. It was a good summer that we had, but I couldn't see the rest of my life laid out in front of me the way you could. You wanted me to grow up and become my dad, with a mortgage and a membership in the Rotary Club. I didn't believe in that war over there, but when the draft notice came, I was almost relieved."

"So I made you up?"

He chuckled. "Sort of. Lord, girl, you did go on and on about true love and forever and ever."

"And the war? What happened over there?"

"Confusion. I killed people. Saw buddies die. It was hell on earth. Then when I got back, I missed it. Life was flat. No adrenaline rush. No life and death. To make up for that, I drank too much and got into fights. At least up here, I can sleep with my gun and go hunting every day. It's better. Down there I'd be dead or in prison."

"I thought you'd be different."

"Yeah, I know. You expected a broken man who took your picture out and looked at it every night before he went to sleep."

Charlotte laughed. "No, not that. I thought you'd be angry. Or full of regret."

"Maybe once, but not anymore. What about you? You got a husband and kids?"

She told him about Stan and her three grown children, pointing to Suzanne waiting below with George and Sammy White Feather.

"Tough about your husband, but I'll bet you're a great mother."

"Oh, I love my children dearly, and I always kept them clean and well-fed. But I let them think life was simple."

"Will you go back there—to Newberg?"

"No, I don't belong there anymore." She had said it spontaneously, without thinking. Did she really mean it?

They sat for a while longer, basking in the warm sunshine. Down below someone was playing "Waltzing Matilda" on a harmonica.

"It's very beautiful here."

"I like it."

"Do you need anything?"

"Like what?"

"For me to come here again? Or write to you? I guess you don't want me to send you books."

"Actually, I've got some books. No, I don't need anything at all." And he reached out to touch her cheek.

"Would you have recognized me?" she asked.

"I think so. You're still pretty."

She smiled. "Thanks. You look like a mountain man."

"Yep, that's what I am. The old man on the mountain."

She stood. "Well, I guess I'll be on my way," she said, and handed him the packet of letters she had collected during her search.

"Some of these have messages for you. It was good to see you again."

Charlotte scooted down off the rock and took a few steps, then turned back. "Would you say my name?"

He grinned. "Charlotte Louise Vogel—1515 Iowa Street. Your phone number was JEfferson 4-1491."

"No, just *Charlotte*. You never called me by my name."

"And you never stopped saying mine. Over and over. 'Cory Lee' this and 'Cory Lee' that. Good-bye, Charlotte. I wish you well."

❦ Suzanne watched her mother pick her way down the steep hillside. The mythical Cory Jones stayed up above on his rock. Suzanne shaded her eyes against the glare of the sun, wanting to get a better look at him, but all she could see was a bearded man silhouetted against a cloudless sky.

On the way back down the mountain, Suzanne linked arms with her mother. "So, how was it?"

"I made him up."

"What do you mean?"

"I was experiencing the greatest love the world has ever known, and he was a horny boy making out with an available girl."

"I'm sorry."

Her mother laughed. "Don't be. It all makes sense now. What a ninny I was." And she began to hum, then sing out loud: "Waltzing Matilda." Suzanne joined in until they couldn't think of the rest of the words, and then they just hummed.

Suzanne had never felt closer to anyone in her life than she now felt to her lean, tanned mother in jeans and hiking boots. Even her beloved father seemed remote. How strange to think that if her father hadn't died, she never would have truly known the woman who was her mother.

Her mother's journey was over. But she sensed that another was just beginning.

"I love you, Mom," she said, reaching for her mother's hand.

"I love you, too, Suzanne. So very much."

❧ The next morning, they said good-bye to Mr. Simms and drove north to revisit Central City, where they'd stopped briefly last summer. They spent their last day poking around the old mining town—turned tourist attraction. They visited the opera house and the shops, ate lunch in an old saloon, had their picture taken with their faces poking through a backdrop that turned them into crusty old prospectors. Charlotte felt almost drunk with the pure pleasure of being with her daughter this way—a day with no agenda, just being together, doing what would be remembered always.

That night, Charlotte called Eric while Suzanne was in the shower.

"We're on our way home," she said.

"Everything okay?" he asked.

"Yes. Really fine. I was just thinking about you and wondered if you'd like to try again?"

"*Try again?* Do you mean in the carnal sense?"

"Yeah. Carnal was what I had in mind."

"Well, I'll be damned. I mean, yes. Sure. I would like to try again. Do you have a time and place in mind?"

"Not really. Just when it feels right."

❧ Charlotte made her last walk through the house, making sure every surface was spotless and ready for the next tenant. Not a sentimental walk-through, unlike the heart-wrenching last time she walked through the family home on Schoolhouse Road. Or when she and Bernice said good-bye to the home of their childhood. In her entire life, she'd only lived in three houses. Her mother before her had only lived in two. Stable people in a stable town. And now she was moving on—she and Suzanne, their possessions loaded into a U-Haul truck and the station wagon.

Brady and Eric had helped her move out and would help them move into their new home in Lincoln. When Charlotte tried to tell Brady how decent he was being about Suzanne's decision, he'd cried and allowed her to embrace him, to pat his back and soothe him. "Crazy, isn't it?" he asked. "Me helping her leave?"

"No, not crazy. Gallant maybe. Dignified, definitely."

"Maybe this way, she'll come back someday."

"Maybe. But at least you can stay friends, think good thoughts about each other. I'm proud of you, Brady."

"Yeah, thanks." He blew his nose and picked up a box to carry out to the truck.

Then he had turned around. "Suzanne said I could keep George. Can you believe that? She's letting me keep old George."

Charlotte locked the back door behind her. She walked out into the backyard to cut some sprays from the rose of Sharon bush, then went around the house to where Suzanne was waiting for her in the shade of the front porch. George was watching Brady and Eric close up the back of the truck.

"I think you have a visitor," Suzanne said, nodding toward a boy sitting on his bicycle in front of the Methodist church.

Charlotte handed Suzanne the flowers and walked over to where Tommy Braunsmeyer waited.

"Are you leaving because of me?" he asked, nodding in the direction of the U-Haul.

"No, I'm leaving because it's time," she said.

He was such a scrawny little kid, not yet into puberty as most of the boys his age were. Charlotte had always wanted to fatten him up.

"My grandma says you got fired because of the paper I wrote."

"No. I lost my job because I didn't tell you *not* to write that paper. It's not your fault. Don't ever think that."

"My grandma made me burn it."

"She means well, Tommy. Just lay low for four years. It will be different when you go to college. You can get a scholarship. I know you can."

"If I go to Lincoln then, will you still be there?"

"Maybe so. If I am, will you come see me and tell me all about your classes?"

"Yes, ma'am. I'd like that."

Charlotte held out her hand. Tommy hesitated, then he took it.

"You sure it wasn't my fault?" he asked.

"Absolutely."

"I think you're a good teacher."

"Thank you. I tried to be. You were a good student. The best one I ever had. Don't ever forget that, Tommy Braunsmeyer. You were the best student this teacher ever had."

❧ In theory, Charlotte didn't believe in entombment. Cremation was better. Scattering ashes to the wind. Placing no demands on progeny for floral offerings and cemetery upkeep, no guilt when gravesites remained unvisited for what was perceived a disrespectful period of time.

Yet, at particular times, like today, she needed to be here in this old cemetery where her forebears were buried. Both of her parents now. And Stan. She felt closest to them here, which she knew was illogical in both the physical and the metaphysical sense. The dead didn't know she was visiting. Still, she was here, making a pilgrimage. Her final visit as a resident of Newberg.

Suzanne had come with her. They went first to the shared gravesite of Hannah and Harry Vogel, placing a spray of flowers at the base.

"I'd like to think they're together in heaven," Suzanne said.

"Me, too," Charlotte said.

Suzanne placed a single flower on the small grave of her lost baby and another spray on her father's grave. She told her father that she loved him, then, sensing that her mother needed to linger alone, walked back to the station wagon. The U-Haul was parked outside the gate, with Eric, Brady, and George waiting inside.

Charlotte ran a hand over the top of the granite marker. She had thought she would pour out her heart, tell Stan about finding Cory. She thought she'd explain how she should have looked for him years ago, should have put that summer in perspective. But if that *had* happened, and if Stan hadn't continued to think about Elizabeth over the years, they would have been different people, and they wouldn't have had the same marriage. It had worked out in the end. They had navigated their way through the heartache and stood firmly side by side at the helm of their family.

"We're moving on, my darling. Suzanne and I. But I'll carry you with me always. And I will be back."

Then she cried, and knew she would always cry when she came here. She and Stan had loved each other as best they could. Which in the end, turned out to be a very great deal indeed.

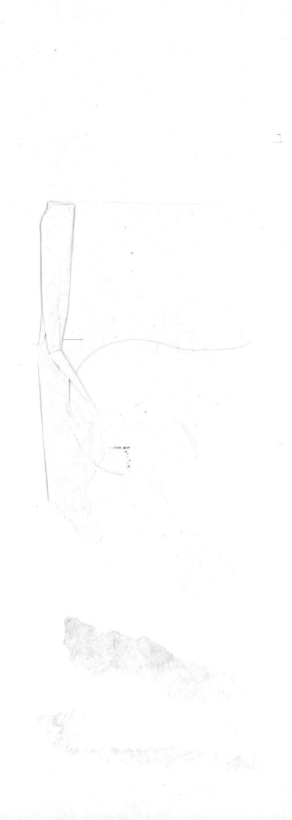